CW01497741

Spire Publishing
www.spirepublishing.com

Shepherdess

by

Brian Crowther

Spire Publishing
www.spirepublishing.com

Spire Publishing June 2008

First published in Canada and Great Britain 2008 by Spire Publishing.
Spire Publishing is a trademark of Adlibbed Ltd.

A cataloguing record for this book is available from the Library and Archives Canada. Visit
www.collectionscanada.ca/amicus/index-e.html

Designed in Toronto, Canada
by Adlibbed Ltd.
Printed and bound in the US or the UK
by Lightningsource Ltd.

ISBN (10): 1-897312 -37-7
ISBN (13): 978-1897312-37-7

Spire Publishing
www.spirepublishing.com

To Kath and family
and all the Border Collies

To Joan,
Thank you for looking
after all our Pets.
Brian. xx   3/7/08

Chapter one

Life can be likened to a candle, initially; it is shining and new, like the newly born lamb. The light is small at first until the wax heats up and penetrates the wick. It develops, burning brightly, often leading the way. At other times it is unstable, often dim and flickering as a draught or breeze catches it.

So it can be likened to human characteristics, sometimes good, sometimes bad. These changes are brought about by outside influences, as the nature of the being remains constant. The candle in the wind, the candle in still air. Its light shines forth when held on high, when placed low its light is often shielded and dims. Once the candle is lit it burns until the last remaining drops of the wax are melted onto the wick, and then it dies. This is so true of life, once life starts there is no return to the former state, there are so many influences on the journey until the final resting-place is reached.

This was the situation that Robert Mason now found himself in; his breathing was shallow and laboured as he fought against the inevitable. The candle at his bedside on the small, roughly made table burned brightly although it was now, like Robert, nearing the end of its time.

A gentle knock was heard at the door followed by a pause, again the visitor knocked, louder this time. From somewhere in the darker recesses a dog growled its warning followed by a low throaty bark. A young girl rose from the side of the bed and crossed the room towards the door. The dog now emerged and growled again. Another dog watched attentively but made no sound as if it knew there was no danger. The young girl's hand reached down to the dog and fondled its head. "Its all right Tess" she whispered. The latch squeaked as it was lifted from the iron sneck set in the wall. The door creaked loudly as its hinges resisted the movement. The candle flickered violently as the draught from outside blew across the room and then it regained its steady flame as the door was shut.

"Thank-you for coming" said the girl softly "he's over there". Footsteps crossed the flagged floor and the minister looked down at the face of the man lying on the bed.

Mason was not a religious man and yet, he felt it right that he should seek solace in his final hours with the man of God. Like many of his time that live and work in the countryside he could best be described as a pantheist, regarding God as being the material universe and force of nature.

Going through the mind of the parson as he looked at the face of Robert Mason was the usual thought in these circumstances. Why, in their last hours on this Earth do those of little faith seek the solace of the disciple of God? Mason had never set foot in the church in the small hamlet of Martindale.

Well he remembered the day when Robert Mason arrived in the area with a young child to take up the position of shepherd for the estate of Lord Farrington. He had been deeply concerned that a man with a small child and no wife to care for it had taken up residence in the lonely croft at the head of the Fusedale valley.

He had taken it upon himself to visit the shepherd at his earliest opportunity and so that warm August day many years ago he found himself walking along the track up the valley of Fusedale. It was a good hours walk and by the time he reached the little croft he was very hot indeed and in need of some refreshment. Mason was working outside the croft carrying out a repair to the sheep pens in preparation for the forthcoming gathering and sheep washing. The young girl whom he guessed to be around three years old was playing happily with a rather dilapidated looking doll.

"Good morning t' you sir," cried the parson, "I'm Michael Winterton from the church in Martindale," Mason looked up and nodded to the parson but carried on with the work on the pen. Although he knew that Mason lived there alone with the child he politely enquired about the lady of the house only to be told curtly that there wasn't one. Somewhat rebuffed by the shepherd's tone Winterton enquired of the reason for the absence of his wife. "Because she's dead," came the reply in a more saddened tone. "I'm very sorry t' hear o' your loss, was it recently?" replied Winterton. Thinking that maybe this was why the shepherd had chosen to take up this lonely station in Fusedale. "T'was about three years ago now, she died shortly after the young one was born."

"I see, so was that the reason that you took up this employment with

Lord Farrington then, to get away and start a new life?" enquired the parson.

"Aye, that and the troubles," continued Mason.

"And what would those be, if I might make myself so bold as to enquire?" said the parson. Mason fiddled with a binding on the crosspiece, which he was attaching to an upright to form a gate to the enclosure.

"Let's just say my marriage to Anna was disapproved of, not only by my family, but also by the likes of your crowd, I'll say no more on the subject." and with that he half turned away from the parson.

"But what d' you mean by that?" said the parson.

"Lets just say that I was let down by God at a time when I needed him most, I've said all that I'm saying on the subject, so if you've nothing more to say I'll bid you good-day'."

"But what of the child, how can she have a Christian upbringing? "

Robert Mason turned to the parson and looked him straight in the eyes.

"She'll not be needing any of your Gods, I can look after her."

The parson was at a loss for words, here he had come up against a person who had experienced deep problems in his former life and had now rejected his faith. The parson could be quite dogmatic and stubborn at times and it seemed that he had met his match in the form of Robert Mason. The fact that Mason clearly rejected the church preyed on the parson's stubbornness and from that day their paths rarely crossed and when they did it was only to exchange the niceties of the day in a resentful tone.

The parson took exception to the fact that the young girl was never christened or, as she grew older, allowed to form her own opinions and take up the Christian faith. He was certain that her father actively influenced her non-commitment to the Lord and the church.

Yet during his time in the dale Robert Mason had never carried out any wrong acts or said anything untoward about any other person in the district. He was a most diligent and conscientious shepherd and set much store in producing some of the finest sheep in the area. Indeed, Lord Farrington had been known to remark on more than one occasion that he had the best shepherd in Cumberland.

Mason had also fulfilled his duties as a parent to good effect. He saw to it that his daughter attended the little village school on a regular basis and even in times of inclement weather when the journey along the dale was difficult. She was well spoken and well read and had a very broad educational knowledge; indeed it was far superior to many of her classmates from the village. Her teacher attributed this to her father's efforts in the evenings and weekends. It was this, which suggested to some that Robert Mason was more than an ordinary shepherd and had probably descended from some upper class family and fallen from grace for some reason.

As the girl grew, she became proficient in housekeeping, being in charge of the small croft, preparing meals and generally taking care of the day-to-day duties that any good housewife would undertake. By the time she had reached the tender age of seventeen she was a competent in many aspects of shepherding.

So, Robert Mason had led a good but unreligious life in the dale and if he did not accept the way of the Lord, Winterton still felt that it was upon him to ensure that he departed this life with his blessing.

"How long has he been ill?" said the parson turning to the girl.

It's well over a fortnight now," she replied, "he is so weak now and not eating anything at all."

"I fear he will be not be of this earth for very much longer," said Winterton gravely, "we must pray for him."

The parson and the girl knelt at the side of the bed and so the last rites were read and prayers for the soul of Robert Mason were uttered. The couple rose to their feet, the parson carrying out the task with a little difficulty and creaking of joints.

He looked into the face of the girl.

"You look tired my child," he said, noting the paleness of her face with the all too obvious telltale signs of one who has spent much time crying.

"Yes," she replied, "it has been hard looking after him and all the sheep as well."

Winterton looked incredulous.

"You mean that you've been doing his work as well as caring for him?"

"It was my father's insistence that I looked after the flock."

"But could you not have got help from someone?" he asked.

"My father would not hear of it, he can be very stubborn at times," she replied. 'He only sought help at the gathering and washing, he was certain that he would soon be well again, but now I don't-."

She turned and sank down on the edge of the bed and buried her face in her hands and sobbed uncontrollably.

Winterton placed his hand on the girl's head and uttered a prayer.

"You must be strong my child and the Lord will give you that strength." With that he turned towards the door. He was needed no longer and he quietly made his exit, he had prayed for the soul of a man about to meet his maker.

The evening turned to night and a chill spread through the air as was common when the sun went down in early spring. The girl sat huddled in the chair at her father's bedside. Tess lay at her feet providing warmth for her legs from her long fur. Moss the elder of the two dogs still remained in his corner but gazed up at the girl and sighed as if to say 'I'm here for you'.

The young girl sipped hot sweet tea, which she had just made and warmed her, hands on the pot.

She questioned her own strength as to how long she could go on caring for her father and look after the flock. She realised that he was much worse, he never responded during the parson's visit. His breathing was still shallow and laboured. She leaned forward and tucked the covers around her father's shoulders; her eyes searched the closed eyelids of this dear man.

The girl lowered her face and her soft lips gently kissed his brow. He jerked as if convulsed and his eyes half opened revealing lifeless pools of blue.

"Is that you, is that you Elfie?" he whispered.

"Oh father," she cried. "Yes, yes I am here," the tears welling up in her eyes again.

He whispered again

"Bring the light closer that I may see your face."

She reached out and took the candle from its holder and held it near to her.

Robert Mason gazed into the face of his daughter. Compassion and love were intermingled for that brief moment. His eyes seemed to gain some of their former brightness and his lips parted forming a gentle smile. He sighed heavily and the eyes closed. His breathing seemed shallower than ever now.

Elfie replaced the candle in its holder noting that it had perhaps an hour to burn; she delayed replacing it just yet. She pulled a shawl around herself and tried to make herself comfortable in the chair. She tried desperately to fight off sleep but gradually she succumbed to the fretful escape.

The night was still except for the bleating of sheep, which surrounded the croft for the night. The candle flickered in the gentle draughts, which from time to time passed through the room over the sleeping pair. This was the scene until the last particles of wax were consumed and then the flame slowly diminished and died.

Chapter two

The shepherd's croft was situated at the head of a long, narrow valley. On clear days the southern edge of Ullswater could just be discerned from the doorstep of the dwelling. On many days in summer it was usually obscured by a misty haze. In winter, low cloud obscured visibility for days on end, so typical of the vagaries of Lakeland weather. The eastern side of the valley was flanked with rough crags at its lower end which had a forbidding appearance even on the brightest of days. The barrier of crags extending upwards over sixteen hundred feet was only broken in a small number of places to give access to the higher grazing plateau above. Further southwards up the valley the crags gave way to steep sided grassy slopes providing mid level grazing. Westwards, gentler fells rose in a graceful sweep much of their lower slopes covered in thick bracken or heather. The lower fells were connected to their higher counterparts by a sweeping wide ridge, which effectively sealed off the lower ground of the valley floor.

Several streams issued from the higher ground, tumbling down over mossy rocks before converging to form the main stream that passed close by the shepherd's croft. The sparkling clear water provided all the domestic needs for the occupants of the croft and also a plentiful supply in connection with the needs of the flock. Beyond the inbye many parts of the lower valley were marshy as the stream spread out finger-like in places. Marsh and cotton grass grew in abundance in many of the peat-ridden areas forming large sphagnum bogs and presenting a sucking trap for the unwary traveller who strayed from the main track down the valley.

The early spring sun shone down on this track reflecting in the many puddles which had formed from the overnight rain. There was a chill in the air discerned by the vapour from the nostrils of the horse that now pulled a small cart along the track. At the head of the horse walked Mick Jarrow, the son of Davy Jarrow who farmed at the foot of the valley.

Davy himself walked at the side of the cart his right arm resting on a rough coffin, which was strapped to the cart to prevent it sliding about as it journeyed along the rough track. Shepherd Mason was now on his final journey.

Davy Jarrow was a good friend of Robert Mason, possibly his only real friend in these parts and the two had worked closely at times in the furtherance of sheep farming for Lord Farrington.

The provision of transport to the shepherd's final resting place was now his last act of friendship.

Some distance behind the cart another figure looking tired and frail walked slowly along. Elfrida Mason looked neither left nor right, her eyes transfixed on the lumbering cart which carried her father's body. Back and forth around her skirts and then around the cart ran Moss in an act of final gathering for his master. Occasionally, he barked to warn off Tess the younger dog who was in a playful mood and disrupting Moss in his final task.

Moss was ageing and much of his work was gradually being taken over by Tess whom Elfie had reared and trained from an early age. The cold, damp and hostile climate was taking its toll on Moss and often now he was stiff in the morning, particularly if he had been working hard the previous day.

The hard conditions got to everyone who sought the life in the higher Lakeland valleys and today was seeing the departure of another of its victims. The little procession moved steadily along until it reached the intake fields around Dale End Farm. The farm was owned by Lord Farrington and was leased to the Jarrow family who had farmed there for some thirty years or so. At the entrance to the farm stood Mary, the wife of Davy Jarrow who now came forward accompanied by her younger son Andy and her daughter Liza and the group joined the sad procession beside Elfie.

"My poor child, I am so, so sorry f' you,"said Mary. "When t' day is over you mum come and stay wi' us until y' get y'self sorted out, will y' do that my child?" Elfie was silent for some time and then she spoke,

"It's very kind of you to make me that offer but I cannot accept."

"Why's that m' dear?" asked Mary.

"Because there is much to be done, lambing time will soon be upon us," replied Elfie.

"But surely my child, y' cannot be thinking o' such a thing, it's far too great a task f' the likes o' a young girl like yourselves," said Mary with a somewhat incredulous tone in her voice.

With that Elfie turned away and moved a few paces nearer the cart signifying that she did not wish to be pressed further on her future.

The lake grew larger as the forlorn procession neared. It gleamed and shimmered in the sunlight, looking at its best as if to say its farewell to the shepherd from the valley head.

The group now passed through Howtown. In all, nearly two hundred people lived in and around the area and several of the villagers were gathered in small groups outside their cottages to witness the passing of the little funeral procession. Snippets of conversation floated through the air.

'Ah, the poor child, to be left on her own in that wild valley.'

'What'll she do now, Where will she go?'

'She needs looking after; see how thin and pale she be.'

Elfie showed no visible reaction to the comments but deep down she knew that these where the questions that soon she would be asking herself.

A few of the villagers joined the procession, whether or not they were being supportive or just curious could not be ascertained, but at least it gave some comfort to Elfie as if some of the residents of Howtown cared even if she did not know them personally.

The cart now slowed down considerably as the track steepened over the Coombs. The route zigzagged to ease the gradient but even then the horse struggled somewhat as it was usual to harness a pair for trips over the pass. Eventually, the horse won the battle and the summit was reached. Now there was a steady descent towards the church of St Martins.

The church stood in an isolated position and was the parish church for Martindale and its surroundings although plans were afoot to build a new church nearer to Howtown. Save for a large yew tree at the rear of the building, the church was completely open to the surrounding fells.

The interior of the church was a simple affair; the altar furnishings consisted of a wooden table, a cross and two candlesticks all made from wood. In a corner stood a stone font which had at one time been a standing stone on the roman road which ran over the fell top of High Street. At one point it had been used by the locals for sharpening tools, the marks still being visible, but was later it was hollowed out and placed in the church to be used as a font. The windows in the church were of plain glass as it was felt that stained glass was not needed with such beautiful scenery visible to the eye whichever window was looked through.

Reverend Winterton now paced backwards and forwards outside the church door, he was still unsure how best to conduct the service, or more realistically what words of comfort he could offer about a non-believer.

He looked up to see the funeral party now approaching the church. He hurriedly went round to the back of the church where Jos Leyburn the sexton was sitting on a pile of earth next to the newly dug grave. Leyburn was eating bread and pickles and continually swigging from a bottle, which obviously contained some form of alcohol.

"Will ye make y'self scarce and show a bit o respect, come back in half an hour to lower the coffin, and keep off the grog till we've finished," said Winterton contemptuously.

With the scolding still ringing in his ears, Leyburn disappeared behind the trunk of the yew tree and scrambled over the wall out of site.

The funeral party had increased along the way and now numbered about twenty as it arrived at the little church. As soon as it stopped Elfie suddenly looked up and about at her surroundings. Her eyes were drawn to the bunches of daffodils which grew in profusion around the churchyard. The flowers were just starting to open out to display their yellow trumpets as if to herald the spring. Elfie moved to one side and stooped down at one of the clumps of flowers, gently she plucked a small bunch and then arose, and clutching the flowers she walked back to where the coffin was being unloaded. She reached up and placed the flowers on the coffin and then stepped back out of the way.

Winterton came over to the girl and offered his condolences on her loss. Mick and Davy Jarrow, Ned Walkden and his son John shouldered the coffin. The Walkdens farmed at Howtown and had joined forces with Robert Mason on many occasions at dipping and shearing times. The little group assembled in a dignified order and Reverend Winterton led the party into the church.

Chapter three

Elfie startled as if being suddenly awakened from a deep trance. Indeed, she had been staring down at the grave before her. The rough coffin now laid at the bottom of the hole, on its lid, a handful of earth cast by Reverend Winterton and the poignant bunch of daffodils so hurriedly placed there earlier by Elfie. How long she had remained there after the funeral party had dispersed she did not know. It was as if she had been transfixed in time neither past nor present and the future unknown.

"Time t' go now lass," the hand of Jos Leyburn fell heavily on her hunched shoulder. " I need t' finish of now an' I've gotten a long trek back 'ome after that."

"Yes, oh yes," she replied, "I'd best be away now."

"Are ye sure yer alright getting back 'ome across yon fell," said Leyburn in a gruff tone.

Elfie now composed herself,

"Yes, I'm quite alright now," and rising to her feet she quickly extracted herself from his hand which had been gripping her shoulder.

Leyburn was not the most desirable person to be stood alone with in a quiet churchyard. With that thought in mind she quickly thanked him for his labours and promised to pay him next time she was in the village, though when that would be she did not know. She hurried away from the scene and set off along Martindale, which was the shortest route back home. Soon the metallic clunk of steel hitting stone and earth could be heard as the gravedigger started to fill in the hole; the noise receded as she progressed on her way.

Martindale is a long valley with a verdant green floor of fields, each enclosed by walls built from a mixture of slate and limestone. The head of the valley is dominated by the Nab, a large conical shaped mountain. The valley splits here, forming the deep sided valley of Rampsgill to the left and Bannerdale to the right. Beda Fell forms the barrier to the next valley on the right and the rugged crags of Pikeawassa and Branthwaite Crag form the barrier between Fusedale, it was over the latter that Elfie now proceeded.

This was the pedestrian route back to the croft and the shortest way into the upper reaches of Martindale, she had accompanied her father on a number of sheep gatherings in this valley and knew the route well. The path started to climb steeply and as it rose a cool breeze could be felt blowing down the valley bringing the colder air down from the fell tops. The long grasses turned in its direction so that their broad blades formed a green carpet in front of her. As she climbed the steepening path above Nettlehow Crags reality and the seriousness of her situation started to flood back into her mind. Problems started to manifest themselves before her eyes.

How was she, a mere girl going to cope with a flock of sheep and about to lamb at that? Would she be allowed to stay on in the valley now that her father was dead, after all, he was the shepherd not her? Would she be allowed to stay on at the croft and carry on the work? Was she capable? Under her fathers guidance she had become proficient in many of the tasks associated with sheep farming, but who would guide her now?

All these doubts swept back and forth through her mind, round and round, first one problem and then the next until they had gone full circle and back to the original thought, new problems were continually added on, no sooner had she considered one when the next one manifested itself. Elfie put her hands over her head as if to try and block out the thoughts from her brain.

She had been walking fast as she was accustomed to in her daily work with her father around the valley and up onto the fells. The unconscious effort of climbing the steep path caused her to break out into a sweat and beads of moisture formed on her forehead. She swept her arm across her brow to wipe them off. The sweat running down her temples entered her eyes causing them to sting, something in the recesses of her mind told her that it was not just the physical effort which caused her to sweat so profusely, but rather a kind of fear of the situation that she now found herself in.

Elfie stopped and pulled up the coarse material of her dress and wiped her face and neck. She then walked on for a few more minutes to a point where the path turned and the gradient eased; the young girl flopped down in the heather, her long skirt fanning out around her. She lay back against the heather, which formed a comfortable couch and gazed up into the spring sky. It was a brilliant blue, almost cloudless save for the mare's tales of high cirrus clouds, which heralded a change in the weather; the

18

observer knew the signs well. As she gazed she passed from the trials of the day and the problems of the future into a dreamless sleep where calm and contentment abound.

Elfie lay therefore some considerable time in a state of sublime peace and would have lain considerably longer had it not been for a feeling of hot moisture gently moving across her cheek. This feeling was accompanied by numbness in her legs and then the altogether common sound of sheep bleating. She opened her eyes and met with two brown eyes gazing down at her. The moisture on her cheek was caused by Tess gently licking her as if to reassure her that she had at least one supporter in the world. Looking about she saw several sheep which had now gathered around her. They were heavily pregnant ewes which should now be down on the valley floor.

She soon realised the cause of the numbness in her legs, it was Moss who had taken advantage of the comfort of her skirts and lain across the lower reaches of her body. He eyed the sheep casually and then his mistress, awaiting a command to sort out the woolly infiltrators that dared to invade his space.

The sheep continued to surround her on three sides until only the path forward was visible from her semi-recumbent position. The girl's eyes were drawn to the path, as she looked she spoke aloud,

"This is the answer, I must go forward like the path, this is now my life."

Elfie rose to her feet, pushing Moss from her legs as she did so. He turned and stood beside the girl who was now his mistress, her arm dropped gently to her side and her hand fondled the soft fur around his ears. She pulled and twined the wispy strands around her fingers gently teasing out the tangles that frequently formed thereabouts.

"Yes," she said out loud, Moss turned his head towards her cocking it to one side and lifting one ear, she smiled down at him, "between us we'll resolve all the problems that lie ahead, won't we old chap?"

Tess, not wanting to be left out of the conversation gave a loud bark.

"And you too Tessy girl, we'll need your help as well. Away Tess," cried Elfie and the dog ran round behind the small group of ewes and started to move them forward. Moss left Elfie's side and flanked the ewes from the right without need of a command.

Elfie followed behind with a spring in her step as if some great burden had suddenly been lifted from her shoulders. She was resolute, this was her life, and she would not give up that easily.

Elfie continued up the path until the gradient eased and the path turned to cross the col between the two higher fell tops. This was a delightful area and one, which she had visited many times by the path up from Fusedale. Tiny tarns glinted in the sun, bordered by reeds, wood rush and cotton grass, which swayed gently in the cool breeze now sweeping across the fell top. Lingy heather grew abundantly interspersed with barren patches of brown peat. Many edges of the peat had been hollowed out by the resident sheep to form a resting place and protection from the weather.

The girl strode on behind the sheep and the two dogs, her movements mimicking the swaying grasses. As she moved forward she reached the edge of the plateau and the valley opened up before her and swept down towards Howtown and Ullswater where not many hours before she had walked in despair. There was her past, full of memories and experiences and now she hoped her future.

Life had been lonely enough save for the companionship of her father. Few people visited the dale and social niceties were confined to a few infrequent visits to the village on business. There had been the occasional dance at the village hall after the washing and shearing. Elfie was always accompanied by her father and they had always left early before any festivities commenced as he sought to spare his daughter from the excesses of drunken farmers and the likes of unsavoury suitors.

Now she would be alone in the valley that now lay at her feet. The decisions would be hers. Success or failure rested squarely on these young shoulders. She had developed most of the skills needed to manage the flock, yet she now needed the confidence to match her abilities. Even then she could not do everything single-handed. She would need help; perhaps she could get this from the Jarrow's.

On this beautiful spring day, tinged with extreme sadness Elfreda Mason gazed down the valley. Did her future lie here, could she stay? Then she was away down the path to the croft following the dogs and the bleating ewes.

Chapter four

Two pools of the deepest blue would best describe the eyes of Elfrida Mason. They were delicately set below a broad forehead, which was topped with tousled blonde hair that reached down to well below her shoulders. Its colour would suggest that she was perhaps of Norse descent, but in fact a trace of her ancestry would have uncovered German origins on her mother's side of the family. The hair, beautiful as it was, was neglected and unkempt due solely to the difficult times the girl had experienced over the last few weeks.

The high cheekbones of her face gave her an aristocratic appearance; her cheeks were a little hollow, serving to accentuate the former. Her nose was small and slightly turned upwards at the tip, on either side, a small band of delicate freckles swept from the nose down to the cheekbones. Her mouth was set below an upper lip which had a slight pout to it emphasising her full red lips. Her face had a reddened appearance due to exposure to sun, wind and general rough weather.

Her body was of a good shape with neat breasts set high above her trim waist. She had well proportioned hips and strong legs, developed through all the walking she took part in around the valley and on the fell tops. The looks of the girl did not portray her age, giving her the appearance of a young schoolgirl attending one of the posh schools which existed thereabouts around Penrith.

Yet it was the eyes that the few who had the opportunity to meet her remembered her by. They could be cold and piercing, scornful and enquiring and generally displaying harshness in keeping with the surroundings of her upbringing. Just sometimes they revealed her inner feelings and amusement. First her lips would break into a smile and then her eyes would enrich the smile with a warmth and brightness, which could charm any oppressor.

The first rays of sunlight filtered through the ragged material which formed a curtain on the window of the girl's bedroom. The ill-fitting window frame allowed a draught to act on the curtains causing them to move too and fro. This action deflected the rays of the sun falling upon a feather pillow which was distorted and scrunched up almost into a ball indicating that the owner of the head laid there upon had spent a restless night of repose.

The rays danced across the face of the sleeping girl who had only managed to achieve a deep slumber before the dawn broke. The sunlight continued to tease the delicate eyelashes on the tightly closed eyes causing alternate ripples of dark and light.

The sunlight strengthened and continued its flickering like the candle in the wind but with ever increasing intensity. This was new life, a new beginning, a new awakening.

The light acted on the inner senses of the sleeping girl until she gently awakened. Then she startled and sat bolt upright on the bed. Elfie gasped out loud and then looking around her, she gave out a reassuring sigh. She was where she belonged, not where her dreams had led her to believe she was. Was it the intensity of the sun's rays or the intensity of the dream that aroused her?

She lay back on the bed again, stretching her limbs and arching her back in feline fashion, bringing all the joints and bones in her young body to life and preparing them for the day's labour ahead.

Then the covers were flung back and in one swift movement her feet touched the cold flagged floor making her grimace slightly as the weight of her rising body pressed them ever more firmly onto the cold stonework. She pulled back the rough curtains allowing the sunlight to filter into the room, bringing with it both light and a degree of warmth.

She moved towards a small, tarnished mirror whose silvering had seen better days; it hung on the wall by a nail driven through the crude wooden frame surrounding the glass. Elfie peered long and hard into the glass and scrutinised what she saw therein.

A tired face, pale and wan looking in the early morning light looked back at her. The hair was tousled and unkempt giving her the appearance of a vagrant. Her nightdress was showing signs of considerable wear and was badly discoloured around its lower edges where it touched the floor. Looking round the room she saw an air of neglect.

All of her waking hours and indeed many when she should have been resting had been spent in the process of caring for the dying man and looking after the flock of sheep. The womanly chores which she normally attended to had been pushed to the back of her mind.

She flinched visibly as reality was suddenly borne home to her. Her thoughts erupted as she spoke out loudly to herself.

"This is not you that you see in the mirror, this room is not how you would let it be."

She sank down on the edge of the bed. There was so much to do, but where to start?

The sheep and the imminent lambing were the main priority, but first she must restore herself in order to maintain the former.

Grabbing the small bag which hung by a cord on the headboard of the bed she moved across the room. Gathering up a rough towel which hung over the back of the chair she hurried out into the main room of the croft. She made a mental note to reorganise this part of the dwelling as soon as she had some spare time. Elfie pulled open the door and stepped outside inhaling deeply, filling her lungs with the crisp, fresh morning air. The two dogs ran around her whining impatiently to be off on the day's business.

The girl ran down to the stream, which glinted in the morning sunlight. The water flowed fresh and fast after the heavy downpour which had taken place during the night. The stream tumbled down through a jumble of rocks which were adorned by small rowan trees. At present they were devoid of foliage. Near the base of the rocks was a deep pool formed in a rock basin, which provided a natural bathing place and also served as a dub for the washing of sheep.

In a trice, the nightdress fell to the ground in a crumpled white heap on to the surrounding grass. Gasping out loudly, she eased her nakedness into the icy water. She grimaced as the cold invaded the intimate parts of her female form. As the water reached her upper body she continued to squirm until only her head was visible. Then she ducked under the water for several seconds, holding her breath, rising out of the water and drawing in a deep breath, she shivered visibly. Droplets of water adorned her upper body glistening in the early morning sunlight as if she was covered in diamonds.

After the initiation, Elfie reached for the bag and emptying out the contents she proceeded to bathe and wash her hair. Now that her body had accustomed itself to the cold she relaxed in the soothing waters until she felt cleansed and rejuvenated and then she climbed out of the pool and stood on the grass. She felt free and unrestricted, standing there in her nakedness, previously on such occasions for the sake of modesty she had to wait until her father was away on the fell before bathing.

Taking the towel she dried herself off, the roughness of the material causing redness on the sensitive parts of her body. This done, she gathered up the nightdress which had lain discarded on the ground and wrapped it around her body. She sat down on a large boulder beside the stream. The top of the boulder was hollowed out and formed a primitive chair.

So many times she had sat in this place without a care in the world, more recently and of course less frequently she had sat here hunched up with all the burdens of her father's illness resting heavily upon her shoulders.

Elfie recalled the happy times and tears welled up within the deep pools of those blue eyes. Despair could be contained no longer and she wept out in anguish, loudly and uncontrollably. She had contained her feelings for so long in those difficult weeks, bottling up her emotions and with no-one to share her problems. Now the healing process could begin.

Thinking fondly of the man, who despite his sharp, curt attitude had raised the girl in his most caring way, she rose and walked slowly back to the croft.

The shepherd's abode was a small single storey construction built from random slate and stone blocks, some of the materials had come from the small quarry further down the dale and brought to the site by horse and cart. However, much use had been made of whatever was available and yet the building was thick-walled and sturdy to stand the forces of nature around its location at the head of the dale.

The inside was relatively dark even on the brightest of days due to the fact that there were only three windows and these were quite small. There was a window on either side of the door and one in the rear wall. Entry through the door brought one into a good-sized living room. Built into the gable end was a fireplace with a crooked chimneybreast reaching up to the roof. To the side of the fireplace was the bed of the shepherd with the foot end tucked into the space formed by the protruding chimneybreast. Over the bed was a rail set into the wall at one end and suspended from one of the beams at the other. Hung from this rail was a thick curtain attached by large wooden rings, which reached, almost to the floor. Draped from this rail was a further length of material at right angles to fill the gap above the bed head. There was an easy chair and a rocking chair in the centre of the room and a dresser set against the back wall. Set into the deep recessed window was a simple wooden seat. The floor was flagged with thick, smooth stone slates which were polished from the traffic of feet which had passed over them for many, many years. The slates sloped downwards towards the door which was an advantage when mopping out or if rain forced its way in around the door when the wind was driving it in that particular direction. A large bit-rug made from hundreds of pieces of cloth sewn together covered the floor near to the fireplace. An oil lamp was suspended from the ceiling which also provided a little additional heat in winter when it was lit. In the lighter months candles were used as the source of light as the working days dictated long hours out of doors. The wall adjacent to the main door had a doorframe without a door leading into a small kitchen which contained a stone sink and a tap connected to a pipe which ran out into the stream at a higher level and so provided a source of running water without the need to collect it in a bucket. Unfortunately it froze up in winter and the bucket had to be resorted to for collection of water. There were a number of shelves and two cupboards which contained a goodly store of food and provisions. A small table and two stools made up a dining area. Halfway back across the kitchen was a rough planked wall with an ill-fitting door. Entry through the door gave access to Elfie's own little bedroom. This room had been built by her father when she was about nine years old to give the young girl her deserved privacy. The room was only six feet square and the window in the rear wall of the building let light into this area. Elfie had a narrow bed, a small chest of drawers and her clothes hung on a rail secured to the crude wooden wall, also on this wall was her mirror.

Across from the house was another building of similar construction and size. At sometime in the past this had also been a dwelling but it was now used as a store, workshop and at times a place for sheep and their lambs if they were in need of extra care. In this building was a store of wood which was brought up by cart from Dale End Farm by the Jarrows. Peat, which was cut from further up the valley was also stored here for the shepherd's fire. There was also an assortment of tools and some foodstuff.

Elfie now busied herself in the little kitchen. In one corner stood a small cast iron stove which when lit heated up very quickly by means of a grid which controlled the air entering at the base. This device enabled the stove to draw up very rapidly. Robert Mason had acquired the stove from a Romany caravan and installed it in the kitchen with a flue pipe through the outside wall. It was possible to boil a pan of water quite quickly on the stove when it was lit and this was what Elfie had just done.

A good stock of oats enabled her to prepare a large bowl of porridge and this was the staple diet for the shepherd first thing in the morning, providing sustenance and energy for the day ahead. Elfie could not enjoy the luxury of porridge made with milk but through the addition of sugar or treacle the mixture was quite palatable. The porridge was always followed by a substantial pot of tea. The little stove could be damped down and kept alight all day if necessary.

Elfie's father always believed that the dogs should be fed at night so that they could digest their food as they rested. The girl was of the opinion that they, like humans needed food to work on and so since she had been in control whilst her father was ill, she had taken to giving them half of their food in the morning and half at night. They were fed on a mixture of dried meat and biscuits which was prepared in bulk and then stored for the two of them in the outbuilding.

Moss and Tess ate greedily as if it was their last ever meal. When they had finished wolfing the food down they would swap empty dishes in case there were a few morsels left, but this was never the case.

Elfie had dressed in a hodden grey wool skirt which almost reached down to her ankles. It had been purchased at a market during her last visit to Pooley Bridge with her father. As such, it was in good condition, but the rigours of shepherding would soon necessitate repairs. She was well able to carry out sewing repairs, but unlike many of the farmer's wives thereabouts she did not possess the skills or indeed the equipment to produce her own clothing. To that end, clothing had to be bought at market stalls as having no family there were no hand downs.

On her upper body she wore a thick woollen jumper and then a sleeveless jerkin made from suede leather. This garment would be essential when walking on the higher fells as the temperature would be several degrees below that of the valley. She had a stout pair of boots on her feet, it was essential to keep her feet as dry as possible as much of the ground was often wet and boggy.

Moss and Tess were sat outside the door waiting for the day's work to commence. As they set of on the rounds of the sheep the two dogs stayed close to the heels of the shepherdess, they knew that the ewes were broody at this time of the year and any confrontation had to be avoided at this critical time in the ewe's pregnancies.

The flock was composed entirely of Herdwicks, a sturdy, coarse-woolled sheep. They are a fairly small breed of sheep and have distinctive grey mottled legs and faces. The nose has a rimy appearance resembling hoar frost and this feature is a sign of good breeding. Their fleeces keep out the worst of weathers and they survive off little herbage making them ideally suited to the harsh conditions of the Lakeland fells. The breed has a 'heafing' instinct which means that they become 'heafed' to their own piece of the fellside and almost always return that part of the fell. It is thought that they were introduced by Norse settlers in the 10th and 11th Centuries. The word 'Herdwick' meaning pasture where the sheep are kept, deriving from the Norse 'Herd-vic' (a sheep farm).

Most of the twinters, sheep approaching their second birthday had been bratted to prevent them from being serviced by the ram. A young sheep can become stunted in growth or even die if she lambs at too young an age. Therefore the bratting took place in early November and is in effect an apron of coarse, heavy-duty cloth sewn over its bottom. The brat remains in place until February and then the ewe lambs as a thrinter or three year old.

With the exception of a small number, the ewes were thrinters or older and lambing was imminent for most of them. The round of the flock was completed and as yet no lambs had been born.

Elfie then cast her eyes to the fells, a common practice at this time of year. She was looking for wiley ewes which had escaped the gather and she knew from a count of the sheep that there were still a number higher up on the fellside, she recounted her journey back from the funeral when she had then brought down a small group that had evaded the gather.

Looking upwards she espied around ten ewes near some rock outcrops on the north-eastern slopes leading up towards Loadpot Hill. The girl set of in the direction of the sheep following a faint trod used by both sheep and shepherd to gain an easy passage through the long bents, reeds and grasses which grew so abundantly in the area. The dogs ran excitedly around her feet anticipating the forthcoming challenge.

Tess was rapidly acquiring Moss's craft and was now taking over the more difficult herding tasks. She was perhaps a bit on the strong side with the amount of eye – 'the eye of control' which she displayed and could at times remain transfixed, willing them without movement into a state of stalemate. Elfie had to watch out for this habit and give additional commands to move Tess into action. Her father had noted this trait in the young dog and was of the opinion that the dog would not make a good worker. He teased Elfie about this, which only deepened her resolve to prove him wrong. This she had done and her continued efforts were slowly overcoming the problem and Tess was developing into a first class sheepdog.

Moss on the other hand was more free eyed and had method in his work with the sheep; he had confidence to move the sheep with quiet authority. However, he stood no nonsense from the stubborn and wayward creatures and had the courage to 'grip' the sheep in face-to-face confrontation.

A Merlin flew low over the rough peat hags and curlews made their bubbling cries as they hopped about in the long grasses. The girl reached a level platform flanked by a low rock outcrop, here she paused and observed the errant ewes some considerable distance above her.

"Come by Tess," she commanded in a low voice to the dog at her side and immediately it set of flanking left up the hillside, she moved at great speed until she was parallel with the five ewes below a rocky outcrop. Here she slowed and crouching low on her belly moving at an angle to gain a position slightly above and behind the sheep. Tess then stopped eycing the sheep.

"Come on," cried Elfie in a loud voice and the dog moved forwards making the sheep move down the hillside towards her.

When the sheep were nearing her she gave the command 'away to me' and Moss flanked right up the hill and moved in behind the ewes and brought them down to a spot near where the girl stood. He then lay down watching the sheep, ready to move if they fell out of line. At the point when Moss had taken over, Tess set off up the hillside under her own initiative this time, she knew what she had to do. She circled round and soon came in behind another three ewes and this time moved in decisively, bringing the group down towards where the girl waited. The first group of ewes had now settled and so again she commanded Moss to flank right to pick up this second cluster, this he did expertly and soon they joined the first group. Moss again lay down close by, expertly watching for any signs of rebellion.

This now left only two ewes to be fetched, this being a more difficult task for the dog as now there was little flocking instinct with small numbers of sheep. The ewes split on her approach, Tess stopped, eyeing the two and making a decision, very swiftly she outflanked the ewe which was the furthest away and drove it back towards the other ewe which had stood there nonchalantly observing the proceedings. She then moved in at close quarters and expertly moved the two ewes down towards the others. Sensing that the approaching ewes might make another bid for freedom Moss set off in a wide arc to the right and moved in to assist Tess. All this was done with no command from the shepherdess. Soon all the sheep were huddled together in a group with the two dogs adjacent to each other at their rear. The dogs knew their job better than their mistress.

"Come on," called Elfie and the dogs set of towards her, she stepped back a little so as not to impede the progress of the sheep and then she fell in behind the group with the dogs at her side.

"Good boy, good girl," she said and the two dogs looked up approvingly at her.

As she walked on behind the sheep she noticed that the last three which had reluctantly been brought down by Tess bore different smit markings on their fleeces to those of her own flock. Ellfie remembered this happening on a number of occasions, particularly when the sheep were brought down for washing or shearing. Her father had identified the marks from a book which he kept in a large chest at the foot of his bed, a chest which she had not been allowed access to as it was kept locked. 'The Shepherd's Guide as the book was called had been written back in 1817 by Joseph Walker of Martindale. It contained descriptions and illustrations of all the markings used by farmers and shepherds in the

Cumberland area. From this it was possible to discover who the errant sheep belonged to. It was usual to keep any sheep, found penned up until the next meeting of the local Shepherds Society. Then they had to be taken to the meet and reclaimed by their owners. Unmarked sheep were penned separately and often-lengthy arguments broke out as to who had the rightful ownership of them.

Once penned, Elfie could also examine the clip marks on their ears for further evidence and then she could consult the guide, but first she would have to find the key for the chest.

Reaching the valley floor the sheep were expertly driven through the gate to the inbye. Elfie then opened the gate to a small pen and by simple commands from the girl the two dogs separated the errant sheep from the other group and drove them into the pen. Elfie quickly closed the gate and secured it with a length of rope wound round the posts. The other sheep had now mixed in with the rest of the flock and a round of loud bleating ensured as a chorus of welcome to the wanderers.

As Elfie made her way back to the cottage she became aware of a noise coming from further down the valley. At first she could not discern what it was and then she realised that it was the sound of a horse galloping. Standing on a large rock she could to see down the valley and was able to discern a horse and rider approaching on the track which ran down the side of the valley. Elfie stepped down from her viewpoint and walked back to her house.

Chapter five

Elfie was sat on the stone bench outside the door of the croft listening to the approaching hoof beats. As the horse rounded the last bend in the track and the house came into view the rider pulled on the reins and slowed the horse to a steady trot. The girl looked in the direction of the approaching rider and discerned the figure of Jacob Farrington, the son of Lord Farrington who owned most of the land hereabouts including Fusedale. The dreaded moment had arrived sooner than expected. Jacob had the task of management of the many tenanted farms and a number of employees who worked as shepherds for his lordship in various parts of the eastern end of Cumberland. He could only be here for one purpose.

The manor was a good ten miles away and Jacob had obviously set off early in the day to reach Fusedale at this early hour. He was an impressive sight mounted on his dark chestnut coloured mare. As he drew nearer she looked up at his face, he had dark brown hair which surmounted a handsome face. Blue-grey eyes, somewhat piercing were set widely above an angular jaw. His sharp features hid inner warmth in his character, his forthrightness was obviously inherited from his father, who was intensely disliked by those in his employ. Often, Jacob displayed these traits but could also be kind and gentle to the few who could penetrate his armour, conversely, it was known by some that he also had a devious side to his nature.

The horse was pulled to a halt and the man sprung down from the saddle with ease and agility. Rarely did he visit the valley as Robert Mason was a competent and trusted employee requiring little supervision and when he had visited he paid little attention to the girl as his dealings were with the shepherd. He was somewhat taken aback by the rough beauty of the girl that now stood up and approached him. Elfie spoke first.

"Good morning sir, what brings you to the dale at this early hour?" Farrington was silent for a minute or more as he surveyed the young woman stood before him and then he spoke in a soft tone.

"You are Robert Mason's daughter, I believe?"

"Yes," was the simple reply.

"Then I am afraid that I am the bearer of bad news, I have a letter here from my father." At that he reached into his inner pocket and pulled out a folded piece of paper which he opened out.

"I will read it to you," he said.

"Sir, I would prefer to read it myself if you please."

Jacob handed the letter to her, clearly failing to conceal the look of surprise on his face that this girl who had spent all her life in this lonely Lakeland valley was able to read. Elfie witnessed his expression and showed this by giving him a short piercing stare, then her eyes fell to the piece of paper in her hand and she read the words contained therein.

The letter offered condolences on the death of her father and complimented him on his work as a shepherd. It then went on to say that she would have to vacate the cottage within the week as a new shepherd would have to be employed and that the dwelling went with the job. It was signed on behalf of Lord Farrington by his estate manager.

Elfie shook visibly and handing the letter back to Jacob she took a few faltering steps backwards. The back of her knees hit the stone seat by the door of the croft and she sank down heavily onto the smooth stone slab.

"I'm sorry that I have to be the bringer of bad news to you, particularly so soon after the loss of your father, but it is his lordships wish and I have to act on it," said Jacob in a dispassionate tone.

Tears welled up in the girl's eyes and then she sobbed uncontrollably. Jacob was not prepared for this reaction; rather, he expected a fiery outburst as was common with the girl's father, but none of the parental trait seemed evident in the young girl.

After a few minutes of silence between the two of them Elfie regained some of her composure. She looked up at the young man, her ruddy cheeks streaked with the run of her tears. She wiped them with the back of her hand and then in a faltering voice she spoke.

"Sir, I had not expected such a turn of events and so soon. I was looking to carry on with my father's work; it is all I know, all that I care about."

Then she sobbed out loudly again. Jacob was touched by the girl's sorrow and dismay but was unsure as how best to proceed, he had a job to do but could not carry it out whilst the girl was in such an uncontrollable state.

Suddenly, he found himself seated beside her. The mighty Jacob, son of Lord Farrington had had his armour pierced, his feelings penetrated by this forlorn girl before him. An arm, heavy with compassion found its way around her shoulder and he pulled her towards him. Her head fell against his chest and she sobbed quietly. He had never been this close to her before having given her nothing more than a cursory glance when he had called to see the shepherd. Somehow, now he felt puzzled, this was different, he had never comforted a woman in distress and he now felt deeply emotional.

It was several minutes before Elfie gained her composure and then she pushed away the comforting arm that had lain so caringly about her shoulder. She stood up and turned to look down on Jacob who remained seated with a somewhat puzzled look on his face. Some of the parental defiance welled up inside her as she started to speak, at first falteringly and then with a positive air.

"Since my father has been ill these many months I have cared for him and your sheep. I have done this task single-handed and I doubt that you have any idea how hard I have toiled to keep things going. And what is my reward for this, a letter from him who neither knows nor cares about me?

He is not aware of my skills, I have worked along side my father for as long as I care to remember, I have learnt all the aspects of the job and I have proved my capability over the last months when my father was too ill to venture outside the house, let alone tend the flock. I cannot leave this place, it is my home and all that I care about, I would sooner die than leave here."

All this time Jacob had sat there and when the outburst had as he thought finished, she flashed a defiant look at him.

"You want a shepherd, a good shepherd don't you, then look no further than the end of your nose, you've got one, I will do the job and do it well."

With that said, she flounced off into the croft slamming the door behind her.

Jacob sat there for a few minutes quite stunned by the outburst and at first unable to decide how best to proceed. Then he stood up and gathered his resolve, this mere slip of a girl was not going to talk to him like that, maybe she had a point, perhaps she was able to do the work but his father would not agree to it, hadn't he told him to 'get rid of her'.

He turned and knocked loudly on the door, there was no answer from within. His temper rising he again knocked on the door much louder this time. Still there was no answer; he was loosing his patience now. He banged the door forcibly making it rattle on its hinges.

"Miss Mason, open this door at once, you are only making things more difficult for yourself'.

The door opened and Elfie stood there looking flushed, she bit on her upper lip.

"Oh sir, I did not mean to be discourteous to his lordship or indeed yourself, but you must give me a chance. The flock is one of the best in the area and the ewes are about to lamb, it is me who has tended them and got them to this stage. I beg you to give me a chance, at least let me try, do not dismiss me."

Then she fell silent and again tears welled up in her eyes, she brushed them aside with the sleeve of her jacket.

"It remains to be seen by the number of lambs they produce and more importantly by the prices they fetch at market later on. But I do acknowledge your labours, it cannot have been easy for you over the last few months," said Jacob.

Elfie's eyes looked down at the floor.

"It was not easy sir," she replied. "Save for a bit of help from the Jarrow's when they could spare time to bring up supplies I have worked single-handed." Elfie looked up at Jacob and her face broke out into an appealing sorrowful expression.

"I'm sorry, but I cannot go against my father's wishes, you really must leave."

Elfie looked questionly into Jacobs face.

"His lordship wouldn't know he has never been hereabouts or was likely to for that matter."

"That is true," said Jacob "but word could get back to him."

There was a pause for moment and then Elfie spoke again, she knew that she was fast losing the chance of staying,

"If your father has never been seen hereabouts who is likely to tell him about me?"

Jacob now faced a dilemma; whilst he acknowledged her capabilities he also had his father's wishes to contend with. He looked at Elfie whose eyes looked up into his face trying to read his inner thoughts. The puzzled feelings he had experienced earlier again swept over him. His innermost thoughts milled about in his head, he felt compassion for the girl, and yes, he wanted to help her, but how?

"You can stay for the time-being, I will speak to my father and try and persuade him to give you a chance, but I cannot promise anything. I will come back and see you within a few days." He then bade her good day, turned and went forward and sprung lithely up onto the mares back. Pulling the horse's head back, he clicked its flanks with the heels of his boots and rode swiftly away from the croft.

The girl stood there some time listening to the sound of the receding hoof-beats as the horse and rider proceeded down the valley. She then turned and sat down on the stone bench and leaned back against the wall of the house. She was aware that the diminishing hoof beats did not fade away to nothing but seemed to stop whilst they still had a degree of volume to them.

Chapter six

As Jacob Farrington rode away along the valley track he was deep within his thoughts, he had experienced something in his encounter with the young Miss Mason which he had not known before. He was totally unprepared for the emotive event and was unsure as to how best to deal with his emotions.

The track passed through a natural cutting in the rock outcrop and because of its height it blocked off the view up the dale. It was at this point that the rider drew hard on the reins and pulled the horse to a halt. Jacob dismounted, leaving the horse to take the opportunity to graze on the sparse vegetation at the side of the track.

Farrington climbed up over the rocks until he could see the croft again. Elfie was clearly discernable sitting outside the dwelling where he had left her but a few minutes earlier. From his viewpoint he was unable to see her face but could see that she was sat leaning forwards and appeared to be holding her face in her hands. Curiosity gave way to compassion as he viewed the scene and again he experienced the same feelings as he had when he was sat beside her on the bench outside the house.

Young Jacob Farrington had been raised through his childhood and formative years in a strict manner. His mother had died during the birth of his younger sister Marianne and it was shortly after this family bereavement that the young Farrington was sent away to be educated at a boarding school in North Yorkshire. Each Christmas and summer he returned home to the hall and it was during these visits home that he observed a change in his father. From being a kind, caring parent his father was becoming embittered and intolerant. He barely showed any interest in his teenage son and seemed to be completely absorbed in the affairs of the estate. The only thing, which seemed to please his lordship was when his son emulated the very qualities that he himself exhibited. And so it was that the young Farrington when away from home was introvert, albeit keen to learn and when at home, unhappy and uncertain.

Upon the completion of his education, Jacob Farrington returned to the manor and was put to work under the watchful eyes of Tom Larson, Lord Farrington's estate manager. The task was to learn all aspects of the management of the vast estate. Young Farrington learned quickly and soon became proficient in management and agricultural skills. Indeed, so innovative in his approach to land management, he introduced a number of radical changes which produced excellent results in efficiency. It was to this end that at the age of twenty-one he was assigned to oversee the northern acres.

This description was an understatement, as the area was quite vast and contained no less than eighteen farms and nine large flocks of hill sheep. These were spread over a vast tract of land including high fells and remote valleys. Most of the flocks were farm based with the exception of two, which were managed by shepherds. One flock was located in Cawdale and the other in Fusedale where he now stood.

Farrington's gaze left the young girl and he lifted his eyes to view the surroundings. His eyes followed the contours of the fell sides; he noted the rocky promontories and deep clefts, which cut into the hillsides. He saw the small streams which cascaded down to join the little river which sidled idly along the valley floor. The area held a fascination for him and he thought deeply about how the girl could have been raised and coped with the remoteness of the place. It was harsh and virtually untamed, and yet, it had a strange brooding splendour. Surely some of the environment was within the girl, she was her surroundings, like the valley, mysterious, brooding and yet somehow simply beautiful and so much yet to be discovered. If he explored this valley for a lifetime, could he ever come to know all its intimate secrets, every rock, every cleft, all the grasses, bogs and bracken? Could he ever come to know Elfrida Mason?

As he gazed he though he caught sight of a figure moving across the hillside directly opposite where he stood. He looked hard, he saw the movement again and then it was gone out of sight, who or what was it? He looked long and hard but saw nothing, it was probably a sheep, but it had not moved like a sheep. He dismissed it from his mind and his eyes again were drawn towards the croft. He then saw Elfie get up from her seat and look down the valley in his direction. He lowered his stance, could she see him? He then saw her turn and walk indoors.

Jacob turned and climbed down from his vantage point, he called to the horse which had spent the last quarter hour grazing quietly, it trotted over to him obediently and stood whist he mounted it. With a pull of the reins he turned the horse and set the animal at a steady trot. This was uncharacteristic of the man as a fast canter or gallop was his usual want. He was deep within himself, his mind was in turmoil.

The errand he had embarked upon had not turned out as expected; it seemed such a simple task. But now, instead of issuing his father's instructions to the late shepherd's daughter by serving notice on her to quit the dale, he found himself pondering on ways to retain her. He had been surprised by her manner; she was not the rough country girl that he had imagined with coarse vocabulary, but with a rather more refined air like that of some middle class girl. There was a gentle simplicity and determination intermingled with a large degree of sorrow, only to be expected at this time.

It was her simple attractiveness, which affected him most, those blue eyes, though sorrowful had an expression of wildness about them. This girl was not going to give in easily to his father's wishes and he was not sure that he wanted her to do so in any case. So why was he so unsettled.

In looks Elfie was not unlike Amelia Bancroft, although Amelia's eyes were more of a grey-blue than the startling deep blue of Elfie's eyes. Perhaps it was this likeness between the one who was firmly ensconced into his life as possibly his future bride and this child of the valley whom he had just so briefly come to know.

Jacob Farrington had of late been showing considerable interest in Amelia who was the older daughter of Sir Richard and Lady Bancroft of Overdale Hall. The interest had developed to such an extent that he had invited her to join him to meet his father at the manor this forthcoming weekend.

Farrington travelled on down the valley passing through the village of Howtown and then joined the road along the shores of Ullswater. Reaching Pooley Bridge he then turned south along a road that would eventually lead him to his home. Jacob turned off the road and passed through the gates of Thornthwaite Manor.

The drive was long and swept down through open parkland bordered by mature trees of oak, beech and sycamore. The trees were changing from large light coloured bud s to foliage of bright green as nature progressed with the awakening of springtime. The grasslands hereabouts were lush for the time of the year and so rich in texture and colour compared with the wild dale which he had now completely left behind him. The dale had gone from his thoughts, but not the girl.

The hall was a fine building in gothic style, set at the lower end of the open parkland, behind it was a large pine forest. Thornthwaite Manor boasted a fine pair of ornate iron gates set in an arch of stone as the entrance to the inner sanctum of the estate. It was through these gates that Jacob now proceeded. He turned the horse to the right and passed through a further stone arch and entered a large flagged courtyard bordered by a number of stables in an L shaped formation.

Watson, the young stable boy was completing the saddling of a fine black mare. At that moment, a voice boomed out from a doorway in the hall and the lad quaked visibly at the sound.

"Is that wretched horse of mine ready for me boy?"

It was Lord Farrington who had appeared at the top of a small flight of stairs which led down into the courtyard.

"Yes sir, it's ready for you now sir," replied Watson.

"And about time too," growled his lordship as he descended the stairs and approached the horse. He turned suddenly, catching sight of Jacob as he entered the courtyard.

"Where the blazes have you been till this hour, you've taken you're time." Jacob said nothing.

"Have you sorted out that dammed business over in Fusedale?"

Jacob did not answer the question; instead he dismounted from his horse and led it to where Watson was standing holding out the reins of the black mare for his Lordship. Jacob handed the reins of his horse to the boy and took the reins of his father's black mare from him. He led the horse to the stairs where his father now stood. He patted the horse on its flank and passed the reins over to his father. Lord Farrington stood looking at his son with an incredulous look on his face.

"Have you lost your tongue boy?" growled his father, "I asked you what you've done about the shepherding over in Fusedale."

Jacob looked his father directly in the eye.

"I've given the girl notice to quit as soon as a new shepherd can be engaged," he said. "Lambing is imminent and she is well able to look after the flock, they can't be left unattended."

"Well you had better get it sorted out soon, I don't want a lass looking after those sheep, they are some of the best in these parts as well you should know."

"Yes father, I am well aware of that, Mason was a good shepherd."

"Aye, that he might have been," said his lordship condescendingly, "but I didn't care for the fellow."

"You don't care for anyone," muttered Jacob.

"What was that you said?"

"I said, I'll get the job done," replied Jacob. "I've put word round in the village and enquired at a number of farms, I'm sure I'll find some-one willing to take on the job, though heaven knows it's a lonely spot up there."

"Good' said his father, just you remember that the northern estate is your responsibility, you see to it that it runs well."

With that last remark his father mounted the horse, turned it sharply and cantered out of the courtyard.

Chapter seven

What Jacob Farrington had seen and dismissed as a sheep on the other side of the valley had indeed been a person quietly observing the scene. Farrington's arrival at the croft, the letter given to Elfie and the subsequent discussion had all been noted by the watcher. The discourse which followed the reading of the letter and the obvious despair were clear to the person located at their hidden vantage point. Farrington was also seen to leave the girl sat outside the lonely dwelling and ride off down the dale, only to stop when he was out of view, dismount and then spend a considerable time looking back towards where the girl remained, obviously distressed. The watcher was puzzled, although the person knew enough about the recent events in Fusedale to reach the conclusion that Elfie had been served notice to leave the valley. This much the observer could deduce from what was seen and from their prior knowledge, but why did Farrington carry out his own secret observation?

Since the death of Robert Mason and the removal of his body by horse and cart for interment at the church in Martindale, Mick Jarrow had not seen Elfie. Throughout the difficult task of placing the shepherd's body in the rough wooden box, securing it on to the cart and walking the horse down the valley Elfie had seemed to be in a timeless trance, only vaguely nodding when his father spoke to her as he tried to explain what they were going to do. There was no recognition between the two of them and Mick had reluctantly left the girl on her knees by the newly dug grave.

Now Mick Jarrow was in a part of Fusedale which he frequently visited. High up on the flanks of Pikeawassa he had a commanding view of Fusedale and of course the dwelling of Elfrida Mason. He often came to this spot of an early evening on the pretext of checking the flock, which he jointly managed with his father down at Dale End Farm. The Jarrow's flock grazed the northern end of Fusedale and linked up with that part grazed by the Masons sheep. Although the two flocks were heafed to their own area there was a degree of mixing and from time to time the two families exchanged their sheep if they had strayed and then been gathered at various times during the year.

Today the young man was early and therefore came across the scene which he had just witnessed. Over the last few months on his visits he

41

had seen her going about her duties on her own whilst her father was ill. Thinking back earlier he recalled seeing her moving cheerfully about the valley, sometimes high up on the eastern flanks. At times he could just discern the sweet sounds which wafted gently through the air as she sang or hummed softly to herself. The sound was music to his ears and the sight of her coursing the valley, effortlessly and gracefully, her long dress swirling about her legs was a joy to the young man. Just to catch a few glimpses of her was enough to satisfy his mind and then he would return to the farm refreshed and cheerful like the feline girl he had just observed.

Mick Jarrow was an honest and hardworking young man. He was of Irish decent; his parents had come to England to escape from the poverty of the potato famine which crippled Ireland back in the eighteen forties. Davy and Mary Jarrow were newly wed when they arrived in England and after some considerable time traveling up country they found work on Lord Farrington's estate. They worked hard initially, labouring about the estate and then took up the tenancy of Dale End Farm. Mary eventually bore three children, Mick, Andy and Liza.

Mick worked along side his father on the farm, the other two children being quite a bit younger were still at school during the week but as was common they turned their hands to aspects of farming during the evenings and weekends. By keeping costs down through family employment the farm was moderately successful and profitable. Mick was a shy, retiring kind of person who took life as it came, happy to work on the farm and really with only one ambition in life to make Elfie his bride. This was little more than a pipe dream for the young man as he rarely got the chance to talk to her, let alone court her. Always she was under the watchful eye of her father and any chance to converse with the girl on the rare occasions when he did get near to her where quickly nipped in the bud by a disapproving look from her father.

And so it was that Mick came to admire her from afar and wish within his heart that someday he might have the chance to tell her how much he wanted her, how much he loved her. The sight of her set his heart beating fast and to the young man this must be love, he knew of nothing else. How he could find the words to express his feelings was beyond his imagination, and nagging away in the recesses of his mind was the thought of rejection. He had absolutely no way of knowing if she cared for him at all. True, she had no suitors that he was aware of as she rarely left the valley. When she did accompany her father on visits to the market she was guarded by him making the chance of conversation most unlikely. On the odd occasion when they did cross paths she would smile sweetly at him and he would half grin and then turn shyly away, not sure how best to react and to avoid any confrontation with her father.

His mind wandered back to a time a couple of years ago when a chance meeting took place in Howtown. Elfie had become temporarily separated from her father amongst the market crowds. Mick was wandering aimlessly around the market having left his father talking to a farmer he had not seen for some time. Suddenly, there she was in front of him and on her own. He followed on behind her and as she turned a corner between some stalls he cut through and appeared as if by magic in front off her.

Summoning up all his reserves of courage he spoke to her.

"Er, good morning Miss Mason."

Elfie was taken aback by his sudden appearance.

"Why, Mick Jarrow, you startled me." she replied with an obvious look of bewilderment on her face.

"I - I saw you from across the lane and wondered if you might be going to the dance in the village hall tonight, seeing as you're down in the village."

The flush on the young man's face paled dramatically as a stern voice spoke from behind him.

"If she is or if she isn't, it's no concern of yours."

Robert Mason had realised that his daughter was no longer close by and had set off to find her, find her he did, talking to young Jarrow.

"I'll mind you to keep your nose out of my business," and on that remark he took her arm firmly and led her away. Mick stood rooted to the spot, open mouthed and dejected. All his courage had been dragged from his soul by the words of Robert Mason

"He meant no harm," said Elfie as her father led her away from the scene of the encounter.

"That's as maybe, but you don't want to be wasting your time with him," he retorted.

"Why what's wrong with him father, he seems a nice enough young man and from a good family at that?" Her father did not answer.

Elfie went on, "you were unkind to him father."

"Ill hear no more on the matter, when I'm no longer here you'll do as you please, till then you'll do as I say."

On that note the matter was dropped and Elfie walked on slightly behind her father, her lips pouted and a look of obvious displeasure on her face.

The conversation between father and daughter was unheard by the young man but now those words rang true, Mason was no longer here to watch over his daughter, his chance was here and had it not been for the intervention of Farrington life could have been simple, that is if she had a mind to accept him as a suitor. Ever since the rebuff from her father the young man had been careful not to converse with her, perhaps now, he could call on her on some pretext in an effort to further their meagre acquaintance. He was puzzled by Farrington's mirroring of his own actions.

Presently Mick Jarrow saw Elfie rise from the place where she had remained since Farrington's departure. He also saw her look down the valley in the direction of the departed horse rider and then go inside the croft. He looked across the valley to where Farrington stood and saw him mount up and ride off down the valley in the direction of Howtown.

There was nothing left to see and so he rose from his seat in the dead, dried bracken, located the sheep track a few yards below which had served him as path to his vantage point and made his way across the fellside. Quickly he dropped down to the valley floor; he picked his way across the marshy sections and crossed the stream in one long jump. His feet sunk into the marshy ground on the other side causing the momentum of his body to thrust him forward and his hand plunged into the soft, wet ground turning them a dark brown from the peat contained therein. He picked himself up and with a few more strides he was soon on the path which Farrington had departed on, but of course the rider was well away from the area by now.

Mick walked on swiftly down the track and soon reached the farmhouse, he was able to cover the ground very quickly being a young athletic lad used to climbing the hillsides around the dale as part of his work with the sheep. His father Davy being somewhat arthritic was happy to be relieved of this more demanding side of farm work. The young man entered the farmhouse and moved directly to the kitchen where he could hear his mother and father talking. Davy Jarrow was sat at the table devouring a large cheese and pickle sandwich which Mary had made for him from bread newly baked that morning.

"Ah there y' are Mick, would y' be wanting a pot o' tea and a bite t' eat"

There was still a trace of the Irish in the soft lilt of her voice.

"Ay, please," he said pulling a chair up to the large meticulously scrubbed kitchen table. His mother was a stickler for cleanliness and inclined her head towards his boots. "An I s'pose y've walked through 'ouse wi' them on, an look at t' colour o' y' hands."

Mick grinned, "I fell jumping a bog, t' were farther than I thought." A pint mug of hot tea and a sandwich that would have fed two men was served up by his mother and Mick tucked in heartily to the food.

"I was thinking it must be about time to take some wood and stuff up to the Mason's place, she must be getting low on stocks by now."

"That poor child up there on 'er own," said Mary. "I've done plenty o' baking, you mun take some o' that as well."

"That would be good, it might cheer her up a bit," said Mick.

"You've always had an eye for her, haven't you lad?" said his father somewhat philosophically. "But I don't know that she's going to be in need of anything."

"Why do you say that father?" said Mick looking up from the remains of the plate in front of him.

"Well I happened to talk to young Mister Farrington this morning as he was on his way up Fusedale and he told me that he was on his way to serve notice on her to leave that cottage up there and he was looking out for another shepherd to take on the job. In fact he offered me the work but I turned it down as we've enough on with our lot here."

The words rang round in Mick's head confirming what he had observed that very morning.

"That can't be right," he said "I reckon she's as good as any shepherd around here, I can vouch for that, I've seen her working away up there, she knows what she's about."

"How come you know so much?" said his father.

Realising that he was getting himself into deep water if his father deduced that he was spending his time spying on the girl, he retorted,

"Well, what bit I've seen of her looked alright to me and her father must have taught her a lot," he said trying to play his knowledge down.

"That well may be, but it seems that his lordship doesn't see it that way and wants her out, so I think you'd be wasting your time going up there now."

"Well I don't think t'would harm to find out what be going on," said his mother. "An' if she has t' go, what's she going t' do, I don't s'pose she's got anybody." Mary moved over to her son placing a hand on his shoulder.

"You go up an' see her, an 'mind y' tell 'er she be welcome 'ere if she be 'omeless."

"Thanks mother, you're a kind soul, I'll go up and see her tomorrow."

With that said Mick pushed his chair back from the table and strode out into the farmyard. He'd go tomorrow and he'd got the rest of the day to summon up the courage to enquire of her circumstances face to face. He knew it would not be so difficult now that her father was no longer around.

Chapter eight

Throughout the night the moon had silvered the valley; bright stars had twinkled in the clear night sky. As the dawn started to break, a fitful wind had made its presence felt and brought with it a veil of low cloud. The grey swirling masses had settled on the mountaintops and into the high niches in the crags. Nature did not wish to reveal its upper magnificence this day; it was more concerned with events on the valley floor. Like the early morning wind the young girl had spent a restless night in her bed and the shortage of sleep had left her slumbering in the early hours of the morning. The trials and tribulations of the previous day had taken their toll on her mind and yet sleep had eventually taken control of the young shepherdess.

This morning the normally tranquil air of the valley had been replaced with urgency. The usual steady bleat of the pregnant ewes had given way to a considerable increase in their cries and intermingled with the deep sound was a more persistent, lighter sound of the newly born, lambing had begun. It was these new sounds which filtered through to the unconsciousness of the sleeping girl causing her to stir in her bed.

Elfie's head moved from side to side as awareness of the day returned to her, with it came an alertness to the sound of the flock outside the dwelling.

The sounds were different to those which normally woke her in the mornings; it was as if every ewe was calling out her name. As the mind attuned itself, everything registered with her as she picked up on the sounds of the newborn lambs.

Elfie arose quickly and dressed, there was no time for breakfast until she had checked outside and assessed the state of the flock. Within minutes she was outside, taking hold of a short length of rope which was attached to a ring set in the stone by the door she called Tess over to her and tied the dog up. "You'll have to wait here a while girl" she said. Whilst good at fetching the sheep Tess had yet to learn the art of moving around the flock unobtrusively at lambing time. The sheep become very defensive and could easily become agitated at this critical time. Moss on the other hand was a master at this and could move around without disturbing the ewes and be available to gently move the sheep about or collect the errant ewe, which was not performing her duties to her new born.

Elfie's eyes were drawn to a ewe on a small knoll near the house, the animal was laid down in the final stages of producing her offspring and then, there it was, a small, frail creature' eyes wide open at the shock of the change to its life. The ewe stood up and moved away and did not seem to show any interest in the lamb. Quickly, Elfie moved over and picked up the lamb and placed it in front of the mother. The ewe looked down at the pathetic, slimy bundle in front of her and then instinct took over as she lowered her head and started to clean up the little creature. Contact was established, the lamb half sitting with its legs splayed out at unnatural angles around it. Soon it would find the place to suckle and all would be well for it, Elfie would check on it later.

Elfie continued her inspection of the flock, finding another five lambs, which had been born, in the early hours of the day, these young ones were faring well and had already found the teats on the ewes and were feeding contentedly or sleeping after taking their fill. All seemed to be going well, there were many, many ewes standing around watching the proceedings in anticipation of their turn to lamb whenever nature desired it. Then the girl came across one ewe, which was bleating, in an obviously anguished tone. A quick, visual inspection of the animal revealed a malpresentation.

The head of the lamb was visible but the forelegs which should have accompanied the head were not there. Elfie had seen this happen on a number of occasions in the past and knew what action her father had taken. Now she would have to try and extricate the lamb herself as she knew that its legs would be tucked under its chest. If she did not act swiftly the lamb would die and probably the mother too.

Elfie rolled up her sleeves and grasped the wool on the rump of the ewe with one hand, and then with the other hand she pushed the head of the lamb back inside its mother. This done, she then thrust her hand and arm inside the sticky, warm interior of the animal and felt the head of the lamb again. She then traced down from its head to its neck and chest and finally reached the forelegs. She could feel the legs doubled up underneath the chest. She gripped one leg and with some twisting and effort managed to release it and pull it so that it laid along side the head. She repeated this task and soon the other leg was in the correct position.

Then she grasped both legs together and with one big pull her arm came out of the sheep followed by the legs and the lambs head. Now the lamb was correctly presented, the ewe gave a groan of relief and then with an almighty thrust the remainder of the lamb was forced out of the animal's body into the world, a new life was born. Elfie cleared away the mucous from the face of the soggy bundle but it appeared lifeless. The blood red cord was severed and lay trailing on the ground. Next she picked up the lamb by its hind legs and swung it to and fro several times to clear its lungs and then it cried out. Elfie cried out too, but in elation, it had worked, she had done it all by herself. The ewe turned to look at Elfie and the lamb, she was sure that she could detect a look of relief in the eyes of the animal.

"There you are my dearie, here's your baby," and she placed the lamb on the ground in front of the ewe. The power and instinct of centuries of birth came to the animal and she lowered her head and started to clean up her offspring.

First she sniffed at it to ascertain that it was indeed hers and then she started to lick its face. The lamb started to wriggle and then made a hopeless attempt to stand up. Soon enough it would find the strength to stand and then it would find the place to nurture itself on its mother's milk.

Elfie stood up, thrilled with her efforts, she walked across to the stream and cleaned herself up and then continued her patrol, checking all the newborn and those which were imminent. This was how it would be for several days to come until all the ewes had given birth.

It was late in the afternoon before there was a lull in the lambing; some twelve lambs had been born so far. There was one set of twins which was an uncommon event with hill sheep. The ewes find it hard enough to feed themselves through winter when carrying one lamb and provide enough milk to feed it after birth. The odd set of twins would provide an opportunity for fostering should a mother loose her lamb.

Elfie was feeling tired and light-headed as she had not eaten since the previous evening and even then she had little appetite after the words exchanged with Jacob Farrington. She went inside the house and came out with a plateful of cheese, pickles and bread. She sat down on the bench by the door and tucked in heartily, the first time she had eaten with any enthusiasm for many days.

The girl surveyed the scene around her and felt justly proud of her efforts. As she sat there she became aware of a different sound other than the bleating of the sheep, it was a faint rumbling sound. She stood up and strained her eyes down the valley. A horse drawn cart was heading up the valley track but she could not make out who it was due to the distance.

Her heart sank as she felt sure it was Farrington returning again, though he usually came on horseback.

As she watched the progress of the horse and cart she was able to discern the figure of Mick Jarrow. A wave of relief swept through her body and then a secondary fear arose, what if he'd been sent to collect her belongings? But no, surely not, there was no-one to tend the flock at this critical time. As she watched she saw the horse and cart stop and Mick got down from his seat and seemed to be looking at something on the ground but she could not make out what it was. He then appeared to pick something up and put it in under his coat, climb aboard and set of again. He disappeared from view as he went behind the rock outcrop that Jacob Farrington had used as his vantage point and then appeared in full view again as he reached the bend in the track which turned towards Elfie's dwelling.

He stopped a few yards short of where Elfie stood and climbed down from the cart. Cradled in his coat with just its head visible was a newborn lamb.

"Hello Mick, what brings you up here?" The smile on her face was one of relief that it was he and not Jacob Farrington.

"Er, my father said I should bring you up some wood and food an' stuff as you'd be running low, and - and my mother has sent you some of her baking as well."

Mary Jarrow had given him a basketful of cakes and bread when she knew he was heading up the valley on his visit. The lamb inside his coat bleated, bringing him back to the present, it was as if he was in some kind of a hypnotic trance being before the girl of his dreams." I found this little fellow down the track its just been born but the ewe is dead."

He pulled out the little lamb and held it offered it to Elfie. She took it off him and cradled it in her arms like it was a newborn baby.

"It'll need fostering, do you know how to do that?" he enquired.

"Oh yes I've seen my father make a coat from a dead lamb and set it with its mother." But so far there haven't been any stillborns, though I expect there will be before I've done. I'll have to put this one to the bottle until there's a foster mum, there's a set of twins so I've got a bit of a queue for fostering."

"Twins eh! Its not often that happens around these parts," replied the lad.

For once Mick felt relaxed in her company, no longer did he fear her father would suddenly appear from nowhere and reprimand him for talking to her.

"H'- how are you managing?" he asked gazing at her with a concerned expression on his face.

"Oh, I'm not doing too badly really," she replied. "I've been so busy that I haven't had much time to think about things apart from his Lordship's threat to me."

"Threat," said Mick, his eyes widening in pretence that he had no knowledge of the previous day's events. Elfie's face took on a defiant expression.

"Yes, Lord Farrington wants me off his land, he said that the tenancy does not pass down to me, so he's looking for another shepherd and then I've got to go."

"You can come and stay with us a while, my mother said that if' - and then he checked himself realising that he was going to give away his prior knowledge. There was a silence for a minute, then her eyes flashed him an impatient look.

"Go on, your mother said what?"

"She said that if you couldn't manage, that you could come and stay with us till you got yourself sorted out," he replied somewhat unconvincingly. But his reply went unquestioned.

"You must thank your mother for me and tell her it's very kind of her to think of me." The fiery expression subsided from her face and a warming smile took over, Mick was relieved.

"Really, I just want to carry on living here and look after the flock." Her eyes filled up and she dropped them to the ground, "but I don't think they'll let me, even if I can. I've worried about it ever since my father died."

"It'll be easier when the lambing is over, it's the hardest time, I could come up and give you a hand every now and again,"

Elfie raised her head and their eyes met; a solitary tear ran down her cheek, she wiped it away. They looked at each other for quite some time in silence. From somewhere deep within, emotions and feelings were intermingling, neither of them understood these feelings but somehow the seeds of a bond were being sown. For the first time in her lonely life someone other than her father had offered to help her and perhaps it seemed, show an interest in her.

Her lips parted slightly and her eyes took on warmth that was rarely expressed by her.

"That would be very kind of you to do that, but really, do you have the time with all your own work down at the farm and anyway, wouldn't your father mind?"

"He won't mind at all," said Mick in his enthusiasm to come back and see her, though he knew full well that his father would object if he were neglecting his work to traipse off up the valley to see a girl. A whole new world was opening up for the young man, it seemed that all his hopes and dreams of the past were suddenly being realised.

He turned and went back to the cart and lifted down the basket containing the food and his mother's baking.

"Where shall I put this?" he called out cheerfully.

"What is it?"

"Some baking my mother has sent up for you."

"That's so kind of her, just put it by the door and I'll see to it," the smile broadening on her face.

'God she is lovely,' he thought.

"I'll put the wood and these sacks in the store for you if you like."

"Yes that is kind of you."

Mick led the horse down to the store and unloaded the contents of the cart and stacked them in the store place.

"These will keep her going for some time," he mused.

Elfie watched on, still nursing the lamb, for the first time in her life she was in charge, making decisions and she now had a willing helper. Mick then turned the horse around in the direction of the farm. He walked back to where she stood, the lamb had settled into a contented sleep in her arms.

"I'd best be off now, but I'll come back tomorrow as soon as I can, and mind you look after that little fellow."

He reached out to stroke the head of the sleeping lamb. His hand slid from fondling the little creature's head to touching Elfie's hand. He could not believe his own boldness. For a few seconds they gazed silently at each other, and then Mick's face turned a bright red and he half turned away.

"Hey, it's alright," the smile on her face changing to a puzzled expression.

"Thank you Mick, for bringing the food and stuff, I'm sure I shall enjoy your mother's cakes, and I hope you get the chance to come back tomorrow. But if you are too busy I will understand. By the way, I found some errant ewes but I don't know the 'smits', can you look them up for me?"

He nodded.

Mick withdrew the hand which still rested on hers. He turned and sprung up onto the seat of the cart almost as if he was floating on a cloud, which indeed he was at this time. He turned and waved and then with a flick of the reins the horse set off obediently. After a few minutes he turned to look back. She was still stood there looking in his direction, still nursing the lamb in her arms. How he wished it was he who was being cradled in those arms. He half waved his hand and then flicked the reins again.

"Hup," he cried and the horse obediently increased its speed to a trot, the cart lumbered and bumped along the track. The croft and Elfie slowly receding into the distance.

The next day dawned brightly; the sun rose and peeked over the fell tops bringing warmth to the valley. The dale became awake with the growth of buds and grasses teased into life by the brisk spring air. Elfie was up and about early, eager to see if there were any new additions to the flock.

A couple of lambs had been born in the early hours, one was happily feeding from its mother but the other one nearby was clearly having difficulties. Elfie moved slowly nearer so as not to agitate the mother, she stooped and inspected the udder of the ewe. There seemed to be a blockage of the teats, with a little dextrous massage she was able to stimulate the flow of milk. She then nudged the lamb to the mother and the eager creature found the teat and was able to suckle eagerly at first, then more contentedly as its need for nutrition was realised.

Some way further from the croft Elfie came across a dead lamb. Above, a number of crows were circling, awaiting their chance to descend for a meal. The mother was hovering nearby looking agitated waiting for a response from her new born which sadly would never come.

Elfie needed to act quickly, calling Moss over she gave him the command to circle behind the ewe. She picked up the dead lamb and with help from the dog she was able to lead the ewe towards the outbuilding next to the house. Here she quickly constructed a makeshift pen and then got the ewe inside it.

The next job was to skin the dead lamb and put the coat onto the orphan which she had been rearing in the store. She fetched a knife and deftly cut of the majority of the skin from the dead lamb. Then she wrapped this around the little orphan and secured it with some twine. In a day or two the adoption would hopefully be complete and the skin could then be removed.

The girl then took the lamb to the ewe.

"There you are my darling, your baby's alright now."

The bereaved ewe backed away suspiciously eyeing the new lamb with distrust, but eventually she could smell her substance on its coat. She moved forward and looked down at what she thought was her offspring with approval, Elfie pushed the lamb towards the full udder and soon it started to draw milk. Elfie backed away quietly, all should now be well. Moss came to her side and she patted his head.

"Well done Moss, you're a good dog."

The crows which had been hovering had now backed off. The shepherdess would have to be vigilant as it was only necessary for the mother to leave her newborn unattended for a short while and then they would strike. Their first point of attack would be the eyes and even if driven off at this stage the damage would be done and the lamb would have little chance of survival.

The days ahead would be a testing time until the lambs were strong enough to accompany their mothers for protection and even then the weak would always be at risk. Several lambs would be lost to the crows and possibly the eagles that lived thereabouts before the lambing season was done.

Chapter nine

Jacob Farrington had left Thornthwaite Manor early that morning for the long ride over to Fusedale. He rode at a steady pace along tracks bordered by fields which were now turning to a lush green after the winter snow was now but a memory. He was musing over the events of the last week since his meeting with Miss Mason. After a recent visit to Penrith he had informed his father that he had procured the services of a shepherd and that he would shortly be going out to Fusedale to assign the man to the job and would of course ensure that Mason's daughter would be away within the same day. His father had shown little interest in the subtleties of the new employment and had only expressed his satisfaction with a series of curt one-syllable comments.

Farrington of course had made his mind up to engage the girl to continue with the shepherding. He wanted to keep her in the dale, though he was not sure why. One thing he was sure about was the wrath of his father should he find out. Jacob thought that it was unlikely that his plan would get back to his father as he knew that he rarely ventured away from the immediate vicinity of the estate and rarely came into contact with people from the outside world. Jacob was willing to take the chance; he felt a strange attraction to the girl and wanted to know her better. He was not sure why and again knew that he was putting his relationship with Amelia at risk as well if his plans backfired on him.

The sun was giving warmth to his face as he rode across Askham Moor. He had taken the old route which by-passed Pooley Bridge as he had no business there this particular day. He rode on passing Ketley Gate and then the circle of standing stones known locally as the Cockpit. At some time during the darker history of this moor the area had been use for the barbaric sport of cockfighting. The earthy scent of peat and marsh rose up from the moor filling his head with its clear acidic scent. A little further on he branched right leaving the course of the old Roman road over High Street and commenced the long steady descent down towards Ullswater. Majestic peaks now started to rise in front of him heralding his approach to the wild wilderness of mountains ahead. Reaching the valley floor, he turned to join the road which would take him to Howtown and then up into the valley of Fusedale.

His mind was alive with the anticipation of seeing the girl of the dale. Although he had seen her on a number of occasions previously he had never been struck by her wild beauty, now he was intrigued by her and felt the urge to know her more intimately.

Soon he riding along the track to Dale End Farm,

"Good morning Davy" he called out to Mick Jarrow's father as he passed the end of the lane down to the farm. Davy looked up from the ewe and her lamb which he was bothering with.

"Aye, good day to you sir."

Farrington disappeared from view along the track leaving Davy Jarrow wondering if he was on his way to order the Mason girl of the land.

When Jacob reached the vantage point of his last visit he again dismounted and climbed up onto the rock outcrop, he looked eagerly up the dale in the direction of the croft. He scanned the area but could not see her anywhere. He returned and remounted the horse and set it at a steady trot for the last remaining part of the journey.

Reaching the dwelling he pulled on the reins and the horse came to a halt. He jumped down from the animal and looked around him. Everywhere there were sheep with their lambs and the incessant bleating filled his head. He walked over to the door of the croft and knocked on the door. The door was slightly ajar and he cautiously pushed it open and peered inside. God, it's so primitive in here he thought, she must be worth better than this. He pulled the door to and looked around him; she must be somewhere he thought.

He walked over to a little knoll and up onto it to gain a viewpoint and then he saw her.

She was on her knees in a hollow beside a ewe and its lamb. The two dogs that were stood nearby watching the proceedings suddenly saw the young man and started to bark. Elfie looked up and saw Jacob.

"Lie down," she commanded the dogs, which they did obediently but still giving out a low warning throaty growl.

The girl stood up and walked over to where he was standing, she had a slightly submissive look on her face. As she reached him she looked into his eyes as if trying to solicit an answer to that most important question and then she dropped her gaze.

"Good morning Miss Mason, the lambing appears to be going well."

She looked up at him again, warming to his compliment.

"It is sir, there's been a good number born so far."

Jacob looked at her for a minute examining the features of her face, he traced down from the blue eyes, along the high set cheek bones to the sensuous lips, like Mick Jarrow, he longed to kiss them.

"Sir?"

He came back to the present and his mouth broke out into a smile.

"Ah yes, as you know, my father wishes you to vacate this place," he paused.

Elfie's heart felt heavy and a deep churning commenced in her stomach.

"However, I have decided that you can stay, well, for the time being, perhaps we should say six months. That would see the lambing through, the gather and shearing and the sale of the wethers. Then we shall see how well you have done. Mind that you don't let me down, I am going against the wishes of my father and I can only justify my decision if he did find out by showing him that we have had a successful season."

Elfie was silent for a moment and then she beamed up at him wringing her hands together in excitement. Tears welled up in her eyes. But this time they were tears of joy.

"Oh thank you, thank you sir," she cried with elation. "I won't let you down." Then the smile drained from her face.

"But what if you father finds out, what would happen then?"

"It's highly unlikely, he leaves all the management of the northern acres to me, he's not really very interested in what goes on, though for some reason he seems to have a dislike of your late father and that is why he instructed me to dismiss you."

Jacob walked over and sat on a large elongated boulder which gave a good viewpoint down the valley. Ullswater glinted in the morning sunlight.

"It is very beautiful up here, well in the summer at least, I can quite see why you are so keen to stay."

Elfie walked over to where he was sat.

"Please, Miss Mason, sit down for a few minutes, we have a few things to discuss."

She joined him, sitting a little way apart from him. At that Jacob outlined the conditions and expectations that he had required from her father and now these expectations fell on her. She readily agreed to the terms, nodding and smiling in agreement to his every request.

"So I will come back in a week or so to see how you are going on and if you have any problems you can call on the Jarrow's for help. I will inform them of our arrangement on my way back."

There was a silence for a few minutes and then he spoke, this time in a gentler inquiring tone.

"You have lived here all your life then," he asked.

"As long as I can remember, though I know I wasn't born in these parts though."

"And where were you born then?"

"Well, that I'm not sure about," she replied.

"Tell me then, you're obviously educated, which most of the folk round here are not, did your father teach you?"

"He did sir, and then I went to the school in Martindale when I could, weather permitting. My father was an intelligent man and really above shepherding, but he loved the life up here, though I sometimes felt that he was trying to hide away from the world - I don't know."

"It must be very lonely now for you," he said trying to look into the blue eyes which averted his.

"I haven't really had time to get lonely yet, but I have lots of books to read to pass the time on. So when I'm not so busy I can do that and I also need to do some work on the house to get it straightened out, its been neglected of late."

"I'm sure it does," he remarked, giving the little croft a disdainful look.

"Well Miss Mason, I hope things work out alright for you and as I said, I will come back to see how you are getting on a week or so." He rose to his feet and smiled down at the girl. Her pleasure at the outcome of their meeting was clearly evident in her face and she smiled back sweetly at him. He could scarcely hide his pleasure, contact had been established and he had gained her confidence. He was a man of his word, he would not let her down even if he risked the wrath if his lordship. She was lovely, of that he had no doubt; he had taken the first steps to win her over although he was not certain how best to proceed with his new found conquest. He whistled and his horse came obediently over to him, gathering up the reins he sprang up lightly settling into the saddle.

"Till next time my dear," and then with a deft click of his heels on the flanks of the horse he was away down the track at a fast canter.

Elfie mused on his last remark for a little while and then dismissed it from her mind. She rose and called the dogs over to her, "its alright my beauties, we can stay,"

Tess jumped up in excitement; she grasped the dog's paws and danced around, the dog trying its best to follow its mistress's steps. Then happily she went back to finish tending the ewe that she had left earlier.

It was early evening and the weather had kept fine throughout the day, now the clouds were parting, allowing the remaining evening sunlight to filter through. It brought much needed warmth to the valley giving a rise in temperature when normally it would be turning chilly. Elfie was taking advantage of this unexpected warmth and was sat outside the house. She had covered the stone bench with a thick fleece for added comfort and was sat reading a book. This was her first chance of relaxing after the work of the day due largely to a lull in the lambing.

Every few minutes her eyes would leave the pages of the book and gaze down the valley. She was trying to discern movement, other than the grazing sheep. She was in fact trying to discern movement of the human kind. Her eyes would return to the book and then her mind would drift from the text to recent events. The elation after Jacob Farrington's visit, now her future looked promising at least in the short term.

Then their was her meeting with Mick Jarrow and for the first time in her life, the seeds of a friendship with someone of her own age had been sown. She hung on his last words to her, "I'll come back tomorrow as soon as I can." It was this anticipation that interacted and distracted her reading.

Again, she looked down the valley and thought she saw someone approaching; she looked long and hard and then disappointedly went back to her book. If only he would come, would he come? She wanted to share her success with today's lambing; she needed his approval that she had done all the right things. Most of all, she wanted to tell him about Farrington's visit and that she now was a shepherdess in her own right. Perhaps he would tell her about his visit to the market. When lambing was over she too could venture into Howtown, free to do as she pleased.

She needed to know about the next shepherds meeting so that she could return the errant sheep, which she had brought down, from the hill. Mick would be able to tell her about this, he may even have identified the markings and know whom they belonged to. There was so much to talk about.

She read on determined not to keep looking down the valley, trying to contain her disappointment. Another two pages and she could not resist another look. This time she saw something moving quickly along the track. As she continued to watch she was able to make out a figure walking at a fast pace. Was it he? She followed the figure with her eyes until it disappeared into the rock cutting. It was gone for a few minutes and then appeared in full view, now she could make out whom it was. Her face lit up, it was Mick walking at a fast pace along the track towards the croft. As he drew near her eyes dropped back to the book pretending that she was not aware of his approach. When he was within earshot, he called out and waived his hand. At first she pretended not to hear, he called out again. This time she looked up unable to contain her excitement any longer, her eyes sparkled and her mouth formed into a most beautiful smile. Her eyes softened as she looked up at him.

She closed the book and laid it to one side,

"Mick, I didn't expect to see you today," she remarked in a nonchalant tone.

"I said I'd come back again after the market, don't you remember?"

Elfie averted her eyes, "perhaps you did, er yes I think you said you might, but really, I didn't know whether you meant it or not," her eyes returned to look at his face, waiting for his reaction to her casual words.

Mick grinned at her,

"Yes I did mean it, and I always keep my word."

"I'm glad that you do, it's nice to know that there's someone I can trust now that I'm on my own now."

Mick sat down on the bench beside her. Elfie then proceeded to tell him in an excited way about her day and her success with the orphaned lamb.

"You did well lass with that on your own, 'specially when you haven't done it before."

The girl positively glowed; she was not used to receiving praise. Whatever she had done for her father was expected of her and he rarely expressed his pleasure if she had done well.

"There's more to the day," she said and promptly launched into telling him about Farrington's visit and the outcome.

Mick listened attentively, happy just to enjoy the sound of her lilting voice.

"So you see, now I'm on trial as the shepherdess, are you pleased for me Mick?" She asked the question in a teasing manner.

The young man was delighted, his love was staying in the valley, it seemed that there were now no obstacles to developing the friendship. He could not resist putting his arm around her and giving her a big hug.

"I'm really happy that it's all settled for you now," he said, quickly withdrawing his arm, his face reddening with the embarrassment.

"It's alright," she smiled at him and took hold of his hand.

"I need friendship and help now," her eyes took on a serious look, "perhaps I will find it in you."

She then stood up and twirled carefree about in front of him.

"You've heard my news, now tell me about your day," she teased.

She sat down again and he started to tell her about his visit to the market, she listened and questioned him on various aspects. When he had finished she boldly announced that she would go to the market when the lambing was over.

"I don't know whether you should do that, well, not on your own," he said, a concerned expression showing on his face.

"Oh really, and why is that?" the tone of her voice clearly expressing her disapproval of his attempt to impose restrictions on her wishes.

"Well, there's some rough characters about you know."

"You mean like Jos Leyburn the gravedigger," she retorted.

"Oh Jos is harmless enough really, but there's some who aren't and they might not take kindly to you and try and take advantage of you, they might not be used to the idea of you being a shepherdess."

"Well they'd better get used to the idea," she replied, a scornful look invading her face.

She was silent for a minute, thinking her next words carefully.

"Then perhaps you'll come with me to protect me, my knight in shining armour, Sir Galahad."

He gave her a puzzled look, not quite sure what she was talking about.

"Don't you know about King Arthur and the Knights of the round table?" she asked in a mock scolding voice.

"N-no I don't," he said, clearly showing his embarrassment, as he was sure he ought to if Elfie said so.

She giggled at him in a girlish manner.

"You take me to market, and I'll tell you all about King Arthur and lots of other famous kings as well."

They sat some time together talking about their lives so far and the day-to-day goings on. Mick was quite well informed about the goings on at the lakeside. Elfie was very interested and amazed at some of the tales that he told her. The more things he relayed to her, the more she realised that she was living in an isolated world up at the top of the dale. She had a good knowledge of history and literature, gained through her reading, but little knowledge of the immediate outside world.

At length he looked at the book beside her.

"What are you reading?"

"It's about Ulysses, its Greek legend."

It was beyond him.

"What's Greek legend?" he ventured.

"Well, it's like an adventure story about his travels and all the people and things he met, it's only make believe but it's exciting to read. Do you read Mick? I can lend you some of my books." Mick was not very adept at reading and writing.

"Don't really have much time for that sort o' thing," he replied as a concealment of his inability. Elfie expanded on the story,

"It sounds interesting," he remarked at length, "but I don't think I could manage to read all that,"he confessed.

"Then sometime I will read it to you," she replied, giving him a coy smile.

"Aye, perhaps you can when we're not too busy with everything else."

Elfie's mind wandered back to her sheep and the errant ewes came to the fore.

"Did you look up the smit of those ewes for me? You said that you would."

Mick had obviously forgotten.

"Er no, I haven't had time yet," he replied.

"Really, Mick," she scolded him gently "you're supposed to be helping me."

"I'll look them up tonight," he said, anxious to please her.

"We could look them up in my book, if I could only find the key for the chest; perhaps you could force it open."

She led him into the croft and pulled the chest out from the foot of her father's bed. It was a solid oak affair with a curved lid. The wood was held together by two broad iron bands secured by coach bolts. The bands were formed into hinges at the rear. The front edge of the lid was secured by a substantial hasp fitted with a large padlock.

Mick looked at the lock for a minute.

"You'll never shift that without the key."

"Well I can't find it," she said impatiently.

"Didn't he tell you where he kept it?"

Elfie groaned, "I wouldn't be trying to force it open if I knew where he kept the key, here, can't you force it open with this," and she handed him a bent poker.

"You've been having a go at it, haven't you," he teased.

"Well, what if I have, anyway the pokers bent and now that's no good now." He took the poker from her, placed it on the floor and stood on it with his boot, pressing it back into shape.

"There, at least I've mended that for you."

Elfie took the poker off him and looked at it as if to confirm that it really was straight again and then she placed it back on the hearth.

"You need something a bit stronger," said Mick.

"Father had some tools somewhere in the outhouse, I'll have to find them and see if there's something there that'll do, I'll find them for next time, then you can have a go at it."

Mick grinned at her.

"Right miss, next time, I must be getting back otherwise they'll be wanting to know where I am."

"Yes, Mr Jarrow, sir, its getting dusky outside and we don't want you getting lost on your way home do we," said she in a sarcastic tone.

"As if I would, I could find my way back blindfold."

"Then perhaps I'll tie a sack over your head sometime and then see if you can," she replied jokingly.

He stepped outside the house and she followed him pausing on the doorstep. Mick turned and looked at her framed in the doorway. To him she was pure delight, beautiful in a wild kind of way, perhaps a little untamed, a bit rebellious. But also he sensed deep warmth within her, warmth that he longed to share.

"I'd best be off then," knowing full well that it was the last thing he wanted to do.

"And when shall I see you next?"

Her lips pouted as if to entice him back to her.

"Tomorrow for sure," came the reply.

"For sure," she echoed his words.

Mick felt totally at ease with the girl now and able to tease her a little, he enjoyed her responses. Gone were the barriers of the past and now she seemed to be warming to him. He clicked his heels together and saluted her.

"Goodnight Miss Mason," he said with a cheeky grin.

"Get of with you now," she said laughingly, "I didn't know you used to be a soldier."

He turned and marched away from her shouldering an imaginary rifle.

She watched as he went, his march turning to a brisk walk.

He turned and waved to her, she waved back and became aware of her heart beating rapidly inside her chest.

"Silly me," she said softly under her breath, "its been a good day, time to sleep now."

She went inside, the dogs now following her. She stooped to fondle their ears, "my beauties, I bet you're hungry, lets see what I've got for you."

She closed the door and shut out the approaching night.

Chapter ten

April made way for the month of May. It had been a mixed month for weather; bright sunny days with a cutting edge of wind to them intermingled with gusty winds and heavy showers. Many days saw the hills brooding under their mantle of low cloud. As the spring had progressed the climate improved and it now seemed unlikely that it would revert back to wintry conditions. It was not unknown though for it to snow in May, although this was usually confined to the fell tops.

The few trees that grew at the dale head were now fully clothed. These were mostly rowan trees, small and somewhat gnarled in their appearance before they sprouted their leaves. Now they were green and had the white bunches of blossom adorning them. The trees clung steadfastly to the rocky edges of the beck, their twisted roots reaching down to take in the sweet mountain waters.

Like the weather, the shepherdess had experienced many changes in the preceding months. The loss of her father, the trauma of whether or not she would be allowed to remain in the dale, her newfound friendship with Mick Jarrow and the lambing season which she had tackled virtually single-handed. The lambing had consumed her life almost entirely, but now it was drawing to a successful conclusion. There were only a handful of ewes left which still had to produce their offspring. Many of the ewes were now returning to the higher sides of the valley, their lambs increasing in size and becoming more robust as each day dawned. It was essential to get the ewes back to the higher ground to reduce the risk of infection due to the density of their confinement on the valley floor.

Farrington had not been seen in the valley since his visit some three weeks earlier. Elfie was ever conscious that he would be back any day now, hopefully, he would be pleased with the progress of the flock and not go back on his word.

Mick continued to call on Elfie some three or four times a week. Sometimes it would be a brief visit combined with a round of his father's flock with a little extension to take in Fusedale. Other times he would arrive early evening and stay for an hour or more. Mostly they sat and talked and on his last visit he had told her that he had looked into the markings on the errant sheep and believed that they belonged to a farm further down the valley towards Pooley Bridge. There was to be shepherds meet on the forthcoming Friday, the first in the month. The Jarrow's also had a number of ewes which did not belong to them and so the couple had agreed to take them to the meeting together.

Mick came up to see Elfie on the Thursday evening before the meet. This time he had brought the little cart with him, pulled by the mare affectionately known as Bonnie. The horse had at one time been such but was now ageing and this showed. She was not worked hard and now only pulled the cart when small loads needed moving. This time it was some supplies for Elfie and another supply of baking which Mick's mother had produced. Mary Jarrow was concerned about the young girl's solitary existence and was actively encouraging Mick to help and support her. His father was not too sure about the relationship as he was of the opinion that young Mick was thinking more about life at the upper reaches of the dale rather than concentrating on his work here at the family farm. This was a misconception as Mick worked harder and quicker to fulfil his duties so that he could spend some time helping Elfie.

Davy did not realise this and only saw Mick heading of up the dale three or four times a week. Mary had chastised Davy for his mumblings about Mick.

"T 'lads doing no 'arm, 'es only 'elping lass out a bit, an' anyway, it's only natural at 'is age that 'e be taking an interest in t' girls. An' anyroad me an' you were not much older than 'e be when we met."

Davy scowled at his wife.

"I've nowt agin the lass, in fact, she's right pretty like, but I don't want it affecting his work here."

Mary gave her husband a knowing look.

"So you've noticed she be a pretty 'un as well 'ave you, then you mun keep y're eyes to y'self otherwise y'll 'ave me to contend with, now leave lad alone and let 'im get on wi' his own life."

When Mick Jarrow arrived at the croft that evening he could not see Elfie anywhere at all. He waited some time but she did not appear and so he called out loudly.

"Elfie, Elfie, where are you?"

A voice came back to him from some distance away.

"I'm up here."

The lad looked in the direction of the voice and spotted the girl some distance away on the hillside. He waved his arm frantically and set off in her direction. Presently, he reached her, she was sat on a small knoll, the dogs layed down a short distance in front of her as if on guard. They got up and wagged their tails when they saw him, accepting him now as a friend, he posed no threat to their mistress.

Elfie was watching a ewe in the process of lambing. The head and forelegs had just appeared. She smiled up at him.

"This is the last ewe to lamb as far as I know," she said.

"Lucky you," he replied, "we've still got a good few left to produce. Usually it's the other way around; yours have always been the stragglers in the past." He knew that his teasing comment would draw a swift response. She gave him a sharp scolding look.

"Our ewes have always lambed on time," she retorted. "And they've done even better this year cos I'm looking to them."

She could not hold the stern face any longer and broke out into a mischievous giggle. Mick enjoyed teasing her to the point of annoyance but his eyes always gave him away. Elfie was always drawn by his teasing remarks but quickly realised that that was all it was, there was no unkindness in Mick. They sat for some time without speaking, content just to watch nature take its course as the ewe completed the production of her lamb.

"There now, isn't that just a little beauty of a lamb, the last of the year and all?"

The ewe bleated and looked round at its newborn, then shuffled round and started to clean up the little creature. Several minutes later it was contentedly suckling on its mother.

"We can leave them to get on with it now," said Mick, "come and see what I've brought up on the cart for you, there's some of mother's baking."

Elfie's eyes lit up in anticipation, Mary Jarrow's baking was delicious. During the last few weeks there had been little time to spend cooking and she had existed on a meagre diet. The two walked down to where the horse stood waiting patiently, two happy souls content in each other's company and the simplicity of it.

They unloaded the cart together; some items went into the store and others into the house. When they had finished they sat down together on the bench beside the door. They gazed down at the reflection of Ullswater in the early evening sun, every so often they would look at each other, their eyes would meet and she would give a little laugh.

"It's so beautiful up here Mick, it's just lovely, but it's so lonely sometimes."

Her face took on sadness.

"I suppose it must be now that you're on your own like," he replied.

"Since I came back here after the funeral the only people I've seen are you and Jacob Farrington and I don't want to see him again so soon really. I mean, while he stays away I'm still here, but I worry that he'll change his mind, do you think he will Mick?"

The young man thought for a moment and then replied.

"I don't think he will, but I suppose you never can tell, he'll only do what's in his best interest, I expect. Anyway, don't look so glum tomorrow were going to Howtown, that'll be a day out for you and you won't be lonely then, will you?"

Elfie brightened, "yes I'm really looking forward to tomorrow, it will be such a change, me going to Howtown on my own, well not really, with you I mean."

"The shepherds meeting's in the afternoon, so if you bring down the ewes first thing we can put them with ours and drive them all down together and be there around midday. Who knows, you might get some back yourself."

"I don't think I'm any short, but you never can tell, there must be quite a few up on the fell tops that evade the gather every year. I don't think we've ever managed to count them exactly," she replied.

"Aye, we're same I suppose, we only know roughly how many we've got."

"Will there be anything else going on in the village?" she enquired.

"I don't suppose so, it's only on market days that you get the travellers and things, but you've got to go to the big markets at Keswick or Penrith to see all the things that go on."

"Like what Mick?"

He paused a moment as if to recollect what there was.

"Well, there's like stalls selling all manner of things and sideshows and the like."

Elfie's eyes widened, "could we go there some time, would you take me. I've never been out of this valley."

Mick thought for a moment.

"Aye perhaps, in summer after the shearing. Tell you what though, sometimes there's a bit of a dance in the village hall in Howtown. I've been a couple of times with Andy and Liza. I'm not very good at dancing though our Liz is, little Andy's just daft with it and messes about. Can you dance Elfie?"

"I've never tried, come to think of it, but I don't suppose it's that difficult, it's only country dancing isn't it?"

"I suppose it is really, it's nothing fancy like," he replied

"We must go sometime then Mick, will you take me?"

Mick would have taken her there and then if there had been a dance. His reply however did not reveal his inner desires.

"Hey young lady, hang on a minute, first you want to go to the meet, then it's the fair at Penrith and now it's dancing, I've got to work as well you know."

"Yes, and so have I, but I'd so like to go."

"Then we shall, when the clips over, I promise you."

Elfie leapt to her feet excitedly, "come on then Mick, show me the sort of dancing you did."

Mick sat there reluctantly for a moment or so. Elfie looked at him impatiently and then grabbed him by both hands and pulled him to his feet.

"Come on then."

Still holding her hands he took a few steps forward and a few steps back. Then he sidestepped forwards and then back. He then put one arm around her waist and waltzed her around. Then looking rather flushed and embarrassed he released her and stepped back a little.

Elfie looked up at him.

"That was very good Mick, come on now, there's no need to be shy, it's only me you're dancing with, nobody is watching."

He grinned back at her, the high colour in his face receding as quickly as it came.

"Well, er it's sort of like that, you watch the other dancers a bit to get the hang of things and then have a go."

"I don't reckon anybody is bothered as long as you're enjoying yourself," she said.

"You're probably right," said Mick. "Then you will take me then?" she said emphatically.

"Next dance there is we'll go to it," he replied, barely concealing his delight at the prospect.

"That's settled then," said Elfie. "Now, first thing tomorrow I'll be down with the ewes and then we can go down to Howtown."

Mick nodded.

"You had best be off then," said Elfie.

He looked at her for a moment with a longing gaze and then walked over to the cart. He was up in the seat in a moment.

"I'll see you in the morning Miss Mason then." A cheeky grin pervaded her face.

"Yes Mr Jarrow, go on with you I've got things to do here afore bedtime." With a gentle flick of the reins, the horse set of obediently. Like so many times previously, she watched him disappear along the track. If only he did not have to go she thought.

Chapter eleven

Elfrida Mason was up and about early the following day. She prepared and ate a hearty breakfast for the first time in weeks; this was due largely to the provisions which Mary Jarrow had sent up for her. The two dogs hurried back and forth anxious to be off on the days work and also anxious to be fed.

"Today's going to be different my beauties, we're off on a long walk into Howtown and you've got some herding to do as well." Tess listened attentively turning her head from side to side, anticipating the words of her mistress. Moss nuzzled up to Tess and gave her a push to one side with a deft flick of his hindquarters. 'You're not having all the attention,' he seemed to be saying.

The eager pair were duly fed and then it was off outside to perform whatever tasks they were asked to do. Elfie did a circuit of the ewes with the newest lambs to ensure that all was well. Another few days and these too would start to return to the higher ground. Weather conditions were improving by the day with a marked change in temperature for the better. The movement of the flock would give Elfie a break from the intensities of the lambing season and provide her with the opportunity to attend to essential domestic tasks before the onset of the gather and washing in June.

Elfie made her way over to the makeshift enclosure where the errant ewes had been contained.

"Right, lets see if we can get you lot down into Howtown."

She opened the rickety gate and the ewes wandered out reluctantly as if surprised by their new found freedom and then they made a run for it.

"Away Moss," and the dog was quick to run out and get in front of them. Tess instinctively, without command flanked to the left. Moss turned the ewes and brought them back to where his mistress stood. After a few more skirmishes and attempts for freedom brought rapidly under control by the two dogs, the group set off along the track down the dale. The dogs took control without any commands from Elfie; they were experts and knew exactly what was expected of them in moving the sheep along the track. The ewes accepted their lot and meandered down the rough track towards the Jarrow's farm.

They passed through the rock cutting and proceeded at a good pace. Further along, the track descended a steeper section with a ruined croft on the left and then the farm came into view. Elfie could see two figures stood near the entrance to the farm track and as she approached closer, she was able to see that it was Mick and his father. The two men were stood by a small stone enclosure. As she drew near, Davy Jarrow opened the gate to the enclosure and Mick blocked off any further forward approach of the ewes. The sheep obediently turned through the gate to join another six or so that were contained therein. The gate was closed and secured.

"Morning to you lass," said Davy.

"Good morning Mr Jarrow, hello Mick," she replied.

"Kettle's on an' there's some scones if you'd like before we set off," said Mick, leading the way towards the farmhouse door.

The girl was ushered into the large kitchen. There was a big, sturdy table in the middle of the room surrounded by a number of chairs. A fire burned brightly in the range at the other side of the kitchen bringing an inviting warmth and cheeriness to the surroundings. How different it was to the drab surroundings of her own little abode. Mary Jarrow was busying herself near the fireplace. Mick's sister Liza was arranging clothes on a creel before hauling it up ceiling-wards.

"Sit y' self down lass," said Davy and almost immediately his wife produced a large teapot which she placed on the table. Liza set three large mugs on the table and then they were filled with the steaming beverage.

"How are you, m' dearie?" Mary pulled out a chair and sat herself down next to Elfie, "how are you getting along now?"

"Oh I'm not doing too badly now," Mrs Jarrow, "I'm staying on up in Fusedale and the lambing has gone really well."

"Aye lass, so Mick's been telling us, in fact that's all 'e talks about, what goes on up in Fusedale."

Elfie's face broke out into a broad smile, "He's been very helpful to me and I do thank you very much for the baking and things that you sent up to me. It really was very kind of you, I haven't had much time to do anything other than tend the sheep, it's been a real help."

"Well I'm only t' glad t' be able t' elp y' out," said Mary pushing a plateful of newly baked scones in front of the girl, "ere you 'elp y'self t' these."

Despite a good breakfast the girl tucked in hungrily.

"These are delicious," she said between mouthfuls.

Mary warmed to the praise; more often than not her cooking was taken for granted. She eyed the girl up and down.

"Y' looks as though y' could do wiv a bit o meat on y' bones like."

Mick grinned at Elfie, "she works too hard, never stops," he said in reply to his mother's comments.

"That's more then can be said o' you lad," retorted Davy.

"Hang on a bit, father, I do all that's asked of me an' more besides," said Mick grudgingly.

"Now you two give up squabbling," scolded his wife.

A brief silence reined and the two finished off another scone each and downed the pots of tea.

"We'd better be off now," said Mick," we've a fair way to go yet."

The couple rose from the table and made their way towards the door.

"Thank you very much, Mrs Jarrow, that was really kind of you."

"Y' welcome anytime, an' mind y' don't go starving y'self up there," said Mary her big smile accentuating the dimples in her rosy cheeks.

Elfie gave Davy Jarrow her most charming smile, "Goodbye Mr Jarrow, Liza," and stepped outside with Mick close on her heels.

"She's a nice lass, an' got real manners an' all," said Mary, "I reckon she'd make Mick a good wife."

Liza started giggling; her father threw her a cold look.

"Don't you go pushin' 'im into anything, I need 'im 'ere t' work y' knows."

"Aye Davy, I knows that, but 'es besotted wiv 'er, y' can tell by way 'e looks at 'er, 'e could do a lot worse y' knows."

"Aye, s'pose 'e could," and with that said, Davy rose and walked out of the kitchen, he had nothing more to say on the subject at present. As he ventured out into the farmyard he was just in time to see the couple heading away from the farm chatting happily together with the group of ewes being herded on in front by Elfie's two dogs.

As the group were nearing the junction with the old track into Martindale they were confronted by the sight of a horse and rider bearing down on them at great speed. It was likely that the rider had as yet not seen the little procession due to a bend in the track which was shielded by a high hedgerow. Within a few seconds the rider was upon then, he hauled tightly on the reins bringing the horse to an abrupt halt in front of them. Gravel and stones were scattered about them and the horse reared up onto its hind legs, snorting and frothing. The sheep turned and fled back up the lane hastily pursued by the two dogs.

"You fool, you could have killed us," shouted Mick, "can't you see we were bringing sheep down the lane?"

Elfie's face flushed to a bright red, she had recognised the rider, Mick as yet, had not, as his view had been obscured by the rearing horse. It was then to Mick's dismay that he realised it was Jacob Farrington. Elfie turned to see where the sheep had gone and was relieved to see that the dogs had already overtaken the sheep and turned them into a field through an open gate.

"You had better watch your tongue Mick Jarrow," retorted Farrington angrily, now bringing his horse under control and stroking its neck to calm it down.

"But you were going a bit fast sir," replied Mick.

"Don't you argue with me," said Farrington, "anyway, there is no harm done, your wretched sheep are in that field. At least your dogs know how to control them even if you don't," he continued, with a sneer breaking out on his face.

Mick was generally a calm, unruffled person, but this time he was incensed and did not want to lose face in front of Elfie.

"There's nowt wrong with our herding, it was you who came upon us too quick like."

"Mick, don't argue, it's alright," said Elfie laying a calming hand on his arm.

"I'm sure Mr Farrington was as startled as we were coming upon us on that blind bend in the track."

"Ah, yes Miss Mason, at least you talk sense," said Jacob. At that, he dismounted from the horse and walked over to the couple. He looked directly at Elfie and mused on the figure stood before him, then he spoke.

"And what might you be doing down this end of the dale?"

The girl thought for a few moments, her indignation at his question clearly visible on her face. 'It was none of his business what she was doing – or was it?' she thought. She threw him a wild look as if to show her contempt, but diplomacy overcame confrontation as she replied.

"Mick and I have collected together these stray ewes and we're taking them to the shepherds meeting in Howtown."

Farrington flashed a look of scorn at Mick.

"I see, it's you and Mick is it?"

Clearly he was both surprised and annoyed at the answer given by the girl. Had this fellow stolen his prize from under his nose? Was he now too late in his conquest?

"And we're going to see if there are any of our sheep to be claimed as well," added Elfie as a soother, as if to confirm that she was engaged on business connected to her shepherding.

"I see, and it's our sheep as well, is it?" replied Farrington in a sneering tone. "I think that you should be at your station attending to the sheep that I have entrusted to your care, don't you? Instead I find you traipsing around the valley-"

Elfie interrupted "But sir, the lambing is over and the ewes are returning to the higher ground for a few weeks before they are brought down for the washing. So there isn't a lot to be done with them at the present time."

Jacob Farrington was clearly displeased.

"Very well Miss Mason, you go about your business then, go and take your sheep wherever, but mind you, I shall be back to see the results of your work very shortly indeed."

With that said he turned abruptly away from the couple and walked back swiftly to his horse, kicking stones from under his feet in an aggressive manner as he went. He remounted his horse and settled himself comfortably into the saddle.

"I shall expect to see you on your own ground next time, you see to that young lady."

Farrington left reined the horse and turned it in the direction in which it had come, kicking its flanks hard with the sides of his boots, he set it off at a gallop and disappeared along the track.

The two stood there sometime dumfounded, and then Mick spoke.

"What do you reckon all that was about, who does he think he is? He's no right to order you about, he doesn't own you."

"I know," said Elfie, "but it's a bit tricky at the moment, I don't want to upset him and for some reason I seem to have done just that."

"I reckon he'll calm down in a while, I've seen him row with my father and storm off and then next time he comes around he's forgotten it all."

"Well I hope he forgets about today's little episode, it sounds as if he intends to come back very soon though, doesn't it?"

"Aye it does, but I shouldn't worry, it'll have blown over by then and when he sees all your lambs I expect he'll be satisfied," said Mick in a reassuring tone. "Come on then," and grabbing Elfie's hand he half pulled the girl towards the gate where Tess and Moss stood guarding the ewes.

"Let's get these sheep into the village."

Elfie dragged reluctantly behind him.

"Listen, it'll be alright, really, send your dogs in to fetch them out and we'll be on our way as if nowt had happened."

Elfie gave him a sickly smile, her stomach was churning over nervously. She composed herself and commanded the two dogs and within a few minutes the group was again proceeding along the lane as if nothing had happened.

The track widened at its junction with the old road over to Martindale and the route dropped gently down through a wooded area with a mossy beck accompanying the road. The aroma of wild garlic and bluebells filled the air with a fragrant purity. Soon they reached the village and stopped for a few minutes. Elfie looked around her, it was now sometime since her last visit which had been in the company of her father. Now she was a free spirit able to do as she pleased. It seemed that the only shadow on the horizon was Jacob Farrington.

"Where's the meeting then Mick?"

"It'll be at the far end of the village by the inn," he replied. "We'll get this lot penned up and then find out what time the meeting starts."

There were very few people about and those that were gave the couple nothing more than a cursory glance. When they reached the inn they saw a number of pens erected in the little square opposite. Mick went over and opened up one of the pens.

"You bringing 'em strays in like?" said a voice behind him.

Mick turned to see an old fellow leaning on the gate on the next but one pen.

"Aye we are," he replied.

"An' where are y' from then?" said the old man, sauntering towards them.

"Up Fusedale," replied Mick. "Send 'em in Elfie."

With a couple of commands the two dogs had the ewes safely in the pen and Mick secured the gate.

"Them your dogs then lass?" said the old man eyeing the young girl up and down.

"Yes they are," she replied, rolling her eyes.

"Good uns like."

"Yes I trained this one myself," she answered as she fondled the ears of Tess who had now returned to her side. "I've just-"

"What time is the meeting?" interrupted Mick.

"Three o'clock sharp," said the old man.

"Come on, we'll call at my aunts house and get a pot of tea."

"I didn't know that you had an aunt in the village," remarked Elfie.

"Well, she's not my real aunt, but a family friend and I've always called her auntie, we all have."

Mick took a firm hold on Elfie's arm and led her quickly away from the square. When they were out of earshot of the old man Mick slowed down and turned to Elfie.

"Perhaps you shouldn't be telling folk about your business," he said in a low voice. "You don't want it getting back to Lord Farrington."

Elfie's face reddened, "Oh Mick, I didn't think of that, do you think the old man will tell him?"

"I shouldn't think so, he probably doesn't even know him, but gossip spreads and that could eventually get back. Just as well to be careful though until you're properly established like."

The couple returned to the square beside the inn having spent a pleasant hour with Mick's 'auntie'. Most of the pens were now full, there was a good number of Herdwicks along with Scottish blackface, a few Dales bred and Swaledales and an odd Cheviot. A number of men were now gathered around the pens looking over the sheep contained therein. Several passed comment about the presence of the Cheviot ewe as the breed was seldom seen in these parts.

"We had better be having a look ourselves an' see if there's any of ours in there," said Mick.

They made their way around the pens but could not see any sheep bearing the Jarrow or Mason smit.

"That's good," said Mick, "at least we don't have to drive any back to the farm, we can leave as soon as those we brought in are claimed."

After a few minutes there was a loud call to order by an elderly man who was stood on a box. Elfie and Mick joined the ranks.

The man on the box deliberated for some time about a number of aspects relating to farming and in particular sheep and market prices. A long and lively discussion ensued with much forceful argument from the crowd. Eventually, the meeting was called to order and the reclaiming of the sheep commenced. The pens were numbered and as each number along with a description was called out various men came forward to claim their sheep. A lot of ribald comments were called out at times.

"Y' want t' get them there walls o' yours mended an' then y' ewes waint get out."

"Tha's allus fetching th' sheep back from 'ere, thal' be 'aving y' own pen in a bit."

There was much good humour and laughter amongst the men.

The ewes brought down by the young couple were claimed by two farmers.

"That's good," commented Mick, "we had three with one mark and four of the other, so that's them sorted now."

"So we don't need to stay any longer then, Mick?"

"No we can get back now."

The couple left the men still sorting out the remaining sheep and set off back through the village towards the road that would take them back up to Fusedale.

"I suppose the next thing will be the gather for washing," remarked Elfie, thinking ahead.

"Might be for you, but our next big job is the hay, we've only a few fields but its still a fair sized job when there's not so many of us to do it."

"I can come and help out a bit, when are you planning to do it?"

"It'll probably be in a couple of weeks, 'pending on the weather, and then we'll all be getting together for the gather."

The pair had now left the confines of the village and reached the track turning off to Fusedale, the two dogs now relieved of their work sniffed interestingly at new scents along the route. Soon they reached the small woodland; the trees were almost in full leaf now giving coolness to the air. Moss and lichens abounded on the rocks on either side of the track giving numerous contrasts of the shade of green. Emerging from the shade of the wood, the pair reached a grassy area near to the beck.

"We could stop here a while and enjoy the sunshine, there's no need to rush back as father will only find me something else to do," said Mick.

They strolled over to the edge of the beck. The crystal clear water tumbled down over a series of little waterfalls before entering a small shallow pool. Dragonflies played above the water, darting backwards and forwards, their wings shimmering in the bright sunlight. A dipper was stood on a small rock protruding from the water, looking for its next tasty insect. The bird upped and was away as the couple approached.

Elfie flopped down on the grass. She pulled off her boots and socks and dangled her feet over the edge of the banking. Then slowly she lowered them down into the pool, she grimaced as the cold water encircled her feet. Despite the warmth of the day, the water was icy cold.

"Aren't you going to cool off then," she enquired of Mick who was stood there watching her. He seemed to be daydreaming. "Mick, are you listening?"

"Oh, er yes," came the reply and he joined her on the bank, he started pulling off his boots and socks.

"Mick Jarrow, when did you last wash your feet?"

The young man looked embarrassed.

"It's my socks that's mucky and they've dirtied my feet," he replied.

"Then I'd best have a word with your mother about washing your socks then, hadn't I?" teased Elfie.

"Cor, don't do that, you'll get me into bother." Mick plunged his feet into the water, "God, its cold," he gasped. "You won't say owt to my mother will you?"

"As if I would, but I'll be checking up on you next time I see you, and then again I might just tell unless you do as I ask," she taunted.

The couple sat by the beck for some time, dipping their feet into the icy water, splashing each other and laughing and squealing like two children.

Elfie got up and moved away from the beck and lay down on the grass. Mick moved nearer and sat there gazing down at the girl. Elfie had closed her eyes and was laid there contentedly enjoying the warmth of the sun. The young man looked down adoringly at her. What was going on in her mind, he wondered. Did she really care for him? She seemed receptive and enjoyed his company, but was there more to it than just this friendship?

Mick Jarrow was a positive person and had already mapped out his future plans in his mind. His father was getting older and fast approaching the stage where he would relinquish much of the running of the farm to him as the eldest son. The lad was also at the stage where he sought some independence from the general family life and indeed he wanted to form his own family. Nothing would suit him better than to have Elfie as his wife. It was a dream he had harboured in his mind from an early age after his first meeting with her. It was an ideal he had nurtured through his formative years and now needed to see his ideals through to fruition.

There was a cottage attached to the farm which had been empty for some years now. He was sure it could be renovated and then he could live there if only she would marry him, but would she, how could he find out? He was too shy at this stage to ask her and was content with her friendship, although he knew that he should not delay his proposals too long. He knew that sooner or later other suitors could arrive on the scene as Elfie broadened her acquaintances, she was very attractive and others would also see her this way and want to win her over. This was an overwhelming desire in the mind of Jacob Farrington, but his motives were not about the simple ideals of marriage.

Mick felt confident that his parents would approve of him marrying the shepherdess and indeed, his mother had suggested it in a subtle sort of way.

As he looked long and hard into the face beside him he felt an overwhelming desire to kiss the soft lips of the girl. He lacked confidence and had little experience of girls other than his sister. How could he approach the tender subject of love when he knew so little about it and yet, he was sure that he was in love with her.

Her eyes opened, first a little, initially to prevent the intrusion of the sun's brightness and then they were opened wide and looking directly into his.

"You're staring at me Mick Jarrow, aren't you, what are you looking at?"

He hesitated, "er I was just thinking er-."

"Go on then, what were you thinking," she asked, a hint of impatience in her voice.

"Y-you're pretty." He blurted out the words.

"Is that all I am then?" she said, teasing him with a coquettish smile, her eyes twinkling up at him.

Mick was on the spot now, she was probing his inner thoughts and he was unsure how to respond. He reached forward and pulled a long stem of grass from a clump that protruded from the smooth grass on which they now sat. Mick moved a little nearer and tickled her cheek with the coarse blade, she giggled girlishly.

"You haven't answered my question Mick."

"Well I don't know what to say," he muttered.

"So - all I am to you is a pretty face then is it?" she chided.

Mick knew in his mind that he was in danger of losing this situation, he was on the verge of expressing his feelings to her and now he was floundering. He took a deep breath and summoned up all his courage, his inner mind was telling him to win her over.

"Can I- can I-"

Elfie looked up at the young man, her eyes searching his for the rest of the question.

"Yes," she said, as if now she had anticipated the question.

"Can I kiss you?" His mind raced, the blood pumped around his body and his face flushed bright red, his mind asked the question, had he done the right thing?

Elfie closed her eyes again. Mick looked down at the soft lips that were gently parted as if waiting for his response, he was so near and yet the final act was so far away in his confidence. There was a long silence between them and it seemed that the pair existed in another dimension, another world.

"Why are you waiting then," she whispered, her words jolted him back into reality. She lay there motionless before him, her eyes still closed but her lips now pouting somewhat. He leaned forward towards her face which darkened as he cast a shadow over it. So gently their lips met, so soft, so warm, the feel of a young girls lips was an experience so new to him. As their lips remained together there was no movement between them as Mick was frozen to the spot in a surreal ecstasy. The warmth of her lips passed to his, this surely was the nearest thing to heaven that he had ever experienced. Then her arms were around his neck, pulling him firmly towards her. The impassioned gave way to fervent passion. Then Elfie released her arms from around his neck, slowly he drew away from her, like waves receding on the shore the passion subsided. Overwhelmed with what he had done, the lad was visibly shaking.

Her eyes opened and looked directly into his and then she turned her head to one side, presenting her neck and long hair to his view now. There was a long silence between them. Mick felt that she had responded favourably, but what was she really thinking? After a minute she turned back towards him, she smiled warmly and reached out her hands.

"Pull me up then," she said with a cheeky tone in her voice.

Then she was up and sat beside him. Was she cross with him? He did not think so, but the uncertainty gnawed away at him, he felt that the chance to put forward his proposals was quickly slipping away, at least for now. There would be other opportunities he was sure, but when?

"Go and get my boots and then we'll be off," she ordered.

Mick obediently fetched her boots and his from where they had left them at the side of the beck. They sat there and Elfie chatted away about the events of the day, but made no reference to the immediate events as they put their footwear back on.

Back in the lane they wandered along towards the farmhouse. Mick needed to know her feelings.

"You didn't mind me er- you know?"

"Kissing me," she replied.

"Yes," said Mick.

"Why, should I have?"

"I don't know, I've never kissed a girl before."

"You've never kissed your sister Liza then?"

"Well, yes, when she was little, but that's not the same is it?"

"No it's not," she replied, giving him a knowing glance, "and I've never kissed a boy before, so there we are."

Mick knew he wasn't going to get an answer today as the farmhouse came into view.

Chapter twelve

A veil of low cumulus cloud had moved in from the northeast and filled the valleys. The effect of this was to create a dull, damp atmosphere and though whilst it was not raining, moisture particles formed on the few small trees thereabouts, causing them to drip profusely. Similarly, the grasses were adorned with water droplets which released in a kind of symmetry and slowly ran down each stem to the eagerly awaiting ground. The recent weeks of dry weather and light winds had dried the ground out considerably.

Elfie had just returned to the croft after an early morning walk around the few remaining sheep in the valley. In the mist they were difficult to see until she was almost upon them and then they moved lazily away as she approached, disappearing from view again. This little group of ewes and their young seemed to prefer the valley floor to the higher slopes. Elfie had developed a kind of affinity with them and made a point of checking on them most days although it was unnecessary. They could be likened to her pets as she knew each one individually and its characteristics. Usually they followed her about, but today they seemed reticent and persistently moved off into the mist as she came near. The girl knew that sheep can be fickle creatures and their actions today gave no cause for concern.

Her intention was to help with the haymaking down at the farm, but the present weather would mean a delay in the proceedings. To cut in these damp conditions would result in it 'looking a bit black' if it was left lying in wet fields. This affected its feeding value making it only useful for feeding to adolescent stirks rather than dairy cattle.

Since the visit to Howtown, Elfie had seen little of Mick. She knew that his time would be taken up with work around the farm as this was a busy period in the farming calendar. He had only been able to steal a brief visit the previous evening and it was then that she had agreed to help out with the haymaking. Although she knew it would be hard work it was a chance to socialise and to be with Mick even though they would both be fully occupied on different tasks. Hopes were now dashed, at least for the time being as it was necessary to have a couple of dry, settled days before the cut. The area had its own miniature climate and so it was just as likely to change back to fine weather, but the clouds needed to move first and this required a wind as the air was motionless.

Now that the lambing was well and truly over Elfie found herself with time to spare and had put this to good use in the house. She had cleared out a number of items that she felt were no longer of use to her. This included her father's clothes except for one thick coat, which although it was rather large and heavy upon her slender frame, it would provide protection from the winter elements. She had decided to keep her small bedroom as it was and so she had dismantled her father's bed and put it in the outbuilding.

Remaining in the corner of the room were a number of items and today Elfie set about sorting and disposing of them accordingly. There was little of any use or value to her. This task completed, there remained but one final item, the locked chest. Over the last few weeks it had gone to the back of her mind as other events has taken precedence. Now her curiosity was renewed, but how to get into it?

She scolded Mick in her mind 'he was going to get it open for me, but I bet he's forgotten'. Her recent efforts clearing the croft had failed to reveal the location of the key. She knew that it must be secreted away somewhere, but it was obviously in a place know only to her father. Thoughts raced round in her mind. 'I'll have one more search, and then if I can't find it I'll jolly well smash it open. 'I'll role it over a cliff or something, or take the wood axe to it, oh I'd better not though, there might just be something valuable inside.'

The key had to be tucked away in some nook or cranny, but she had never seen her father locate it. In fact she had only seen him looking in the chest a couple of times. The padlock was quite large so she reasoned that the key had to be two or three inches in length. She decided to check one wall at a time rather than darting about from place to place as in her earlier efforts.

She commenced the search by feeling in all the cracks in the walls. Every now and again a spider would run out, disturbed by the probing fingers. Each time this happened she would let out a squeal and then scold herself for being so silly. The search of the first wall revealed nothing; all that she had gained was blackened fingers from the years of dust in the nicks in the walls. Next it was the turn of the wall with the fireplace.

Despite her thorough search no key was found. Uh, she stamped her feet in frustration. On to the third and fourth wall, but again, no luck.

Elfie flopped down in the chair and sighed heavily. She was beginning to feel exasperated, would she ever find the key and see the contents of the wretched chest. She looked around the room again and again as if trying to will the key out of its hiding place. Her eyes gazed up at the roof and beams, and then like a flash it hit her, the beams, she had not looked up there, it was a likely place.

She went and fetched the stool, climbed up and started a systematic check of the beams. Small pieces of wood and dust fell down on her as she slid her hands along the rough timbers. Ouch, a splinter went into her finger, she pulled it out and continued. She carried on feeling along each beam, coughing every now and then from the dust which she was disturbing.

Then her fingers touched something, dislodging it, it fell to the floor giving a metallic clunk as it hit the flagstones. Elfie looked down, there at her feet lay a large, somewhat rusty looking key. She stepped down off the stool and bent to pick up the key. She blew the dust of it and the placed it on the mantelshelf.

She stood silent for some time, now she could open the chest, but there was a reluctance, what would it contain? She went off to wash her hands. Returning to the room still drying her hands on her skirt, she went over to the mantelshelf and took hold of the key. In a flash she was kneeling on the floor in front of the chest as if it were some kind of sacred altar. The key slid easily into the padlock, her hand turned it and with a resounding click it opened. She removed the padlock from the hasp and gingerly lifted up the lid of the chest, the hinges creaked a little as if offering their final resistance to the intrusion of the secrets contained therein. Then it was fully open, Elfie gazed down into the chest her eyes wide open.

The contents were covered with a thick cloth of a velvet-like texture. On top of the cloth lay the book which she had wanted to consult some weeks previously. It was the record of sheep smits written by Joseph Walker of Martindale. Elfie briefly flicked through the pages as if to confirm that it was indeed the book that she had seen her father look at on a number of occasions. The blocks of two sheep were printed three to a page showing the smit and lug marks from both angles. Her mind wandered back for a few moments when she had looked at the illustrations with her father. Her thoughts quickly returned to the present and she closed the book and placed it on the floor beside her. This was an expected content and her mind now focussed on what the cloth could be hiding. She hesitated for a few moments, then in one swift move she pulled the cover away to reveal the contents.

There were a number of books which she quickly looked at. Half a dozen or so novels, a book on animal husbandry and another on mathematics. She placed these on the book of smits, she could look at these in more detail later. Next there were a couple of notebooks, which contained several hand written entries. The girl briefly read some of the notes which seemed to be about woollen and cotton materials and which contained a number of numerical quantities. There were a number of names of companies and addresses in places such as Bradford, Manchester and London. There were other places, which she had never heard of too. These notebooks puzzled her considerably, but she placed them atop of the others on the pile, eager to discover more.

Next out was a large bag, which obviously contained soft materials, she opened it and pulled out a number of items of clothing. A jacket and trousers, a waistcoat and a number of shirts. Elfie studied them, they were of a good quality and clearly the clothes of a gentleman, had they been worn by her father in his former life? She held them up, they appeared to be about his size and so she concluded that they had been worn by him in the past.

The clothes were placed on the chair and then she was back on the voyage of discovery. A leather bag of some considerable weight was the next item out. She released the cord and placed her hand inside, she pulled out a small pouch like bag which she quickly opened. Her fingers probed inside and withdrew a gold ring. It was a beautiful piece of jewellery with delicate engravings around its circumference. The girl gingerly slid the ring on to her third finger, "this must have been my mothers wedding ring, oh if only I'd known her," she said out loudly in a slightly faltering voice.

Her mind went back to the leather bag, she tipped the contents out onto the floor. It contained a quantity of coins; there were florins, shillings, crowns and sovereigns. Elfie gasped with surprise and delight, the fact that the chest might contain money had never entered her mind. She sorted through the coins putting them into piles of the same value and then counted them. Eighteen shillings, twelve florins, four crowns and fifty-seven sovereigns, a small fortune. Elfie could not believe her eyes, she counted again and then a third time arriving at the same amount each time. She sat for some time staring at the money, pondering where it had come from. She was clearly aware that her father had made a living albeit meagre from keeping sheep but it did not equate to what now lay in front of her. So was it from some previous employment or some family fortune? Her mind was now in a turmoil trying to imagine what had been and then suddenly the more important question, what was she to do with it? What if some one robbed her? A wave of panic now swept over her, no, she reasoned with herself, no one ever comes up here except Mick and Farrington and she was sure there were no robbers hereabouts. Still, better be safe she reasoned and gathering up the coins, she placed them in the bag and went to hide them in her bedroom.

She was quickly back beside the chest again, eager to see what else it would reveal to her. The young girl's thoughts went back to the money again and she now felt a feeling of security sweep over her. The realisation that she was no longer the poor shepherdess of Fusedale eking out a meagre living intrigued her. Although it was not a large fortune, it was certainly sufficient to improve her standard of living, maybe buy her own flock. Her mind was in a turmoil but she resolved to keep her secret to herself. At least for the time being.

She looked back into the chest again, there was one item remaining, a wooden box with a close fitting lid. She lifted it out, it was made of a dark brown wood with ornate veneer inlays on the lid and a small silver handle. She opened it up, unsure what she would find. Inside was a quantity of small, leather bound books, she picked one out and opened it. By looking at the pages with their neat hand written entries she soon realised that it was a diary. She picked out another and yet another; each was the same, page after page of dated entries. She carried the box over to the table, sat down and began to read.

Chapter thirteen

The next day dawned brighter than its predecessor although it was still cloudy. The wind had got up somewhat during the night and was now blowing quite strongly up the valley. The grasses bent and swayed under its influence as if to mirror the clouds scurrying across the sky.

"If this wind continues and the sun comes out properly then the grass will dry out quickly and Mick will be able to get on with the haymaking," said Elfie out loud. She was walking back from the steam where she had been carrying out some washing, having got rather dusty from her search around the croft yesterday. She scanned the sky for signs of impending weather changes. Through small breaks in the clouds she was able to catch glimpses of a bright blue sky with no traces of higher cloud.

"I think it looks promising Tess," said the girl to the dog walking along side of her. Tess wagged her tail and looked up adoringly at her mistress, her head inclined to one side as if to beg the question, when are we going onto the fells? The two dogs had been inactive for the last couple of days as Elfie had been searching for the missing key and then reading her father's diaries. Although she had not read them in their entirety, she was now half way through them.

"Yes, today things will dry out, tomorrow will be haytime, won't it girl?" The dog wagged its tail again in agreement. Moss now appeared by her side, he had been engrossed in some new scent that he had found but now wanted to know what was going on. She reached down to fondle him.

"There old boy, I've just been telling your sister that we might go down to Dale End tomorrow and help out with the hay."

Reaching the door of the croft she knelt down for a moment and tickled both of the dog's heads, they had their favourite spots, Tess behind the ears and Moss under his chin.

She was about to get up and go inside when she heard the sound of a galloping horse. She looked up to see a rider approaching, and knew that it would be Jacob Farrington.

"So, he's back," she mused, "well, at least we're at home this time, aren't we my beauties?"

She rushed inside and moved the pile of diaries, her circumstances had now changed somewhat but she did not want him knowing about her affairs. She was back, stood in the doorway as the rider approached the croft. The girl was aware of a feeling of calm as she looked at Farrington as he dismounted from his horse; generally, his visits brought a feeling of trepidation to her, this time it was different.

Jacob slapped the flanks of the sweating beast and it wandered off to graze and drink from the trough at the side of the outbuilding, clearly, he had ridden it hard as so often was his want.

"Good morning Miss Mason, I take it that I find you well," he said in a condescending tone.

"Yes sir, I am," came the reply from her in an almost lyrical tone.

She now had a secret which changed how she related to his lordship's son.

"Shall we go inside and talk?" he asked in a bold tone.

"Oh, no, I would prefer to sit outside if we must talk, it is a much better today."

Farrington raised a questioning eye brow.

"Very well then," he answered rather curtly and went and sat down on the stone bench at the side of the door. Elfie remained standing. Jacob looked at her for a moment and then his expression softened.

"Come, Miss Mason, be seated, we must talk about how you are progressing. You remember that I said I would come and discuss things with you last time we met, don't you?"

Elfie did not answer but reluctantly took a seat at the other end of the bench and stared down at her feet for a few moments, and then she looked at him and gave him a wry smile.

"I'm not cross about what happened the other day; it was probably my fault for going too fast."

Elfie was a little taken back by his apology.

Farrington went on, "but that sweetheart of yours needs to be a bit more respectful."

"He doesn't mean any harm sir," she replied and then in a scornful voice,

"he's not my sweetheart either. I was just helping him out with the ewes at the shepherds meet."

Why she denied her affection for Mick she was not sure, but her comments had a profound effect on Jacob. He moved up next to her and put his arm around her. She froze.

"Come Miss Mason, we are friends surely, haven't I done you a great favour by helping you to remain here in the dale?"

Elfie was silent for a short while.

"Yes, yes, you have been very kind to me."

"Well then, perhaps it's time you repaid some of my kindness then my girl."

"I don't know what you mean sir," a tremble evident in her voice.

In her mind she had a pretty good idea of exactly what he meant.

Farrington removed his arm from around her; in his mind he knew that he was rushing things. This girl was spirited but also innocent and he also thought her somewhat naïve. She would need gentle handling, he needed to gain her confidence. Elfie relaxed now that the threatening arm had been withdrawn.

With a new found confidence she enquired, "what do you mean about repaying you?"

"I'm sorry Miss Mason, perhaps you misunderstood me, what I meant by repayment was doing a good job looking after the sheep and the likes."

"Then I can assure you that I am doing that, but now that the lambing is over there's not a lot to do. The next thing is to gather the sheep in for washing and clipping, but I can't do that till the hay is in and I can get some help."

"Yes, quite," replied Farrington. He sat silently for a few minutes, clearly deep in though, and then he spoke.

"Perhaps you should consider your future here though; it will be hard up here in winter. Surely, there are other things that you could do- I could probably find you work at the manor."

Farrington's voice quickened into an excited tone as ideas flooded into his head.

"Yes, yes, that's it, there are plenty of things that you could do, and you'd be well looked after, comfortably, I mean, none of this hardship. You would even have your own room."

These were wild ideas, but he was sure that he could fulfil them. He could present the best possible reason as the girl's welfare, although he knew that deep down he was trying to possess her.

Jacob Farrington loved Amelia, but this girl fired up a passion, which he did not experience with his betrothed, he needed to have her for himself. His face coloured up in his excitement of the plan that he was constructing. Elfie noticed his flushed appearance, but was unaware of the deep reason for it.

"Well, what do you say Miss Mason, do you not think that it would be better than your lonely existence here?"

Elfie was in a quandary, she did not think it prudent to refuse his offer outright as it would offend him and possibly affect her present position, but neither did she want to work at the manor.

"Well then," he urged.

"I would have to give it some though sir."

She knew that she needed time and that this reply was not a refusal, it might be enough to satisfy him for the time being, but she knew deep down that it would not pacify him for long. It was becoming clear to Elfie that Farrington always got his own way eventually and that he was impetuous.

She added, "my real love is here though, shepherding."

"I realise that my dear," he said in an endearing tone, "that's why we are where we are at this moment, but my offer would give you a better life, free from all the harshness of this God forsaken place."

Elfie flashed him a disapproving look.

"You know nothing different than this dale, why – I bet you've never been further than Howtown have you?"

"Yes, I have, I've been to Penrith two or three times," she retorted defiantly.

"And what did you think of it there?"

"It's alright I suppose, but I'd rather be here really."

Farrington realized that the conversation was drifting away from its real purpose.

"I'll tell you what Miss Mason, you have a good think about what I've said and then we'll talk about it next time I'm here."

"And when will that be?" she replied in a forthright tone.

She knew that by having this information she would know how much time she had to think things through. Furthermore, she could also make sure that she was about.

"Shall we say two weeks from today if that is agreeable to you my dear?"

Elfie gave him a wry smile.

"You think carefully on my words Miss Mason."

Jacob rose to his feet and clicked his fingers, the horse came obediently over to him and he took hold of its reign. If only this girl was as obedient as this horse he thought to himself.

He was quickly ensconced in the saddle and deftly turned the horse around.

"Till next time then?"

"Yes, till next time," this time she gave him a broad smile making him wonder if he was winning with the girl.

"Walk on then" he said to the horse. As he moved away he looked over his shoulder at her. She gave him a half-hearted wave. Yes, perhaps she was warming to him. He turned forward again putting the horse into a steady gallop and then he was away.

Elfie sat down again on the bench and thought things through. Events were changing her hitherto steady, uncomplicated life. She knew in her heart that she wanted to be with Mick, to get to know him better, yet at this stage she did not really know whether or not she loved him, she was uncertain about love itself. There was the revelation of the diaries which she was about to continue discovering, and then there was the money. Now there was Farrington's offer, life was getting complicated for this simple shepherdess.

Elfie spent the rest of the day in a state of transition. Skimming through the diaries, she was forming a mental picture of her father's former life and circumstances. Her thoughts continued to move between Mick and Jacob Farrington. What was behind his offer? Perhaps it was a genuine desire on his part for her to have a better life. Maybe he was right, life at the manor would be a lot easier than here, even if she was in service of some kind and if that was what he intended?

The day drifted into early evening as she flitted about the croft, sometimes reading, sometimes moving things about or tidying up, not really wanting to eat as the turmoil rolled about in her head. The two dogs watched her with sulky expressions in their eyes; this was not their kind of day.

There was a loud knock at the door, the two of them rushed forward and took up their places behind it. Tails wagging, there was no threat, they sensed the person outside was friendly. Elfie stopped what she was doing and went to see who it was. It was Mick standing there, a broad grin on his face.

"Oh Mick, am I glad to see you," her best welcoming smile spreading across her face.

"Is-is something up, - its not Farrington again is it?"

"No it's nothing with him," she replied, denying the suggestion that somehow he was involved.

"I've just got such a lot to tell you."

There was a pause as they looked at each other intently.

"I'd just come up to tell you that we're starting haymaking first thing tomorrow and we'd be glad o' your help."

"Yes, I was expecting you to start tomorrow now that the weather seems settled, I'd be glad to help out, look, I've just boiled the kettle, I'll make us a pot of tea and then we can talk. I've so much to tell you Mick," she repeated in an excited voice.

Mick went to sit down in the only comfortable chair. Presently, Elfie appeared with two pots of steaming hot tea.

"There you are Mr Jarrow, sir," she said, a mocking look on her face.

"Thank you, Mrs Jarrow," he replied, and waited for the reaction to his remark.

"Don't you mean Miss Mason?"

"Sorry, yes I do, he replied somewhat nonplussed, just a mistake,"

"Or wishful thinking on your part, eh," she chided.

"Well-er."

"You just be careful what you're thinking," she interrupted.

Mick looked a little dejected. Secretly, Elfie rather liked the sound of Mrs Jarrow, Elfrida Jarrow? She revealed nothing of her inner thoughts as she sat down in the chair opposite to him. She looked directly at him but said nothing, Mick's face coloured a little and he shuffled his feet nervously and looked down at them. Then he mustered up some courage and spoke,

"Er, go on then, what have you got to tell me then?"

A cheeky little smile spread across her face and Mick immediately warmed to it.

"You remember that chest that you couldn't open for me?" Mick nodded.

"Well, I've got into it," she sat back, a look of triumph on her face.

"How did you manage that, it's a strong lock?"

"I found the key," she replied in a jubilant tone.

"And is it full of treasure then?"

"Don't be silly, but it's full of diaries, well - half full."

Mick looked a bit disappointed.

"Diaries, what do you want with diaries."

"They're my father's, and I've been reading them and now I know about my past and where I came from."

An interesting expression now formed on Mick's face as he pondered what she was about to reveal to him.

"Go on then," he urged. "Where do you come from?"

"I was born on a farm near Appleby, would you believe?"

"Well I suppose you've got to be born somewhere, but what's so special about that?"

"That's not special in itself, but my father's life is – I'll start at the beginning, though I've only briefly read the diaries. I will read them some more when I've got the time."

She wriggled herself into the chair to get more comfortable and took a long drink from the mug of tea clasped in her hands.

"My father came from Lancashire, Manchester to be exact. His father owned mills around there which he had set up due to the decline in handloom weaving."

"Weren't they the people who weaved in their attics or something?" interrupted Mick.

"Yes, but the work was being taken over by the mills and this was how my grandfather was expanding his business. Anyway, it seems that my grandfather inherited a large farming estate near Settle. My grandfather had the farm managed and it was used to supply the mills with wool.

My father's older brother John was put in to run the farm when he was old enough, as he did not want to work in the mill. It seems that my grandfather did not get on with him and more or less banished him to the farm. My father went to a boarding school at Giggleswick which was quite near to where the farm was. It seems that my father used to spend his weekends with his brother on the farm and got very interested in farm work and started to neglect his schoolwork. My grandfather found out and soon put a stop to it. He wanted him to work in the mills, so when he had finished at school he was put through an apprenticeship, which I think is some sort of training. Then he was eventually put in charge of one of the mills.

Then he met a girl called Anna, she was the daughter of a wealthy German banker in Manchester."

Mick was listening intently; it was like a story to him.

Elfie went on, "They must have fallen in love and wanted to get married, but the families were against it as they were of different religions. She was a Catholic and he was Methodist or something."

"But did that matter?" enquired Mick.

"Apparently, it did, so it seems, they were not allowed to marry if they had different religions. So their parents tried to stop them from seeing each other but they carried on in secret. Then they were found out and Anna's parents forbade her to see my father ever again."

"Aw, that's a shame if they loved each other, it doesn't seem fair, does it?"

"No it doesn't," replied Elfie, "but that did not stop them. Do you know what they did next?"

Mick could not think, he just sat there listening to the excited girl.

"They ran away together to Scotland, and, in the middle of the night at that, would you believe?"

"How did they do that, Scotland's miles and miles away?" said Mick.

Elfie's was wide eyed as she continued with the story.

"Well, it seems that my father arranged a lift on a mail coach going north and she crept away from her house in the dark and they met up and boarded this coach. My father had heard that you could get married once you got over the Scottish border without having to go to a church and all that. But, when they got to Scotland they couldn't get married right away as someone called Lord Broughton had brought in a law to stop this kind of thing. The new law said that you had to live in Scotland for three weeks before you could marry. So they did not know quite what to do, but they had to act quickly as it was not uncommon for the families to come looking for them. So they travelled on quite a way into Scotland so that they were away from the border if anybody came looking for them. My father got a job on a farm and they lived in a little room over the barn for a month or more."

Elfie downed the rest of the tea in one go, then she continued with her tale.

"They then travelled back to a toll house on the border where they had first made their enquiry and got married there. Then they travelled around the borders looking for permanent work and eventually my father got a job on a sheep farm near Hexam for a short while. Eventually, he got permanent work on a big sheep farm outside of Appleby.

"I've heard of Appleby," interrupted Mick.

Elfie ignored his comment.

"Then Anna became pregnant and that's how I came about."

Elfie leaned forward and placed the empty mug on the floor.

"So that's it, Mick, Anna Mason was my mother."

Mick was obviously enthralled by the excited girl's tale, he was quite happy to sit and listen to her all day if need be.

"Well, it's quite a story, what happened next and where's your mother now?"

Elfie swallowed hard as if to choke back an emotion.

"My mother died shortly after I was born," she replied sadly. "There were some complications with the birth"

"Oh, that's so sad," said Mick. "So you never knew your mother at all then?"

"No, no I never had the chance, but I suppose it's a long time ago now."

"I bet she was lovely, your mother, if she was anything like you," said Mick in a supporting voice.

Elfie gave him a thanking smile.

"My father was heartbroken and with no-one to turn to he travelled down to his brother's farm. His brother took him in and helped him through. My father stayed on at the farm and worked there for quite some time. I was looked after during the day by a Mrs Hawkins who was the wife of one of the farm labourers. They lived in a cottage next to the big farmhouse. That's how it was for a few years until my grandfather found out about it all. Apparently, he threatened to take the farm away from

John if my father remained there. So rather than let this happen my father left the farm and came here to work for Lord Farrington."

Elfie fell silent for a few minutes, Mick too said nothing, he was trying to take in the story that had just been relayed to him. After a while he broke the silence.

"So now you know all this, where does it leave you now?"

"Well, I know I'm not a peasant's daughter or anything like that, in fact I come from a wealthy family, although I suppose it's not much good to me now is it? They wouldn't want to know me after all that's happened in the past. I suppose I'm part German as well."

"What about your uncle in Settle, he would be alright with you, wouldn't he?"

"I hadn't really thought about that, I don't know where he lives apart from the name of his farm and anyway, why would I want to find him?" concluded the girl quite decisively.

Mick thought for a minute, "he is your uncle after all, he might be pleased to see you."

"Maybe, but he might be dead by now and fathers relatives in Manchester certainly will be,"

"Their not forced to be," replied Mick.

"Oh, they must be Mick, they were all much older than my father," she replied emphatically as if to close the book on this chapter of her life.

"Really, why would I want to change things, I'm happy here, yes- I'm sure I am unless his lordships got other ideas?"

"What do you mean by that?" asked Mick.

"Nothing really," she replied, although the previous conversation with Farrington was still milling around in her mind.

Mick glanced out of the window, the evening was drawing in as the light started to fade.

"I think I'd best be going, there's a few days hard work ahead."

He rose to his feet, as did Elfie.

"So you'll come down to the farm tomorrow then?"

"Yes I will," she replied, "and not a word to anyone about what I've been telling you, mind. At least till I've had a chance to finish reading everything."

Mick nodded. Elfie moved closer to him and gave him a peck on the cheek. Mick quickly put his arms around her and pulled her closer. He kissed her gently on the forehead, not daring to kiss the lips he had so enjoyed only a few days previously. Elfie smiled broadly, a dreamy sort of expression on her face. They parted a little but still remained holding hands.

"I'll see you tomorrow morning then," Mick confirmed.

"Yes, you will."

They parted on the doorstep and Elfie watched him as he walked away. He turned several times to wave at her and then he was lost from view in the approaching evening gloom.

Chapter fourteen

Haymaking is one of the most important jobs on the farm calendar. Whilst the grass is growing tall it has to be saved and then stored so that the stock can eat it and enable them to thrive during the coming winter. To a shepherd, this date was not as important as it was to the farmer with his cattle. The sheep did consume some hay in winter but were adept at locating their own food in all but the most difficult conditions. Haytime was important to Elfie in another way, it was by helping with this task that she could in turn receive help with the washing and clipping of her flock. This support between farmers and shepherds was an important part of the yearly cycle of events.

The shepherdess hurried along the track towards Dale End Farm, eager to be of service, but also with another motive, that of being in the company of Mick. Her feelings for the young man were steadily developing. When she was with him she was playful and teasing and careful not to expose her inner feelings to him. Conversely, when she was away from him she experienced a deep longing to be with him. In time, her feelings would materialise into a true relationship. She was experiencing a deep fondness, which would surely turn to love.

As she approached the farm she could make out three figures already cutting away at the grasses and she estimated that they were already halfway across the first field. Walking down the lane from the farm she was also able to make out Mick's mother and sister Liza armed with hayforks. Within a few minutes she had joined them at the entrance to the first field.

"Morning Mrs Jarrow – Liza," she called out cheerily.

"Aye lass," replied Mary Jarrow, "we was beginning t' think you wasn't coming like."

"Oh yes, I told Mick I'd be here, I didn't think you'd be starting as early as this."

"Oh aye, t' lads 'av been out wi' leys for well o'er an hour now. Come on then, we need t' turn grass t' dry it like, an' then they'll fetch cart an' tek it t' barn," replied Mary.

Liza stepped forward and gave Elfie one of the two rakes that she had slung over her shoulder. Without further ado, the three of them formed a line and started to turn the hay over with the forks. Little mice scuttered out, disturbed for a second time after the initial cut. And so the morning progressed, by the time they had reached the point that Elfie had observed on her approach the men where into the next field and the newly cut grass lay at their feet. Due to the lay of the land the fields were fairly small and numbered eight in total. If the weather conditions held the work would be completed in three days.

Just before noon, Mary sent Liza back to the farm to fetch the lunch. By now the weather was getting quite hot and Elfie was ready for a break. Liza returned shortly with a large basket containing the food that Mary had prepared earlier.

"We'll sit 'ere in t'corner, it's bit shady, go tell lads t'lunch is ready," said Mary.

Liza climbed onto the wall and started shouting and waving her arms at the men.

"A' said go an' tell em, y've, got a voice like a wild animal, screeching like that."

Liza glared at her mother then jumped down off the wall and ran ahead to the next field.

Elfie smiled briefly, not certain whether to agree with her of not, then flopped down onto the ground by the wall and leaned back to rest. Her back suddenly felt cold as her dress, damp from the sweated labour pressed against her skin. She squirmed to get comfortable.

Mary perched herself on a fallen wall-stone beside her.

"I daresn't get down so low else I'll niver gerup agin," she remarked.

She pulled the basket that Liza had fetched from the house over towards her and lifted the cloth covering the contents. Inside there were bread rolls, cheese cut into small blocks and a jar of pickles.

"Help y' self lass, y've worked hard this morning – ah! here come t' lads."

The three men approached through the gate into the field. Elfie did not recognise the third figure but guessed that he would be from a farm further down the valley. A big grin broke out on Mick's face when he saw Elfie sat on the grass beside his mother. He walked over and sat himself down next to her. Elfie passed the basket to him without speaking, Mick dived in greedily.

"Go steady wi' it lad, 'e'll eat 'is share an' ours an' all," scolded Mary.

Mick passed the basket to his father who acted just as greedily as his son in taking out a large quantity of the food.

"I dunno what they'll be like of a night when they've done, 'appen they'll eat us an' all," chuckled Mrs Jarrow and at the same time pulling the basket away from her husband.

Liza came and sat down directly in front of Elfie and Mick and stared at them. Mick picked up a handful of grass cuttings and threw them at her.

"Give up staring like that, y' cheeky little beggar." Liza got up sulkily and moved some distance away.

"See now y've gone 'an upset 'er agin, 'e's allus doing that," said Mary in a cross tone.

"Come and sit by me Liza and have some food."

Elfie beckoned to the girl invitingly and with a bashful expression on her face Liza came and sat beside her.

"You tell me if he bothers you again," remarked Elfie, a forceful tone in her voice.

Mick laughed, "and what are you going to do about it then?"

"You'll soon see," retorted Elfie. "You should look after your sister, I wish I had one."

Davy Jarrow observed all this with a disinterested look on his face. He pushed the cap on his head back a bit and spoke for the first time since joining the little group.

"I reckon we'll finish third field by middle 'o afternoon an' then we'll cart this first field an' next un off t' barn. Bob Colton said he'd come up with 'is cart later on, so we should be able to shift it all between us."

Mick looked a bit puzzled, "we'll have a job to get third field in afore it's dark, won't we?"

"Well, we'll see, lasses al after make it into 'cocks' to stand overnight and then we'll shift it first light" -

Mary broke into the conversation now.

"An oos going t' feed y' if I'm making haycocks then, can't it lie till morning?"

Davy flashed her a cross look.

"You know it can't lass, it'll get damp."

Mary was swift to reply.

"Then why don't y' shift first two fields to barn, an then cock 'alf o' t'other field?"

"I'll do it as I've a mind, woman," growled Davy.

"An you'll do it as I say, if y' want any supper, shift first two fields an' then cock third field while me an' Liza mek supper. Andy 'll be 'ome from school later on an' 'e can 'elp as well.

Mary stood resolute her arms folded across her ample breasts.

Elfie looked on, a mused expression on her face, not really knowing how serious this confrontation between husband and wife really was.

"Do as mother says, or else there'll be no supper," crowed Liza in an amused voice.

Davy glowered at the girl, "you watch your tongue, or else."

He then rose to his feet, "we'll see then," he muttered and ambled off in the direction of the field to be cut. Mick and the other lad got up and followed obediently.

"E's a stubborn old beggar, if he thinks I'm cocking t'hay till it gets dark he mun think agin. Come on, we'll get this field turned agin an' then get on t' next un, shall we?"

By late afternoon Mary and the two girls had turned the first field again and raked the grass in the second field into rows. A horse and cart was seen to enter the first field, it was Bob Colten and his lad Danny.

"Run and tell yer father Bob's 'ere and send Mick to fetch our cart an all. We should be able t' get this lot in afore dark."

Elfie was beginning to wonder who really was in charge of the haymaking. Mary was clearly giving out her orders and she could well imagine the reaction in the field where the men were cutting.

Presently, Liza came skipping back.

"Mick's gone f' cart an' father's on his way back here."

The mischievous grin on Liza's face only served to confirm Elfie's suspicion of the reaction when the message from Mary was received.

Obviously, Mary's instruction had been carried out, but was he on his way back for another argument with her.

Bob had now walked over and was talking to Mary when Davy appeared.

"Well, come on you women, never mind standing there talking, lets get hay onto Bob's cart.

He gave a half knowing wink to Elfie. Perhaps he's not as awkward as he seems after all, she thought.

The first cart was fully loaded and with Elfie and Liza firmly ensconced in the hay it set off along the track to the farm. Presently, the cart came to a halt halfway along the track, pulling in closely to the wall. Mick's cart coming in the other direction was just able to squeeze past. The lad was unaware that the two girls were seated in the hay. As he got past Liza called out loudly to him in a cheeky voice.

"Ho, Mick, aren't you going to say hello to Elfie then?"

Mick swung round rather suddenly on the seat of the cart and overbalanced, this caused him to fall rather awkwardly into the back of his cart. Both Liza and Elfie laughed hysterically at his undignified fall. Mick regained his seat and shook his fist at the two girls, casing them to laugh even more.

"Now, you mind you don't fall of again Mick," cried Elfie in a cheeky voice. Their cart jerked forward and moved off again before any further banter could be exchanged.

The hay had to be stored in the sink mew off the bank barn. This was because the barn was built on a slope to make use of the contour of the ground. The cart was backed up an incline to the door of the barn and the hay was unloaded down into the mew. When this was full the top floor would be used for the remainder. In winter the cattle would be kept in the lower part of the barn where the hay could be easily fed to them. Once unloaded, the cart and its occupants set off back to the field.

Again in the lane the two carts met, this time Mick's cart stopped and the empty cart hedged past in the narrow lane. The two girls crouched down below the shelving's of the cart. These raised the sides of the cart for light loads but would be taken of when the haymaking was completed. This meant that Mick could not see the two girls.

"Where's the two lasses Bob?"

"I think they fell into mew," cried Bob jokingly.

As the two carts pulled away the girls jumped up and shouted out.

"Oy Mick."

Mick turned in his seat, careful this time not to fall off.

"Beat you up next time," shouted Liza, shaking her fist vigorously at him.

"Yes we will," echoed Elfie, laughing quite giddily.

The banter continued each time the two carts passed until finally the two fields had been cleared. The two girls remained at the farm after the last load whilst the men went back to make haycocks from the remaining cut grass.

Into the evening as the daylight faded the men toiled hard stacking the remaining cut grass.

"Its been a good day, eh lads," said Davy. "Another couple o' days an' we'll be done."

Back at the farm Mary and the two girls were getting the supper ready. Much of it had been prepared earlier in the day. The beef which had been part boiled was put back on the fire again together with a pan of potatoes and carrots. Two large fruit pies were put into the oven to warm. A flagon of beer was put on the table.

"You've been a big 'elp to us today lass," said Mary.

"It's been fun really, so much different to what I normally do and nice meeting other people as well."

"Well I daresest say y' father were a bit restrictive like, but anyway, will y' 'elp us tomorrow then?"

"Oh yes, I'd love to."

"Then y'll stop night then?"

Elfie was a bit taken back by the offer, having never spent a night under a roof other then the croft for as many years as she could remember.

"Well, I wasn't expecting to stop the night, Mrs Jarrow.'

"Aw y' don't want to be traipsing up that valley and back agin int' morning. Y' can share a bed wi' Liza, that's if y' don't mind sleeping wi' a silly bit o' a lass."

Elfie had never shared a bed before, but she replied. "If it's not putting you to too much trouble and Liza doesn't mind then."

"I don't mind," piped up Liza, quite excited at the prospect of a 'sister' for the night.

"Then that's settled," said Mary, a beaming smile spreading across her face.

Weary footsteps were heard approaching the kitchen door and the three men appeared.

"We're right done for," said Davy, sitting down at the table. "I 'ope supper's ready."

"Is it ever not?" retaliated Mary.

Soon the group were all seated around the big kitchen table and tucking in to the beef, potatoes and carrots. The men downed gulps of ale in between mouthfuls of food. The hard work had clearly created a thirst that would take a few mugs full of ale to slake. The fruit pie went the same way as the first course, being eagerly consumed and then the men pushed their chairs back from the table and stretched out heir legs.

"That were a right good meal lass," said Davy.

"Well y' wouldn't 'ave got it if y' 'adn't listened to me out in field, would y'?"

"Go on then, y' were right as usual."

Mary gave Davy a condescending look.

"Mick nearly fell off cart today, wasn't looking where you were going, was you?" said Liza in a cheeky tone of voice.

"It were you lot cheeking me off," replied Mick.

"Well it probably served y' right 's all I can say," chuckled Mary.

Good humoured conversation continued for a further half hour or so as the table was cleared and pots and pans washed up in the large stone sink. Then came the round of yawns, these were followed by the nodding of heads and the sudden jerks back to consciousness as the satisfaction of the meal, hard work and the toil of the day took its toll on the weary bodies.

"I'd best be getting back," said Bob, "I'll give Jack 'ere a lift to village, then we'll be back first light in t' morning."

"Aye, well thanks very much lads," said Davy.

The two men thanked Mary and were then quickly on their way.

"Well that's me done for, I'm of to bed," said Davy.

"Me too, it's been a hard day," echoed Mick.

Mary, Davy, Andy and Mick said their goodnights and trooped of up the stairs leaving Elfie and Liza still sat at the table.

"Well then, are you going to show me to my room for the night then Liza?" enquired Elfie in a teasing tone.

"D – d' you love Mick like?" blurted out Liza.

Elfie was a bit taken back.

"Oh, I don't know about that, but I am very fond of him. Come on then, I'm done for."Liza turned out the big oil lamp on the table and taking a smaller one from the dresser lead Elfie up to her bedroom.

Chapter fifteen

Elfie awoke from a deep, dreamy sleep, still tired from the previous days labour and yet somehow comfortingly rested. As she awoke she became aware of deep warmth to one side of her. She moved a hand towards it and felt the soft form of the young girl's body beside her. It was then that she fully realised where she was, not in her primitive little room where she had slept for most of her years, but in a warm, comfortable bed albeit shared with Liza Jarrow. She snuggled down again enjoying the luxury of the well-filled flock mattress, so much more comfortable than her own and the soft pillow that moulded to the shape of her head. She made a mental note to do something about her own bedding when she returned. Perhaps she could buy some at the next market; after all she had some money now, or maybe make some up herself if she could find the materials to do so.

There was a sharp rap at the door, then Mick's cheerful voice called out.

"Come on you lazy lot in there, it's time you were up and out working."

Liza just grunted and entrenched herself deeper into the bedcovers.

Elfie got up and washed herself in the bowl on the dresser whilst Liza slept on. She then went over to the window and pulled back the curtains, it was early, but already the sky was brightening to a vivid blue as the first rays of the all-warming sun peeked over the distant hills. She went over and shook the sleeping girl

"Come on Liza, it's a lovely morning."

"Go away an' let me sleep," came back the reply.

Liza was not a morning person, waking and rising presented a challenge to her on most days. Her mother Her mother constantly scolded her for not getting up when called.

"I'm going downstairs now, don't say I didn't wake you."

Elfie retreated from the girl's bedside and left her to her slumbers.

The delightful aroma of food cooking met her nostrils as she reached the top of the stairs. Mary had been up for well over an hour preparing food for the day. Elfie descended the stairs and walked towards the kitchen, now she was met by an oaty, milky smell. She popped her head around the kitchen door.

"Good morning Mrs Jarrow."

Mary paused from stirring the big pan of porridge balanced on the range top.

"Ah, there you are m' dearie, did y' sleep alright?"

"Oh, I did that Mrs Jarrow, it was so warm and comfortable compared to my own little bed – where's Mick, have they started already?"

"Lord no, 'e's outside, you go on an' see 'im," she replied with a knowing smile. "An tell 'im breakfasts ready in a few minutes."

Elfie wandered outside into the farmyard, a few hens scurried across in front of her and then she was assaulted by two furry black and white animals. Moss and Tess had spent the night in the barn and were anxious to greet their mistress. They jumped up and down in delight, Tess twirling as she left the ground and landing rather ungainly at the girl's feet.

"There, there my beauties, have you missed me?"

Much tail wagging and licking ensued before the two of them settled down.

Mick was by the door of the storeroom watching the proceedings with a grin on his face. When Elfie caught his eye he quickly turned back to sharpening the leys with a handstone. The stone scraped away on the metal ley causing an eerie screeching sound.

"Morning Mick."

Mick stopped what he was doing and turned in the direction of the voice.

"I hadn't seen you, have you been here a bit?"

"You had seen me, you were watching me playing with the dogs, why are you so shy sometimes and other times your not?"

"I dunno, didn't think I was shy like," came his reply in a bashful voice.

"Well, anyway, breakfast's about ready."

"Right, I've just about done here, got to keep these things sharp y' know."

There was a long pause and then Mick spoke again.

"How are you anyhow, I didn't get much chance to talk to you yesterday?"

He reached out and took hold of her hand.

"But it was nice having you around though."

Elfie felt the warmth from his hands pass to hers and she smiled sweetly at him, then Davy Jarrow appeared from the direction of the barn.

Mick quickly released Elfie's hand and she felt the warmth recede.

"You finished them leys yet – morning Miss Mason."

"Yes they're done, we're just going for breakfast and then we're away again."

Davy scowled at the lad and walked past on into the farmhouse, the couple followed meekly behind and on into the kitchen.

Liza had appeared by now and was serving up the porridge, setting great steaming bowls of the stuff on the kitchen table.

There was a loud rap on the kitchen window and the faces of Bob Colten and Danny appeared cheekily at the windowpane.

"I knew you lads ad be 'ere, can't resist m' breakfasts eh, well come on in then," cried Mary cheerfully.

The two quickly appeared in the kitchen and took up places at the table. Liza filled two more bowls with porridge and set the bowls before them.

The porridge was eagerly consumed and then followed by bacon and bread and large mugs of tea.

Davy rose to his feet.

"Right then lads, lets get started, we'll take the cart up with us and cut grass till lasses join us and then they can load up and bring it back."

With the decision made, the men left the kitchen and headed off in the direction of the fields leaving Mary, Liza and Elfie to clear away the breakfast things and pack up food for dinnertime. In less than an hour they were back in the fields, turning the newly cut grass and then gathering the cocks and loading them onto the cart.

As the morning progressed, the sun rose high into the clear blue sky, pouring its warmth down onto the workers toiling in the fields. An air of tranquillity pervaded over the scene, an ambience of peace, man in harmony with nature in a timeless landscape.

When the rays of the sun started to recede over the northern rim of the fells another three fields had been cut, the grass had been turned several times and then carted off to the barn. The lower mew was now almost full despite much use of the hay paddle to compress it. The last cut was cocked and then the weary party made its way back to the farmhouse for supper.

"We should be finished tomorrow," remarked Davy as he left the kitchen, full from his evening meal and tired from his labours, he made his way upstairs to bed. Mary was soon to follow leaving Mick, Elfie, Liza and young Andy still seated at the kitchen table.

"You should be in bed now Andy", said Liza in a matronly overtone.

"Isn't it time you were off to bed Liza, you know you can't get up in a morning?" Mick intervened, obviously knowing that the two would soon be arguing.

"I'm waiting for Elfie," she replied, looking first at Mick and then at Elfie for a reaction.

"I'll be up in a moment, I just want to talk to Mick about the gather next week."

Liza looked nonplussed and without speaking she upped and flounced off up to her bedroom with Andy close on her heels.

"She's a droll 'un sometimes, - well, what about the gather then, s'pose it's the first time you being in charge like?"

In truth, she had a pretty good idea about the proceedings for gathering in the sheep from the fells, washing them and the subsequent clip. It was largely a matter of deciding what order the flocks would be gathered in, on which day and then everyone pitched in and helped out. It would be a week of hard work, more taxing than the haymaking, but nothing she could not cope with.

"My father will decide the order that we fetch them in and then we just get on with it till its done."

Mick got up from the table and went to sit down in the rocking chair by the fireplace. The fire was nearly out having done its job of providing heat for cooking the supper and boiling water. Mick prodded the remaining embers sending a few sparks lazily up the chimney. Elfie took up a chair beside him. She sat there a short while and then stretched out her arms and yawned loudly.

"I suppose I'd best be getting off to bed, it's been a hard day."

The infectiousness of the yawn passed to Mick.

"Another day and we'll be finished and then I expect you'll be getting back up the dale then?"

Elfie thought for a moment before replying to the question.

"Yes I will – to get ready for the gather, but it's been really nice staying here Mick, it's so cosy – and people to talk to as well. It's so lonely now

that my father's gone, perhaps Farrington was right when –"
She stopped mid sentence.
A puzzled expression appeared on Mick's face.
"What do you mean, Farrington was right?"
"Oh, it's nothing, really it's not."
"No, tell me what he's being saying," said Mick firmly.
There was a hint of anxiety in her voice as she spoke.
"Well, when he came to see me a few days ago he said that he could find me work at the manor and that I could live there and," she stopped speaking.
"What did he say that for?"
"Well, he reckoned that I'd be better off and life wouldn't be as hard, that's all really."
"So what did you tell him then?"
"I said I'd think it over."
"But – but you're not going to are you?" the anxiety was evident in his voice.
"No, I'm not, but it's a bit difficult because I don't want to offend him, you know what he's like, he could make it hard for me."
There was a long silence between them. Mick was worried in his own mind. The last thing he wanted was for Jacob Farrington to spirit her away, he might never see her again. He reached out and took her hand.
"Promise me you won't go Elfie."
"Oh Mick, there's no fear of that happening, I've just got to find a way of putting him off, but I don't know how long I can do it for. I want to work on the land, not as some servant waiting on people or clearing up or what else."
Mick knew the solution, but he simply could not summon up the courage to say the words out loud. Marry me; marry me, the words just buzzed around in his head. It was the answer, he felt sure that their friendship was progressing and yet he did not know how deep her feelings were for him. Many times she displayed affection for him but equally she could be dismissive. It seemed as if she was not ready to be serious about their relationship. Perhaps she needed to prove herself now that her father was gone, he must be patient with her.
Elfie released his hand and rose from her chair as if to go but promptly

sat down on Mick's knees, the action almost tipping him out of the rocking chair. Giggling loudly, she wrapped her arms around his neck and cuddled him.

"I'm not going anywhere without you," she whispered in his ear. Then giving him an extra hug with those heavenly arms, she announced, "I'm off to bed now, see you in the morning."

She left Mick pondering, there she goes again, firstly she comes on all strong sitting on his knee and then just as quickly she goes of to bed.

He resolved to ask his mother when the haymaking was over what the best course of action would be. He was convinced that his mother approved of her from the little comments that came out in general conversations. He sat awhile and then taking up the poker prodded the last remaining embers, a few sparks rose reluctantly up the chimney. Mick put the poker down and took himself off to his bed.

The men breakfasted early the next day and were in the fields as the sun rose, anxious to get the work completed by early evening. Mary was busy in the kitchen preparing the dinner and supper. This was to be a special affair to celebrate the end of the haymaking. All the helpers would be joining them around the kitchen table to partake of the meal and a liberal supply of ale.

There was a slight commotion at the door as Liza preceded Elfie into the kitchen.

"Lawks above, av niver seen 'er up so early 'afore," exclaimed Mary.

"She dragged me out 'o bed," shrieked Liza, trying to stab Elfie with her elbow as she was propelled forward.

"Well, y've done a better job than me, I could niver get 'er oot 'o bed this soon, y' mun stay agin if y' can work miracles like this lass."

"It's not so difficult just a bit of pushing and tugging and she was out of bed."

"An I nearly broke me back falling onto floor," retorted the girl.

"You big story teller Liza Jarrow, you tripped over the rug running away from me so that you could get back into bed at the other side."

Mary laughed heartily.

"Come on then lasses, get summat to eat an' then we's away t' fields, see if we can get finished t'day."

111

By late afternoon the last field had been cut and turned. The work had been greatly assisted by the arrival of John Poskit and his son Frank. John farmed at the foot of Martindale and was a good friend of Davy Jarrow. The Poskits had only a couple of fields to cut as most of their farming involved a large flock grazing the fells. John was now ready to get on with the gather as he probably had the largest flock thereabouts. By helping the Jarrow's he could be assured that Davy and the other farmers would assist him in getting his flock washed and clipped early on.

It was all hands to the haycart now to get the grass into the mew. Mick and Bob Colten were kept busy back and forth with the carts. The women were now loading the carts in the fields whilst the men were piling the hay into the mew which, because of its height, was now a more physically demanding job. Elfie had little chance to talk to Mick except in the general conversation and friendly banter which ensued each time the cart was loaded.

Early evening saw the work done. Mary and the girls had returned to the farmhouse leaving the men to finish off in the mew. Half an hour later the men were sat on the flags outside the house. Mary had put a large jug of ale and some mugs there and the men were eagerly slaking their dry throats.

"You lads 'll be stopping f' supper, eh?" Mary directed the question to the Poskits and Coltons as she appeared at the door.

There was a chorus of 'aye' from the men.

"Be ready in ten minutes or so then," Mary went back inside.

When the men appeared in the kitchen, the table was set with a large pot of mutton stew and dishes of carrots, potatoes and onions. To follow was plum pudding and custard and a further liberal supply of ale. The men took up their places at the table and tucked in eagerly to the food before them. There was little conversation as the hunger and thirst of the hard days labour was slowly satisfied. Mary observed the proceedings with a wry smile on her face. She was pleased that the work was over and her arguments about how the work should be done had proved correct.

Davy glanced up from his plate and caught her eye.

"A supper fit for a king eh lads! She knows what she's about does my Mary."

Mary knew that this was the only acknowledgement she would get for her efforts and there was little chance of him accepting that she was usually right.

After the meal was over the men retired to the chairs around the fireplace. Liza fetched more ale for them. The kitchen had an air of contentment, the job was well done and the men talked quietly on a variety of farming related subjects.

When the dishes had been washed and the table cleared Elfie made her move to leave. She glanced over to where the men were sat. Mick was earnestly engaged in discussion, forceful opinions were expressed coupled with laughter and good humour.

"I'm going back up home now Mrs Mason."

"Right lass, well, I can't thank e enough, y've been a real big 'elp 'ere these last few days."

Mary then looked over in the direction of the men and in particular to Mick.

"Mick," she called, "Elfie's off on her way now."

Mick seemed a bit reluctant to leave the group as he was obviously enjoying himself. Mary called again, this time in a firmer tone.

"Elfie's going now, Mick."

The lad got up and came over, a slightly sheepish look on his face.

"Sorry, we were just talking about the new fangled machines for haymaking."

"It's alright, you don't have to take me home you know."

"That 'e does," interjected Mary, giving the lad a hefty dig in the ribs with her elbow.

He winced, "y-yes I'll see you home Elfie."

"Really Mick, there's no need, I'm perfectly alright walking back up the valley."

"No, come on, it's a nice night," he remarked as he opened the door, "look, there's a brilliant full moon."

"Now think on lass, y' not long 'afore y' come back agin."

"Thank you Mrs Jarrow, I hope to see you soon," she replied politely.

"Night lass," called one of the men and the others responded similarly. Elfie gave them a half wave and followed Mick out into the moonlight.

The night sky was a dark inky blue interspersed with thousands of twinkling stars. The moon silhouetted the mountains making their shapes clear and well defined. The smell of the newly cut grass hung in the air giving it a sweet fragrance. The couple were silent as they walked along the track a little apart. The two dogs ran back and forth eagerly scenting rabbits and other nightlife.

"You'd no need to walk back with me Mick."

Elfie was intent on probing his feelings having felt somewhat rebuffed at his lack of attention when she was about to leave. Feelings of loneliness were already starting to invade her mind. It had been good over the last few days and had given her a glimpse into another way of life. The food, the company, the chatter and good humour had made her realise that she had led a very lonely existence at the top of Fusedale.

"N-no I did want to walk back up with you."

"Well it didn't seem like it to me'"

Mick moved closer to her, taking her hand, he gave it a squeeze. Elfie warmed instantly to his advance.

"Alright, I'll forgive you this time."

She pushed hard on his hand causing him to wobble and trip over a stone.

"Clumsy oaf."

"Nay, you pushed me and made me trip up."

Elfie pulled his hand again only this time pulling him back beside her.

The pair continued on their way laughing and teasing each other until they reached the croft.

Elfie now stood in the doorway with her back to the door.

"You'll let me know when the gather is going to start then?"

"Yes, I expect we'll have an easy day tomorrow and then get started on it day after like."

The girl relinquished the hand she had held for the last half-mile or so and then with both hands she pushed Mick slightly away from her.

"You can get back to your pals now."

Mick looked a trifle dejected at this comment.

"I'll come up tomorrow then?"

"Only if you want to," she replied.

"I do."

He moved closer to her again. Their eyes met as if to search the depths behind them in an effort to read each other's thoughts. He could feel the warmth of her body and her sweet, earthy scent. Simultaneously, their arms wrapped around each other and their bodies moved even closer together. She gazed up at him, her facial features clearly outlined in the moonlight. Her soft lips parted slightly and she drew breath and then their mouths met. Blood surged through their bodies as they embraced. Then she pulled away from him.

"They'll be waiting for you back at the farm."

"No they won't."

He moved forward to kiss her again. Her hand reached behind her and her fingers sought the latch to the door. The door creaked open and she stepped backwards.

"Goodnight Mick, thank you for walking me home, I'll see you tomorrow."

She turned and went inside closing the door behind her and leaving a very puzzled young man standing outside.

Why did she behave like this, one minute so warm and tender, next, polite, formal and dismissive? He wandered back down to the farmhouse, his mind pondering the events of the last few days.

Chapter sixteen

"Lie down y' stupid dog."

The young dog ignored the command of its owner and ran forward scattering the ewes to either side. Walter Mawson leaned on his crook observing the proceedings.

"That's a drowning dog tha's got there Ewan," he called.

"What d' you mean Walt?"

"I mean, it wants drowning like, it'll niver be any bloody good at fetching ewes."

There was a round of laughter from the other men who had been watching the display.

At that moment Elfie was approaching the group with her two dogs.

"Ere, int that Masons lass?" enquired one of the men.

"Aye, she's taken over up at top o' Fusedale," informed one of the group.

"Bit on a strange chap her father, he-" the conversation was abruptly halted as she approached the group of men.

"Come to gather with us lass then?" enquired Walter.

Elfie smiled and nodded a little nervously.

"Now, this lass 'll show you how to control a sheepdog, just you watch her with that pair."

The girl positively glowed at the praise which had just issued from Davy Jarrow. Mick stepped out from the midst of the group.

"Yes Elfie, show 'em how it should be done."

Her face coloured considerably and she felt somewhat embarrassed at the attention. The group of men fell silent and each looked at her in anticipation.

With two quiet commands, the dogs were away, Tess eagerly outflanking the ewes whilst Moss worked them into a group on the lower slopes. Within a short space of time the two dogs had gathered a dozen or so ewes and were bringing them back along the track towards the men. All it took was a few commands in the form of whistles and a couple of verbal commands.

"See what I mean Ewan, y' want t' give yon dog t' lass an' see if she can train it for you," said Davy.

"Nay, I'll make it do afore so long," Ewan replied.

"Well done lass," piped up Sam Gregory, "I reckon you'll be a big help to us over next few days."

Mick gave Elfie an approving nod and winked at her. The girl could not recall an occasion when she had been the centre of attention before or indeed received such praise.

"Alright lads, lets get to work, an' tie that silly bloody dog o' yours up Ewan," said Davy Jarrow.

The dogs accompanying the group were set to work on the fellsides. Some of them ranged right up to the summits whilst others concentrated on the lower slopes. The farmers and shepherds followed the dogs giving commands either by whistling or shouting. Within a couple of hours all the sheep had been brought down to join those already gathered on the easier ground.

Ewan was busily engaged trying to count the sheep that had been penned.

"What d' y' reckon then?" called Davy.

"Looks like we've got most of 'em, though there'll alus be a few that gets missed."

"Aye, but we might get 'em in t' next gather of Mawson's lot with them being kept next to each other, there's alus a few that cross over."

By lunchtime all of Ewan's flock had been contained in makeshift pens on one side of the beck adjacent to the farmhouse.

Before the sheep can be clipped they have to be washed and the fleece allowed to dry out for a few days. The first flock to be gathered is washed and then whist they are drying out the next flock is brought down and washed and so forth until all are done. By that time the first ones are ready for clipping.

The beck by Ewan's farm entered a circular pool and by damming it at one end the water level could be raised sufficiently for the washing process. After putting on additional clothing, one of the men waded out into the pool until the water level was almost up to his waist. The sheep were then flung into the pool one by one. The washer had to dig his hands into the fleece, working, rubbing and squeezing the wool so as to get as much dirt out of it as possible in the time available. The sheep was then released and swam to the other side of the pool. As the sheep emerged from the pool they were evidently astonished by the burden of the extra water that their fleece had been saturated with. Many staggered about for some time until by degrees they approached their natural weight as the water ran off them.

Some of the sheep went completely under the water and came up snorting the water out of their noses. The noise of the bleating was incessant, particularly when a ewe was separated from its mother.

The washing continued at a steady pace throughout the afternoon with a change of washman about every hour. This being considered the amount of time a man could bear being in the cold water.

On completion, the men moved on to gather the next flock. The work continued late into the evening until all of Mawson's flock had been gathered and penned with a view to washing them first thing the following morning.

"I reckon that's a good days work there lads, we'll wash 'em first thing and then start on t'other valley," cried Davy. "We'll do Sam Gregory's and Will Blake's tomorrow with a bit o'luck and then finish off with mine and Mason's the following day."

With a chorus of approval, then the work weary men trudged off back to their farms. Davy, Mick and Elfie set off back on the track to Dale End Farm, some two miles away.

"So it's the same again tomorrow then?" remarked Elfie.

"Aye, except you're in washing dub tomorrow," piped up Mick.

"Oh no, I couldn't possibly do that," said Elfie, a tone of terror clearly evident in her voice.

"Y' daft beggar, don't tease lass like that, tek no notice of him now."

Elfie was relieved at Davy's words.

"Listen lass," said Davy as they approached the lane that went down to the farm. "Y' mun stop night with us, there's no point in trailing up t' top o' Fusedale to come back down again in t' morning. Mary will 'av a right supper on for us."

"That's very kind of you to offer," said Elfie who was now thoroughly enjoying the hospitality and company which seemed so freely on offer from the Mason's. And so all three of them turned down the lane to the farmhouse, its lights emitting a cosy glow as the last of the daylight faded to night.

It had been a hard day for the girl, but the reward was a hot meal, company and a cosy bed for the night.

The next day continued like the previous and by evening both Sam's and Will's sheep had been gathered, washed and penned up. Will had the largest flock but they had come in easily with the skill of the dogs and shepherds and the assistance of an extra couple of lads who turned up to help with the washing.

Again, Elfie spent the night at the Jarrow's farmstead as theirs was the next flock of sheep to be gathered. Exhausted from the hard work of the day, Mary and Davy had taken themselves of to bed leaving Mick, Elfie and Liza sat by the now dwindling fire.

"It's so cosy here compared to my little place at the top of the valley," sighed Elfie.

Liza had been listening quietly to the idle chatter of the two without her usual interruptions, but now she spoke.

"Why don't you come and live 'ere then Elfie, I'd like you to an' I'm sure Mick would as well, wouldn't you Mick?"

"Er' well' it's not so simple as that," replied Mick. "You don't just pack up and move into someone else's home you know."

"Well, why don't you two get married then, that 'a be a good enough reason I think, don't you?"

There was a painful silence for a few minutes, Elfie scrutinised Mick's face for a response. Mick reddened and coughed nervously.

"Isn't it time you went to bed Liza?"

"Alright then brother, I'll go, then you can ask her, can't you?"

She flashed a wide grin at Elfie as she got up as if to say – there I've fixed it for you. The girl then left the kitchen and made her way up to bed.

There was a silence again in the kitchen Mick looking anywhere but at the girl sat opposite to him. Why, oh why couldn't he summon up the courage to ask her, the subject has been broached, it was out in the open. Elfie had similar thoughts, why doesn't he say something, perhaps he's not that interested in me.

After a few minutes of the dreadful silence between them he spoke.

"Listen Elfie, she's just a silly girl saying things like that, she's –"

He stopped himself. He knew he was turning away from the most important question in his life. He coughed again nervously and his complexion reddened again. Elfie searched his face intently, watching his every expression. Her heart sank a little at his words, why was he so dismissive of what his sister had said?

"But, but, er I'd well" -

"Go on then," she urged him encouragingly.

He blurted it out.

"I-I'd like to marry you Elfie."

His heart was racing now and he was sure she could see his chest thumping away, he'd said it at last. Excited by his own words he went on.

"We could live in the cottage next to the barn, It's a bit of a mess at the moment, but- but I could do it up, we could get some more furniture and" –

Elfie reached out and took his hand.

"Hey, hang on a bit, you're talking about somewhere to live and I haven't even said whether I want to get married to you."

The wind was completely taken out of the young lads sails. It had never occurred to him that she might say no. The colour drained from his cheeks and his heart felt to sink into his boots.

Elfie looked into his eyes and smiled, at the same time squeezing his hand.

There was a pause and then she said, "yes Mick, yes I will marry you."

Mick pulled her to her feet and wrapped his arms around her. She felt a distinct wetness on her neck and pulled away from him a little, tears were running down his cheeks. Tenderly, she wiped them away for him.

"Do you know, you've just made me the happiest person in the world."

He nestled his head into her neck and kissed her, then their lips were together, the warmth and passion passing between their elated bodies and minds

Elfie pulled away from him a little.

"Yes, I will marry you Mick Jarrow, but not straight away."

Mick looked somewhat nonplussed.

"But why not Elfie, what is there to wait for?"

"Well we can't get married just like that, we need to set a date and then there's work to be done back home and all sorts of things to sort out."

"Well, when then?" he asked, a little impatiently.

"Next springtime."

"Next springtime! that's a long time away."

Her lips pouted as she replied, "am I not worth waiting for then?"

"Well, yes but I" -

She placed her hand gently over his mouth.

"Then that's how long you've got to wait and then I give you my word that I will be your wife,- Mrs Jarrow."

There was a solemnity in her voice as she made the reply, almost as if she was making the wedding vows. He pulled her towards himself again, a feeling of confidence filling his mind, now she would really be his.

He kissed her again and held her close for some time. The light from the fire reflected in her face, she is so beautiful and soon she will be mine forever, he thought. Then their bodies parted from the warm embrace and the two made their way upstairs. She turned and blew him a kiss as she opened the door into Liza's bedroom.

"You've been a long time, did he ask you then?" came a drowsy voice from the bed.

"Never you mind, go to sleep," retorted Elfie.

She slipped into bed beside the warm body of the girl. In a few months time it would be Mick that she cuddled up to.

During the early hours of the morning the weather had changed, now low cloud hugged the fell tops obscuring their summits. A damp drizzle pervaded the valley as the group of shepherds, farmers and dogs set about gathering the Jarrow's flock.

"Dammed weather, makes it a lot harder f' dogs," muttered Ewan.

"Might be better for that dog o' yours if it can't see t'ewes," said Sam Mawson in a dry sarcastic tone.

"Appen it'll lift by mid morning, anyway we'll 'ave to get on with it," remarked Davy Jarrow.

He went on. "Ewan and Sam, you go up left by them crags, Will, you come with me, we'll start further up valley and if you Mick and Elfie cross river and do right fell side I reckon we'll have it covered."

There was a chorus of agreement from the group who were anxious to get on with the task. Then they could get back to their own flocks to get ready for the clipping in a few days time.

Mick and Elfie crossed the river by hopping from boulder to boulder. The crystal clear water ran low as there had been little rain over the past few weeks. Elfie's dogs splashed and frolicked in the water.

"Come on you two it's not playtime, there's work to be done," she called to them cheerfully. Tess and Moss obediently joined the couple as they started to climb the flanks of the fellside.

"I think it's lifting a bit," said Mick, "you couldn't see Raven crag before and now it's clearing and coming into view."

A number of ewes could just be discerned to the left of the rock outcrop. Elfie sent the two dogs off. Tess rapidly climbed round to the top of the crag sending the ewes down in the direction of Moss who quickly took control of them. Tess then disappeared into the gloom. Moss brought the ewes down to where the couple stood and then turned and headed back up the hill disappearing out of sight. Presently, Moss appeared again with several ewes in front of him. Tess was obviously clearing the higher ground, seeking out the sheep and driving them down towards Moss. This was the brilliant teamwork that they excelled at.

The process continued as the couple moved higher up the fellside as the dogs scoured the area for ewes. By the time an hour had elapsed there were some forty or so ewes heading down towards the valley floor. Elfie and Mick were now quite high up on the fell, the mist seemed to rise with them and they could clearly see the gathered ewes descending.

"How many do you reckon you've got this side Mick?"

"Probably around fifty, best part of the flock is heafed to other side o' the valley."

"Then we've got over half of them already then?"

"Aye, reckon we have."

Mick was a little higher up than Elfie. He stopped and leaned on a rock waiting for her to catch up with him. When she came along side of him he grabbed hold of her and pulled her close. She pretended to resist his advances by pushing his arms apart, but his grip remained firm.

"You aren't going to get away from me now you know."

Elfie's ewes narrowed and she flashed him her most scornful look, then followed it by a wan smile.

"You don't own me Mick Jarrow."

"No, but I soon will."

She squirmed free from his hold on her.

"You'll never own me, Mick."

"What do you mean, you said you'd marry me last night, didn't you?"

"Yes, and I meant it, I will be your wife, but you won't own me."

Mick looked puzzled.

"We'll get married and live together and love each other and have children, but you can't own me, just like I can't own you. We're free spirits, not pieces of property, do you see what I mean?"

Mick still had a puzzled expression on his face.

"We have to love and respect each other equally, we can't possess each other, that's my view of a marriage. It's like Jacob Farrington" -

Mick interrupted.

"What's he got to do with it?"

"Well, he comes around telling me what to do as if he owns me, the sheep may belong to him, but I don't. He's trying to get me to the manor like I told you.

Mick though for a moment, this worry had slipped to the back of his mind.

"Look, if he comes bothering you again, you tell me and I'll see to him," he remarked in a forceful tone.

"No you won't Mick, he's a powerful man and could cause allsorts of problems for you and me, let me deal with him in my own way."

Mick was anxious.

"I'd kill the beggar if he tried to take you away from me."

Elfie pressed her fingers on his lips.

"Sh, leave it be, I'll handle Jacob Farrington in my own way."

She gave him a peck on the cheek.

"Come on, let's get the rest of these ewes down, there's still mine to do as well you know."

Another dozen or so ewes were heading down towards them followed by Moss. Suddenly, his legs seemed to give way on him and he fell, rolling over a couple of times. He got up slowly and shook himself. Elfie rushed over to him, the dog gave her a bewildered look as if he did not know what had happened to him. The girl bent over him and stroked his head.

"I've never seen him stumble like that before, he's so sure footed, there now, you've been working too hard."

She cradled his soft head in her hands.

"Probably tripped over a rock or something," commented Mick.

"No, no, it's like he lost the strength in his legs, maybe he's getting too old for this game."

The situation was interrupted by Tess bringing down another group of ewes into their midst. Moss moved forward, somewhat unsteadily at first and then he seemed to regain his composure, joining Tess now to move the ewes down the fellside.

"Seems alright now," said Mick.

Elfie was still concerned about the dog.

"I'm going to rest him when we get back down to the valley, do you think we've done up here now?"

"I reckon so, must be getting on for fifty ewes now, we could spend all day trying to track down the odd one or two. We'll get these back down t' valley bottom."

When the couple got back to the bottom of the fell there was already a large group of ewes gathered below the intake wall and a further group heading down the main track.

"I think we've got most of 'em now," called out Sam.

The rest of the group assembled and then after a bit of confused rounding up of the sheep the whole flock was driven down the track towards Dale End Farm.

Elfie walked along the track with the group of men. The dogs were busily engaged in the task of keeping all the ewes going in the right direction and stood no nonsense from any errant sheep that tried to side track them. As the journey proceeded Elfie walked at the side of Mick, with an emerging air of confidence. Things were changing in her life. She now had a prospective husband and the prospect of somewhere better to live away from the isolation of Fusedale. The findings of her father's chest had now given her a modest sum of money of her own and although it was not a small fortune it was enough to enable her to make changes to her life.

But what was equally exciting to the girl was the growing recognition as a shepherdess in her own right. Already, she was accepted into the group of men with whom she had worked with for the last few days. Many of her skills had been recognised and yet, she had an overwhelming desire to take this prowess further. This was partly the reason for putting Mick's proposal of marriage off until the forthcoming spring. This would ensure that she would have fulfilled one year from lambing, through the clip, tupping and back to lambing again. If she was successful she would have maintained the standards set by her father and then she would be established as a competent shepherdess in her own right.

To realise this ambition she needed to maintain a satisfactory relationship with Jacob Farrington, at least for the time being. Then possibly she could establish a flock of her own, bought with her own money. Alternatively, with the recent change of events, she could work along side Mick in the development and expansion of the Jarrow's flock. Whatever happened, she knew that this was what she wanted to do and whilst she was now certain of a future with Mick, she was also sure that it would not just be the role of a housewife. She wanted to be fully involved and use her skills to their best advantage.

By late afternoon the Mason's flock had been brought down from the fells. The beck below the croft had been dammed up to increase the depth of the water in the dub. Davy and Sam were manhandling the ewes into the pool and Ewan and Will were washing them. Elfie and Mick hauled the wet animals out at the other side and pushed and shoved them into the makeshift pen to contain them prior to clipping.

"Another hour should see us finished," cried Davy.

"Aye, I 'ope so, it's getting dammed cold in this water now sun's gone down behind t' fell," retorted Will.

And so within the hour the work was done and the weary men made their way back down the valley to their homes. Only Mick and Elfie remained at the croft to finish off.

"Been a good day's work then?"

"Aye lass, we've done well I think. Give it another couple o' days and then we can start the clip with Ewan's flock and finish up with yours. By the middle of next week it'll all be done. Then we should have it a bit easier for a while."

"There's only one person who's not happy about it all and that's you Moss, isn't it?"

Elfie walked over to the outbuilding where the dog had been tied up and released him. He ran round excitedly, back and forth, barking away.

"No lad we've done for the day now, he seems better for the rest don't you think."

Mick looked at the dog and then at Elfie.

"Suppose you'll just have to see how he gets on now, at least there's not as much hard work in front of him for a time until we start salving in October and then tupping."

The couple sat for some time on the step outside the croft chatting away and watching the changes in the sky as the night advanced. Mick felt happy and relaxed in her company now after the earlier times when he felt both clumsy and awkward. Now, having got a positive answer to his proposal, it was a huge weight off his mind.

Mick liked to tease her and she regularly took the bait only to find out that he was not serious. At times she could be quite naïve, but at other times she was more worldly wise than Mick and so they played this cat and mouse game until she got the upper hand on him.

"I suppose I've got to spend some lonely nights and days until the clip," she said in a doleful tone.

"Well, there's quite a bit to do about the farm, but I'll come back up tomorrow evening."

"Alright then, I've got a few things to do as well."

"Such as?"

"Bits and things," she replied in a dismissive tone.

He knew not to pursue the matter any further. The young man rose to his feet at the same time grabbing her hands so that she involuntarily rose as well. Then he put his arms around her waist and in a simple move, placed her on the bench. She looked down at him.

"This is how it will be when we are married you know, I shall be the boss."

Mick grinned.

"Oh well, we'll see about that."

"Your mother's the boss in your house, isn't she?"

"Suppose she is really," he replied thoughtfully.

Elfie stepped down from the bench and put her arms lovingly around his neck.

"We'll be partners you and me."

Mick hugged her, almost squeezing the breath out of her body.

"You're like a big bear sometimes, Mick Jarrow."

He eased off and their lips met in a warm kiss, which lingered for some time.

"Come on now," she said, pushing him away. "You get back to your farm and make sure you come back here tomorrow."

"You bet I will," he replied cheerily.

Chapter seventeen

Jacob Farrington had spent almost two weeks up in Scotland. Part of the reason for his visit had been to conduct some business or so he had led his father to believe, but mainly it had been for pleasure. The pleasure derived from his being accompanied by Amelia. They had first travelled to Glasgow to see some of Farrington's business acquaintances connected with the woollen trade and then they continued on to Edinburgh.

Jacob wanted to show Amelia some of the historic aspects of the city and its fine buildings. And so they had visited numerous places of interest and Amelia, not being very well travelled had been duly impressed. They strolled along the three parallel streets of Princess Street, George Street and Queen Street both admiring and purchasing items in the many fine shops. Both of them admired the fine Georgian architecture of the area and visited many art galleries and other such displays. The couple had stayed at one of the finest hotels in the city, which had an excellent view of the castle and Arthur's Seat. Indeed, on one fine morning they had undertaken the climb up to the very summit to observe the best views over the city.

They had left the city mid morning and were now settled into the first class compartment at the head of the train bound for Penrith. The warmth and comfort of the carriage and reassuring noise of wheels on the steel track had a lulling effect on the pair. They chatted away contentedly, much of the subject being their forthcoming marriage. They had agreed a date in the springtime next year, now they could put into motion the lavish preparations for their wedding. The next stage was to find a suitable property to live in and the two of them discussed this at great length. Being a rather meek sort of girl, Amelia was in agreement with Jacob's suggestion that they live relatively near to the manor so that he could continue his work managing the estates with relative ease.

By early evening the train slowed from its former fast speed at full steam and drew into Penrith Station. The frantic noise of the engine hauling the carriages now ceased and the only noise was the squeal of the brakes and the porter's announcement "Penrith, Penrith."

Staff from the manor greeted the couple, assisted them with their luggage and led them to the awaiting carriage. Once it was loaded up and the couple seated inside the carriage set of on its journey to the manor.

As they left the town behind Jacob's eyes were drawn in a southwesterly direction towards Ullswater. The tip of the lake could just be discerned shimmering a vivid blue grey in the early evening sunset. His eyes moved from the lake to the rim of mountains on its southern side. He knew that beyond that line of unyielding hills lay the valley of Fusedale. Indeed, he could make out the cleft between the hills, which was the entrance to the valley.

Jacob had enjoyed the last few days enormously and had no doubt in his mind that his future lay with the sweet, demure Amelia seated at his side. She was not a strong willed person and eagerly agreed to his demands and foibles. She was well versed in the complexities of etiquette and would easily become an accomplished host when they entertained guests in their future home. Amelia was always willing to please Jacob in any way that she could and he was well aware of her characteristics and could mould her to fit his desires. Most of all, she had an elegance and was rather beautiful, assets which satisfied the ego of the young man.

And yet, whirling around in the recesses of his mind was that primitive girl at the head of Fusedale. Something about her simplicity and her situation tinged with a hint of rebelliousness attracted him. She had not been in his thoughts over the last few days, but now, retuning to Lakeland his desires and designs on her were being rekindled.

"You are quiet my love, is anything the matter?" came the sweet voice at his side.

"Nothing at all, my dearest," came the reply.

"But you've hardly spoken at all since we left the station or even looked at me, you just seem to be staring out of the window all the time."

Jacob recollected his thoughts bringing them back to the present situation.

"Have I really, I'm sorry my dear, I was just thinking that I will have to spend some time visiting the farms and tenants to see how they are progressing with the shearing of the flocks. It's an important time you know and there's a good income to be had when the wool is sold on."

Jacob returned his full attention to Amelia and the journey continued with the couple contented in each other's company.

Early the following morning Jacob rode over Askham Moor. It was true that he needed to establish the progress with the clipping of the various flocks up and around the valleys, but the real focus of his interest was initially Elfrida Mason. As he rode his horse at a brisk pace over the heathery moor, he rehearsed in his mind how he would approach the girl this time. On his last visit he had made a proposition to her, now he wanted an answer, one that would satisfy his desires. He needed to speed up his plan if he was to get her to come to the manor to tale up some sort of work there. If he was to marry next year he wanted her under his control now, possibly then he could tame her and even find her a position in his own household. Then she would be available to him when he so desired that extra excitement.

He slowed the horse to a trot as he passed the Jarrow's farm, taking note of the flocks gathered in the surrounding pens. Those sheep should have been clipped by now he thought to himself and determined to find the reason for the delay on his return later in the morning.

The horse's pace was quickened as he now rode along the track up to the head of Fusedale. The early morning sun brightened the valley and a light breeze gently turned the grasses on the flanks of the fells. Shortly before reaching the croft he pulled the horse to a halt and dismounted. Jacob then ascended the rock outcrop that gave him a view of the home of the shepherdess. His eyes scanned the area, and he saw the sheep penned up around the croft. Well, at least they are down and ready for clipping he thought to himself, but where was the girl?

He took in the scene for some considerable time and then he caught sight of her coming away from the outbuilding. Jacob was conscious of the quickening of his heartbeat. He climbed down from the rocks, remounted his horse and proceeded at a steady trot up to the croft.

Elfie saw him coming along the track and was now standing next to one of the makeshift sheep pens as he called out to her.

"Good morning Miss Mason, I see that you have the sheep ready for clipping."

Elfie raised her hand and cupped her ear to indicate that she could not hear what he had said because of the incessant bleating of the ewes.

Jacob dismounted and walked over to where she was standing.

"Let us walk a little, it's too noisy to talk here, my dear," he said in a gentle tone.

Jacob strode away from the croft a short distance. Elfie obediently following behind him. They reached a flat bed of rock.

"Come, we will sit here and talk, it is much quieter," he waved his arm in the direction of the rock.

Elfie sat down and Jacob positioned himself close to the girl.

"Now, what I said earlier was, I see that you have the sheep ready for the clipping then."

"Yes. That's right sir, I'm just waiting for the men to come and start the work."

"I see, and when do you think that will be, Miss Mason?"

"Possibly within the next two or three days, all the flocks have been gathered and washed."

"Good, good," he replied almost dismissively. "Now we can talk about the offer that I made to you last time I was here."

There was a pause, the inevitable question had been asked.

"Well, what do you say?" he prompted.

"Er, I haven't really thought about it yet sir."

"Come, come, Miss Mason, you've had plenty of time to think about it."

He moved closer to her and put his arm around her shoulder.

"See now, I could look after you, it would be a better life for you at the manor. I would see that you had everything you needed in return for working for me. You would have your own room, good food and a wage as well."

"And what kind of work do you have in mind for me, sir?"

"Well, you could work in the dairy or with the horses, or possibly in the house, we are always short of people, there are so many jobs to be done. Come on then, what do you say," he gave her a gentle hug as he spoke the words.

"I really need more time to think, and-and there's so much to do hereabouts."

"No you don't need more time," he replied persuasively. He could feel his impatience rising.

With his free hand he cupped her jaw, tilting her head back slightly. He looked at her, his eyes following the contours of her face, the high cheek lines, the pert nose, those soft lips slightly parted. It was too much for him, he wanted her.

131

"I could make you a very happy girl," he murmured, and with that he kissed her firmly on the lips.

In a flash her arms were up forcing his hands away, she wriggled free from his hold and stood up to face him defiantly. Her face was flushed and her eyes took on a rebellious expression. She wiped her mouth with the back of her hand as if to rub away the kiss.

"How dare you force yourself on me," she blurted out almost sobbing the words.

Jacob knew that he had gone too far, he thought for a moment.

"Please do forgive me Miss Mason for being so forward, I was carried away somewhat, but I really could give you a better life away from all this hardship."

Elfie relaxed a little.

"Really sir, I am quite happy here, things have improved of late and -" she paused, realising that she was giving things away.

"And in what way could that possibly be?"

Directing her mind away from her recent discovery in the chest and Mick's proposal of marriage, she replied.

"The lambing has been good this year and the clip should also be, and that's what I'm about, doing the best job that I can."

She knew that these were feeble reasons, but she could not think of any better reason at present.

"I see," came his reply. "But is this all that you want in your life, stuck up here in this desolate valley with no-one to keep you company except sheep?"

She wanted to reply that she had all the company that she needed, but she bit her lip. She looked at him thoughtfully for a moment.

"At present, I'm content in what I do, maybe later on I might change my mind."

Ah, he though, maybe she will change her mind if I pursue her more gently and yet, he needed her to agree sooner rather than later.

"Very well then, have it your way, but remember this, I am trying to help you by letting you stay here I can easily change my mind you know."

Elfie just smiled at his warning shot, not the reaction that he expected.

"I do thank you for your offer sir and maybe in a few months time I may change my mind and do as you ask."

Jacob could not conceal the expression of surprise on his face. Perhaps he was winning over a little at least. He stood up and took hold of her hands. She did not draw away but looked up steadily into his eyes. Yes, he was a handsome young man and maybe he could give her a life of relative luxury, but at what price? How sincere was he, what were his motives? Surely she could never exist along side him on an equal basis

Again, he pulled her closer to him, a mischievous twinkle in his eyes.

"It's alright Miss Mason, I'm not going to kiss you again, that is, unless you want me to."

He was obviously teasing her now and strangely her being responded to his charms. They held hands a little longer and then he gently released them.

"I shall come back in a few days when the clip is over and then we'll talk some more."

She did not reply but simply stood there with a half smile on her lips.

He clicked his fingers and the horse walked obediently over to him.

In one swift movement he was up and seated in the saddle.

"Remember my dear, I only want to do what's best for you, I will see you again soon." With a flick of the reins he put the horse into a fast trot and set off back down Fusedale.

Elfie stood there for some time watching him until he was out of sight. What were his real motives, surely he couldn't really care for a simple shepherd girl so well below his station? But somehow, he aroused a curiosity in her which her instinct told her she must resist.

Chapter eighteen

It was almost a week since the first gather of flocks in and around Martindale and Fusedale had taken place. The weather had been relatively warm and fine for the time of the year. There had been a few heavy showers which served to keep the ground fresh and moist and this was reflected in the greenery of the lower fells and valleys. Lakeland was at its best, stunningly beautiful, nature had removed the harshness from the environment and a serene mellowness pervaded the lower ground.

The sheep were now ready for clipping on the first farms in Martindale, namely those of Sam Gregory and Will Blake. The facilities at Blake's were far better for the purpose of shearing and so Gregory's flock had been driven down the valley to Blake's farm. This action would enable the two flocks to be clipped and marked together on the same site. This was common practice hereabouts and the other flocks would be treated similarly ending with the combination of the Jarrow's and Mason's flocks.

Ahead lay a busy week until all the work was completed and it involved all the family members, wives, sons, daughters and anyone else who could be coerced to help out. When the job was done there would be time for relaxation and a mass get together in the village of all those involved, together with other farmers, shepherds and workers from the other farms within the area. The get together usually took the form of a dance in the village hall in Howtown and was an event everyone looked forward to. It provided an incentive to get the clip completed by the weekend so that everyone could take part in the merriment.

By mid morning everything was organised and the clip was well underway at Blake's farm. The sheep were penned between two buildings. The geld sheep, these being the ewes without lambs were done first and the process was to sort the ewes into smaller groups so that eight at a time were placed in a smaller pen. In this pen two workers picked out the thorns and straw from the fleeces before they were led through to the clippers. The clipping was carried out in the farmyard. This was a rectangular, cobbled area which had been thoroughly cleaned prior to the clip in an effort to keep the fleeces as free from dirt as possible. Four clipping stools were situated in front of the barn. Each one consisted of two pieces of wood about five feet in length and fixed on sturdy legs. The wood was braced by cross pieces. The crude structure tapered from about three feet wide at one end to eighteen inches at the other. The shearer sat at the narrow end. The catchers brought in the sheep from the pen and placed them on their backs onto the stools. Sheep are generally restive when on their backs and this greatly aided the shearer.

The clipping of sheep is an art which has to be learnt and some are more adept at it than others. There is a certain knack to it if the work is to be done without nicking the animals skin. Anyone seen doing this would immediately jeered and reprimanded by the other clippers.

The womenfolk backed up the men with a liberal supply of tea, homemade bread-cakes and jam. The women were also actively engaged in the rolling and packing of the fleeces.

The rolling of the fleece is a skilled job in itself. It is rolled from the inside out, edges to the middle and then tail to the head. Then it is tied round with a band of wool roughly twisted from the neck area. This helps to keep the fleece together in transit.

When the sheep has been clipped it has to be marked with the smit of that particular flock. The shorn sheep are taken to a holding pen and then pushed into a narrow pen where the smit mark is applied to its back. Finally it goes into a larger enclosure to await its release back onto the fell.

This was the scene for the day and the procedures used for many years, handed down from father to son were strictly adhered to. Will Blake and Sam Gregory were engaged in sorting out the ewes in the pen and bringing them forward for clipping. Mick, Ewan, Davy and a travelling shearer known locally as Jed were seated on the clipping stools receiving the ewes and expertly detaching them from their fleeces.

The shearers would generally do a shift of around an hour or so and then change places with the catchers or dispatchers. One of them would also supervise the womenfolk and other workers with the rolling of the fleeces.

When the ewes were dispatched into the exit pen they were forced through a narrow gap towards the rear of the farm. A large stone post adjacent to the corner of the building created an exit through which one ewe at a time could pass. It was here that Blake's elderly father was sloped almost double and as the sheep passed through he held them against his knees and applied a new smit mark. He used the appropriate marker, which he dipped in the tar costral and made the mark on the animals exposed skin. The ewes were then free to enter the large pen at the rear of the farm. Here they huddled at the remotes part of the pen with their companions before being released to the fell or taken back to their farm of origin.

Elfie assisted with the rolling of the fleeces, something which she had done for the last three or four clips and her proficiency in the task was clearly evident. She would dearly have liked to try her hand at clipping but so far the opportunity had been denied her. She has asked Mick to show her how it was done but he has countered this with the comment that it wasn't really women's work and anyway the work has to be completed in the day.

Elfie was not best pleased with his remarks and this was obvious from the steely cold look which she gave him. In order to appease her disappointment he had offered to bring his shears up to the croft one evening and give her some tuition. He had made it clear that it required considerable skill to be able to do the job properly. Elfie dismissed his last words by countering that she could be as good as anyone else given the chance. However, she accepted his offer and secretly looked forward to the chance and also some time on her own with him. She constantly reminded him that she needed to be good at all tasks if she was to become a fully-fledged shepherdess.

Mick was mildly amused at her pursuit of skills and knowledge but knew that he would feel her displeasure if he did not support her.

By late afternoon the two flocks has been clipped and the fleeces rolled and stored in the woolsheets. The sheets could hold several fleeces and enabled the wool to be loaded onto the wagons and safely carted away to the wool merchant.

The workers had been sustained throughout the day with a liberal supply of food and drink prepared in the farmhouse. Now that the work was over for the day the workers relaxed with a final round of the good ale. The usual good-humoured chat and banter ensued before the workers made their ways back home.

Mick sought out Elfie who was finishing off the last of the woolsheets in the shed.

"You ready for off?" he called out cheerily to her over the pile of woolsheets.

"Won't be a minute, just this last one to tie up," came back the reply.

Shortly she appeared from the shed, brushing of wool bits from her clothing.

"Father's already set off back with Ewan, we can probably catch them up."

"Well, I thought we could walk back over Pikeawassa to my place and then you could teach me how to clip, like you promised –remember?"

Mick looked a little forlorn.

"Ee Elfie I'm pretty well done for after today's work and it's along way round to the farmhouse that way."

Disappointment immediately showed on the girl's face in the form of a sulky expression.

"Well, if you don't want to bother Mick, I'll go home on my own."

Elfie promptly turned and marched off in the direction of the track over the fell. Mick stood there silent for a minute or two, this was a side of the girl's nature he had not experienced before. Similarly, it was a side she seldom displayed unless she was intent on having her own way. Whilst her father was alive she was obedient and had always taken a submissive role as he would not tolerate any form of bad behaviour or argument from her. Now she was fully aware that she could manipulate situations and people to her own advantage and whilst she often showed naivety she was nobody's fool.

"Well, are you coming with me or not?" a voice called out to him.

Mick turned and looked in the direction of the voice. Elfie was stood on the track which sloped diagonally upwards to ease the gradient, her hands were on her hips in a defiant pose which also hinted at the provocative. Mick set off quickly, almost running to catch her up.

"If we get a move on we can be back at my place in no time at all."

The girl set off again at a brisk pace, Mick silently following on behind her.

Within a short time they reached the wall which ran along the fell top and the croft came into view some way below them. When they reached the stile Elfie climbed the three stone steps and promptly sat down on the wall top.

"See, we're almost there," she remarked, giving him her sweetest smile.

Mick grinned at her, she was softening again.

"You're trying to kill me off with all this traipsing about after a day's hard work."

"Really," she replied in a surprised tone," well it's not as hard as you'll have to work when we're married."

"Why's that?"

"Because I want us to build up a really big flock and make money for ourselves instead of the likes of Lord Farrington, Isn't that what you want too?"

"I hadn't given it that much thought really, I suppose I was just expecting to take over from my father when it gets too much for him."

"Well I've got plans of my own, that's why I want to be really good at shepherding and perhaps get famous for the quality of our sheep."

"Yes, but we need money to branch out on our own, that's why I was waiting to take the farm on."

"That's alright, but I want to start next year, it could be a few years before your father lets you take over. When we find somewhere to live I can give up Farrington's sheep and build up a new flock."

"I like your ideas but it doesn't get over the problem of how we buy stock and such does it?" he argued.

"Hm," she murmured, a little disappointed that he wasn't as enthusiastic as she was.

"Well I think we can do it."

"But how?"

"You'll see," she replied brightly, jumping down from the stile to the other side of the wall. She knew that she has sufficient money now to buy stock and with good management they would prosper, but she wasn't letting on about it just yet.

"Come on then, I want my first lesson in clipping."

Mick still had a puzzled expression on his face as they reached the croft.

Without pausing for a rest Elfie said, "go on then Mick, go and fetch a ewe and let's get started."

"Mick's face took on a worried expression.

"D' you know what, I've left the clippers behind."

"Oh, you're not getting a way with it that easily Mick, there's some of my father's in the store, I'll go and fetch them."

Mick went over to the pen and secured two gates to form a smaller pen, then he sought out the biggest ewe he could see. Grabbing it by its neck and rump, he hauled the reluctant animal into the little enclosure which he had just created.

"There you are," said Mick, secretly thinking that 'll stump her.

"You've done that on purpose haven't you, got the biggest you could find."

"Would I do that to you Elfie?"

"Yes you would, now go and put it back and get that one there for me," she replied, pointing to a rather dainty looking ewe in the corner of the large pen.

Mick duly got the smaller ewe out of the pen.

"Now, where's the clipping stool?"

"It's over in the outhouse."

The ewe was marched over to the outhouse between them as if it didn't mind succumbing to its forthcoming fate.

"Right, you sit down lass an' I'll put her on her back for you."

With one swift movement the ewe was on its back with its head pressing against the girl's chest. Mick deftly tied its hind feet and the animal lay there helpless.

"Now you start on its belly and work up to its chest, working outwards and mind you don't break the fleece."

Elfie started nervously at first and somewhat clumsily, but she soon gained confidence as she usually did and started to clip quite well.

"It's not that difficult really," she remarked.

"Y' need to get a bit nearer its skin, but not too close mind."

As she proceeded the fleece hung down like a crib blanket. The animal was turned from one side to the other until the fleece was clear of its back leaving only the neck to be cut to release it. Elfie worked away carefully until the work was complete.

"There, I don't reckon I've done too badly for a first attempt, do you Mick?"

Mick surveyed the shorn ewe.

"Well, there's a few lumpy bits but it's not bad for a first attempt."

He took the clipping shears from her and tidied up the bits that she had missed, then he untied the legs and rolled the animal off the clipping stool.

"Right then Mick, go and get me another one."

"Aw, come on Elfie, one's enough for tonight."

"No it's not, if I can get good at it I might be allowed to do some clipping tomorrow."

"Well, I don't know about that, I wouldn't think they'll let you loose on their ewes you know."

"Alright then, but they can't stop me doing my own sheep can they?"

"Suppose not."

"Go on then, fetch me another one."

Mick dutifully took the shorn ewe back to the pen and returned with another. Elfie smiled warmly at him from her position at the end of the clipping stool. Mick took in the expression on her face and glowed inside, she was the nicest thing that had ever happened to him and despite some outward resistance to her whims and fancies deep down he was anxious to please her in anyway that he could.

Within an hour four more ewes had been relieved of their fleeces.

"D' ye reckon I'd be alright at clipping then?" she enquired of him as he returned from penning the last ewe.

"Aye, that last one was pretty good, but that's enough for tonight now. You'll have to keep them penned up until they are marked when we do the rest of them."

Elfie got up from the clipping stool and started to brush the wool off her clothing.

"Come on then what's the joke?"

"You look like a bit of an old ewe yourself with all that wool hanging off you."

"Cheeky oaf," she retorted, "You get off back to your farm then."

"Beggar me, I trail all this way back with you, teach you how to clip and then you thank me by telling me to get off back home."

"Shouldn't insult me should you?"

"Eh, come on, I were only joking.

Elfie flashed him a mischievous smile.

"You don't half tease me," he ventured, "I never know if you're serious or just having me on."

"There's no need to look dejected Mick."

"Well I'm-"

"Come here you big silly thing."

Elfie flung her arms around his neck and gave him a big kiss.

"There, does that make it right?"

He warmed to her, hugged her lovingly and kissed her neck.

"There's one thing you can be certain of, " I love you Mick Jarrow, I really do."

Mick held her close and kissed her lingeringly several times.

"And do you love me?"

"You know I do, I've loved you for a long time now, long before we got together."

"Really, I never knew that," she replied, evidently surprised by his remarks.

The sun had dropped down behind the rim of fells leaving a rosy pink hue in the now fading blue sky. Shades of blue and grey now showed the outlines of the mountains, nature was revealed in another of her guises in subtle hues and colours. Nightfall was imminent.

"Looks set fair for another good day tomorrow Mick," said the girl in a dreamy tone whilst gazing at he sky.

They lingered some while longer in each other's arms and then gently drew apart.

"I'll let you go now Mick, but only till tomorrow mind."

A happy young man made his way back down the valley in the receding daylight.

The clipping progressed favourably at the other farms until the Jarrow's and Mason's flocks remained to be done.

As the last sheep were being clipped Davy Jones called out to those around him.

"If Elfie brings down her ewes first thing, I reckon we'll 'av done t' lot by end of afternoon, d' ye reckon so lads?"

"Aye, its gone well this year," replied Ewan. "Reckon you're right Davy."

Early the following morning the Mason's ewes were heading down the valley under the watchful eyes of Moss and Tess. The sun was just climbing over the rim of high crags and introducing welcome warmth to the cool valley air. Within an hour the flock had reached Dale End and the ewes were promptly penned prior to clipping and marking.

Elfie spent most of the morning helping with the newly clipped fleeces and packing them into the woolsheets. Eventually, the work halted as the call for dinner was made. Most of the workers sat outside the shed and tucked into the ample supply of bread, ham and pickles provided by Mary Jarrow.

On finishing the fleece she was rolling, Elfie went and seated herself next to Mick.

"Now who looks like an old ewe?" she teased.

Mick's boyish grin spread across his weathered face as he tried to brush the accumulation of wool from his clothing.

"D' ye think I could try my hand at clipping this afternoon Mick?"

"I dunno, better ask my father."

Elfie stood up and walked over to where Davy was sat with Ewan and Will.

The girl stood there a minute looking down at the men, not wanting to interrupt their conversation.

"Aye, lass, are y' wanting something?" asked Davy, a questioning expression on his face.

"Yes Mr Jarrow, can I take a turn at clipping this afternoon?"

Davy nearly choked on the bread roll which he had just taken a sizeable bite of. The other men looked equally aghast and turned to look at Davy, awaiting his reaction.

"Bloody hell lass, it's men's work, not for likes on a lass like you."

"Why shouldn't I clip? I've done everything else, like lambing and gathering and the like," she retorted.

"Y' waint take a turn in t' dub though, will y'," chuckled Ewan.

Elfie gave him a scornful look.

"I said it's not lasses work and that's it," said Davy, an annoyed expression pervading his face now.

Elfie wasn't going to be beaten, she rounded on him.

"They're my ewes and I can clip them if I want to," she said almost defiantly.

Davy half rose from his seat, his hand outstretched as if to give her a clout, then he sat down again.

"Now don't you get cheeky with me lass, an' they're his lordship's ewes an' 'e 'll want em doing proper like."

"And I look after them and do everything else, so why can't I clip them?"

Davy was not used to being resisted and certainly by a girl. The others looked on silently awaiting the next move. Mary had been witnessing the confrontation from the door of the farmhouse and she now came over to calm the situation.

"Ere, what's going on?" she exclaimed.

"Lass 'ere wants to clip."

"An' can she clip?"

"Ow the bloody 'ell do I know," he growled angrily.

The group of men had all stopped eating now and sat, mouths open, jaws dropped as the argument unfolded before them. Never before had a woman tried to infiltrate the clip, but then, they had a shepherdess amongst them either. They looked at one another, each thinking that everything she had done so far had been alright, but this was a step too far.

Mary turned to Elfie now, a mild expression of anger on her face.

"Well lass, can y' clip?"

The girl was clearly causing a problem in the otherwise smooth running of the work and she didn't want it on her doorstep.

By now Mick had joined the group and intervened.

"Yes, she can clip and she's not bad for a beginner, we all had to start somewhere."

There was a nod of approval from the men, but Davy continued to scowl.

Elfie calmed down now Mick was supporting her.

"I only want to be good at my work, Mr Jarrow, and I'll only be that if I get a chance to practice, after all, it's only once a year." Her voice had now taking on a pleading tone.

"Sounds fair t' me," said Mary, "give lass a try, an 'if she's no good y' can boot 'er out."

Davy continued to scowl.

"You 'eard me, give 'er a chance." Mary stomped back to the farmhouse.

"You 'eard her, give 'er a chance," chorused the men mischievously, chuckling away amongst themselves.

"Right, if that's how it is y' can take my stool over, an' if y' make a bugger of it, y 're out, right." Davy spit the words out somewhat contemptuously.

Elfie didn't reply, but just nodded in agreement, she felt sick inside knowing that she had upset the harmony but there was no going back, she knew that she would have to get it right.

Dinner over, the girl duly took up her position in the row of men at the clipping stools. She was rather relieved to be at the end of the line with Ewan next to her. She glanced cautiously at him and catching her expression he winked at her.

"You show em lass" he whispered.

Elfie returned a feeble smile.

The next thing she knew was a large ewe being turned on its back and placed on the stool in front of her, she hesitated.

"Tha'd better get on wi' it lass, we've no time to waste," said Ewan.

The girl quickly gathered her thoughts together and composed herself. She took up the shears and proceeded to clip away the fleece. She worked carefully, albeit somewhat slowly clipping the belly and legs as Mick had shown her. Then she deftly tied the legs and rolled the animal onto its side. First one side was clipped and then the animal rolled the opposite way to access the other side. Then she worked her way up to the shoulders and neck and then pulled the fleece clear. She looked across at Ewan who had started at the same time as her. He was now halfway through his second ewe. Untying the legs, she rolled the ewe off the stool onto the floor.

One of the farm lads who was waiting immediately took the animal away for marking and straight away another ewe was on the clipping stool before her.

As she was pulling away the fleece from the body of the second ewe, Davy Jarrow appeared.

"Ave y' finished it lass, lets take a look." He inspected the ewe. "Well, I 'ave to admit, it's not bad for a first go lass, only thing is. Y' ll 'av t' speed up else y' ll be holding us all up like."

"Eh, hang on a minute," intervened Ewan, " she's on t' 'er second ewe, you know."

"Bloody 'ell, I thought she were still on t" first un," replied Davy in an incredulous voice. "Well, I tek back what I said afore, y' right, with practice you'll be as good as many around 'ere.

This was praise indeed from Davy Jarrow. He had a soft spot for the girl to the point of envying his son to some degree and although he would be the last to admit it, he hoped that the two of them would eventually marry.

"Best crack on w' it then lass, how many 'av you done Ewan?"

"This is third 'un I'm on with now."

"Lass is nearly as fast as you then?"

"Nay, she'll non beat me, but she's doing alright though."

Davy said no more as he bundled up the fleeces and took them off to where the women were rolling them.

By mid afternoon Elfie was feeling exhausted and a bit sickly. There was no let up in the work and she was glad when Mick appeared to take her place.

"You alright Elfie, you look a bit pale?"

"Yes, I'll be fine, it's much harder than I thought when you're doing them non-stop. She wandered off to join the women who were rolling the fleeces.

It was a beautiful evening as Mick and Elfie drove the ewes back up Fusedale, assisted by Moss and Tess.

"He's not up to it," said Elfie, inclining her head towards Moss who was following the ewes somewhat lethargically.

Tess was doing most of the work, back and forth, side to side to keep the ewes together.

"Happen he's like me, worn out for the day, I did find it hard you know."

"It's no easy task," replied Mick, "but you did very well and you impressed them all."

"Really, you're not just saying that?"

"No they all said you'd done a good job, especially Ewan, you'll be down for clipping next year for sure."

"If we're here next year."

"What do you mean Elfie?" asked Mick in an anxious tone, he always sounded a bit worried when she countered the normal run of things or his expectations.

"I mean, a year's a long time, who can say what we'll be doing at this time next year."

Mick was about to reply when Moss visibly stumbled before them, but before they could reach him he was up again and plodding after the sheep somewhat unsteadily.

"That's like he was last week when we were gathering," her voice clearly displaying her concern.

"Aye, he's not right is he, it's probably his age, I mean he's getting on a bit now isn't he?"

Elfie didn't answer him at first, she was too busy watching the dog who seemed to stagger about a bit before finally composing himself and then continued to walk on steadily behind the ewes.

"If he doesn't improve I'll have to get him to the veterinary in Penrith, but there's not much for him to do now so he can have a good rest."

The croft was reached and the ewes were left to disperse themselves around the lower ground. Within the next day or two they would return to their heafs on the higher ground.

The feeling of her kiss lingered on the young man's lips as he made his way back down the valley in the now fading light of the halcyon summer evening.

Chapter nineteen

On the next Saturday the people of the valleys of Martindale, Fusedale and the surrounding hillsides were gathering in the little village of Howtown to celebrate the success of the clip. This event marked the end of a hard years work from the tupping of the previous year, the lambing in spring through to the gathering of the flocks and subsequent clip. Throughout the day many of the workers had been engaged in carting the wool to the carriers for onward delivery to the wool merchants in Penrith. Now as evening approached it was time for the get together, to meet up with friends old and new, have a few drinks and mainly take part in the dancing. As usual, the dance took place in the village hall that had been decorated with flowers by the womenfolk of Howtown.

Elfie had been to previous celebrations before but they had only been brief visits. She had always left early with her father before the merriment got into full swing. So in effect, she had not experienced the full event. Now she was looking forward to her first taste of freedom as an individual as she made her way down to the farm to meet up with the Jarrow's.

Mary was busying herself in the kitchen when Elfie popped her head around the kitchen door and called out cheerily.

"Hello Mrs Jarrow."

"Eh, lass, I'm right glad to see you, it'll be right grand t' 'av a night out."

She cast a critical eye over the girl.

"An' are y' going t' dance looking like that?" she remarked, obviously referring to Elfie's somewhat shabby hodden grey dress. "We alllus gets dressed up a bit f' dance like."

Elfie looked somewhat dejected at Mary's comment.

"I've only got three dresses and this is the best one."

"Aw, come on lass, we'll 'ave to make y' up a bit better, I've one or two dresses upstairs. I 'ad em like when I were a bit thinner y' know. Lets go see what w' can do and y' 'air could be a bit better as well." The last comment referring to the girl's tousled blonde tresses that hung loosely around her slender young shoulders

Within a short space of time the plainly dressed shepherdess had been transformed. She now wore a long navy blue cotton skirt which had been quickly taken in by the deft hands of Mary. One of Liza's white blouses was a reasonable fit as the two girls were of very similar build albeit that Elfie had a more mature figure. The two items were complemented by a black velvet waistcoat. The blouse was open at the neck and the buttoned up waistcoat served to lift her breasts giving her a subtle sensuality. Mary had worked wonders on the unruly mop of hair.

"Y' look right lovely lass," she told her as she finished off brushing out her long curly tresses before finally tying then back with a bright red ribbon.

"There now, 'av a look in t' mirror, you're a pretty lass y' know. I reckon our Mick'll be right proud on y' when 'e sees y'."

"Oh, Mrs Jarrow," she exclaimed as she gazed at herself in the mirror turning from side to side to examine her profile, never before had she been able to see herself in a full length mirror.

"I've never been dressed up before Mrs Jarrow, you really are so kind to me."

"Think nowt on it lass, y'll do fur our Mick as far as I'm concerned."

The two of them made their way down stairs to the kitchen where Mick and Davy now stood, mug of tea in hand, having just returned from carting the wool. The two men stood open mouthed as Mary and Elfie entered the Kitchen.

Davy was the first to speak.

"Well, I'll be blown, that's not lass that were clipping t' ewes yesterday is it?"

Mick just stared. Elfie was beautiful in his eyes when she was sat on the shearing bench covered in wool, now she was positively stunning.

"Well y' daft beggars, what d' y' think on her now?"

"Y- You look lovely," was all he could utter.

Mary interrupted.

"Go on then lads, get y' sens ready, then we can be off like."

The evening had a balmy feel to it as the group made their way along the lanes to Howtown. The sun's rays still gave lingering warmth to the valley as it started to slip down behind the fringe of mountaintops.

The little village was bustling with people. Events such as this to mark the end of clipping were infrequent and so when they did take place they drew people in from all around the valleys. The strains of the little band could be clearly heard as the Jarrow's made their way through the village. Outside the inn men and women spilled out into the village square. Cheerful banter and laughter was all around though it was certain to change to a more raucous form of behaviour as the evening progressed and ale was consumed.

The noise from the village hall increased as they got nearer to it. Inside the villagers and incomers were taking part in the dancing with much enthusiasm. In reality, there was more stamping about than dancing as many could not dance very well or else they were already a little worse for wear from the effects of drink.

The more experienced were of course dancing properly to the little band which was comprised of a fiddler, two men on concertinas and a flute player. The accomplished dancers who took up the centre of the floor were engaged in a Cumberland reel. The less able on the sides either tried to replicate it or stomped about clapping their hands enthusiastically.

The Jarrow's stood on the sidelines and took in the scene.

"Next dance an' were away in," said Mary.

"Nay lass, I'm getting to old f' this lark."

"No y' not."

The next dance was announced, it was stripping the willow.

"Come on husband, this un's fun," said Mary as she dragged the reticent farmer onto the floor.

"Are we dancing then, Mick?" asked Elfie to the reluctant looking lad at her side.

"I'm not right good at dancing Elfie."

"Nor am I, but we can have a go, it's not that hard." Taking his hand she pulled him, protesting somewhat onto the dance floor. Once they got into the swing of things the dancing became intoxicating and the couple danced away long after Davy and Mary had given in to exhaustion.

The ale flowed freely both inside and outside the village hall and by late evening many were well and truly inebriated. The Jarrow's although partial to a drop or two exercised some constraint and never went overboard. This was largely due to Mary's rules, due in part to her childhood experiences in Ireland of a drunken, abusive father.

"I'll av no drunken beggars in my 'ome else they'll av me t' reckon with," were her often reiterated remarks preceding such events.

Davy and Mick took heed of her warnings and exercised a good deal of restraint and although they were somewhat merry by late evening they were still a long way off the drunken stupor of some of the locals.

"Lets have one more song, where's old Jack Briggs," came a call. "I'm over 'ere," came the reply. "Come on, Jack lad, give us another song" Jack was propelled forward to the front of the hall and the band struck up 'The falling of the leaves.'

Old Jack was getting on in years and his voice faltered as he sang.

When he came to the chorus the whole of the group of people joined in.

'Oh look at the leaves a little while ago
How beautiful they grow upon the trees
Now they are withered and falling to the ground
Like those leaves we are withering and falling to the ground'

This was followed by 'Old black Joe' and then a hearty, rousing round of 'Old Lang Syne'.

The band then packed up its instruments much to the dismay and protests from the people gathered in the hall.

"Aw, come on lads, just one more," came the call from the people.

"Nay, we're done for, we've been playing since six o' clock, it's time to be off" replied the fiddler.

"A round of applause f' band," came the call, and they were duly cheered and clapped out of the hall.

It was still a warm night as little groups now spilled out of the hall, they gathered in the square still reluctant to leave the pleasantries of the evening. Eventually the groups of people broke up, some walking, some staggering or supported by others as they made their weary ways home.

Elfie and Mick walked on behind Davy, Mary and their children, they all chattered away happily despite the waves of tiredness that now swept over them. Much of this was due to the evening but also to the hard work of the last few weeks.

"Can Elfie stop for the night?" asked Liza as they approached the farm.

"Oh, I can't keep putting you out like this," replied Elfie.

"It's no bother at all, y' more than welcome," said Mary.

And so Elfie turned down the lane to the farm with the Jarrow's.

The following day saw Elfie back at the head of Fusedale. Most of her time was spent busying herself around the croft and surrounding area. The pens that had been used for containing the ewes were stacked away and there were a number of jobs that she wanted to do inside the house as well.

Mick came up to see her in the early evening and the couple spent a pleasant hour reminiscing on the events of the last few days. Mick then headed back down the valley as darkness started to fall. How much better it would be if he did not have to make this journey and the two of them could be together all the time. But Mick was content in his own mind, he could wait safe in the knowledge that his lifelong dreams and hopes would soon come true.

Elfie slipped into bed shortly after Mick had left. She had spent a restless night at the Jarrow's on the previous night which she put down to tiredness from the events of the last few days and off course, the thrill of the dance in the village hall. Never before had she been out so late at night and in the company of others. She felt sure that had her father got to know Mick as she now did he would have approved of him as a suitor.

The happy thoughts buzzed around in her head making sleep difficult to achieve until the brain finally succumbed to the exhaustion of the body.

When sleep did finally come it was deep and restful.

In the early hours of the morning she awakened by a whining sound from one of the dogs' outside her room. She slipped out of bed, the first light of dawn was just breaking and easing itself over the rim of the hills.

The whining became louder and then a paw scratched at the door. On opening it she saw that it was Tess who was trying to get her attention.

"What's the matter girl?"

Tess turned and went over to where Moss lay in his favourite corner. As Elfie approached him her eyes slowly became accustomed to the semi-darkness. As she looked down at the dog he appeared to be shaking and convulsing quite violently. Tess stooped her head down towards him and then looked anxiously up at the girl as if to say 'he's poorly'.

Elfie cried out loudly, "oh Moss, what is it boy, what's wrong?"

She flopped down onto the floor next to him and cradled his head in her arms. Gently stroking his broad head, she spoke to him in a soft voice.

"It's alright my precious, I'm here now."

Moss seemed to calm a little at the sound of the girl's voice.

Tess whined gently, she reached out and stroked her head as well.

"It's alright Tess, it's alright."

Moss seemed to settle somewhat as Elfie continued to cradle and stroke his head. He gazed up at her, those soft brown eyes were pools of the deepest trust, she was with him now. His pain seemed to ease a little and he gave out a low whimper.

Then he groaned loudly and his body convulsed again entering into a spasm of rigidness before the tension left his body again. He gave out a long, low groan and still gazing up at Elfie he flicked his tail feebly a couple of times.

Tess shuffled over and rested her head on his back. She looked up at Elfie in anticipation, she would make it right.

Elfie nestled her head in the thick, soft hair around his neck and gently kissed him. The dog gave out another low groan and then his head lolled to one side, his lower jaw dropped open and his thick pink tongue slipped out and hung there. Tess wined in an agitated tone.

"It's alright girl," Elfie knew it wasn't.

She knew that it was the last breath that Moss had taken and now his body lay in a limp state in her arms. Then the reality of it all penetrated her mind. The dog whom her father had brought home as a fluffy black and white puppy when she was but a little girl had now gone. The dog that she had played with so fondly despite her father's attempts to train it into a working dog was no more. She had watched him grow, he had accompanied them almost everywhere and had become the excellent working dog she knew and loved, he was the last link with her father.

The tears ran effortlessly down her cheeks and splashed onto his back causing a large wet patch on his fur.

"Oh Moss – Moss, what am I going to do without you," she sobbed out loudly

Tess shuffled closer resting her head in the girl's lap. She bent over and kissed her head and stroked her ears.

"Tessy, Tessy girl, now there's only you and me left."

Tess licked her hand softly and with that animal reassurance as if to say, 'we'll be alright.'

The girl and dog just sat there in a crumpled heap beside Moss until the sun rose over the fellside and its warm rays penetrated the croft and a long yellow beam fell on the three of them.

Elfie looked down at Moss and whispered softly-

"Whenever we see the morning sun or a rainbow after the rain is done, or the stars in the sky on a cloudless night, then we will know Moss is alright."

It was a heartbroken girl, eyes reddened with crying that made her way over to the outbuilding with Tess at her heels, head hung low.

She came out of the building with a spade and walked a little way along the track until she reached a little, flat area just above the beck. It was a shady little spot surrounded by a few rocks and a small rowan tree growing to one side.

"Moss loved it here, he could see right down the valley." She gulped the words out to Tess who stood close by her side. The dog wagged her tail and leaned against her legs reassuringly. Elfie put the spade to the ground and within a short time the last resting place of the faithful Moss was ready. She stood back and wiped the sweat from her brow on to her sleeve.

"We'll go and fetch him now," she said turning to look down at the dog sat close by her side. Tess gazed up at her mistress with sorrowful eyes.

She walked back over to the croft with Tess close at heel. She hoped in the deepest recesses of her heart that she would find Moss just asleep inside the building. But it was just a hope; the lifeless body lay where she had left it. Kneeling down, she sobbed uncontrollably. This creature had been her friend, always the same, never cross or bad tempered as her father often was. He was always ready to lick her hand, settle against her feet and just love her in the way that only a dog can.

She knew in her heart that her father had loved her in his own way but the love of a dog is different to that of a human being. Animal love is constant and faithful, unchanging; no matter what happens it is always there.

Her father had looked after her in his rough kind of way; he had protected her, perhaps too much in denying her some of the pleasures of childhood and adolescence. He had educated her to a good standard through schooling and his own input and made sure that she spoke well and yet, there had always been that lack of warmth, that tenderness, that love. Elfie had never experienced the love that a mother can give to her child. Moss had been her best friend, her sole companion and at the head of the lonely dale he had been her protector when her father was away. He had been her confident, she could always talk to him, tell him her deepest thoughts. He listened quietly to what she said, his head inclined to one side, perhaps an ear cocked and those soulful, expressive eyes, watching her every move.

Now he was gone, the pain she felt in her heart was almost too much to bear. She just sat there on the floor, stroking his lifeless body. Feeling the soft, thick fur around his neck, tracing her fingers along the white flash on his head that ended on the crown of his head. And all the while the tears flowed constantly until she could cry no more.

How she longed for someone to comfort her, she felt like she did when her father had died, suffering the loss on her own. She felt the gentle pull of a paw on her arm, she looked down, it was Tess, her eyes seemed to be saying 'you've still got me.' She bent over and cuddled the warm body of the dog.

"We'll get through this, Tessy girl, we will."

Elfie stood up and went to get an old blanket which she wrapped around the lifeless form of Moss. With a little difficulty she lifted him up into her arms. He was a large dog but she drew the strength to carry him outside, his beautiful head lolled from side to side as she carried him to where he would finally rest. Kneeling down on the rough ground, she lowered him as gently as she could into the grave. She sat for some time staring down at the still form of her lifelong friend, saying her goodbyes within the deepest recesses of her mind. Then still sobbing, she took up the spade and covered him over with the freshly dug earth. She collected up small stones and placed then around the mound and piled some up to form a little cairn where his head would be.

"There, he's at peace now, we'll plant some flowers to come up in the springtime Tess and then he'll be with us again."

Tess waged her tail in agreement. They both knew he'd always be there, when she looked around the fells she could still see him running high amongst the crags, searching out the errant ewes.

"He'll always be with us, always here."

She reached down and ruffled the hair on Tess's neck, then slowly made her way back to the croft, a sad, heartbroken girl.

He looked at the pale face and reddened eyes of the girl sat on the bench outside the croft.

"Elfie- Elfie, what ever is the matter love?"

At first she was unable to answer, seeing the one person who loved her just set her off crying again. He sat on the bench beside her and just hugged her and kissed her hair.

"It's alright, it's alright, what is it?"

"It's Moss- Moss, he's dead," she sobbed.

"Oh Elfie my poor thing, what has happened to him?"

"I think it was his heart, it just gave out on him, you know he'd been acting a bit odd for a while."

She cried again the tears seemed endless.

Mick held her close and she started to calm in the warmth of his arms. They sat there, nothing was said, he just held her until she was settled and composed. Then she relayed the dreadful event to him.

"You poor, poor thing, if only I'd known, I could have been here."

"You weren't to know, I've managed, you couldn't really have done anything. He's up there now," she added, waving an arm in the general direction of where she had buried him.

"He was such a love, not just a working dog but my best friend, he still is, he'll always be about up here."

Mick looked a bit puzzled at this remark, but then he understood what she meant.

"Yes he will, and you've still got Tess, haven't you?"

"And you as well," she smiled at him, the hurt made just that bit easier to bear now that she had a comforter.

"You'll always have me Elfie, I love you so much, I really do."

He kissed her tenderly, the very beginnings of the healing process had started. She knew the hurt would get easier to bear. It would take time, just like it had with her father although in her mind she was puzzled how the loss of an animal seemed to have a more profound effect on her than the loss of a human being. It would get easier and she would be able to look back fondly on the happy times with that lovely dog called Moss.

Chapter twenty

During September the lambs had been weaned from their mothers and the ewes now relieved of their responsibilities had started to make their way back onto the fells. A month or more on, they were now being brought down again for salving. This was an essential task carried out annually to kill off lice, keds and ticks which attached themselves to the sheep. The work involved parting the fleece on each side of the animal and smearing a mixture of tar and rancid butter on to the skin by using the fingers. The job, though simple was labour intensive and so as many helpers as possible were enlisted to carry it out. There were many casual labourers who went around the flocks at this time of year to help with help salving and earn a meagre wage.

On completion, the ewes were kept on the inbye to await tupping early on in November. They were then free to return to their heafs until the first sign of snow, then they would be brought down to more sheltered areas on the lower fells. This final task ensured that they had access to easier grazing through the winter.

The autumnal period had been witness to the development of the courtship between Mick and Elfie. It was a known fact that the couple intended to marry in the springtime. A few knowing comments has been passed by both farmers and shepherd who had observed them during the gather for the salving. So often they had been seen climbing the fells together, hand in hand and pausing for the occasional hug or kiss.

"I dare say that wouldn't have happened if her father were still about," commented Will Blake.

"Nay, their right enough them two, I'm right glad f' em, it's nowt f' a lass on 'er own at top o' this valley," replied Sam.

"I tell you I wouldn't a' said no to 'er if I'd bin a bit younger like," quipped Ewan. "She's a right bonny lass."

"Aye, we've seen you watching 'er."

"You keep your eyes to yourself, she's far too young for likes of you," teased Will.

And so the comments and knowing winks which had abounded when the couple were together were proven to be well founded.

The friendship had gone beyond Mick's visits to the croft at the end of a days work. Now they could be seen together on occasions in the village and on an outing to Penrith.

Elfie was a welcome visitor to Dale End Farm and Mary was treating her like another daughter. Davy had his reticent moments, complaining that Mick was being detracted from his work, which in reality was untrue. Mick was no shirker; he simply worked harder and got the jobs done quicker so that he could spend more time with the girl.

"She's good f' our Mick, that lass, brings him out a bit," remarked Mary during one of the periods when Davy was having gripe about all the work that needed doing

"Aye, could do worse I s'pose," came the philosophical reply.

"What d' y' mean, she's no fool, she's got a good 'ead on them shoulders and a pretty un at that, an don't tell me y' 'ant noticed?"

There was no reply, Davy's eyes were closed, feet propped up on the buffet. There would be no sound from him for an hour or so.

Jacob Farrington had not been seen in and around Fusedale since the clip but he was now on his way to pay a visit to the secluded valley. This time he was not following his usual route through Martindale but had instead chosen a wild remote route over the top of Wether Hill. His travels took him from Burnbanks up the steep hillside of the Tail O' Ling. This was not a suitable route for a horse because of the steep nature of the ground, but Jacob was headstrong and liked to take on a challenge. With a little slipping and stumbling the horse and rider attained the summit of Low Kop. Now the ground was easier and High Kop was easily reached. Jacob paused here to look back and reflected on his previous visit. He had purposely left the girl alone to give her the chance to consider his offer. Now he was of the opinion that she had been given sufficient time and he would be looking for an answer when he next met her. It felt good to be out on the open tops and he drew full breaths of the heady air. The ground to the east was much gentler, the High Street range providing a barrier to the Lakeland area. On reaching the Roman Road that traversed the entire range he headed down into Fusedale on a convex slope. The horse picked out a steady route down a rake in the hillside; a misplaced foot here would certainly result in the unseating of the rider.

As he descended, he observed the scene. The recently salved sheep were abundant on the valley floor and the strong smell of the salve reached his nostrils. At first he could not see the girl but then he spotted her, she appeared to be doing something to the ground a short way from the croft. Reaching easier ground he spurred the horse on to a quicker pace and was soon pulling his mount to a halt beside the crouching girl.

Elfie had been aware of his approach but as yet she had given no recognition of this, instead, she continued to plant bulbs into the ground around Moss's grave. Farrington looked down at the girl somewhat annoyed at her failure to recognise his presence.

"What are you doing there Miss Mason?" he asked in a brusque tone.

Elfie continued to push the last bulb into the hole and then padded the soil and grass back into place. She then stood up and turned to face him. His annoyance at this action was clearly visible on his face.

"I was just planting some daffodils."

"Daffodils, and why are you doing that up here may I ask?"

"Because this is where my dog Moss is buried."

"A dog's grave and you're planting daffodils," he replied scornfully.

Elfie's eyes flashed in anger, she rounded on him.

"I loved that dog and I'll see that he's properly remembered if I care to."

She glared at him defiantly.

"Well, just remember who you are talking to, young lady."

The girl was resolute in her anger. What right had he to come down here passing comment on what she did? Why should she cowtow to his demands? She was rapidly developing her independence and had money of her own now, she had skills and most of all she had a future with Mick. She was enjoying turning the tables on Jacob Farrington and stood there looking up at him defiantly.

"My job is to look after your sheep, anything else I do is my own affair.

Farrington was amused by this outburst and his initial anger quickly receded. He dismounted from his horse and walked towards her.

"We're quite the little demon today, aren't we?"

A half smile broke out on his face; Elfie said nothing, continuing to glare at him.

"Come on my dear, we must be friends if you are to continue to work here."

"And what does that mean?"

He hesitated a moment and then said, "well, I mean that we must get on together if you're working for me. Now, how are things going here?"

He smiled broadly at her, his eyes twinkling somewhat as he waited for her reply.

She could not resist warming to him; he was a good-looking young man who could be quite charming when it suited his purpose.

The anger left her voice as she replied.

"The lambs have been weaned off and the salving is done. Mr Jarrow is hiring two rams within the next few days and then I'll put one to the ewes.

"Good, good, you seem to be well organised, I must congratulate you on your efficiency, Miss Mason."

"Thank you sir," she gave him a wan smile.

"Now, about that little matter I left you to think about, have you er -?"

Elfie was expecting this question and her answer was already prepared.

"Yes, I have given it a lot of thought and I've decided that I would like to continue here until next spring and the lambing. By then I will have had a full year shepherding and then I will see what you have to offer me."

Her tone was decidedly assertive, in her mind she knew that next spring she would be Mick's wife and the whole situation would be completely different.

Farrington was a little taken back by the forcefulness of her reply. It was not the answer that he sought, but at least she was now beginning to consider alternatives, or so he thought.

"Perhaps you should consider a change before winter sets in, all the signs point to it being a harsh one this year."

"Well, we've survived a few winters up here and some rough ones at that, so I think I'll take my chance with this one."

"Yes, that's probably true, but you could be warm and comfortable back at the manor and not have to endure such hardship. We have a large flock on the estate; you could take charge of that and have a room in the manor, or perhaps, one of the workers cottages' on the estate."

The last idea was unlikely unless he turned out one of the worker's, but he would be willing to do this if it resulted in satisfying his desires.

"Now, what do you say?"

"Like I said before sir, I'll wait till next spring and then I'll do as you ask."

She had no intention of doing anything like that, but if it appeased him it was worth suggesting.

"Oh very well, have it your way."

He conceded defeat for the time being but replied, "think it over carefully, I'm sure that sooner rather than later would be to your advantage, particularly as I said, in view of the forthcoming winter."

The girl said nothing in reply as he mounted his horse.

He looked down at her for a moment from his elevated position.

"Think it over carefully, I might not make the same offer again and you might not be kept on here."

He flicked the reins of the horse and set off at fast pace back down the valley.

"Now we've upset him Tess, I wonder what he'll do next."

Tess looked up at her mistress and wagged her tail.

"Anyway, it won't be for much longer will it, we'll soon be moving out of here."

The dog nuzzled her outstretched hand.

"Come on, let's go and get something to eat."

Elfie spent much of her free time reading the diaries of her father, trying to piece together his former life. She was particularly interested in his brother's farm in Yorkshire and wondered if he was still alive. If he was, he would be her only relative now or maybe if he had a family she might have some cousins. She considered trying to find out where the farm was and the possibility of paying him a visit but then she put paid to the thought as she reasoned that he probably wouldn't know her anyway even though she had lived there for a short time.

Mick visited her the following evening and brought the tup which his father had hired for her. He brought the animal on the back of the cart in a makeshift pen.

Elfie was delighted to see him and went running along the track to meet him. She jumped up on to the cart and sat beside him, her arms went around his neck and she gave him a big kiss.

"I've missed you, you haven't been to see me for two days and that horrible Farrington's been pestering me again."

Mick drew the cart to a halt outside the croft. Elfie turned to have a look at the ram.

"He looks like a fine tup, strong and healthy."

"Aye, should be a good un, we've got his brother down at the farm for us."

"Did you remember the reddle?"

"Course I did, do I ever forget anything?"

"Well, you forgot to come up to see me, didn't you?"

"Nay, I didn't, it's just that I've been busy with going to the tup fair and the likes."

"Alright, I'll believe you then, hey what's in that basket then, it's not from your mother, is it?"

"Might be."

"Well is it?" she queried, knowing full well that it would contain some of Mary's fine baking.

"She's sent you some bread and stuff, she's too good to you really," he said teasing her. "I hope you look after me as well when we're married."

"Don't expect too much, I'm not a good cook like your mother, but I'm sure I'll learn once I've got a kitchen of my own."

Mick gave her a hug.

"Next time you're down at the farm we'll have look at the cottage next to the barn and see what we're going to do with it."

"That's if we're going to live there, we might want to find a place of our own."

"How can we do that El, we can't afford to."

"Might be able to," replied Elfie, her mind picturing the money hidden away in her bedroom.

"What do you mean?"

"Oh nothing, I'm just dreaming, that's all."

They chattered away happily for some time, then Mick drew the conversation around to Jacob Farrington.

"You say Farrington's been around again?"

"Yes he was here earlier today, trying to persuade me to go shepherding the flocks at the manor and then threatening to throw me out if I didn't."

Mick looked angry.

"Well, not quite that," she continued, "but he hinted as much that if I didn't go to the manor I might not be able to stop here."

"So what did you say?"

"I told him that I would go next spring after lambing."

"Eh, what did you go telling him that for," said Mick, somewhat astonished.

"Mick, it doesn't matter then, we'll be married and living somewhere else, won't we?"

"I hope so, but I don't like him coming here trying to get you back to the manor."

"Well there's no way I'm going there, so he can go on all he likes, it's just a matter of keeping him at bay for a bit longer, that's all."

Mick was silent for a moment, and then he took hold of her hand.

"I must agree with Farrington on one thing though El, why do you want to go on living up here on your own?"

"It's a kind of promise really, you see, when my father was ill I promised him that I would keep things going up here. He was really proud of the flock, so in my own mind I decided when he died that I would keep up his work. After all, there's not much else I can do really. Things have changed a bit since then, things that have made me change my mind, but I'm determined to see the whole year through, just to prove to myself and him that I can. If you think about it Mick, I didn't know any other life, then when we became friends and I came down to the farm I realised that there's more than just shepherding. I want some of the things my father never allowed me to have."

Mick listened intently, it was not often that she revealed her innermost feelings to him, she went on-.

"Like the cosiness of your farm, your mother's lovely food, meeting lots of new people, going to the dance. I've really had such a good time this last few months and most of all I just love being with you Mick, that's really the best part of it. But as I've said before, I don't just want to be a farmer's wife; I want to be running our own farm. I want to build up the best flock around here, buying and selling and all the other things that go with running a farm. So if you marry me you would be getting a partner, not just a wife, can you see that Mick?"

The lad was silent for a while thinking over what she had just said, but before he could speak she went on- "I still owe my promise to my father so that's why I insist on working the flock until next spring."

"I see what you mean Elfie and if you want a joint agreement or what ever you call it I don't mind. We'll work together and have one of the best farms in these parts. The only thing I'm not so sure about is how we find the money to do it.

Elfie gave him a cheeky grin.

"Perhaps I'll go and work at the manor after all."

"Why, what do you want to do that for?"

"So I can rob Farrington, then we'll have some money."

"Don't be daft, you can't do that."

"I know I can't, I'm only joking."

She giggled mischievously.

"Or – I could steal sheep instead."

Mick's jaw dropped.

"You're not serious, aw come on, stop having me on."

"Do you really think I would do that, you haven't got a very good opinion of me, have you?"

She stood up and turned her back on him as if in a sulk.

"I didn't mean it like that El, I'm sorry."

She remained with her back to him.

"Come on Elfie."

She turned round to face him, a wicked smile spread across her face and then she sat down on his knees.

"Silly boy you."

"I never know if you're serious or not Elfie."

"Well, I'm serious about the farm, I've got plans for it and I think I know a way how we can do it."

"But how?"

"You'll see, I'll tell you before we're married."

The two of them kissed and cuddled for some time, then she pulled away from him and looked seriously at him.

"Now Mr Jarrow, what do we do with that tup?"

"Oh heck, I'd forgotten about him, he's still on the cart. We need to reddle him and then he can get on with it."

"Alright then, lets get him sorted and then he can have his fun, I suppose he does enjoy it?" she enquired in a naïve sort of way.

"Reckon he does," replied Mick.

The couple went outside to where the tup had been left on the cart. Mick climbed up and got one of the tubs of reddle and a flat stick. He scooped up some of the liquid and rubbed it onto the chest and forelegs of the animal. The tup resisted but Mick was a strong lad and he held it firm.

"We can let him go now."

He undid the rope attached to its horns and pulled back the makeshift gate of the pen. He then pulled the tup forward and it jumped down from the cart. The animal looked about for a bit as if to familiarise himself with its new surroundings, then it ambled of in the general direction of the ewes.

"He'll be alright now, but he'll need reddling again in a few days. Should have calmed down a bit by then, getting tired like. In a couple of weeks you'll have to do him with a different colour so you can keep a check on when the lambs are due, you know that, don't you?"

She nodded.

"Anyway, I'll come up and sort him out for you."

"They can go back on the fell then, can't they?"

"That's right El, but you need to keep an eye on them now, you don't want them going too high in case weather turns like. Keep them below the intake wall then they'll be fine. Send Tess up now and again to bring them back down. They know best grazings lower down, but there's allus a few daft uns that wander off."

"You'll sort them out won't you Tess." She addressed the remark to the dog who was laid down next to her, head on paws, ears cocked, listening to the conversation

Tess gave little bark and wagged her tail.

"There's a few of them collected up on that flat bit above the wall." She indicated the general direction with her arm. "I'll fetch them down in a few days for the tup."

Mick looked in the general direction and then down the valley.

"I suppose I'll have to be getting on back down; I wish you were coming with me instead of being stuck up here at the other end of the dale."

She gave him her most endearing smile.

"I won't be long now, we're into November and I'm coming down for Christmas."

"Are you, you didn't say so?"

"Well you didn't ask, did you, but your mother did. I've never celebrated Christmas before apart from getting a bit of a present from my father, that was about it."

"It's a big thing down at the farm, specially Christmas Day. We have a turkey or a goose and Christmas pudding as well.

"Never had Christmas pud before."

"You'll love it Elfie, you'll love all of Christmas at Dale End."

"I know, I can't wait, I'm really looking forward to it," she replied excitedly.

"And then spring will be upon us before we know were we are, and then it'll be lambing time as well. Who knows, if you're really good, I might even marry you then."

Mick gave her a big hug, this time he knew the last remark was a tease, he played along with her.

"And if I'm bad?"

"Then I'll marry Jacob Farrington."

"Will he have you though?"

"Well he wants me to go and live at the manor, so he must like me."

"So you'd better be really good to me and then I'll be Elfrida Jarrow next springtime."

Mick knew that he could not persuade her to bring the day forward; she was resolute in seeing the year through to the lambing.

"Anyway, there's not much chance of you marrying Farrington, he's marrying that Amelia what's her name?"

"How do you know that?"

"It's common knowledge in the village, there's a big wedding planned for next year in Bampton."

"Ah, well," she replied, "who cares what he does, in a few months he won't mean a thing to me, we'll have our own place by then- if you're good, mind.

He gave her a kiss.

"You can bet I will, you're all I want."

They kissed again lingeringly.

"Off you go then before you get lost in the dark – see you tomorrow."

"You will sweetheart."

"Hm, sweetheart, I like that, go on now Mick Jarrow."

Mick climbed aboard the cart and the horse dutifully turned and set off back down the track.

Elfie reflected on their conversation. Yes, it would not be all that long before they married. Soon she would tell him about her little fortune and then they could start to plan what they would do and where they would live. In her mind she felt that she wanted to be completely free of the influences of Lord Farrington and his land. Maybe they could find somewhere out towards Keswick or the other side of Ullswater. She wandered back into the croft locked in her thoughts.

Chapter twenty-one

The two under-keepers and the group of beaters had taken up their positions in a long line awaiting the start of the drive. As soon as the shooting party had settled themselves into the butts along with their loaders, the head keeper gave a signal by waving a red flag to start the first line of beaters off walking. They approached from the south across Colton Moor some two miles below Thornthwaite Manor. As the line of beaters neared the shooting butts waiving their flags and shouting to drive the grouse forward the guns opened up. The beaters at the ends of the line had much further to travel due to the contour of the land and so they had to run to keep the line.

The loaders frantically kept passing the loaded guns to the shooters and the most expert were able to lose off four shots as the birds approached the butts. Then they managed another three or four as the birds passed over the line of butts.

A whistle was blown to stop the shooting as the first line of beaters approached close to the shooting party. The dogs were then sent out to collect the fallen birds and return them to the shooters at the butts.

"I say, not bad at all for a first drive," called out Lord Farrington to his friends and guests. "Now lets get the beggars on the way back."

The first line of beaters withdrew. Again, the red flag was waived and the second line of beaters drove the birds back in the opposite direction. When the latter drive was completed the fallen birds were collected up.

The ponies were brought over from where they had been waiting and the panniers on the animals were loaded up with the kill.

"Damn good show I must say," piped up his lordship in encouragement. "Now gentlemen, we'll take lunch."

The whole shooting entourage had about a mile to walk across the heathery moorland to a stone-shooting lodge. A large pot of stew had been sent over from the kitchens of the manor along with corned beef and ham sandwiches, cheese, beer and wine for the shooters. Staff from the manor was on hand to serve up the meal. They were all dressed in pristine outfits, which realistically were unsuitable for the location and terrain.

The shooting party had split into two groups on arrival at the shooting lodge. The gentry entered and sat inside on chairs whilst the beaters and loaders grouped outside in the cold to eat their own food. There was a good deal of friendly banter amongst the beaters as the lengthy lunch break progressed. Towards the end of the proceedings, a carriage appeared on the track leading to the lodge.

"Now 'oos coming?" piped up one of the men.

"Aw, looks like young Farrington an' 'es got some lasses with 'im."

"Nay, 'es not bringing lasses to shoot, is he, I remember last time he did that, it were a right farce," commented one of the under-keepers.

The carriage pulled up at the lodge and Jacob Farrington and another young man alighted and helped down the two ladies, one of them being Amelia. The beaters and loaders stared at the two couples. The two men were dressed in tweed jackets, plus fours and deerstalker hats. The two ladies wore heavy dresses with fur capes. The two couples walked past the men without so much as a sideways glance and went into the building.

"Snotty lot," came the comment from one of the beaters.

"Ah, Jacob, come over here will you," Lord Farrington called out to his son.

Jacob and his friends joined his lordship who was talking to a group of shooters.

"Thought we would join you for the afternoon session, father, how has it gone this morning?"

"Yes, yes, never mind that," replied Farrington senior, "look, this is Mr Jeffreys, he's got a number of farms on the borders and is looking to introduce some hardy stock. I suggested some herdwicks, we have some good stock. You can pick out a few for him to try out can't you?"

"Certainly I can do that, they've just been tupped so if you took them you would have some fine lambs next spring I'm sure, how many are you looking for?"

"Oh, about a dozen or so, perhaps within the next couple of weeks, before winter sets in."

"That shouldn't be difficult, they are still able to travel."

"The best ones are up Fusedale," interrupted his father, "you get up there first chance. Fellow that ran things up there died, damn good shepherd and all, who did you say was managing them now?"

Jacob was silent for a moment and the two men waited in anticipation for his answer. "Dan – Dan Smithies, yes that's it, I'll go see him in the next few days and get things organised for you."

"Excellent, excellent, then if they are successful we will take more the following year," replied Jeffreys.

The conversation was interrupted by the appearance of the head keeper.

"Pardon me sir, but we're ready to move on now."

"Damn you man, we'll go when we are ready," growled his lordship.

"Yes- yes alright then," he relinquished, "We'll be ready shortly."

The head keeper hurried outside.

Jacob Farrington's mind was already up in Fusedale. Yes he would get up there first chance; he hadn't seen the girl for some time, now he had a good reason.

In a short time the shooting party had assembled outside and started making its way to the next line of beaters on Jackson Ridge.

"Do we really have to walk all this way over this rough ground?" enquired Amelia.

"I'm afraid so dearest, we cannot take the carriage as there is no track can we?" he replied in a sarcastic tone of voice. "It's not very far now, there, you can see the line of butts."

The beaters carried out two separate drives as before and then the party moved on to the final shoot of the day which was about half a mile away from the manor. The dead birds were again gathered up and loaded into the panniers on the ponies. They would then be taken and hung in the game larder back at the manor.

The next task would be to carefully sort them out and the best would be put to one side for the shooters to take away with them. The remainder would be sent to the market or used in the household kitchen. An accurate tally would be compiled so that the results could be relayed to the shooting party.

The wind had got up somewhat during the afternoon and the sky was a sullen grey colour. As the shooting party finally made its way back to the manor the first flakes of winter snow were drifting and spinning to the ground. They formed a delicate white carpet on the hardened tracks but disappeared in to the heather and grasses on either side.

Elfie was awakened from her deep, dreaming sleep by a low whining noise, as she stirred and came back to an awareness of her surroundings she realized that it was Tess that was making the sound. The girl stretched out her body under the heavy, warm cover on the bed and then threw it back and alighted gently on to the mat at the side of her bed. She crossed the little room and looked out of the window, gasping out loudly at what she saw. Everywhere that she looked was covered with a thin layer of fresh snow.

The wind could be heard whistling and blowing the snow into little drifts against the walls of the outbuilding. Crossing to the foot of her bed she searched round frantically in the half-light for her clothes. She patted Tess on the head.

"It's alright girl, but we've work to do and quickly."

She was thinking of the few remaining sheep in the parcel of land above the croft. Her voice did not portray the rising feeling of panic inside her but she knew that she must act quickly and bring the ewes down into the shelter of the valley floor before the snowfall got any worse. Finding her clothes, she dressed rapidly and knowing that she would need something to keep her dry and warm she remembered a thick coat that her father used in the winter-time. It was in the cupboard where she had stored most of his belongings since his death being reluctant to dispose of anything. The coat was much too big for her but she put it on and secured it with a length of chord around her waist. Taking an old scarf, she wrapped it around her head, and then calling to Tess she stepped outside into the hostile weather.

There was an ethereal silence as she walked quickly over the lower ground in the direction of where she had last seen the group of ewes. The snow crunched under her boots, it was of a firm texture and she left clear tracks as she went forward. The wind was driving down from the fell tops, its cold penetrated the exposed skin of her face, she pulled the scarf up to protect her forehead. The sky had an angry leaden look about it, a sure sign that there was much more snow to come.

These conditions often happened in late November giving a moderate fall that often thawed as temperatures rose a little before the final onslaught in December. Then the snowfall would be prolonged and heavy cutting off the valley for days on end. This year the girl hoped to spend some time down at the Jarrow's farm so that she would not be isolated on her own at the head of the valley.

The girl reached the gate in the intake wall, Tess deftly jumped over it, her feet barely touching the top rail. Elfie followed through the gate and girl and dog headed uphill to the small plateau between the higher fells. The tops of the mountains were obscured in a great white cloak, which merged with their dull colours. The snow increased in depth as they climbed higher, making progress more difficult as each footstep sunk in and had to be extricated.

Through the swirling grey and white landscape it was just possible to make out the group of ewes compacted together above the higher wall.

"There they are Tess, we'll soon have them down and then we can get out of this foul weather before it gets too bad."

Tess barked in response and shook to remove some of the snow that was piling up on her back and head. The dog ran about excitedly in the snow, these conditions did not seem to deter her from her enjoyment. Every now and then she would push her muzzle into the snow and run forward creating miniature snowballs.

Soon they reached the second wall which was the last man made structure on the desolate high fells. It was beginning to be obscured as the wind whipped into drifts along it base. The wall was quite broken down, serving more as a marker to the higher ground than for its original purpose as an enclosing structure to keep the sheep from straying too high. There were a number of small rock outcrops along the base of the wall and the builders had included these as part of the structure.

Elfie climbed up on to one of the small outcrops and could now see the ewes more clearly. She gave Tess a command and the dog dutifully set off to flank the ewes, there was a bit of reticence from the ewes, but soon they were under control and the dog made its way back down to where her mistress stood.

"Good girl, good girl," cried the girl, "now, let's get back down the valley, it's getting bad up here."

Elfie turned to climb down from the rock outcrop, but as she did she lost her footing on the slippery surface. She fell backwards hitting her side and head on the rocks; she felt a searing pain and rolled over into the gap between the wall and the rocks. The fall had severely wounded the girl and the blow to her head rendered her unconscious. Now she lay in a crumpled heap, a trickle of bright red blood running down her temple and dripping onto the snow. Here it was absorbed by the crystalline flakes and spread out to form a pink surface on the snow.

Tess brought the ewes round to where Elfie lay between the wall and the rock outcrop. She quickly sensed that something was wrong and pawed at the body of the unconscious girl. She sniffed at the bloodstained face and gave out a low whimper. The ewes bleated and shuffled about in an agitated state.

Tess now had a dilemma; she had been given the command to contain the ewes and this she must do. Conversely, her mistress lay on the ground not communicating with her. Tess made her decision and was round the back of the ewes in a flash, she drove the sheep into the cleft where the girl lay. Her task was twofold, contain the ewes and guard her mistress until she was able to give her further commands.

True to its appearance the dark, heavily laden sky gave up its burden and the snow fell fast and heavy covering the girl, dog and ewes stranded high up on the fellside above Fusedale.

Mick groaned out loudly.

"Go away and leave me alone."

"Mother says you're to drink this up cos it'll make you feel better," replied Liza, hovering over the sweating body of her brother huddled up in his bed sheets.

"Aw, one minute I'm shivering, next I'm boiling hot and sweating like a pig."

"It's only a cold you've got."

"Nay, it's more than a cold," groaned Mick, "it's been coming on for a day or two."

"I wish I could stay in bed," retorted Liza, "it's snowing like mad outside."

"It's not is it?" Mick half sat up and then slumped back, "I'll have to go and see if Elfie's alright."

"You're not going anywhere," came an authoritive voice as Mary Jarrow appeared at the bedroom door. "Y' need t' stop in bed f' a few days. Y've got a right fever like, now drink that, it'll do y' good."

Mick took a sip of the concoction that Liza held for him.

"Cor, it's awful."

"Get it down y," grinned Liza, taking pleasure from her brother's dismay.

Mick reluctantly downed the contents of the mug.

"What am I going to do about Elfie?"

"I'm sure she'll be alright," replied his mother. "She's not daft, she'll be inside with a right fire going I reckon. Any 'ow, I'll send our Andy up as soon as it stops snowing t' tell 'er t' come down 'ere, there's no point in being up there on 'er own. But you waint be going anywhere f' a few days in your state. Now, try an' get some rest an' I'll bring y' some soup up in a while, y've got to keep eating y' know."

"I don't want ought to eat, mother."

"Yes y' do, it'll get ' strength up, come on Liza, leave him to rest."

"Can't I go up and ask Elfie to come down," asked Liza as the two of them descended the stairs.

"Y' can both go as soon as it stops snowing."

Chapter twenty-two

Drifting in and out of consciousness she slowly became aware of the blackness surrounding her as she half opened her eyes. Her head was throbbing and she felt sick. Worst of all was the stench, a putrid smell that penetrated her nose acting almost like smelling salts only much stronger. The girl's brain operating feebly after the long period of unconsciousness could not discern what it was or indeed where she was. The smell was almost intolerable. She sniffed the air and as she took breath the smell of ammonia filled her lungs. The smell heightened her senses increasing her awareness. She realised what it was, a familiar smell, which her brain told her, she knew, but much stronger then she had ever experienced. The smell, which in some incomprehensible way was helping to revive her, to bring her to her senses was urine, sheep urine.

She groaned out loudly and immediately something warm and wet licked at her face, pawed at her and whined gently. Elfie tried to sit up, but somehow felt pinned down. She felt about her in the darkness. To one side her hands touched something hard and rough, which she identified as rocks and it was against these that her body was pressed. She reached out again and felt something coarse, yet soft and yielding. Her hands delved into the substance, it was familiar. Pushing in deeper to confirm she realised that it was wool, a fleece. With-drawing them she sniffed her hand as if to confirm, yes it was a fleece.

Strangely, it was warm within the acrid smelling capsule. Tess seemed to be half on top of her. What was happening to her? Where was she? It was totally dark. She listened; she could hear the breathing of the sheep and the muffled sound of their hooves as they fidgeted about within their confinement. The fleece next to her moved about slightly and she was able to stretch her arm weakly above her head. The girl's fingers penetrated something cold and wet. It was loose, her fingers pushed into urgently. It felt like some kind of ceiling above her, bits of it dropped onto her face. She then knew that it was snow. Her arm dropped back to her side, the fingers now wet and cold. Lying still for some time, her mind puzzled over the situation and she again drifted in and out of consciousness.

She came to and then panic struck her and she gave out a terrorised wail. The seriousness of her situation was emblazoned across her mind;

somehow, she was entombed in a snow-hole. As her awareness became more stabilised she tied to recollect her thoughts on what had previously happened to her. Vaguely, she could recollect seeing Tess bringing the ewes down towards her and it was snowing hard, then there was the feeling of falling and nothing else.

Her brain was clearing and thoughts raced through he mind now. She was trapped, the snow must have drifted over them, forming some kind of cave, what was she to do? Her mind went back to a time a few years ago when there had been a heavy snowfall. She had accompanied her father and Moss, looking for sheep that could have been buried. Moss was good at locating the scent and would lead them to places where the snow was deep enough to cover the sheep over. The dog would dig frantically at the spot and Robert Mason would probe the snow with his long crook to feel for any ewes that might be embedded there. Moss was usually accurate in his location and the shepherd would dig into the drift to release the ewes.

Sheep are able to survive for some time in a snow-hole, living off what they can scratch from the ground and their own fat resources. Protected from the wind, they are able to remain relatively warm. Now, Elfie knew that she was buried in the snow along with the ewes, which had huddled around her and the dog.

Some instinct of nature, some higher ethereal force had led the animals to surround and protect her. There was no animosity between sheepdog and sheep, just a common will to protect the injured girl. Some presence was watching over her. Had she been alone in the snow, she would have surely perished.

Elfie lay there sometime, now visibly shaking with fear at the thought of her position. Tess knew the situation was desperate and that her mistress was frightened. The dog shuffled up closer and licked her face. This brought the girl to her senses and calmed her down somewhat.

'We're all alive Tess, we're all alive,' she said slowly. She felt the dog's tail thumping against her leg as it was wagged vigorously; her mistress was alright after all.

"We must try and get out of here and get back home." Tess gave a half excited bark causing the ewes to shuffle about. She tried to kneel up but her head touched the roof of the snow chamber. Next, she tried to push the ewe in front of her in an effort to make it force a way out, but she had no idea of the depth or thickness of the snow.

"What are we going to do Tess, no-one will ever find us here," she said despairingly.

Wriggling about she was able to feel behind her, what she at first thought was rock was in fact the wall and she could feel a draft of air coming from near its base. She wormed her way nearer to the wall and the source of the colder air, yes, - it smelt fresh. With some considerable pushing and shoving the girl was able to get one of the ewes to move around her. It was then that she saw something for the first time in her tomb of darkness. A chink of light was coming through the wall itself. Her spirits rose, the deep snow must only be on one side of the wall in a drift. Perhaps now, she could pull some stones out of the wall and crawl through.

Elfie fumbled about in the darkness, then she felt something upright against the wall. Her hand traced its shape; it was a large, flat piece of slate. Feeling along its edges she was able to determine its thickness, perhaps about two or three inches. She tugged as hard as she could against its top edge and it moved a little towards her and then sprung back against the wall with a resounding clunk.

Then it came to her, she knew what it was. She had found a large slate used to cover a cripple hole in the wall. Its purpose was to allow the sheep to pass through when it was uncovered, but could be blocked off by the shepherd by using a large slate or wooden board. It had obviously not been used for a long time. She tugged away at the slate, it would only move a few inches away from the wall, but each time it allowed light to penetrate the snow-hole and she could just make out the huddle of the ewes in the dim light.

"It's no good Tess, it won't move." She slumped back against the wall, exhausted from her efforts. Tess barked loudly causing the ewes to shuffle about. The dog started to dig frantically at the base of the slate causing clods of earth to scatter over the interior of the hole. Elfie tugged again at the slate, rocking it back and forth, and then suddenly it loosened and came away from the wall at an angle.

"Alright Tess, that 'll do," the dog stopped digging. With one last big tug, the slate came away from the wall and lay flat on the ground. Light and fresh air flooded in through the cripple hole. Tess quickly crawled her way through the hole and stood on the other side barking excitedly, as if to say, 'come on.'

Elfie squeezed her body through the hole and lay on the snow on the other side of the wall. Her eyes were tightly closed, partly as a reaction to the sudden brightness but also from the pain around her ribcage. She lay still for some time until she heard the familiar bleating of sheep. The girl half opened her eyes and looked around her.

It was a beautiful, bright day. The sky was a brilliant blue with not a single cloud in sight. The sun glistened and danced on the clear, white landscape. The fells were ringed with splendour only to be found under these winter conditions. Elfie directed her gaze to where the bleating sound originated from and watched as one by one the ewes emerged from the snow tomb by wriggling through the cripple-hole. The animals stood around her bleating gently. Their presence in the snow-hole had been the reason for the girl's survival. Without them she would have died from exposure

"You were my guardian angels, and you as well Tessie for keeping them all together."

The dog ran around the ewes giving excited little barks.

Elfie raised herself to a sitting position; the dull pain in her chest was now more severe after her efforts to extricate herself from snow-hole. Looking down the valley, she could see the croft and the ewes gathered on the lower ground. She knew that somehow she had to get down the hill. With much effort she came to a standing position but immediately her legs gave way and she fell over. Her head throbbed unbearably; again she tried to stand, but dizzily flopped down again into the soft snow.

Resting for some time she again tried to stand and was able to pull herself up and support her body against the wall. Looking over she could see the depression in the ground which was filled with snow forming her ice tomb. She shuddered at the thought. If I'm going to get down there I've got to get over this wall, she thought. The girl shuffled along to a section where it was broken down, the point that had given her a view down the valley. With some considerable effort the girl launched herself over the wall and landed in the deep, soft snow on the other side. She winced at the pain and waited for it to subside a little before sitting up.

She called to Tess who brought the ewes round to where she sat in the deep snow.

Half crawling, half walking and stumbling, Elfie made her way slowly down the hillside. The snow got up under her already sodden skirt and down into her boots, stinging her legs and making he feel even more uncomfortable. Slowly, but determinedly she made her way down, stopping every few minutes to allow the pounding in her head to subside. After an hour or so of staggering, sliding and crawling she reached the gate in the intake wall. Now, feeling considerably weaker she slumped down against the wall to rest. She felt cold and wet and shivered continuously. Tess licked her face and Elfie gave the dog a reassuring pat. "We're nearly there, we'll make it somehow and then we'll be alright." Pulling herself up on the wall, she opened the gate and the ewes passed through, she pulled the gate shut behind her and stumbled on. The task was nearly done; all that was remained was to reach the croft. The snow was not as deep on the valley floor and progress was a little easier. Finally, they reached the track to the croft and the girl and dog progressed slowly towards the building. Eventually they made it to the door and Elfie staggered inside.

Her one overwhelming desire was to get out of the wet clothing and in to bed to get warm and rest from the pain. Slowly, she stripped off the wet, smelly clothing and boots. She shivered violently from head to foot. Leaving her clothes in a heap on the floor, she made her way to the bedroom. Pulling the covers back she collapsed on to the bed. Dragging the covers around her and over her head, the girl lay there alternating between bouts of sweating and shivering. Eventually, sleep overtook her. Tess lay patiently at the foot of the bed, her mistress was home now, and soon she would be well.

It was a little over a week since Jacob Farrington had agreed to find some suitable Herdwick ewes for Mr Jeffreys to introduce to his border farm stock. He had delayed his visit to Fusedale due to the heavy snowfall and bad weather. Now, with an improvement in temperature and clear, bright days, the snow was beginning to melt in the valleys and lower ground, revealing once again the outline of roads and tracks.

As his mare carried him at a brisk pace over Askham Moor, he reasoned that this early, heavy snowfall might just be the lever needed to persuade the shepherdess off her precarious and fragile position at the top of Fusedale. He resolved that he would try and talk her into leaving the croft and come to the Manor. He toyed with the idea of suggesting that she spent the winter at the manor and return to the dale in the springtime. Would this ploy work? If she did fall in with his wishes, perhaps, after she had sampled the comforts of the manor she might not want to return to her spartan position.

The wet snow scrunched and sloshed under the horse's hooves, a few more days like this and the lowland snow would be gone. Soon Jacob reached the cockpit on the edge of the moor and looked down on to Ullswater. The lake shimmered in the bright sunlight. The rim of mountains gave a dreamy, blue reflection in the still waters. On the rider went until he reached Howtown, there the horse was slowed to a trot as it progressed along the main street through the village. There were few people about to witness his passage. Plumes of smoke rose vertically in the still air from the chimneys of the cottages giving the winter air an aroma of burning wood. Jacob spurred the horse on again as he left the environs of Howtown.

Dale End Farm came in to view, Jacob noted the ewes contained in the inbye, many of them still showing signs of the reddle from recent tupping.

Looking down the lane leading to the farm he could see two figures outside the farmhouse. One of them was clearly Mary Jarrow, the other had their back to him. Davy or that son Mick, Jacob surmised to himself.

The snow lay a little deeper and thicker as he progressed up the valley. What he saw before him confirmed his minds view of the desolation of the place and yet, it had a strange, compelling appeal under its mantle of snow.

"And there's a rare prize awaiting at the top," he said out loudly with a slightly wicked chuckle in his voice. As the horse and rider climbed the last steep section of the track the animal struggled to get a purchase with its hooves as it slithered around on the icy track. Farrington reduced its speed to a walk and the horse progressed in a more surefooted manner. Jacob didn't stop at the rock cutting as was his usual want to spy out the ground ahead, but carried on at a steady pace until he reached the croft. He dismounted and looked around him, similar to Dale End, the croft was surrounded by the ewes and the now redundant tup stood on its own by the beck. The sheep had actively grazed and large areas of the ground were uncovered. He cast his eyes around the area; the girl was nowhere to be seen. He strode over to the croft and knocked on the door, calling out.

"Miss Mason, are you there?"

Tess barked loudly at the knock on the door. Somewhere in her subconscious sleep Elfie was aware of a dog barking.

Farrington knocked again and called out loudly, "are you there Miss Mason?"

Tess ran to the door and barked again.

Again the bark registered in the recesses of the girl's mind, "It's alright Tess, it must be Mick," she drifted off again.

Jacob waited a few minutes for a response then slowly pushed the door open, the hinges made their customary creaking noise as they resisted the movement. He stepped inside; Tess stood there, eyes transfixed, emitting a low, throaty growl.

"Easy now, easy now," he whispered.

Tess realising that he was not perhaps the threat that she first envisaged quietened down.

"Good dog," said Jacob in a soft voice he stooped and patted the dog.

"Alright then, where's your mistress?"

Farrington looked round the interior of the croft, how could anybody live here, he thought, its so primitive?

He called again, "Miss Mason, are you there?"

Tess gave a low whine and walked towards the little bedroom, Jacob followed. He pushed the door fully open and peered inside the dim, drab room. What he saw was a pathetic figure almost white, save for the streaks of dried blood on her temple, huddled in the bed sheets.

"My God, what on earth has happened to you?"

He approached the bed and looked down at the girl, was – was she dead; he half pulled back in horror. Then he put his face close to hers, yes, thank God she was breathing. Drifting in and out of consciousness, Elfie half opened her eyes and let out a low moan, then they closed again.

In her subconscious state she knew that someone was here to help her.

Jacob knelt down at the side of the bed, "my poor child, what is it, what has happened to you?" he asked anxiously.

Her eyes opened again, but she was unable to speak, her lips just parting and closing again.

He looked at the wound to her head, there was extensive bruising but the injury was superficial. He felt her forehead and neck, it felt cold and clammy. Any thoughts or desires he may have felt towards the girl were now changed to ones of deep compassion and concern. He was sure that she was near to death and that he needed to act quickly if she was to survive. She needed a doctor but the possibility of getting one up here to the top of the dale was nigh on impossible, it would be a long ride out and return with a doctor even if he could find one. He was certain that he could not leave her for any length of time. There was only one solution, he must take her back to the manor as fast as possible, there he could summon the family doctor quickly and she could be properly cared for. Who she was and why he had brought her there was of little consequence at this stage. Her life was at stake; there was no time to waste.

He lowered his face close to hers and in a quiet voice said, "you are very ill Miss Mason, I'm going to take you back to the manor where you can be cared for."

The girl half opened her eyes and gave the briefest nod of acknowledgement, she was too ill to care what happened to her now.

Very carefully, he put his arms around her and brought her up into a sitting position, she groaned loudly at the movement of her pain-wracked body. Then he wrapped the frail body in the bed sheets. He was strong, she was weak and in one swift movement he had her cradled in his arms like a child and was carrying her outside.

Calling the horse to him, he then lifted her and placed her in front of the saddle. The girl lolled forward against the neck of the horse but he held her firm with one hand as he swiftly seated himself in the saddle behind her. Cradling her firmly against his chest he took the reins with his free hand.

"I'll soon have you where you can be cared for my dear."

He turned to look back at the croft; Tess lay by the doorstep, looking anxious and unsure what to do.

"Alright dog, you may as well come too."

Jacob gave the reins a gentle tug and the horse set off at a gentle pace with Tess following closely at its heels.

The person Jacob Farrington has seen talking to Mary Jarrow was indeed Mick. The lad was now feeling much better and had got up with the intention of walking up the dale to see how Elfie was. Mary felt that he was not yet up to it and wanted him to stay in bed another couple of days. She was of the firm belief that rest and complete recovery was essential before returning to arduous farm work, but Mick was having none of it.

"You were going to send Andy up to see if she was alright," he argued.

"Aye that I was lad, but weather were too bad at time, so I couldn't send 'im then, I were gonna sent 'im today."

"Look mother, I'm feeling alright, I'll just walk up and see her, I wont stay long," retorted Mick in a firm tone.

Mary knew it was no use trying to stop the lad.

"Well, alright then, but mind y' not out long" she scolded.

Mick set off up the track to the top of the valley. He felt weak from the effects of his illness but his determination to see Elfie was enough to spur him on. He was approaching the ruined croft below Groove Gill when he saw a horse and rider coming down the track steadily towards him. As it drew near he recognised the figure of Jacob Farrington but could not make out what the bundle of cloth was in front of him. Then as horse was upon him he could make out the pathetic face of Elfie swathed in the blankets.

He cried out to her, "Elfie, what are you doing, where are you going?"

She made no response to his call, merely looking at him through half closed eyes with a blank expression on her face.

"Hey, what are you doing, where are you taking her," he shouted up to Farrington. Mick repeated his words and tried to grab the reins of the horse. Jacob cracked his wrist with the loose end of the rein in his hand.

"Elfie, Elfie, tell me what you're doing," he implored.

Farrington released his boot from the stirrup and kicked out at the lad.

"Out of my way Jarrow, she's coming with me back to the Manor."

"Elfie, it can't be true, tell me –"

Mick tried to block the horse's way.

"Damn you man, out of my way," cried Jacob, with a menacing look in his eyes. He kicked out again causing Mick to stumble and fall to the ground.

Mick lay stunned for several minutes and then pulled himself shakily to his feet. He stood rooted to the spot watching Farrington riding steadily away from him. The lad was beside himself, what did this mean? Had Elfie really decided to go to the manor? Why was she wrapped up in blankets and why didn't she speak to him?

Mick set off down the track trying to catch up with the couple. It was not until they reached the bridge where the track turned off above the farm that he eventually caught up with them.

"Please, Mr Farrington, tell me what's going on," he cried out imploringly.

Jacob turned and looked at the lad, "I've told you, the girl is coming with me to live at the manor, now get on your way or there'll be trouble for you – and that family of yours."

Mick ran along side the horse and looked up at Elfie, their eyes met and then she turned her head away from him. The lad stopped in his tracks and watched as the horse and riders continued on their way. Eventually, he set off again and turned down the track to the farm, feeling utterly bewildered and devastated.

He stumbled into the kitchen where his mother was busying herself with the ingredients of some of her luscious pies. Mick pulled a chair out from the table and slumped down on it, head in his hands in utter despair.

"You're back soon lad, did y' see 'er then?"

There was no response to her question.

Mary turned to look at him.

"Aw lad, are y' alright, I told y' not t' go out so soon like, didn't I?"

Mary stopped what she was doing and came over to him, pulling a chair out she sat down beside him.

"What is it lad, what's the matter?" she asked tenderly.

Mick looked up at her, the tears streaming down his cheeks.

"Oh mother, its Elfie, she's –" he sobbed uncontrollably.

Mary took his hand, "come on now, what is it?"

"She – she's gone off with Farrington," he blurted the words out in a choking voice.

"Nay lad, she wont do that."

"She has, I've just seen them riding away on his horse, and she wouldn't even speak to me."

"Oh Lord, it can't be," replied Mary in an indignant voice, "what's she thinking on?"

"Farrington said she was going back to the manor to live there, I know he kept asking her to."

"Did he?"

"Yes he did, but she always said she wouldn't and now she has, what am I going to do?" he started to sob again. "I can't live without her."

Mary cuddled him in her arms.

"Nay lad, there must be a reason or summat, you two were getting on just grand like, weren't y'?"

"I'll have to go and fetch her back."

"No lad, y' can't do that, it'll mek right problems for us all if y' went over t' manor, y' know what them Farrington's are like. No lad, y'll 'av t' stop 'ere an' see if she comes back. I'll talk t' y' father when 'e comes in, see what 'e 'as t' say. Now you get back up t' bed, or y'll be laid up agin."

Mick got up and trudged off up to his bedroom.

Mary gave out a deep, worried sigh. What to do, they seemed so set on one another and now this has happened, what did it all mean?"

She talked at length to Davy when he came in. He too could not understand it, but he was adamant that Mick should not go over to the manor. As he said, "there was no telling what he might do when he got there, and the Farrington's where not the people to cross swords with. Best wait and see what happened."

Farrington pressed on with his journey crossing Askham Moor. He cradled the limp body of the girl in his left arm whilst urging the horse on at a brisk trot. There was little time to lose but speed had to be balanced with the need to keep Elfie on the back of the horse. Jacob was relieved to reach the long, sweeping drive down through the parkland to Thornthwaite Manor. Turning through the large archway the horse proceeded at walking pace around to the courtyard at the rear of the building.

Jacob shouted in the direction of the stables and a young stable boy came running out and over to him

"You, boy, find Taylor and get him here immediately."

The young lad ran off and was soon back with Taylor the head stable man accompanying him. Jacob had just lifted Elfie down from his horse and was cradling her body in his arms.

Taylor gazed open-mouthed at the bundle in his master's arms, but before he could speak Farrington was giving him a command.

"Taylor, get the carriage and go and fetch Doctor Blaymire here as quickly as possible, tell him it's an emergency. Don't let him argue with you, tell him I'll double his fee, go on man, get on your way."

Taylor ran off in the direction of the stables.

"And you boy, take my horse, oh, and the dog, er, tie it up in the barn and look after it, carefully now."

Farrington turned and went in through a side door and into a long corridor. He quickly walked to the end of it and kicked the door open into the kitchen.

"Cook, where's Mrs Riley?" shouted Jacob.

Before the cook could answer, Mrs Riley appeared in the doorway to find out what all the commotion was about.

"Ah Mrs Riley," Jacobs voice quietened somewhat. "I've got a very ill girl here. I want you to make up a bed for her in one of the spare rooms, light a fire and warm the bed; I've sent Taylor off to fetch the doctor."

Mrs Riley stood gaping at the bundle in Jacobs's arms.

"Go on woman, get on with it."

Mrs Riley scowled at Farrington, then calling two maids; they scurried away to carry out his orders.

Jacob carefully sat Elfie down on a chair near the range.

Mrs Eddleston, the cook was already making a pot of tea for the girl.

Bringing it over, she raised the pot to the girl's lips. Elfie half opened her eyes and drank down a little of the tea.

The heat from the range and the warm drink seemed to revive her somewhat and she looked around with a dazed expression.

"Who is she sir, she looks so poorly where did you find her?"

Farrington did not answer the woman's enquiries. Instead he kept his eyes firmly on the girl seated on the chair.

"You're going to be alright my child," he said gently, " Your going to be alright, the doctor is on his way."

Chapter twenty-three

Elfie was sat up in bed, comfortably propped up on several feather pillows. A good fire burned away in the grate of the moderately ornate fireplace. The winter sun streamed in through the window, its brightness enhanced by the snow and formed a pool of light at the foot of the bed. The whole room had a cosy air, which was a new experience to the shepherd girl. After several weeks of illness she was now feeling much better and today was the first one sat up in her bed. She had been near unconscious for two weeks and it had been touch and go as to whether or not she would survive. The doctor had visited her on a daily basis and one of the servant girls had been assigned to watch over her every hour under the watchful eye of Mrs Riley.

The girl had been bed bathed, spoon-fed and cosseted in every way. The care and attention had paid off. Doctor Blaymire had declared that she was well on the road to a full recovery and that he now only needed to visit her if there were any problems or cause for concern.

Much speculation had taken place amongst the staff as to who the girl was and where she had come from. Some were of the opinion that she was a vagrant or gypsy girl that Jacob Farrington had found on his travels. Others thought that she was the daughter of one of the farm workers that he had taken pity on.

Suzie, the young girl assigned to care for her had tried to find out who she was but with little success as Elfie had been too ill to converse. When she did talk a little, Suzie was puzzled by how well she spoke, not the voice of a gypsy or farm worker.

Today, Elfie had improved dramatically wanting to sit up in bed and Suzie has assisted her and then gone off to tell Mrs Riley of the improvement in her condition. Shortly, Suzie returned with Mrs Riley and they entered the bedroom.

"See Mrs Riley, see, she's much better today," said the girl, excitedly.

Mrs Riley smiled at Elfie, "well, I must say, you are looking much better this morning."

Elfie gave the middle-aged woman a weak smile, "yes, I do feel a lot better and I am very grateful to you all for looking after me."

"Young Mr Farrington brought you here and instructed us to look after your every need, then he went away on business down to London. He didn't even tell us your name or where you came from."

Elfie looked a little dazed but then collected her senses.

"You say Mr Farrington's away, I need to see him. When will he be back?"

"It'll be another couple of weeks, he's expected back for Christmas."

"Is – is it nearly Christmas," replied Elfie in an astonished tone.

"It is my dear, you've been very poorly for several weeks now."

Elfie looked at her surroundings and then at the anxious faces of her carers.

"Do you know where Tess is?" enquired Elfie.

"Tess – who's Tess? replied Mrs Riley, somewhat puzzled by the question.

"She's my sheepdog."

"Just a minute, -yes, Will the stable boy is looking after a collie dog, that'll be her I reckon. Came at the same time as yourself, and came in my kitchen as well, she did."

Elfie gave a sigh of relief, "Is she alright?"

"I expect so, Will's a good lad, and he'll look after her."

"How long have I been here?"

Mrs Riley smiled at the girl, having now spoken with her she too was of the opinion that Elfie was not from a working background.

"It's been several weeks now, we all thought that you were going to die, whatever happened to you?"

Elfie's recollection of the events leading up to her arrival at the manor were very hazy.

"I don't remember all that much really. I was out getting the sheep in up on the hill when I fell. Next thing I remember was waking up in a snow hole with the sheep."

Elfie went on to recall how she managed to escape from the snow hole and struggle back down to the croft. "After that I don't remember much at all."

"Lord above," exclaimed Mrs Riley.

Suzie, who had been listening to the tale, broke into the conversation.

"You say you was out with the sheep, what did you want to do that for?"

"Because that's what I do," replied Elfie somewhat indignantly. "I'm a shepherdess for Lord Farrington."

"Well I'm blowed," remarked Mrs Riley. "That explains why Mr Jacob brought you here and what's your name then?"

"Elfie – Elfrida really, but everybody calls me Elfie."

There was a silence for a moment as each took stock of the new information.

"I – I really need to go home – Mick will be wondering where I am."

"Who's Mick?" enquired Mrs Riley.

"He lives at the farm at the foot of the valley, he –" Her head fell back against the pillow.

"There now, you must rest, you've done enough talking for today. Suzie will go and get you some tea, but you're far too weak to be going anywhere just yet. "

The two women left the room, locking the door behind them.

After a couple of days Elfie had improved further. When Mrs Riley had made her morning visit she slipped out of bed, her legs felt very weak as she took her first tentative steps over to the window. Looking out, she could see in the distance a long area of rising ground culminating in a steep, pointed mountaintop with further high ground rising beyond. The girl felt sure that she was looking at Kidsty Pike with High Street rising beyond it, although she had never seen it from this angle. Looking down she noted that she was up on the third floor of the manor, below was a courtyard and stables. She could see one or two people walking about below, obviously stable hands.

Then, she saw a young lad come out of the building followed by a collie dog attached to a length of thin rope. Elfie's heart missed a beat, it was her beloved Tess. Frantically, she fumbled with the window catch in an effort to open it but it would not budge. Her hands slid down the glass in desperation, then the boy disappeared out of sight.

She carried on watching and then saw the boy return with the dog and go back into the stable again. At least I know where Tess is, she thought, perhaps he'd been taking her for a walk. Elfie left the window and went over to the bedroom door and turned the handle, it was locked.

Sitting back down on the bed she conceded that she was some kind of prisoner in the house. Was this what Farrington meant by coming to live at the manor – to make her a prisoner? Surely, he wouldn't do that – or would he?

Elfie lay down on the bed, a feeling of desperation sweeping over her. Thinking logically, she knew that she was too weak to go anywhere so the best plan would be to build up her strength over the coming weeks.

In a few more days Jacob Farrington would be home, then she resolved to see him and confront him over his intentions.

Elfie spent the following week in her room, reading books that she had persuaded Suzie to obtain for her from the library. She spent a lot of time at the window observing the goings on in the courtyard below. The girl noted that there was an increasing bustle as deliveries were made and more people seemed to be coming and going. Enquiring from Suzie about the activity she was informed that Christmas was almost upon the manor. Elfie took great comfort from regular sightings of Tess being taken for her morning walk with the stable lad.

It could be said that Elfie was a model patient, cooperating fully with Mrs Riley's requests to rest and eat well. This was paying dividends and she was getting stronger by the day. The housekeeper promised that as soon as Jacob Farrington returned she would speak with him and ask him to come and see her.

A few days later, Jacob was ushered into the room by Mrs Riley.

"See now, sir, how well she looks, she's getting better by the minute."

"Yes, I must say, it's an amazing transformation from the frail girl that I brought here some weeks ago."

Farrington turned to the housekeeper, "You can leave us now, Mrs Riley, I wish to speak with Miss Mason in private."

Mrs Riley looked somewhat nonplussed, remaining standing by the bedside.

"Go on woman, you heard what I said," cried Farrington in an abrupt tone.

Mrs Riley flashed him a cold look and quickly scurried out of the room, muttering to herself. Jacob sat down on the edge of the bed.

"You do realize that you were in a very bad way when I found you, a few more days and you would have surely died, you do know that?

The staff tell me that you said you had been trapped in a snow hole on the fells, is that true?"

"Yes, I was," the defiant attitude of their last encounter no longer evident.

"And how did that come about then?"

Elfie explained in detail the events that she could remember.

Jacob listened intently watching the expressions on her face with great interest. "That's quite remarkable, you were very lucky and even more so, that I found you."

"Yes, I am very grateful to you for saving my life."

"Then perhaps now, you realize that it is not a suitable place for a young girl like you to be on her own in winter, anything could happen and no-one would know would they?"

"I'm sure that I would be alright, it was just a freak accident, I want to get back to the valley as soon as I can."

"Well, you're certainly not well enough at present and I think you should reconsider what I proposed before."

He moved a little closer to her and took hold of her hand, giving it a gentle squeeze.

"You see, you could live here, a nice warm room, good food, and in return, some work around the manor."

He placed a hand under her chin and gently tilted her head back, he looked at her intently. The old thoughts raced through his mind, there was a wild charm about her, and now that she was here he must find a way of enticing her to stay.

She pulled her head away and looked directly into his eyes. She could see a warmth in them and there was an air of gentleness about him. But she was aware that his moods could change dramatically if things were not going his way and Elfie was sure that there was some underlying motive to his offer.

"I will think it over, sir."

"You must my dear, it's for your own good. It's Christmas next week, I shall be very busy, what with guests and shooting parties and the like, but I will come and see you as soon as it's all over. I will instruct Mrs Riley to see that you have everything that you need." Jacob rose to his feet. "And we will talk some more soon."

Elfie sat back against the pillow after he had left and let out a long sigh. She felt trapped, locked in a room and now Jacob was starting to pressurize her into a decision. If only she could get away, back to Mick, he would look after her. Perhaps, if she played along with the situation she would get stronger and then the opportunity to escape might arise.

The girl continued to improve over the coming days, she saw Jacob on several occasions from her window, but he did not visit her in her room. Most of the time he was in the company of other men or setting out on horseback.

On a couple of occasions she observed him in the company of a young lady whom she took to be his fiancé.

She asked Mrs Riley if she might have some clothes, instead of spending all her time in her night attire now that she was spending most of the day out of bed. Mrs Riley had duly obliged and sent Suzie to find some suitable clothing for the girl. Now dressed in a full skirt and white blouse elaborately trimmed with lace and a woollen jacket to complete the outfit, she felt quite the part in her room in the manor.

At least I've got some clothes, she thought, her mind now actively planning a means of escape. A few more days and she felt that she would be ready. She had asked if she might take a walk in the grounds but the request had been denied on the pretext that she was not yet well enough and also that it was very cold outside. Elfie felt sure that it was on the orders of Jacob Farrington that she was not allowed out.

Presently, Jacob came to see her again and as before, ordered the housekeeper out of the room. Elfie was seated by the fireside reading one of the books when he came in to her room.

He looked down at her for some time before he spoke. "I see that you are up and about and looking almost fully recovered."

"Yes, I am sir, I'm feeling so much better now."

"Good –good," he replied in an almost agitated tone. "Have you given your consideration to what we discussed the last time I was here?"

Elfie was silent for some time as if in contemplation, then she replied. "What kind of work did you have in mind for me sir?"

"Well, what about some work with the domestic staff?"

From her expression he could see that this was a non-starter, "or, perhaps in the dairy, eh?"

"What about the offer of shepherding you told me about earlier," she replied as if to give a commitment if the work was suitable?"

Although the suggestion was a vague idea in Jacob's mind, his expression did not portray this as he replied.

"Yes, that is quite possible, but first you ought to take on some light duties until you are really fit and well, don't you agree?"

"Then there's the flock in Fusedale, I really wanted to get back to them and see the lambing through," replied Elfie in a pleading tone.

"Oh, don't worry about them, I've given the work to the Jarrow's."

Elfie was aghast and the displeasure was clearly evident in her expression.

"What do you mean, are they taking them over?"

"Well, yes they are, you see, you were very ill, so I told the Jarrow's that you would be staying here at the manor from now on."

"But – you've no right to do that."

Jacob's tone hardened, "yes I have my dear, you were ill, not expected to live, clearly you couldn't carry on, so I had little choice."

Elfie rounded on him, "so, you are saying that I haven't any work in the dale anymore?"

Jacob hesitated, before he replied, "I had to do something, but listen, you have work here just as soon as you are well."

Elfie was incensed, and sprang up from the chair to face him full on. She glowered at him as if she was about to spit in his face.

Jacob took a firm hold on her arm.

"Now, now Miss Mason, don't get so angry, everything I did was with the best intentions, there is work for you here and you can have this room and –"

She interrupted him, "and be locked in all the time?"

"No, that was only until you were well again."

Jacob then pulled her towards him.

"You see Miss Mason, I am really very fond of you, I could make you very happy here and you would be well cared for."

She tried feebly to wrestle free from his grip but he was too strong for her. He bent forward and kissed her gently on her forehead.

"You see, anything could be yours."

He lowered his head and kissed her full her lips. She did not resist but stood there motionless. Their lips parted.

"There, you see, there's nothing to be afraid of, really there isn't."

She allowed him to kiss her again, this time more lingeringly. His arms wrapped around her and slid down to her waist.

There was a knock at the door. Quickly he released her and stepped back. The door opened and Mrs Riley entered the room.

"What is it woman?" he asked in an agitated tone.

"There's a man downstairs to see you, says it's urgent sir."

"Who is he?"

"He didn't give his name sir."

"Oh, very well, tell him I'll be there shortly."

Mrs Riley left the room giving Jacob a sideways stare.

"Right, Miss Mason, you seem to be coming round to my way of thinking, I shall see what I can arrange for you."

He left her, still shaking slightly and wondering what would he have done next had the housekeeper not intervened.

Jacob caught up with Mrs Riley as she descended the stairs.

"Who is this fellow, Mrs Riley?"

"I don't know sir, I've never set eyes on him before, but he said it was most important that he spoke to you, he's waiting in the kitchen."

"In the kitchen, what's he doing in there?"

"It was Mr Barker sir, he sent him there, he said he was a farmer, he's been there ever since till we found you."

Jacob hurried through to the kitchen to see a man sitting at the table with a mug of tea in front of him, he recognised the man immediately, it was Davy Jarrow.

"What do you want Mr Jarrow?" enquired Jacob in an abrupt voice.

Davy quickly came to his feet. "I'm sorry to trouble you sir, but since you came to see us about taking Mason's flock on, our Mick's disappeared, gone off like, he has."

"And you've come all this way just to tell me that?"

"Well, we're so worried about him and where he's gone like."

"So why should it concern me?" retorted Jacob somewhat impatiently.

"Well, with you telling us that Elfie Mason had come to live here, I was thinking he might have been here to see 'er and tell 'er where he was going. He were right upset like, stopped eating an' that. They were going to be wed next spring an' all."

Jacob's tone softened at seeing Davy's obvious distress.

"No Mr Jarrow, I don't think he's been here, you can ask the servants, er – Mrs Riley, has a young man been around enquiring about Miss Mason?"

"Well, now you mention it Mr Barker said a young fellow had been here asking about her last week."

"What did you tell him," interrupted Davy anxiously

"I didn't," replied the housekeeper curtly. "It was Mr Barker that spoke to him."

"Go and fetch Barker, Mrs Riley, lets get to the bottom of this."

There was a silence between the two men as they awaited the arrival of Barker. Presently, Mrs Riley returned accompanied by a dapper middle-aged man immaculate in his butler's outfit.

Farrington turned and addressed him.

"Barker, Mrs Riley tells me a young man was here enquiring about Miss Mason."

Barker stared at his feet momentarily as if looking for an answer.

"Yes, that's right sir, scruffy looking individual if you ask me."

"Well, what did you say to him, man?"

"He wanted to see that Miss Mason upstairs, I told him it was out of the question and sent him on his way."

"Did he say where he was going?" ventured Davy.

"No he just turned and left when I said he couldn't see her."

"There Mr Jarrow, that's the best we can do for you, I'm sorry we couldn't be more help to you," said Jacob in a condescending voice.

"Well thank you anyway," replied Davy touching his cap, "I'm sorry to have troubled you."

Mrs Riley ushered him out of the kitchen.

After Davy left Jacob turned to Barker.

"If the lad comes back, you make sure to send him away. He's not to see that girl, do you understand?"

"Certainly sir, I'll see to it if he turns up again."

Elfie had been drawing Suzie in to her confidence and they talked at length when she brought up her meals. The two off them were becoming friends, Elfie telling her about her life in Fusedale and Suzie telling her snippets of information and gossip about the goings on at the manor.

She was a pretty, rosy-cheeked girl, a little on the plump side but with a disposition that was eager to please. Elfie seriously considered as to whether or not she would become her ally and help her to escape, but she knew that she would need to develop the friendship much further before she broached the subject. Since Farrington's advances Elfie was also aware that she did not have much time left to effect a plan before he returned.

The following evening when Suzie took Elfie her dinner she told her about the man who had come to the manor looking for his son who was looking for Elfie.

"D' you see Miss," she babbled excitedly. "This man who's going to marry you came a looking for you."

The information had been gathered from her seat in the corner of the kitchen when she overheard the conversation. Now, when she relayed it to Elfie it all came out muddled.

Elfie grasped her arm, "You say that Mick has been here looking for me?"

"Ooh, I don't know anyone called Mick, no – wait a minute, that man mentioned a Mick."

"That's him, you say he came here, to the manor?"

"That's right, but Barker sent him on his way."

"Barker, who's Barker?"

"He's the butler, he's in charge, an' then this fellow came today, looking for him, er, - a Mr Jarrold."

"Jarrow," corrected Elfie, "And what did he say?"

"He said that after Mr Farrington had been to see him about his sheep he'd taken off and he wanted to know if he'd been here looking for you."

So it was true, mused Elfie, Jacob Farrington had given the sheep over to Davy Jarrow.

"Thank you Suzie and if you find out anything else you will tell me, won't you?"

"Oh, yes Miss," replied Suzie, anxious to please her newfound friend.

Elfie slept very little that night, tossing and turning restlessly in her bed. The moonlight beamed in through a chink in the curtains causing a light to dance about the room as it reflected in the mirror. The result gave an almost ghostlike aura to the bedroom.

The girl's mind switched between the various events of the day. She went through Farrington's advances and what he might do next. Davy Jarrow's visit to the manor and most worrying of all, Mick's efforts to try and see her and being turned away. Now it seemed that he had left his family and the farm and gone away somewhere on his own, but where to?

Her brain was in turmoil and each event kept visualizing itself and played in her head. When sleep did come it was fitful and each time she would wake up suddenly with either Farrington or Mick vividly in her mind. At first light she was up and dressed and prodding the embers of the fire in an attempt to rekindle the flames. The fire cooperated with her and soon she was able put on some more wood. Soon the flames brought a new warmth to the room as it started to burn the wood. She moved over to the window and looked out anxiously, all was quiet below in the courtyard except for the crowing of a cock somewhere in the distance.

Now she resolved to get away as soon as possible, but how? She half flung herself into the chair in desperation. How was she going to get away from this place? Breakfast arrived and went with little interest from the girl. The only comfort of the morning was seeing Tess being taken for a walk. How she longed to be with her dog again. To feel her soft, warm fur, the wetness of her tongue as she licked her hand.

The longing for her dog, to find out what had become of Mick and Jacob Farrington's seemingly encroaching attentions were now paramount in her thoughts. She paced about the room most of the day, deep in thought, hatching out a plan of escape.

That evening when Suzie unlocked the door and entered the bedroom to clear away the dishes from Elfie's evening meal she was taken aback as she could not see the girl in the room. She looked around the room in astonishment, where was she? Then suddenly, she could not see anything except a white blur.

Elfie had hidden behind the door and in one swift movement she had pulled a pillowcase over the servant's head and shoulders, pinning her arms to her sides. Suzie started to struggle and cry out but Elfie stifled the noise by cupping a hand over her mouth.

"Be quiet Suzie, I'm not going to hurt you."

Elfie removed her hand from the girl's mouth, she was quiet and stopped struggling. She then pulled her captive's arms behind her back and deftly tied her wrists together using a length of bed sheet she had torn up for the purpose. Next, she pulled the pillowcase off her head and at the same

time pushed her down into a sitting position on the edge of the bed.
Suzie's eyes where enormous as she stared at Elfie in startled surprise.

"W – what are you doing?" gasped Suzie.

"I'm getting out of here," replied Elfie. "Now, you must tell me, which is the quickest way downstairs and out into the courtyard without being seen?"

Suzie's jaw dropped wide open in a stunned silence.

"Come on Suzie," cried Elfie in an agitated voice, "you've got to help me. I'll repay you for helping me."

"But what if Mr Farrington finds out?"

"Don't be silly, who's going to tell him, you won't, it'll just look like it is, I tied you up."

Suzie gave Elfie a mischievous grin. "Can't say I blame you miss, locked in here like. You go along the passageway to the left an' you'll see a back stairway going down. Be careful when you get to the floor below, there might be folk about. Then go down again and you'll come to the hallway leading to the kitchen."

"Right, then what?" asked Elfie anxiously.

"The door at the end leads into the courtyard, but you mun be careful as you'll have t' get past kitchen door."

"You're a good girl Suzie, now I'm going to tie you to the bed post and put a gag on your mouth, then no-one will ever know that you told me anything."

Elfie quickly carried out the task, then gave Suzie a hug and kissed her cheek. "Thank you, I won't forget you," she whispered.

Then she slipped out of the door and looked anxiously along the passage and then headed in the direction of the stairs. Quickly, she descended to the floor bellow and cast her eyes up and down the corridor; there was no sign of anyone. Down she went again and reached the ground floor and looked along the hallway leading to the kitchen and the outside door, she could hear voices coming from the door leading into the kitchen. She ducked back into the stairwell as she saw two girls and the butler come out of the kitchen carrying trays of food. She froze in fear behind the door as they went past her. Would anyone else come out of the kitchen? She eased the door open again and looked up and down. She could not hear any sounds, so she tiptoed up to the kitchen door and peeped in. she could see the cook, Mrs Riley and another girl preparing something on the kitchen table, they had their backs to her. Mrs Riley half turned to look at the kitchen door and then turned back. "Where on earth has that girl Suzie got to, I'll have to go and look for her in a minute?" remarked Mrs Riley.

There was no time to waste, this was her only chance, swiftly, she crept past the kitchen door and along the hallway to the outside door. She looked cautiously through the glass pane in the door, she could not see anyone about. The door creaked open and then she was outside. It was dark which aided her cover as she headed towards the building where she knew Tess would be.

Reaching the door, she lifted the latch and pushed the door, it did not move. She sighed half in panic, half in exasperation. She tried again, this time putting her shoulder to the door, it gave way and she half stumbled inside. Elfie gasped out loudly at what she saw. There was the stable lad filling a dish of food for the dog. Tess saw her and ran over whimpering in excitement and jumping for joy. The lad stared in surprise.

"Who the 'eck are you?"

Elfie stared hard at him, then quick as a flash replied, "master's sent me to fetch the dog."

She turned and headed for the door.

"Hey, I've never seen you afore."

Elfie did not reply. She saw a coat hanging behind the door and grabbed it as she went past.

"Oi, that's m' coat," cried the indignant lad.

But before he could catch her she was through the door, pulling it closed behind her. She hung on to the sneck handle as the lad tugged at the door in an effort to wrench it open. Then she let go and the door opened suddenly, pulled by the lad, causing him to loose his footing and fall in a heap on the floor.

Elfie literally leapt over a low wall followed by the eager dog, together; they ran across a field and disappeared into the woodland on the other side. By the time the stable lad was back on his feet the girl and dog were out of sight.

Chapter twenty-four

The excited stable boy ran into the kitchen.

"A lass 'as been an' taken that dog and m' coat an' all."

"Calm down lad, what on earth are you talking about?"

"It's true, Mrs Riley, this lass came into barn an' took off w' m' coat an' that dog I were looking after, I'm telling you, she did."

"What was she like, this girl?" asked Mrs Riley in a puzzled voice.

"She'd long white hair, said master 'ad sent her t' get dog, I've never seen 'er afore."

"Oh no," exclaimed the housekeeper, realising what must have happened. She hurried off up to the room where Elfie had been kept. Gasping for breath she pushed the door open to find Suzie still gagged and tied to the bedpost.

"Oh my lord", she cried in alarm.

Quickly she untied the mumbling girl.

"How did this happen?" she demanded.

"Oh, Mrs Riley, she was hid behind the door an' jumped on me and tied me up, I couldn't stop her." The girl started to cry.

"Alright Suzie, alright, it's not your fault, but heaven knows what Mr Jacob will say when he finds out that she's gone. You go down to the kitchen and get y' self a drink and I'll go and find Mr Barker and tell him what's happened."

Barker was quite incredulous as the tale of events was relayed to him.

"You'll 'ave to tell his lordship, Mr Barker."

"No – no, his lordship doesn't know anything about the young woman being here. Mr Jacob made me promise not to inform his lordship about her."

Mrs Riley was somewhat taken aback by this revelation but did not question it.

"I'll have to find Mr Jacob and tell him, he'll be in a right rage when he finds out. Now you go back to the kitchen and tell the staff, not a word to be said for the time being."

Half an hour later, Jacob Farrington burst into the kitchen and glared angrily at the staff huddled around the kitchen table discussing the event.

"You lot were supposed to be looking after her," he growled angrily.

Mrs Riley wasn't frightened of Jacob, as she had had much to do with his upbringing.

"Now wait a minute, it's not our fault, she tied poor Suzie here to the bed and she set about young lad here as well, there wasn't much any of us could do."

Jacob stormed over to the stable boy, "which way did she go?" he demanded.

"I –I, er didn't see, sir, she were too quick."

"You useless boy, letting a girl get the better of you," scolded Jacob. "Now, go and saddle my horse up immediately, I'll have to go and find her and fetch her back. She's not well enough to be out," he added as an explanation for his anger and haste.

Elfie had rested up in the woods for a short while after the turmoil of the last hour. Tess just rested her head on her lap, so glad to be reunited with her mistress again. She licked the girl's hand and gazed up constantly at her face.

"There, there, Tessy girl, it's alright now, we've just got to find our way back home now, haven't we?"

From her study of the landscape from the bedroom window she had ascertained that she must be several miles away from Fusedale, possibly ten or twelve miles. Elfie had made out the long sprawl of the Highstreet range as it lead down to its terminus with Askham Moor. She estimated that she would need to travel in a northerly direction until she reached Askham Moor which she would then need to find her way across its large, featureless expanse. Hopefully she would reach the Roman Road crossing the moor and that would take her to the track leading down to Ullswater.

Sat resting in the woods she cast her eyes to the sky. It was a restless night with a strong southwesterly wind scurrying blackened storm clouds across the sky. These were interspersed with clear windows in the clouds when the stormy moon shone through and the stars were clearly visible.

The girl knew quite a lot about the stars from what her father had told her and during the breaks in the clouds she could easily discern the North Star.

And so she set off this time in a northerly direction, stumbling and twisting over the uneven woodland ground, dead bracken crunched under her feet and she constantly stopped to listen, terrified that someone might hear her. At times she thought that she was being followed and she repeatedly glanced behind her. She scolded herself for being foolish, no-one was following her yet, but they soon would be, she thought. Eventually, she reached the edge of the woodland and the fields beyond. Elfie climbed the field wall and reached a rough road on which she could make out wheel ruts. She reasoned that this was a track leading to Bampton and Askham. Then as the clouds scudded across the sky the moon and stars were blackened out and it started to rain, light at first and then a heavy downpour. She was glad that she had stolen the coat of the stable boy, at least she had some warmth and it kept her dry. Elfie hurried along the road with Tess eagerly trotting along side her mistress. She was anxious to put as much distance as possible between herself and the manor. She constantly looked back as she progressed along the road, half expecting to see some-one riding after her.

The rain eased off and the clouds broke up giving glimpses of the moon and stars. Thankful for the extra light to make way finding easier, she hurried onwards. The road seemed endless, flanked by fields and a scattering of houses. The ones nearest to the road emitted a cosy glow from the lights inside them. How she longed to be inside one, sat perhaps by a cosy fire. She considered knocking on one of the doors and seeking shelter for the night, but she decided against it. The best plan was to press on and get as far as she could before she was pursued.

Eventually, she came to a fork in the road; the left one seemed less used than the right, which appeared to dip off downhill. Now she was unsure which way to go. Then she spotted a guidepost next to the wall and stooped to read what it said. A carved hand on the left side had Pooley Bridge written under it and a similar one on the right side said Askham. Elfie studied for a moment and decided that the left road would lead her over Askham Moor. She thought that Askham itself was further east, but she was not totally sure. Pooley Bridge was at the end of Ullswater and so she took the left fork which was little more than a track. The ground rose at first and then opened out onto a vast expanse of heathery moorland. The track across, albeit narrow was quite clear and easy to follow, even when the moon was obscured.

After some time she reached a large standing stone, known locally as the copstone. Elfie sat down on the grass with her back to it looking back the way she had come, anxious to see if she was being followed, but it seemed that she was on her own. She felt weak after the physical effort of the last couple of hours. Although she was almost fully recovered from her illness, the confinement of being in the room at the manor had left her legs and body feeling weak. A few years ago she had crossed Askham Moor with her father en route to Askham village but the approach from Bampton was unfamiliar. She reasoned that the track that she was now on would meet up with the old Roman road that led up onto High Street. Then instead of going straightforward to Pooley Bridge she would be able to head off left and then down towards Howtown. Dale End farm was her objective.

The girl was anxious to see Davy Jarrow and find out what had happened to Mick. She wondered if he had come back. What could have been said to make him go away like that? Her heart sunk as she pondered the situation. What if she never saw him again?

Rising to her feet, she set off once more, anxious to complete her journey and reach the farm. Her feet and legs were wet from the slushy remains of the snow and the heavy showers. Her body shivered from the cold but moving again started to restore some of her body heat. On and on across the moor, when the rain showers came there was no shelter and it was a case of gritting her teeth and baring them out. The moon danced and dived behind the rain clouds. Then there was a long clear break in the clouds which cast much needed illumination onto the moor. Elfie was able to make out a broad track ascending on her left and rising then more steeply over higher ground. This has got to be the Roman road, she thought.

At this point she turned left and followed the rising track until she reached a large stone circle on her left. Elfie gave out a short, excited gasp.

"This has got to be the Cockpit," she said out loud. Tess gave an excited bark. She remembered her father pointing it out to her on that visit to Askham. He had related a grizzly tale of cocks fighting in the circle and wicked men putting wagers on the birds to win.

"We must turn off soon Tess."

The dog gave out another bark.

"Sh, we don't want anyone to hear us."

The track dipped and crossed a stream and then climbed up again. Soon they reached a track going off to the right. The girl and dog turned along this one and the ground started to fall away to the right with the track now going downhill. Then she could see it in the distance below, Ullswater, gleaming in the moonlight. Her heartbeat quickened, now she was alright, she had made it across the moor; she was on the last leg of the journey.

It was then that she heard the dreaded sound, distant at first, but becoming steadily louder and louder. It was the sound of a horse, galloping at great speed. Panic surged through he body as she turned to look behind her. Although there was nothing to be seen, the sound of hoof beats continued.

She felt a sudden bump to her back and shoulders; in turning to look back she had inadvertently walked into a wooden gate across the track. It was situated in the intake wall and was partly obscured by bushes and a clump of trees, which darkened the area. The girl fumbled with the rope, which tied the gate closed. Her fingers released it and she slipped through, the gate closed behind her under its own weight. A short distance from the gate she turned again to look behind her. Then she saw the horse and rider, silhouetted against the moon as the clouds rolled to one side. It was a fearsome sight; the noise grew louder by the second and the horse approached at a good speed.

Tess dropped to the ground, the hackles along her entire back fully raised. Elfie just stood there, rooted to the spot in a paralysis of fear. Suddenly, the clouds covered the moon, plunging the track into darkness and obscuring the view of the approaching horse and rider. Then, in the blackness, came the sickening sound of wood cracking and splintering as the horse hit the gate full on. Digging in its hooves as it screeched and scraped to a halt, stones and gravel were thrown up from the track as the animal, remaining upright stopped abruptly.

The rider was thrown off the horse over the shattered gate. Propelled through the air at an alarming rate before hitting the ground to the left of the track. The body hit a small rock outcrop as it landed with a terrifying sound of shattering bones. Then came an eerie silence, save for the horse which had extricated itself from the remains of the gate and now stood panting and frothing by the side of the track, seemingly none the worse for its encounter with the gate.

Elfie remained motionless as the events unfolded before her. The eerie silence continued to pervade her surroundings until the crumpled figure on the ground coughed and groaned loudly.

She ran over to the body lying there, distorted beyond the normal limits of the human frame. The girl looked down at the figure, a large gash in his head exuded blood, the eyes stared up at her with a desperate expression. It was Jacob Farrington.

Instantly, she was on her knees, cradling his head against her legs, trying to support and comfort him in any way that she could.

The twisted face looked up at hers.

"Why – why did you run away?" he croaked.

She did not answer him, but simply cradled his head gently now; the blood from his wounds ran down her arms and soaked into her dress.

His throat made awful gurgling sounds and his body convulsed from the pain in his back which was clearly broken from the shape of his body as it lay on the ground. In the dark wetness of the night she just knelt beside him, stroking his forehead in an effort to sooth him, she could do little else. Tears welled up inside her and ran down her cheeks profusely.

"I didn't want it to end this way," she sobbed.

His eyes brightened a little on hearing her voice.

"I could have looked after you, I think it was you I really wanted and loved," he said hoarsely. He gave an agonising groan.

"Sh –sh, rest now."

His hand reached up slowly and touched her face.

"Couldn't you have – have loved me?" he asked now in a quiet, failing voice.

Elfie gazed down at him through tear-filled eyes.

She leaned forward, close to his face now and gently kissed his bloodstained lips.

"Yes – yes, in another world, in another time, yes I probably could," she replied tenderly.

A half smile came to his lips, then his body convulsed violently almost twisting itself from her hold. His head slumped to one side, lolling loosely and uncontrolled. He was still now. The vibrant life and energy of the young man had ebbed away. Elfie continued to hold him for some time before releasing him and laying his head and shoulders gently on the ground. She stood up and looked down at the motionless figure of Jacob Farrington.

"No, no anything but this," she murmured.

The rain came on heavily and beat down on the two figures. Large drops fell on his face, washing away the blood and grit. Somehow he looked at peace with his world. Did he really love her? She would never know, but somehow, her final words had brought some peace to his soul as he departed the living world.

She stepped aside from the reality of her situation. Would anyone know why he really died or would it look like a simple riding accident? He was pursuing her, but was she in any way to blame for his death? She was never party to any of his actions and was simply trying to escape from his clutches. It would be hard to come to terms with the events of the night, but terrible as they were, she was not responsible for his death, yet would the Farrington's see it that way?

There was nothing more she could do at the scene of the accident and so with one final look back at Jacob's distorted body she set off again towards Dale End farm. As she approached the farmhouse a couple of dogs barked from somewhere in the depths of the farmyard, Tess responded with a warning growl. Everything was in darkness as its occupants slumbered in their cosy beds.

By now, Elfie was soaked to the skin from the rain, her hair a tousled, bedraggled mess. Her hands and face were dirty and her clothing was covered in bloodstains.

She knocked loudly on the farmhouse door. The hour was early and she was not heard. She waited and then banged the door loudly and then sank down in the doorway, sobbing in desperation.

It was some time before the door opened and Davy Jarrow peered out into the darkness. Then his eyes caught sight of the sodden figure huddled by the doorstep.

"Who the hell are you, what do you want?" he asked angrily. To Davy it looked like some vagrant had landed on his doorstep.

The girl got up and clung to him, sobbing loudly. He half pushed her away from him, and then he saw her face.

"My God it's – it's you Elfie, it's – yes it is you."

He took hold of her and half carried her inside the house and into the kitchen.

He shouted out at the foot of the stairs, "Mary, Mary, for Gods sake come down here quickly."

Davy sat the girl in a chair and lit a lamp. He riddled the embers of the fire and put on some wood, which quickly burned to give out some, much needed warmth.

Mary appeared at the kitchen door, not sure what all the commotion was all about. Her eyes fell on Elfie and she gasped out loudly.

"Oh my Lord, my poor child, whatever's 'appened to y'?"

Mary looked at the sodden, bloodstained clothing.

"'As someone attacked you, what on earth is it?"

Mary started to cry as she knelt down beside the girl. Looking up into her face, she took hold of both of her hands. "You poor dear, who's done this t' y'?"

Elfie looked at the kindly face and then up at the anxious face of Davy.

"I was running away," she sobbed and Jacob Farrington came looking for me. He – he's dead now."

"Dead?" said Mary and Davy simultaneously.

"Yes, he fell off his horse and now he's dead, I didn't want it to happen like this." She sobbed uncontrollably.

Mary stroked her head. "You're safe now – you're with us now."

"Oh Mrs Jarrow its been so awful these last few weeks, I was locked in a room at the manor."

"Locked in?" retorted Davy.

"Yes, but I managed to get away and then he came looking for me."

"Where is he now?" interrupted Davy.

"On the track down from Askham Moor, his horse hit a gate and threw him off and he fell onto some rocks." Elfie sobbed.

Mary held her tightly, "It's alright, m' dear, it's alright."

"Someone will 'ave t' tell his lordship, we'll 'av t' get word to him," said Davy in a solemn tone.

"In t' morning Davy, this child's more important now."

"Aye, an' I've lost a son on account of her," retorted Davy in an angry tone,

"You left 'im for yon Farrington an' now it's gone 'orribly wrong for 'you."

"Eh, don't you go starting that argument again," rebuked Mary.

Elfie released her self from Mary's hold and sat upright on the chair, she looked directly at Davy.

"No – no, it wasn't like that at all, I was ill and he took me back to the manor and I was too poorly to do anything, then he kept me locked in a room.

Mary interrupted," never mind all this now, lets get you into some dry clothing, Davy, get some tea made for her."

Mary ushered the girl upstairs to the bedroom, stripped off her wet clothing, cleaned her up and redressed her. She then put a blanket around her shoulders.

"It really wasn't like Mr Mason said."

"I know m' dearie, I believe y', but our Mick's gone an' 'es teken it 'ard 'e 'as, but when y' tell us the real tale I'm sure 'e'll understand."

The pair went back down the stairs to the warming kitchen and the three of them sat by the fire drinking tea as Elfie relayed the events of the last few weeks to them. Both Mary and Davy listened intently without interruption as Elfie recalled going out to fetch the ewes in when the snow came and how she awoke in a snow hole. She then went on to describe how she eventually escaped and got back down to the croft. The following events were very vague in her mind as she was so ill. But she could recall part of the journey on horse back to the manor and of seeing Mick on the way.

Elfie went into detail about her stay at the manor and how they kept her locked in her room. She knew about Davy's visit to the manor as this was relayed to her by Suzie the maid. She told them about her plans to escape when she was feeling stronger after Jacob had visited her.

She vividly described her flight from the manor and how Jacob Farrington met his death.

"I –I couldn't do anything for him, he just lay there groaning with blood pouring from his head." She started to cry again. "It was so awful, there was no-one to help. I just sat with him and tried to comfort him. It was horrible, I didn't want anything like this to happen and it seems like it was all my fault." She fell silent.

Mary reached out and took hold of her hands. "Y' did all y' could pet, but it's not your fault, 'e shouldn't 'av kept y' there agin y' will, should 'e, Davy?"

Davy shook his head, still trying to comprehend what had gone on.

"I know he was trying to help me, I would have died if he hadn't found me, but he was always trying to get me to go and work at the manor, he was up to something, but I don't know what."

"Aye, our Mick said that," replied Mary.

Davy had said nothing at all through the tale but now he spoke.

"I'm sorry lass, I were wrong about you."

"You weren't to know Mr Jarrow."

"No, but I shouldn't 'av thought it, trouble is, it won't bring our Mick back."

"And you've no idea where he's gone?" enquired Elfie.

"None at all, after 'e'd been over t' manor he just said 'e couldn't stop here any longer an' that 'e were going to seek work somewhere else. 'E did say 'e'd let us know, but we've never heard from 'im."

"It's many a week now," added Mary. "Davy's 'ad t' take on a couple of lads 't 'elp out an' with 'aving your flock an' all it's made it 'ard f' you 'asn't it?"

Davy nodded in agreement.

"So where's my sheep now?" enquired Elfie.

"We brought 'em down 'ere and penned 'em for time being, it were too much trailing up top of dale to em."

Elfie's thoughts went back to the vision of Jacob's crumpled body ling up on the hillside.

"What will you do about Mr Farrington?"

"We'll 'av to get word over t' manor, I'll send one of the lads over, 'e can tell 'em we found him up on track an' then it's up to them I suppose."

The three of then sat for some time discussing the events, then Mary asked, "what 'll y' do now m' dear, y' know y' welcome t' stay 'ere as long as y' want y' know."

"Thank you Mrs Mason, I don't suppose I can go back up there now, and anyway, I've nothing to do if my flocks down here. But I'll earn my keep until I get sorted out and decide what to do.

Davy suddenly stood up in a very abrupt manner.

"'Ere, hang on a minute, I've just remembered, he left the kitchen and returned a couple of minutes later brandishing a newspaper.

"It were in 'ere, Ned Walkinton give it me, he came across it a few weeks ago."

He rummaged through the pages. Although he was not a good reader, he could get the gist of things.

"Ere it is, you read it lass, he thrust the newspaper at her with his thumb clearly indicating a advert in the public notices.

John Mason - Farmer

If the kindred of John Mason late of Catrigg Farm near Settle in the county of Yorkshire who died on the twelfth day of November will send a satisfactory statement of their relationship either by letter or in person to Mr John Blackburn Solicitor of Settle Or Mr Jack Blow solicitor of Penrith. They may hear something to their advantage.

The deceased was fifty five years of age never married and was born in Blackburn he resided near Settle aforesaid for thirty years

His only known relative was his brother Robert Mason last know of in Cumberland

The girl read the words over and over again.

"Well, what is it lass, is it 'owt?" asked Mary impatiently.

"Yes – yes, John Mason was my father's older brother, I knew he had a farm somewhere in Yorkshire, but I've never seen him."

"So how d' y' know about 'im then, did y' father tell y' about 'im?"

"No, he told me very little about his past life. But when he died I found some diaries in a chest, which he kept locked. They told me everything about his former life. My father used to stay at his brother's farm when he was at boarding school in Giggleswick. After my mother died, my father went to work for his brother. I was only a little girl then so I don't remember much about it. Oh, you don't know how my mother and father ran away to get married do you?"

Again, Elfie related some of the story as Mary and Jacob listened intently.

"Then when his father found out about it all we had to leave the farm and that's how we ended up in Fusedale.

"Well I niver," remarked Mary, incredulously.

"I reckon y' need t' see yon solicitor as soon as possible," remarked Davy wisely. That fellow – your uncle like, well 'e might 'av left y' some money or something. Did the farm belong t' your uncle?"

"I think it belonged to his father, that's why he threatened to take it away from him if my father didn't leave, it's all very complicated, you see."

"Aye, sounds like it lass, but y' never know, y' might be in for something, or at least y' father was, an I s'ppose it passes down t' you if y' father's dead like, don't y' reckon, Mary?"

"Lord, don't be asking me, I've no such idea 'bout such things."

"I've got a bit of money of my own," said Elfie. "I've never told anyone but my father left me some in the chest, I was going to use it to start up when me and Mick got married."

"Now, Mick kept saying you had some plans," replied Mary, "but 'e couldn't see 'ow y' could afford to do 'em, now that explains it."

"Best thing is t' get all y' belongings and bring 'em down here an' then get y'self off to yon solicitor. But y' need t' get some sleep, you've 'ad a rough time on it. Go up and get a few hours and then we'll sort things out like," said Davy in a very caring tone.

"Aye, Mick's bed's empty, you go on up there," Mary added.

Elfie undressed and climbed into the bed. It felt good to be back at Dale End. The ordeal of the last few weeks was over, but relieved as she was her heart felt empty. She longed for Mick, perhaps she ought to go and look for him but she'd no idea where to start. Surely they'd hear from him in a while and then she could let him know all that had happened. The girl drifted off into a fitful sleep.

Chapter twenty-five

The following article appeared in the Penrith Journal.

On Friday last an inquest was held before Alfred Walker-Blades Esq. coroner for the Borough of Penrith and a highly respectable jury at Parkside House on the body of Jacob Farrington son of Lord Farrington and the late Lady Farrington of Thornthwaite Manor.

The body of the deceased was found on the track leading from Askham Moor to Howtown. It appeared from evidence at the scene that the aforesaid was thrown from his horse as it crashed into a gate across the track whilst riding in the very early hours of the morning. It is unclear as to why the deceased was out riding at this early hour as there were no other witnesses other than a stable boy who saddled up the horse. The stable boy did not know of the exact reason for the journey other than to say that Mr Farrington was going out to find someone. No other staff at the manor gave a reason for the journey.

Examination of the body revealed multiple injuries to the back and head.

The coroner summed up the evidence at length and commented on the folly of riding during the hours of darkness. The jury returned a verdict of death by misadventure.

Lord Farrington was made aware of the circumstances surrounding the death of his son Jacob. He was incensed to learn that the Mason girl had been retained in Fusedale despite his orders that she should be dismissed. His anger was compounded when it was revealed that Jacob had brought the girl back to the manor and installed her in one of the rooms in the west wing.

Much of his anger was vented on Barker and Mrs Riley. They both argued that they were following the instructions of Jacob Farrington. His lordship was embarrassed that his son had been trifling with a girl of the lower classes and so his instructions to his staff was to keep silent about the why's and wherefores of the ride across Askham Moor. So it was only the stable boy who 'put his foot in it' to some extent when interviewed by the constable. This action did much to absolve Elfie from any blame surrounding his death.

213

His lordship, in his grief and bitterness sent his agent to Fusedale to ensure that the girl was immediately evicted from the area. The agent found the croft empty and on making enquiries at Dale End Farm was informed that the girl had left the area to a destination unknown.

Several days before these events Elfie had travelled with Davy on the horse and cart to the head of Fusedale. She had taken what possessions she wanted and loaded them on the cart for storage at the farm.

The following day, not wishing to impinge on the hospitality of the Jarrow's, she hired Daniel Gray the carrier to take her to Pooley Bridge. There she took the coach to Penrith to visit the office of Jack Blow the solicitor.

The coach was quite impressive after the cart of Daniel Gray's. It was of the high built pattern drawn by four handsome, clean-limbed horses. Elfie took up her seat with the other occupants who seemed to eye her disdainfully. I'm not as well dressed as they are but I'm just as good as them, she thought. There was the usual bustle around the coach, loading it up and then the horn was sounded. The coachman tightened the reins and the journey began.

The coach climbed up the steady gradient from Pooley Bridge, passing little whitewashed cottages along the roadside. The winter sunshine lit up the fell tops and reflected them in the still waters of the lake. It was but a short journey of five or six miles before the outskirts of Penrith were reached.

Presently, the horn was sounded and the coachman reined in the panting steeds, bringing them to a halt at the edge of the market square. Elfie alighted from the coach and enquired of the coachman where she might find the offices of Blow's the solicitor.

Elfie was ushered into a rather dim upstairs room, which overlooked the main street of the town. A large desk was set at an angle in the corner and the walls were covered by bookcases containing books, files and papers and the like. The volume of papers extended onto the desk and behind the piles sat a small, bearded man with spectacles perched on the end of his rather large nose. He was busily working away and did not look up at the girl. Elfie coughed nervously and then the man looked up peering at her over the top of his spectacles.

"Yes, what is it?" he asked in an abrupt manner.

"I've come about this advert you placed in the journal." She handed over the page to the man who took it from her and read it very carefully then placed it on the desk before him.

"And who are you?"

"My name is Elfrida Mason, I'm the daughter of Robert Mason named in the advert, sir."

"Hm, I see," came the reply. "Can you prove who you are?"

"Yes sir, I can, I have my birth certificate here." She fumbled in her pocket and brought out the certificate, neatly folded and handed it to him.

Again, he read it carefully and then placed it on the desk in front of him. Then he got up and rummaged around in a pile of folders on a chair behind him, occasionally, he cursed as papers fell out on to the floor. Eventually, he found what he was looking for and sat at his desk again. Placing the folder in front of him, he took out some papers.

"Now, sit down, sit down then, he pointed to a leather chair as if now he had determined that she was of some importance. Elfie perched herself nervously on the edge of the chair.

"Now, Miss Mason, tell me about your circumstances.

The girl coughed nervously and then spoke, "I have lived in Fusedale most of my life with my father who was a shepherd for Lord Farrington. My father died last year and I have carried on with his work until recently.

"I see, and what about your mother?" Jack Blow enquired, peering at the papers before him.

"She died shortly after I was born."

"Right, things seem to be in order," said Mr Blow suddenly. "What I can tell you is that your father's brother, your uncle in fact, died last November and left the farm to your father. As your father is dead, which I will need to confirm, then it would seem that the estate will fall to you as next in line.

"But I thought that the farm belonged to their father," exclaimed Elfie.

"And how do you know that?"

"From diaries that my father left to me."

"Well it seems to me from the papers before me that your uncle inherited the farm upon his father's death some twelve years earlier. Of course, I do not have the full details, these are held by Blackburn's solicitors in Settle. I am only acting as their agent as this area is the last known residence of your, er late father whom it appears was the only known relative.

Elfie sat back in the big chair, taken aback by the information relayed to her. It was difficult to comprehend at first and then the realisation started to sink into her mind.

"Well, what do I do now?" she asked eagerly.

"I will write you a letter of introduction which you must take to the solicitors in Settle, they will then expedite the matter.

The pen scratched away noisily as Mr Blow wrote the introductory letter on his officially headed notepaper. Elfie looked around the room as he wrote and concluded how awful it would be to be confined to a room such as this each and every day. The letter completed, the writer placed it in an envelope and sealed it and then wrote the recipients name on the envelope.

He then thrust the letter at Elfie.

Taking it from him, she asked, "Can you tell me anything about the farm or the will,"

"No," came the abrupt reply, "as I said, I don't have the details, you'll find out when you go to see Blackburn's solicitors in Settle. Now, if there's nothing else I'll bid you good day."

Elfie felt somewhat intimidated by the sombre and abrupt methods of the man and thanking him, left his office as quickly as possible. Glad to be outside in the fresh air she took stock of her surroundings. It was market day and the town was bustling with people. Elfie wandered along the main street and around the market square, fascinated by the range of goods on display. She spent considerable time browsing and was particularly interested in the clothing, aware that what she was dressed in was well worn and had seen better days. Eventually she purchased a dress and a short jacket, though little different to what she already wore, the condition was much better. Perhaps, when I've inherited this farm or money or whatever, I might dress like a lady, she mused.

The bag of clothing tucked under her arm, she asked for directions to the railway station. The rather devious looking man that she asked offered to accompany her there.

"That won't be necessary," she replied curtly and hurriedly made off in the direction that he had indicated. At the station she made enquiries about trains to Settle.

"You can't get a train from here to Settle, Miss, well not directly," the man in the ticket office informed her.

"Oh, I thought that the railway ran down that way."

"Aye, the line goes that way, but not from here."

"So how do I get there then?"

The man in the ticket office thought for a moment and scratched the back of his head. "It's like this, Miss, either you take the train north to Carlisle and then change on to the Midland line. That goes down through Garsdale to Settle or you could take the train to Skipton and catch another train back to Settle. Either way it's a long way round. The best way for you would be to go by coach to Appleby and meet up with the train down from Carlisle."

Elfie looked puzzled from this outpouring of information.

"I've not done any travelling before, will I be able to get to Settle within the day?"

"Yes Miss, the coach from Penrith leaves at 10 am to meet the midday train at Appleby, so you should get to Settle by late afternoon. My advice would be to book a seat on the coach, otherwise it might be full."

"And can I do that here?"

"Not by me, you need to go to that little wooden building outside the station, you can book there."

Anxious to discover what was in store for her she booked a seat on the coach for the following day, and then she caught the coach back to Pooley Bridge. It was early evening before she arrived back at Dale End Farm.

"Hello my dearie," came Mary's cheery greeting as she entered the kitchen.

"I were thinking y'd gotten lost out there, kettle's on 't boil if y' want a drink o' tea, supper 'll be 'alf an hour.

Elfie, deep in thought, made herself a pot of tea without speaking.

"Come on then lass, tell us what 'appened, what's it all about?" enquired Mary.

Andy appeared at the kitchen door and called out, "Liza, Elfie's back."

Shortly, Liza came into the kitchen and promptly sat down at the side of Elfie.

"Nay, don't you be sitting down, there's things t' do," scolded Mary.

"But I want to hear what Elfie's got to say," protested the young girl.

"Then y' can listen an' work, come on now, - now don't keep us guessing lass, tell us all about it."

"Well, I've been to see the solicitor and he told me that my uncle died and left his farm and everything to my father and seen as he's not alive it all falls to me as the next dependant.

"Well I never, where's farm, what's it like?" asked Mary, eagerly.

"It's near Settle, that's all I know, I've got to go and see a solicitor down there to get it all sorted out. When I was a little girl I lived there for a while before we came up here, but I can't remember much about it really."

"So, will you be rich then, Elfie?" asked Liza.

"I don't know, the man in Penrith didn't seem to know much about it, he said that he was just acting as an agent for the solicitor in Settle, so I'll just have to wait and see. But it's so exciting, I only wish Mick was here to share all this, it might be just what we were looking for to live in, I do wish I knew where he was, Mrs Jarrow," she said her voice almost faltering.

"So do I love, 'appen 'e'll turn up in a bit, but I'm right pleased about it for y' though, y' deserve summat better than what y've had, it'll 'av been 'ard f' y',"

Elfie smiled at Mary's words. "I'm going to go to Settle tomorrow. I can get a coach to Appleby and then the train down to Settle. I'll have to find somewhere to stay when I get there till it's all sorted out and then I'll be back to tell you all about it."

"Can I come and live with you, Elfie?" asked Liza, imploringly.

"You'll be able to come and stay for a while, but your place is here isn't it?" came the wise reply. "Come on, let's get supper ready before your father gets back."

Early the following day, Daniel Gray picked Elfie up from Dale End. He was going into Penrith and agreed to take the girl so that she could catch the coach to Appleby. It was a cold morning; a change in the weather had brought a thick frost to the area, decorating the trees and grasses in an adornment of shimmering silver.

They reached Penrith just in time, the Appleby coach was preparing to leave and Elfie was quickly ushered aboard and the coach set off. Elfie was able to take a seat next to the window. The route followed the line of the old Roman road passing Brougham Castle. A good pace was maintained on the well-maintained road. Reaching Temple Sowerby, the coach stopped to pick up a small group of people. It then followed the banks of the River Eden into the town of Appleby. The coach came to a halt at the bottom of the long sloping main street. Elfie obtained directions from the coachman and headed off in the direction of the railway station.

There was a fair amount of time before the train was due, so she found a seat on the platform. Opening her bag, she took out the lunch bag that Mary had packed up for her and tucked in hungrily. She was unsure when the next meal would be or even where she might be by early evening. Elfie did not know whether she would make it to the solicitors that day, then there was the problem of where to stay the night. Like the train journey, all this was a new experience to her. and she felt a bit scared. How she wished that Mick was about, he would have looked after her.

The train was an impressive sight as it rounded the bend into the station. People alighted and others boarded as the stationmaster paced up and down impatiently and porters slammed the doors shut. The compartment she boarded contained to elderly gentlemen puffing away at pipes and filling the carriage with a smoky haze. In the corner was a younger man with his face buried in a newspaper. Elfie took a seat opposite to him. The guard blew his whistle and waived his flag. The train pulled majestically out of the station.

It soon gained speed on the gentle downward gradient. The sound of steel rolling on steel and the sway of the carriages gave a relaxing air to the journey.

Elfie had never travelled south before and looked out of the window with great interest at the passing countryside. Kirkby Steven was soon reached and the train came to a halt. The two elderly gentlemen got off leaving just Elfie and the young man in the carriage. When the train set off again the man put down his newspaper and surveyed Elfie.

He was a good-looking young fellow probably aged around twenty-three. He had a fair complexion with light coloured brown hair. His eyes were blue in colour and seemed to have a mischievous twinkle about them. Elfie caught his eyes and turned shyly away, averting her eyes out of the window.

"I'm glad those two have got off, aren't you? The smell of those pipes was beginning to get on my chest, - do you mind if I open the window?"

Elfie shook her head. He reached over from his seat and released the strap which secured the window, lowering it about halfway. "There, that's better."

The fresh air entering the carriage brought in the earthy scent of the surrounding wild moorland as the train started the long climb up to Garsdale Head. The young man settled back into the corner and smiled at Elfie.

"I'm sorry, we haven't been introduced, my name is James, - James Irving, and you are?"

He was well spoken and clearly not from a working class background.

Elfie turned to look at him and couldn't help but warm to his smiling face.

"I'm called Elfie," she replied.

"That's an unusual name."

"It's Elfrida really, but everyone calls me Elfie."

"And where are you travelling to, might I ask?"

"I'm going down to Settle."

"That's a coincidence, so am I, do you live there?" enquired the young man.

"No, I live in Fusedale."

"Never heard of it, where's it near to?"

"Pooley Bridge."

"Never heard of that either, it must be a really small place."

"Oh, it is," replied Elfie, have you heard of Penrith?" He nodded. "Well, it's about twelve miles from there, in the middle of the mountains and lakes."

"Ah, Lakeland, Cumberland and Westmorland, I once went there when I was younger, with my parents, let me think. Yes Keswick it was called, very beautiful if I recall."

"It's all very beautiful," sighed Elfie.

"You've always lived there?"

"Yes, for most of my life."

"I bet you live on a farm, don't you?" he said, almost teasingly as he eyed up her clothing.

Elfie gave him a grin, "if you must know, I'm a shepherdess."

"Really," he replied in an interested tone. "So what brings you to Settle?"

"I've got some business to attend to," came the curt reply.

He chuckled. "So you're not going to confide in me, what is it, eh?"

"Bit nosy, aren't you," she replied cheekily. "Alright then, I've inherited a farm and I'm going to see the solicitor about it."

"Ah, I see, so you might be going to live down there, then?"

"I might, I don't know very much about it as yet, - anyway." She plucked up courage and asked, "What are you travelling to Settle for?"

"I'm going for an interview, I'm a teacher, you see."

The reply explained the good manners and well-spoken voice that she had been listening to.

He went on, "I teach geography and there is a post at Giggleswick School –"

"My father went there," she interrupted.

"Really," came the reply. That probably accounted for her well-spoken voice, her father must have been of some standing if he attended that school.

"So, where do you live now?"

"Carlisle, I teach at a school there, but Giggleswick is a better school, so I'm hoping I will get the job. My interview is tomorrow."

The train pulled into Garsdale station and after a halt to take on water it set off again on the descent towards Dent station.

The two of them chatted away. Elfie felt at ease with the young man and told him much about her life in Fusedale. A man and a woman boarded the train at Dent station and came and sat in the same carriage as Elfie and James.

The train pulled out of Dent and proceeded around the head of Dentdale before plunging into Blea Moor tunnel. There was no light in the carriage and an eerie silence befell the occupants, save for the sound of the wheels on the track and the whooshing sound of air. Eventually, the train bust forth from the tunnel into the bright air again and made its way across the spectacular Battye Moss viaduct situated at the foot of Whernside.

"Have you got anywhere to stay in Settle?" enquired James.

"No, I've never been before."

"Neither have I, but I'm sure there will be somewhere decent in the town, perhaps you would care to join me?"

Elfie hesitated at his suggestion.

He grinned at her, "It's alright, I'm perfectly harmless."

"Maybe, I'll see when I get there."

The train sped on through Horton in Ribblesdale and Elfie observed a mountain standing proudly alone. It seemed to rise up from the surrounding countryside like a crouching lion.

Noting her interest, James remarked, "not as big as your Lakeland mountains eh!"

"No, but it's very graceful, I wonder what it's called?"

"I believe it is called Penyghent, we're in the limestone area of Yorkshire now. You can see the silver grey of the crags and walls, that's limestone."

"Mm, it's very beautiful, not as barren as where I live."

Presently, the train pulled into Settle station.

"Settle, Settle," called the man on the platform. The two of them alighted from the train and walked the short distance into the market square.

"I've got to find this solicitors, it's supposed to be in the market square."

"What did you say it was called?"

"Blackburn's," replied Elfie.

"We're right outside it," said James, pointing to a brass plaque at the side of a door. "Shall I come with you?"

"No, there's no need to, really." As pleasant and genuine as he was, Elfie did not feel that she wanted him involved in her personal affairs.

"I apologize, I'm being too forward aren't I? I can wait outside for you and then we can look for some accommodation together."

His company for the evening would probably be alright, particularly as she had never stayed away on her own before, she consented to him waiting for her, then she went inside. She handed the letter of introduction to the clerk behind the desk who opened it and read it carefully.

He raised his hand, "one moment please."

The man disappeared through a door behind him and then returned a few minutes later. "Mr Blackburn can see you at 9-00am tomorrow morning."

"Oh, is it too late today then?"

"Indeed it is miss, we will be closing very shortly."

"Very well, I'll come back tomorrow. Can you recommend anywhere I can stay for the night?"

"The Talbot Arms in the main street is very good, they have several rooms and should be able to accommodate you."

"He can't see me until tomorrow," said Elfie in an annoyed tone of voice to the young man waiting outside for her. "But he says the Talbot Arms is a good place to stay."

"The Talbot Arms it is. A good meal and a bed for the night is what we both need, then tomorrow, you can inherit your farm and hopefully, I might get my new job."

Chapter twenty-six

Elfrida Mason sat nervously on the cane-backed chair outside the office of Mr Blackburn. Her mind was constantly portraying the events of the last few days before her. Now she hoped that the full picture of how she was to benefit from her late uncle's will would be revealed. She had no idea if it was a thriving farm or whether it was a run down affair or even where it was located.

The girl had enjoyed a pleasant evening in the Talbot Arms in the company of James Irving. He had proved to be a thoroughly pleasant and agreeable young man and seemed to take an interest in her. She felt that he was above her station in life but nonetheless this did not prevent him from socialising with her throughout the evening in a most enjoyable way. Elfie could not help thinking that he was the kind of person she could have got attached to if she hadn't met Mick. No mention of him was made during the course of their conversation. They took breakfast together and James enquired if he might see her again that evening to which she agreed.

The ornate, oak panelled door opened and a dapper, middle-aged man appeared.

"Miss Mason, would you please come in, er – do please take a seat," he waved an arm in the direction of a leather- bound chair on the other side of his desk. He opened a large file in front of him and smiled at her.

"I believe that Mr Blow in Penrith has verified that you are the daughter of the late Robert Mason, brother of the late John Mason, so we don't need to go through those formalities again. Now, you re the sole survivor of the Mason family line and it is as such that you inherit Catrigg Farm."

He shuffled through some papers in front of him, Elfie sat in silent anticipation.

"It is a considerable acquisition, comprising of a substantial farm house, two cottages and some eight hundred acres of grazing and moorland."

Elfie could not believe what she was hearing and sat there wide-eyed and open-mouthed.

"One of the cottages is occupied by a farm-worker and his wife and the other by a dairy-maid. There are some thirty or so dairy cows and approximately three hundred sheep, which I am given to understand, graze on the adjacent moorland. There are also two farm-workers employed on a temporary basis." Mr Blackburn sat back in his chair and surveyed the girl.

"Gracious, I'd no idea it was like that," she exclaimed at last.

"Yes, my dear, you are a very fortunate young lady, but do you know anything about farming, because you will need to if you intend to run it.

"Well, yes I know all about sheep, but not much about cattle and dairies and the like. I was a shepherdess in Cumberland until very recently."

"Ah, well that knowledge will stand you in good stead. Now, there is a lot of paperwork to formalise and sign which I can prepare within the day. What I propose is that you go out to the farm and have a look round, you may not want to get involved in the running of it, you may prefer to sell it instead."

"Oh, no, I wouldn't do that," she replied, quickly.

"Well, go and see it first, then come back and see me and we can finalise things. One way or the other, I have to transfer it into your name, and then it is up to you what you do with it. Now wait here a moment and I'll get Mr Foster to organise the transport to get you there, it's only about thirty minutes away from here.

Within fifteen minutes Elfie was seated beside a young man in a horse and trap and they set off along the main road out of Settle towards Stainforth. Shortly, they turned off the main road into Langcliffe village.

"It's a bit of a pull up this next bit, Miss," were the first words of the driver since leaving Settle.

The horse pulled the trap up a steep, winding road for some considerable distance before emerging on a plateau like expanse of moorland interspersed with numerous limestone rock outcrops.

"I think it's somewhere on here to the left," remarked the driver again.

Shortly a track came into view on the left and they turned down it towards a number of buildings in the distance. After a short distance the driver alighted and opened a gate leading into a walled lane and then they presently entered a farmyard.

"Here you are Miss, Catrigg Farm, now do you want me to wait for you or shall I come back later?"

Elfie was silent for a moment as she scanned the surroundings, there's probably a lot to see she thought.

"I think you'd best leave me here and come back mid afternoon. I've got to see Mr Blackburn again later on."

"Very well Miss, I'll be back in good time."

Elfie got down from the trap and stood in the farmyard taking in the surroundings, somehow there was a familiarity about it.

There was a large farmhouse, built in traditional dales fashion, with a large barn attached to it. Beyond that stood the two cottages that Mr Blackburn had mentioned. The whole area had a well-kept air about it and the external appearance of everything was clean and tidy. Much better than the Jarrow's farm noted Elfie, so someone obviously took a pride in the place. In the surrounding fields she could see numerous sheep, which were clearly approaching lambing.

She walked towards the first cottage of the two, which had its door slightly ajar. On the windowsills were wooden boxes containing snowdrops, which were just staring to flower. Things seemed to be much further on down here, she thought.

Elfie raised her arm hesitantly, then knocked on the door and called out "hello." There was no reply. She knocked again, harder this time and called out loudly, "hello, is there anyone in?"

Presently, a plump middle-aged woman appeared at the door, her hands covered in flour.

"I were just in the middle o' baking now."

She looked long and hard at Elfie. Similarly, Elfie looked at the face of the woman. It was a kindly face, twinkly eyes and well-weathered rosy cheeks; her grey hair was tied back in a bun. Elfie knew the face but before she could speak the woman leaned forward and grabbed her in her arms in an emotional embrace.

"Your Robert's daughter, aren't you?" She then held Elfie at arms length and gazed at her face. "Yes, as soon as I saw you I knew it were you. Tears started to stream down the rosy cheeks of the woman.

Then suddenly, Elfie knew, it was Mrs Hawkins, the woman who had looked after her when her father worked at the farm all those years ago.

The woman poked her head around the door in the direction of the barn.

"Edgar, Edgar, come here, it's Robert's daughter come back."

A tall man with a weather-beaten face came out of the barn towards them.

"What is it lass, what's up?"

"See Edgar, it's Robert's lass, remember, Ellie, no, Elfie?"

The man stood in front of her, pushing his cap to the back of his head he took a long look at her.

"Aye, reckon it is lass, it's them eyes I remember, what's it all about then?"

"Well, you probably won't believe it," replied Elfie in an excited voice, "but I've inherited this place in my uncle's will. I've just come from Blackburn's solicitors in Settle to take a look around."

"Well, I'm blown," said Edgar after a minute or two of stunned silence. "Is that kettle on lass? You've best come in an tell us all about it."

They went inside the little cottage and took up seats around an immaculately scrubbed kitchen table; Mrs Hawkins produced three mugs of steaming hot tea. The couple listened intently as Elfie explained the how she came to inherit the farm and a little about her background and life in Fusedale.

"I allus wondered what happened to you when you left 'ere, you were but a bairn really," remarked Nell.

"I can only vaguely remember being here, it was such a long time ago and I was only little.

Edgar sat quiet for some time, deep in thought, then he spoke. "What are you going to do miss, I hope you're not going to sell it up like?"

"No – no, I'm not, I'm going to come and live here, it's what I planned to do when we got married, I mean having a farm somewhere, now this has come up so unexpected. So now I am still going to do it, but it'll be on my own. I just hope I can meet up with Mick again," she added sadly.

"Anyway, I want to have a good look round," she said in a more positive tone. "Will you show me, Mr Hawkins?"

"Right, we'll go then, I expect you'll be sound enough with ewes and that, they're due to lamb in a few weeks. We'll be needing all the help we can get, then you see. It's been hard since master John died, an' I'm not as young as I were y' know." I'll show you round farmhouse first."

The farmhouse was a long building with mullioned windows. It was built in traditional style with a stone slate roof. Elfie noted the date over the door.

"It's very old," she remarked.

"Aye," replied Edgar. "Master John only lived in part of the house, some of the rooms haven't been used for many a year now.

"He never married then, my uncle?"

"No, reckon he never met anyone he really liked, he were only interested in farming, didn't socialise much, you see, but he were a grand chap."

They entered a large room from the through passage, there was a large inglenook fireplace at one end. The walls were painted blue with delicate stencils. An array of chairs and a low table were set in the room along with a number of rugs on the flagged floor.

"This were parlour, like," commented Edgar, "but it were hardly used, spent most of his time in kitchen, I'll show you."

Elfie followed Edgar into a large kitchen which was not unlike the one at Dale End. A large fireplace contained a hob grate consisting of bars and a grate fixed between two stone slabs. Kettles and pans hung over the empty fire grate suspended on a reckan crook. A large iron kail pot also hung over the grate. Elfie surveyed the room. There was a comfortable looking rocking chair, a large table and chairs and cupboards and shelves against the walls. It had a deserted air about it. They looked at a further two rooms downstairs which were mostly empty, save for a few odds and ends of furniture. An open staircase led to a landing with several doors leading off. All of these were empty save two which contained beds. The larger of the two contained a four poster bed which had a pleated alpaca canopy with fringe. A number of limestone pieces were suspended on cords from the posts. Elfie looked at these with a puzzled expression.

"What are these for?" she enquired.

"They're witch stones to keep away evil spirits," replied Edgar with a grin on his face. "Lots of people around here have 'em if they're suspicious like, don't hold with it myself."

Elfie went over to the window and took in the view of a solitary mountain.

"Is that Penyghent?"

"Aye, miss, but how do you know that?"

"Oh, a man on the train pointed it out to me on the way down."

The couple went back down the stairs.

"I'll show you the barn an' dairy next."

Elfie followed Edgar around the barn and then through into the dairy. This consisted of a room with stone shelves and a range of utensils and equipment for butter and cheese making.

"It's butter in winter and then when cows go out to grass we make cheese, we make that until about October.

"You have dairymaid, I believe," commented Elfie.

"Aye, Hannah, she's been here about two years now. She an' missus look after milking and that."

"And she lives next door to you, then?"

"She does, she used to do a bit in the house for master John, cleaning and such, she's a good lass. You do any dairy work were you come from?"

"No, just sheep, but I reckon I'll learn."

Edgar pushed his cap back on his head. "Well, as long as you're willing you'll be alright. There's a lot to do though, it's been hard since master John passed away, he took charge like and made sure everything were done right.

"Yes, I can see that by looking around, but I'm sure we will get things sorted."

"Well, I'll be honest with you miss, me an' your uncle worked well together, it weren't like a boss an' worker, we all worked together and that's how I hope it'll be if you take over."

"I'm sure it will be, Mr Hawkins, I've never had anyone work for me before, so it's all new to me and I'll need all your advice and knowledge."

The two of them walked back over to the cottage.

"We'll be putting the cows out in a bit, a couple of lads from village help out three or for days a week."

"Gosh, it's a long way for them to come."

"No, not really, they come up from Stainforth village, it's less than a mile away down through woods. You've come up from Langcliffe village."

"Ah – I didn't know there was another village further on."

"Oh, aye, an' then there's Horton."

"Horton – we came through there on the train."

Next they went into the mistle, the pungent smell of silage met Elfie's nostrils.

"There's thirty or so milkers, they go out early spring."

"So are they milked in here?"

"That's right miss, I'll show you the fields now."

They entered a field adjacent to the barn.

"There's around three hundred ewes, mostly Swaledales, most of 'em in fields now."

"Right, I had Herdwicks, they're quite a bit smaller then these but very hardy for the fells, you know," commented Elfie.

"Aye, well, these are tough old blighters, they'll stand up to most winters.

"So, how far does the land extend," asked Elfie, trying to comprehend all that was being shown to her.

"Well, lets see, it goes down to top o' crags and woodland to the west an' then over to Lancliffe Road where you came up. Then down to Cowside beck and across to Catrigg beck an' the force. An' there's a parcel of rough grazing at Overclose. Reckon it 'ad take you 'alf a day or more to walk round it all."

"It's unbelievable, but what's the force?"

"Oh' it's a big chasm where Catrigg Beck goes down, there's a lot o' that sort o' thing round here, it's the limestone, it lets water in like. One minute you've got a beck, next thing it's gone into the ground."

After the tour they went back to the cottage.

"You'll be having something to eat with us," exclaimed Mrs Hawkins on seeing the two of them return. "Y' know, I can't believe it after all this time, so what do you think of it all, are you going to live here?"

"It – it's just perfect, I can't believe it, I'll definitely be staying. But I've got to go back and see Mr Blackburn and then back up to Dale End to get my things and Tess, then I'll be back," said Elfie in a voice full of excitement.

"Who's Tess?" asked Edgar.

"She's my sheepdog, she's a real worker, really good."

"Well, we could do with one of them," said Edgar with a wry grin.

"Haven't you got any dogs here then?"

"Oh, aye, we've two of em, they're kennelled at back o' barn."

"Right, I didn't see them when we went round," said Elfie.

"No, lad's taken 'em, gone up to check on ewes at Overclose, trying to train 'em. Young 'uns a bit daft with ewes."

"I'll probably be able to train them, I trained Tess and she's very good."

"Nay Miss, I reckon you'll not 'av much time to be training dogs once you get started here."

"You're probably right," she replied, philosophically.

There was the sound of a horse clattering into the farmyard.

"Oh, that's probably the man to take me back to Settle."

She went to the door and looked out. "Yes it is, I'll have to be getting back. It's been so exciting coming here and seeing everything, I'm sure I'm going to love it here, I can't wait to come back, really, I can't believe it's all happening to me of all people – really I can't."

She hugged Nell and then Edgar who looked taken aback. "I'm sure we'll all get along just fine and thank you so much for showing me round."

The horse and trap drew out of the farmyard with Elfie waving cheerily at the Hawkins couple standing in the farmyard.

Back at the solicitors, Elfie signed all the documents that had been prepared.

"So, you'll be coming to live down here?"

"Yes I will Mr Blackburn, it's a lovely place, and I can't wait to get started."

"Well, everything seems to be in order. Now, do you want us to keep the deeds here for safekeeping?"

"Well, yes, if that's best."

"Very good, now if you come back and see me in about a weeks time I will have got everything transferred over to you. I need to write to the bank and then of course you will need to go and see the manager there as well."

"The bank?" exclaimed Elfie, somewhat surprised.

"Yes, there's a tidy sum of money as well, didn't I mention it?"

"You probably did, it's just, oh there's so much to take in."

"That's alright, Miss Mason, you come back in a week and then we can finalise everything."

"Yes, I will and thank you very much Mr Blackburn, you've been very kind."

"No at all my dear, that's what we are here for."

Elfie left Blackburn's and went out into the village square. It was still quite busy despite the afternoon drawing to a close. I'm sure I'm going to like it here, but I wish I knew where Mick was, I do so need you, she thought to herself. She was looking in the window of one of the shops when she felt a gentle hand on her shoulder. She turned to see James's smiling face.

"How did you get on?"

"Oh, marvellous, it's a big farm, hundreds of sheep and dairy cattle as well. There's a big farmhouse, and, can you believe it, the woman who looked after me when I was a baby still lives there?"

"Yes, I can believe you, I'm so pleased for you."

"What about you, James did you get the job?" she asked eagerly.

"Yes – yes I did, I'm so thrilled."

"Oh, James, that's wonderful." She gave him a big hug.

"Hey, steady on."

"I'm sorry, it's just – well, everything's so exciting, it's the best day I've had for a long time now. When do you start at the school?"

"In two weeks time, I'm going home tomorrow and then I shall come back the following week."

Elfie thought for a moment. "You'll have to find somewhere to live then?"

"No, I get accommodation at the school."

"Really, so you're all sorted out then?"

"That's right, I've just got to bring my things down, but what about you?"

"Well, I'm going back to Fusedale tomorrow, to sort things out, then I shall be coming back as soon as I can, probably early next week, I've to see the solicitor again that week and then I'll be moving in and become a farmer I suppose."

"That's brilliant, you'll be staying the night at the Talbot then?"

"Yes"

"You'll join me then?"

"If that's what you really want me to do."

"Yes, I do, I'd like it very much."

The excited couple headed off in the direction of the Talbot Arms.

The next day James and Elfie boarded the morning train at Settle station for their journeys back to Appleby and Carlisle.

Again, they had enjoyed a pleasant evening together and had talked at length about their futures. Elfie felt comfortable in the company of James and enjoyed the attention that he paid to her. He was courteous and considerate and far more of a gentleman of manners than ever Mick was. She was aware that he was developing more than a passing interest in her but could not understand why a person of his intellectual background should take pleasure in her company. When she thought about it Jacob Farrington had taken a similar interest albeit in a different manner and as she discovered with an ulterior motive. She shuddered as she recollected those thoughts.

Elfie warmed to James but felt she needed to keep her guard up to prevent the reoccurrence of a situation similar to the one she had escaped from. Elfie reasoned to herself that James couldn't really have the same motives as Jacob Farrington, but to make her situation clear she told him about her relationship with Mick on the journey home.

"So you see, we were to be married this spring but he took off without telling anyone were he was going and all because he thought I'd gone off to live with Jacob Farrington at Thornthwaite manor."

This revelation threw James Irving. He clearly felt that he was in the process of developing a friendship with her. Like others, he saw the simple beauty in the girl and now that she had inherited a substantial property her social status would rise accordingly, something that would have been a concern of his parents. Now, his plans to meet up with her again when they were both living in Settle seemed to have been dashed. Although he had only known her a few days he had become captivated by her simple charm and honesty and of course by those beautiful eyes.

"Have you made any enquiries as to his whereabouts?"

"No," came the sad reply, "I don't know where to start, he could be anywhere."

"You could try advertising for him in the newspapers, though I suppose it's difficult if you don't know whether he's gone north or south."

"I know, I'll just have to hope that he returns home, but how long that will be I just don't know."

"You can't wait for ever though, can you?"

"What do you mean?"

"Er, well, he might never come back and you would have spent your life waiting."

Elfie looked directly into the eyes of the young man sat opposite her.

"I love him James, really love him, so I'll just have to wait and hope that he eventually comes back."

There was a long silence between the two off them as they both stared out of the window watching the majestic grandeur of Swarth Fell and Wild Boar Fell passing by.

James was reflecting on his time spent with Elfie and the information which she had confided in him. At length he spoke. "I don't suppose we could still be friends could we, even if you are still waiting for Mick to comeback?"

Elfie concluded that any desires that the young man may have had on her had probably been crushed and yet, he still sought her friendship. She gave him a broad smile. "Yes, I'd like that, we must remain friends.

Perhaps when I've got settled in at the farm we could meet up "

James looked delighted. "You've only to send a note to me at Giggleswick School and it will find me. I would very much like to see you again."

"Then that's what we'll do."

The journey continued with the two off then chatting at length on a variety of subjects until the train finally steamed into Appleby Station.

"You will write to me, won't you?" he asked as she alighted from the carriage. "Otherwise I'll have to scour all the farms a round Settle until I find you."

"I promise I will, and thank you for your company."

She stood on the platform and watched the train pull slowly out of the station. James leaned out of the window and waved to her. Her hand went to her lips and she blew him the most gentle farewell kiss.

Elfie arrived back at Dale End Farm in the middle of the afternoon. Mary was busy sweeping outside the front entrance to the farm. She liked to keep things clean and tidy but despaired at the farmyard itself.

"I'm back," called out Elfie as she saw Mary.

"Eeh lass, I didn't see y' coming. I'm right glad to see y' back safe an' all. I allus worry when folk go travelling like, specially in them trains an' things. Come on inside an' tell us 'ow y' got on."

Elfie was buzzing with excitement as she followed Mary into the kitchen.

"Sit y' sen down lass an' I'll make some tea, y' mun be hungry after that journey, eh?"

"I am a bit," replied Elfie.

The words had barely left her mouth before a plate of scones and the butter pot appeared on the table.

"There, lass, summat t' push y' on till supper's ready."

Two pots of tea were quickly produced from the kettle which resided permanently on the hearth coals.

Mary drew up a chair, "Now lass, tell us all about it."

"Oh Mrs Jarrow, it's so exciting, but – is there any news of Mick?"

"Nay lass, we've heard nowt at all on him, I'm sure 'e'll be alright, but I'm a bit cross with 'im, going off like that an' not telling us where 'e is. We can only wait an' see, can't we?"

Elfie gave a vexed sigh. "I wish he'd come back, I really need him. This farm's so big; there are three hundred ewes, and thirty or so cows and a dairy. It's going to be a big job to run it all."

Elfie promptly lapsed into a full description of the events of the last few days, from her meeting with the solicitor, the visit to the farm and the return journey home. At length the tale was told but additional things were thrown in as they were recalled.

Elfie sat back on her chair. "So you see, it's just perfect, it's what I wanted for Mick and me, well at least to build up to. But it's here, now, I've even got some workers, though I may need some more when things get going properly. I haven't told anyone before, not even Mick, but my father left me some money in an old chest, enough to get started. Now my uncle's left me some as well, so I'm quite well off really."

"Well, I'm right glad f' y' lass, y' deserve it, but you saying y've got some money explains things."

"How do you mean, Mrs Jarrow?"

"Well, Mick were allus saying y' wanted t' do this an' that an' he allus worried about it y' see, - 'im not 'aving any money to do it – he used t' tell me like. Now that explains things."

"I was about to tell him so we could look for somewhere to live when we got married, then everything went terribly wrong. But it's all come good again except there's no Mick to share it with and I don't know where to find him. But I'm going to put some notices in the newspapers to see if I can track him down. I mean, that notice about my uncle found me, so maybe I can find Mick."

"Eh, I never thought o' doing that, lass, it's a good idea. So what d' y' plan t' do next?"

"Well, I've to go back next week to finalise everything and then I'll go and live at the farm. So I'll have to get my things together, what bits I've got and get them sent down there. You will come down and see it all Mrs Jarrow, won't you?"

"Eh lass, I don't know, it's a long way."

"No it's not," replied Elfie in a firm tone. "Anyway, you could come and stay a few days, oh, please, you must come."

The conversation was interrupted by the arrival home of Andy and Liza.

"Elfie, your back," cried Liza, rushing over to give her a hug.

A shortened version of the of the events was relayed to the two children who both sat there wide-eyed taking in every word.

"When can I come and see you?" asked Liza, excitedly.

"Perhaps in the summer after school, if it's alright with your mother," replied Elfie, at the same time looking at Mary for approval.

"Sounds like a good idea, get y' out 'o m' 'air for a bit," came Mary's cheery reply.

"Is supper ready yet?" Came a voice as Davy appeared at the kitchen door.

"Eh, lass, y' back," he remarked as his eyes fell on Elfie.

He pulled up a chair at the table and a mug of steaming tea was thrust in front of him.

"Go on lass, tell 'im all tale, - Liza, come on, lets get supper sorted."

The following day Elfie got her things together in preparation for sending down to Settle. She spent most of the day frittering about the farmhouse in a bit of a daze. Her mind tumbled ideas back and forth until she felt that she could not cope. How will I manage this, what about that? Things bombarded her brain constantly.

In an effort to escape her inner thoughts she went and fetched Tess and set off down the lane towards the village. She wandered on aimlessly with no real destination in mind but eventually found herself by the beck where she and Mick had first kissed on their return journey from the shepherds meet.

How well she remembered that moment, his naivety and nervousness and her reciprocal actions all made to make that moment so special. Now she felt totally alone but with an exciting and daunting task looming over her.

"If only – if only he'd come back, Tess," she said out loud. Tess wagged her tail and nuzzled against her hand.

"I know girl. Soon we'll be leaving here and you'll have your own farm and a lot of work to do, I hope you'll get on with the other dogs at the farm and teach them how to do things." Tess tilted her head from side to side as her mistress spoke, trying to understand what was being said. Then she leapt up and barked excitedly, she wanted to be off, there had been too much inactivity of late.

"Alright girl, we'll go." She turned and looked back at the beck, a tear rolled down her cheek as she set off back towards the farmhouse.

With her few possessions despatched to Settle all that remained was for her to travel back down to the Dales and this she intended to do on the coming Monday.

Before this there was last thing that she wanted to do, to say her own goodbye to the valley where she had spent most of her formative years. With that prime objective in mind she set off on the track up to the head of Fusedale.

It was a bright, clear day. There was still a good covering of snow on the fell tops and some deep pockets of white in parts of the valley. A fresh wind blew down from the fells bringing a chill to the air. Although the valley was still in its winter garb there was a promise of spring in the air. A few more weeks and it would be lambing time only this time it would be her own sheep that produced. An exciting and challenging time lay ahead.

Elfie crossed the beck above the farm and set off on the long steady climb up the valley. The track ran parallel with the beck for some considerable distance before turning away and climbing steeply to the flatter ground at the head of the valley. The girl thought of the number of times she had made this journey, initially in the company of her father but more recently and more frequently on her visits to the Jarrow's. In so many ways the valley had been good to her, but it had robbed her of the one person she truly loved and longed for.

Soon she passed the rock outcrop unaware that it had been Jacob Farrington's viewpoint and that many times he had secretly observed her.

"There we are Tess, our little house."

The dog barked excitedly and ran back and forth, perhaps now things were back to normal. They reached the place where Moss was buried and the two of them paused. Elfie knelt down and smoothed the grass around the mound. Already, the daffodils were pushing up thorough the ground.

"Soon you'll be beautiful again my lovely, only – I won' t be here to see them." Tears started to stream down her cheeks. "You'd have loved Catrigg, Moss, - if only" – Tess lay, her head resting on her paws. She knew that her best pal lay here.

"Mossy, my lovely friend," sobbed the girl. "One day we'll all be together again."

She stood up, "come on Tess."

They walked on to the croft which now had a cold, deserted air about it. There were still a few items of furniture remaining inside which she had no use for. They might be of some use to the next person to live here although she seriously wondered if anyone would. The ewes were all down at Dale End and although they would return to their heaf up here, they could be maintained from the farm. She looked around her for the last time then went back outside closing the door firmly behind her.

In some ways her heart felt heavy and tinged with regret, but the prospect of Catrigg Farm far outweighed her feelings of melancholy. She headed around the top of the valley and up towards Pikeawassa, here on the flanks of this pretty little fell she picked up the track down into Martindale. As she descended into the valley she could see the little church of St Martins below and this was her next destination. The path followed a long rake down the fell side before plunging into a sea of bracken, which fortunately for the walker had died down for the winter and so did not impede progress.

Reaching the church she lifted the latch on the gate in the wall surrounding the graveyard and made her way to the place where her father lay. She stood for some time staring at the grave where he had been buried the year previously. Time had passed and healed her sorrow, but again, tears ran down her cheeks and a lump came to her throat as she softly spoke. "I'm leaving here father and going to your brother's farm. I'm sure that you would be pleased for me if you knew – maybe you do. So much has happened to me since you died."

She stood a while longer, then whispered, "I love you father."

The girl then turned and walked to the entrance of the church, she paused a while in the porch uncertain whether to enter. The door creaked as she pushed it open and went inside.

In her life the girl had never aspired to any religious inclinations. At school she had learnt about God and read stories from the bible. Yet, in her day to say life she had never practiced any form of worship, indeed, her father's pantheist beliefs had probably dissuaded her. She was happy in the knowledge that some greater power had created the world in which she lived but did not see it as a god to be followed slavishly. The acts of nature, the seasons, the environment were her worldly gods. Unlike her father who had cast religion aside, she had never formed any strong beliefs.

And yet, sitting there in the little church she felt as if a presence was overlooking her. Was it her father's spirit or some deep telepathic communication from Mick? She was puzzled, but felt comforted. Somehow, she knew that things would work out, some unforeseen force was telling her. Whether or not it was some inner sense or some more powerful external force she did not know, but she left the church feeling reassured.

Elfrida Mason had made her final visit to the place where she had spent most of her life, she had visited her father's grave. Whether she would ever see them again she did not know, but it was time to move on.

Chapter twenty-seven

Tess almost bolted as the train, hissing and spitting water vapour from the cylinders and valves which drove the crank levers to the wheels pulled into Appleby Station. Fortunately, Elfie had been prudent enough to attach a length of light rope to the dog's neck and she was able to restrain her.

"There, there, it's alright, it won't harm you."

Tess was not so sure, she had never seen one of these steaming metal monsters before and so she stood cowering behind the girl. With great reluctance the dog boarded the train and immediately scuttled under the seat in the carriage.

"That dog's not used to a train," observed the man who entered the carriage immediately behind the girl.

"No, she's never seen one before."

"Going far, then?" enquired the man as he took his seat,

"Yes, I'm going down to Settle."

"You seeking work there then?" came the question; the man obviously assuming that she was some kind of farm worker from the attire, which she wore.

"Yes, you could say that," replied Elfie. This fellow is far too inquisitive she thought, so she decided to turn the tables on him.

"Might I enquire where you are travelling to, sir?"

"Aye, same as you, lass, to Settle. I've been visiting my sister in Dufton, you see.

"So, do you live in Settle, then?"

"That I do lass." He gave her a broad smile.

Elfie half returned the smile, perhaps he was alright after all, her suspicions were allayed somewhat.

"I own the grocer' shop in the square, don't often get away, keeps me busy you see. But chance came up so I went to see our Meg, my sister that is, er – you say you're going to work in Settle?"

"Well, sort of, I'm going to Catrigg Farm."

"Really, old John's place, knew him very well, he were a right gentleman, shame he died last year you know."

"Yes, well actually he was my uncle and I've inherited his farm."

"Well I'm blown, now, let me think, wait a minute, yes – you must be Robert Mason's daughter, lived at the farm for a bit afore he took off some where."

Elfie couldn't control her surprise. "But how do you know this," she enquired somewhat excitedly.

"Eh lass, there's not much I don't know about Settle folks, and their whereabouts and goings on. I've lived there all my life you see. So – you'll be getting your provisions from me then? John always did, we deliver as well you know."

"Really! Then why not."

"Elijah's the name, Elijah Hall and sons, you'll see name over top of shop in t' square."

"Right, Mr Hall, I'll look out for that, and I'm Elfrida Mason, I'm pleased to meet you." She offered her hand, which he politely shook.

The latest revelations explained the inquisitiveness of the man. He was one who obviously knew everybody's business and if he couldn't find out he'd ask directly. Maybe he could be of use to her apart from supplying groceries.

"I don't suppose you've heard of a young man by the name of Mick Jarrow, have you?"

"Mick Jarrow, no, it doesn't ring a bell. Unusual name that, I'd remember it if I'd heard it. May I enquire who he is?"

"Yes, I was to be married to him, but due to some unfortunate circumstances he went away, I've not seen him since. I really do need to find him."

"And where's he from?"

"From Cumberland, like me, near Penrith."

"I see, well I can't say I've heard of him. But you can rest assured, I'll keep my eyes and ears open and ask around for you, if I hear anything, you'll be first to know."

"That's really kind of you, Mr Hall."

"Well, I've a lot of people coming into my shop and passers through and all. Someone may know of his whereabouts. Do you think he might be in Yorkshire?"

"I don't really know, he's a farmer so he might be looking for work around here, but then again, he might have gone north," she replied wistfully.

"As I say, I'll keep a lookout and if there's anything I can help you with, you've only to ask."

The train sped on and Elfie's mind went over the events of the last few days. She was very sad to be leaving Fusedale behind and it had been an emotional goodbye to the Jarrow's. Mary had hugged her for some time as she made to leave, not wanting to let her go.

"Y 'll be back t' see us – promise?" she said through the tears that rolled down her weathered red cheeks. "We think a lot about y', y're a good lass an' we're all going t' miss y'."

Elfie filled up. "Aw, Mrs Jarrow, you've been so good to me, I'll be back to see you first chance and I'll write and let you know how things are going on"

"Nay lass, tha knows I can't read much."

"Yes, but Liza can, she'll read it to you."

"Aye, you write then, and soon."

At length, Mary let go and Elfie turned towards Davy. "And thank you Mr Jarrow, I hope I haven't been too much trouble to you."

"No lass, y're alright." He gave her a brief cuddle, unusual for Davy as he rarely showed any emotion. "Take care of y' sen and good luck."

"Now where's that lass if she' going t' village wi ' y' – Liza," Mary called out loud.

Liza raced down the stairs, "I'm ready."

"Come on you lot, I've work to do," cried Daniel from the seat of the cart waiting in the farmyard.

The two girls hastily climbed aboard, laughing and giggling as the cart set off.

"I wish I was coming with you instead of going to school, I don't like school really."

"Well you ought to, Liza, the more you learn the better your life will be."

"Hm, suppose you're right, but I still wish I were going with you."

"Well, when summer comes you can come and stay, I said so, as long as it's alright with your mother and father."

The train worked hard as it attained the summit of Aisgill before the descent down into Dentdale. It plunged into the darkness of Blea Moor tunnel before finally emerging into the daylight near Battye Moss and the graceful viaduct. On it went in an urgent manner until it finally steamed in to Settle Station.

Elfie walked through the town accompanied by Elijah until they reached the square and his shop.

"There you are lass, now you know where to find me, and I'll keep my ears open." He gave her a wink and bid her good day.

"And you, Mr Hall," she reciprocated.

Elfie went to the solicitors a few doors away and completed the transaction of the farm into her name. Returning outside, she untied Tess from the railings. "Now, lets see if we can get a lift up to the farm, otherwise it's a long walk."

Tess replied with a short, excited bark.

After some exhaustive enquiries she eventually found the young man who had previously taken her up to the farm. He was duly hired and the girl and dog were soon on their way to Catrigg Farm.

The steep climb out of Lancliffe completed, the cart and occupants reached the high limestone area above Winskill Stones and Catrigg Farm came in to view, nestling in a slight hollow in the extensive moorland.

Elfie's heart started to beat rapidly, partly through excitement and also apprehension about the daunting task that lay ahead. At last the farm is mine, how it goes is up to me, I'm not answerable to anyone now, she reasoned to herself.

"See Tess, that's where we're to live." The dog gave an excited bark seeming to understand every word that her mistress said to her. She jumped up and licked her face. "Steady on girl, I know you'll like it here."

The young man turned the cart off the road and down onto the track leading to the farm. Elfie was quickly off the cart as it stopped in the farmyard with Tess eagerly following. She thanked the young man and paid him for the journey. Then she stood in the farmyard, looking around, her hands clasped to her chest in excitement.

A figure appeared at the door of the cottage next to the farmhouse.

"Why miss, you're back already, y' things only arrived yesterday."

Elfie ran over to Mrs Hawkins, throwing her arms around her neck.

"Oh Mrs Hawkins, I'm so pleased to see you again, everything's sorted out now so I'm here to stay."

"Well I'm fair pleased to hear that miss, now let me make you a nice cup of tea, you must be worn out after your journey down here."

Elfie followed Mrs Hawkins into the kitchen and seated herself at the immaculately scrubbed kitchen table. Soon a pot of tea was in front of her and a plate of oatcakes.

"There now, I'm so pleased to see you again. I've put your things in the house and the bed's made up an' all."

"That's very kind of you Mrs Hawkins."

"Nay, it's least I can do miss, an' I've given everything a good clean, it's all ready for you now."

The two of then chatted a way for some time, then a face appeared at the door. "Any tea going, lass?"

"Aye, look who's here Edgar."

Edgar turned and caught sight of Elfie sat at the table.

"Eh, I'm sorry miss, I hadn't seen you there."

"No, y' too busy looking t' see if kettle's on or if there's owt going to eat," scolded Nell. "Tek y' muddy boots off and come in."

Edgar made his way to the table grinning at Elfie.

"Boots Edgar," shrieked Nell. "He comes in here caked in mud an' allsorts, make a right mess, he does."

Edgar sheepishly removed his boots and sat down at the table.

Nell placed a pot of tea in front of him.

"You got everything sorted out then miss?" enquired Edgar.

"Yes, everything's in order, I'm here to stay."

"That's good, it's coming up to a busy time now."

"Right, well what I'm planning to do is to work along side of you for a few days until I get the hang of things and particularly the dairy side. Then we'll have a meeting of every body who works here to talk about how we're going to run the farm. Does that sound alright?"

"Well, yes miss, it's your farm now, you do as you've a mind and we'll do as we're told," replied Edgar with a chuckle.

"No- no, I don't want to be going about telling everyone what to do, I've such a lot to learn from all of you. I want it so that we all work together and feel that we're all important to the running of things."

"Sounds fine to me miss," replied Edgar. Nell gave an approving nod.

"Good, that's settled then, I'll start first thing tomorrow. I need to get sorted out in the farmhouse and then we'll get going."

The three of them talked for some time before Elfie made her way to the farmhouse and went inside.

The girl stood for some time in the entrance passageway staring at the doors leading off both right and left and the flight of steps leading upwards.

She had difficulty grasping the reality of the situation and couldn't quite believe it was all happening. Could all this be hers or was she going to wake up from some dream? She pushed open the first door on the left, which led into the parlour. The room had a slightly musty smell about it and a damp feeling due to the lack of fires being lit on a regular basis.

"Well, Tess, this is a lovely room." She walked over and looked out of the window, which overlooked the farmyard and gazed at what she saw. She then turned and looked around the room again. The big arched fireplace on the adjacent wall exuded a cold but promising comfort. She ran her hand over the back of the studded, leather sofa and then sat down on it. It was so comfortable. She imagined herself on a cold winters night, a good fire burning in the grate and Tess beside her. Only one thing was missing to complete the vision. "Dearest Mick, how I wish you were here to share all this with me, I need you so much, please come to me," she whispered.

"Come on then Tess, let's explore." She rubbed the dog's ears. They went across to the room opposite and entered the kitchen. It had a flagged floor, immaculately clean. A fire burned in the range, giving the room cosy warmth so typical of a dales kitchen. There was a large table in the middle of the floor and a settle type seat adjacent to the hearth. A rocking chair was placed opposite. Cooking utensils hung on a rack above the fireplace and a kail pot stood on a stand in the earth. Elfie went to look in the cupboards; most were empty save for a few items of food, which Nell had placed there to put her on for the next day or two.

"Looks like we'll have to stock up with food, Tess."

On the back wall was a large dresser, which contained a large quantity of plates, dishes, cups and saucers and the like.

Hm, there's enough stuff here to serve a large family, what a pity it was never used, she thought.

She left the kitchen and went to look in the other two rooms at the far side of the house. Both were empty save for a few items of furniture. One had a large fireplace. Elfie went to look out of the window and gasped in amazement as she took in the view. She could see for miles and in the distance was a large flat-topped hill. Over to the right was a large whale back of a hill of great bulk.

"It's so beautiful, so much more gentle than Fusedale, but you'll love it Tessy. Come on, let's take a look upstairs."

The staircase led to a wide landing with four doors leading off from it. Two of the bedrooms were empty; the third contained a bed and some items of furniture. I could sort out this room for when Liza comes to stay, she'd love it here, was her thought. The fourth room contained the four-poster bed which she had seen on her previous visit. The bed was made up with the cover turned down at the corner. "Mrs Hawkins is such a dear," she said out loud.

She flopped down on to the bed. It was not as soft as she imagined it would be but was still far superior to anything she had slept in before. Elfie completed her tour of the house and returned downstairs to the kitchen. There came a knock at the door and a cheery voice called out "hello."

Elfie opened the door a broad smile enriching her face.

"I've brought you a few things across to keep you going, till y've time to get t' market. It's on Thursday y' know."

"Oh, thank you so much, Mrs Hawkins, you really are too good to me, getting everything ready in here for me as well."

"It's least I could do, specially since y're a relative o' Mr John. Might 'av been a bit different if y'd been a stranger buying place. But y're not, y're Roberts little girl to me, I looked after you then an' I'll look after y' now as well."

Elfie gave her a hug. "I know I'm going to be so happy here, it's like a dream. Best of all everything I do here, however hard it's going to be is for me, not for some wealthy landowner like it was back in Fusedale."

"Aye miss, I'm sure it'll all come good. It were happy enough with Mr John an' I'm sure it's going to stay the same now y've come here."

"Yes, but what about Mr Hawkins, do you think he'll mind having a woman in charge?"

Nell laughed out loud. "Nay he's used to that with me, it'll be no different, an' anyway, 'e'll do as I tell' him. So if y've any trouble you tell me an' I'll sort 'im out."

Elfie giggled at the thought of telling tales on Edgar to his wife.

"No, I wouldn't do that, it's best to be straight with people and sort things out there and then," replied Elfie.

"Aye, perhaps you're right, anyhow, I'll let you get on.

"Yes, and thank you again Mrs Hawkins."

"You must call me Nell, miss."

"Alright then –Nell, oh by the way, do you go into the market in Settle?"

"Sometimes Edgar takes the cart down when we've a need. He'll take you down this week, then y' can see for y'self what there is. Well, goodnight miss."

"Goodnight Mrs Hawkins – I mean Nell and thanks again."

Elfie was up early the following morning having spent a restless night in the new bed. Several times she had awakened with a jolt and sat upright in the bed, heart pounding until she realised where she was. The dawn chorus put paid to further sleep and she had lain in bed listening to it in fascination. It was an enchanting sound and something which did not exist at the barren end of Fusedale. She dressed and made her way downstairs to be greeted by Tess who had spent the night on a rug in the hallway.

"There, there, it's such a big house, were not used to it are we?" The dog jumped up and licked her face. Going in to the kitchen she felt the warmth from the fireplace even though the fire had gone out during the night. The early spring air had a distinct chill to it and there were pockets of ground frost. So to have some warmth in a house was a luxury for the shepherdess.

Elfie spent time cleaning out the fire grate and then relit it with the kindling and logs in the bucket at the side. It drew up very quickly and she was soon able to boil water for a pot of tea and a bowl of porridge, having found oats and salt in the cupboard.

She was sat at the kitchen table when a loud knock came at the door. She opened it to see Edgar stood there.

"Morning miss, I were just giving you an early call, didn't know if you'd be up yet or not."

"Come on in Mr Hawkins, or shall I call you Edgar?"

"Aye, Edgar 'll be fine miss."

"Would you like some tea? The pot's freshly made."

Edgar nodded, looking a bit taken aback.

"Sit yourself down then," she gestured towards the table.

"There you are," she said placing a large mug of tea in front of him.

"Now, what are we going to do first?" she enquired enthusiastically.

Edgar took a noisy sip of his tea. "We'll start in t' mistle miss. Lass and missus 'll be in there starting milking."

Edgar finished his tea and the two of them went outside.

"Right, this is main mistle an' then there's a smaller one round side like."

Going inside the long, low building, Elfie observed the rear ends of the cows. They were kept in pairs in a flagged area known as a boose. Each cow was tied by a cowband to an iron ring set in to the wall. Above the mistle was another floor containing hay. Each boose had a forking hole through which hay could be pushed down into a feeder above the cows. The whole area had an ordered air about it and was relatively very clean. At the far end of the mistle Elfie could see two figures, each sat on a milking stool or coppy as it was referred to locally. As they approached a cheery face looked up from the rear of the cow.

"Good morning Nell,"

"Good morning miss, did you have a comfortable night?"

"Comfortable, yes, but I didn't sleep too well, I didn't know you did the milking."

"Only some of it like. It gets me back sitting and bending for along time, but I give a hand as much as I can though Hannah does most on it."

A plump, rosy-cheeked girl of around seventeen came out from the next boose carrying a wooden pail full of milk.

This is Miss Mason – the new mistress, taken over from Mr John," said Nell.

"Hello Hannah, I'm pleased to meet you," said Elfie in a warm tone.

"An' you miss," came the reply.

"When I've got settled in you'll be able to teach me how to milk the cows."

"Well, yes, if you want me to," replied the dairymaid.

"Yes, I do, now, what do you do with the milk next?" asked Elfie in an enquiring voice.

"It goes in the back can over there ready for carrying round t' dairy."

"I see, so then you'll be able to show me how to make the cheese and butter as well."

The girl did not reply simply giving Elfie a puzzled look.

Elfie interpreted this as the girl not understanding why the mistress should want to get involved in such a menial task. Then she replied, "If I'm going to run this farm successfully I need to be able to do all the jobs that go on here. That way I can understand how things work, then anything I can do to make improvements I will, do you see?"

Hannah gave Elfie a half smile.

Elfie squeezed her shoulder, "I'll see you again later on." Turning to Edgar, she said, "what's next then?"

"We'll get the dogs and have a walk round the ewes, see how they're coming on."

The two dogs were kept in a kennel at the side of the mistal and barked excitedly as they were approached. Tess eyed the pair with some consternation, were these friends or foes?

Edgar let the two dogs out and they promptly ran over and inspected Tess.

"One 'ats nearly all black is Gemm, she's quite a good dog, T'others called Gael, master got 'er from over t' border, though I don't know why 'e bothered, she's daft as a brush with ewes like."

"Here Gemm, let's have look at you,"

The dog obeyed and came to Elfie, who bent down and fussed the dog.

"You're nice, aren't you?"

"Here, Gael," the dog ignored here. "Here Gael," said Elfie in an assertive voice. The dog reluctantly came to her, laid down and rolled on its back in a submissive act. "There, you'll be alright when we get you sorted out," she rubbed the dog's tummy.

Tess came over a jealous expression on her face, her lip curled up at one side as if to warn the young dog – she's mine.

"Now, Tess, you're going to have to get on with these two, It's not good three bitches together."

"They'll sort themselves out," said Edgar.

"Yes, I suppose they will, but I've a good idea who's going to be boss."

Edgar laughed, "aye, let's go an' have a look at them ewes."

They went through a gate into the field which contained about sixty ewes.

"These are early lambers so we've got them next t' house, reckon another three weeks an' they'll start. Mostly Swaledales with a few Rough Fell and Dalesbred in with 'em."

"What's the difference between then, how can you tell?"

"Well, Rough Fell, are slightly bigger than Swaledales an' have a much thicker fleece, they can live on next to nowt. Dalesbred have a bit longer fleece an' little white patches under t' eyes, y' see like yon un there."

"I see, so that one there's a Rough Fell, isn't it?"

"That's it miss, y' right."

The two of them progressed from the inbye to the open moorland, followed by the three dogs. Tess and Gemm followed obediently but because Gael kept darting about, Edgar had attached a length of rope to her to keep her in check. "Don't want her upsetting t' ewes," Edgar had said.

Presently, they dropped down the side of a hill towards a fast flowing beck, which disappeared into a small section of woodland.

"That's Catrigg Beck, where farm gets its name from. It goes in t' force an' then drops down into woods like. Appen it'll drop hundred foot or more. We 'av to keep fence in good order or we can loose ewes an' lambs down it.

The two of them made their way towards the force and peered over the edge.

"Ooh it looks terrifying," said Elfie, staring down into the moss-lined chasm that the silvery-white water plunged into.

"Aye, it is, especially if y' fell in, never get out alive," chuckled Edgar.

They followed the beck uphill for some considerable distance passing groups of ewes grazing thereabouts.

"Do they lamb up here?" enquired Elfie.

"Some do, but end of week we'll bring 'em down towards house, make it easy for us to keep an eye on."

"I see," said Elfie, making a mental note of the proceedings.

Finally, they reached a wide track, walled on either side. "This is road t' Malham an' upper boundary of y' land."

"Really, so how far does it go' left and right?"

"See that road over there by yon farmhouse." Elfie nodded. "Well that goes down t' Stainforth and that's the boundary to northeast.

They climbed up onto a hillock and Edgar pointed out various features.

"Over yonder in that dip is Cowside Road, y' came up it t' farm. Well that goes on t' join Malham Road. That's extent of land over there, but there's a parcel of land on t' other side o' road at Overclose. We graze it mainly in summer, but there's allus a few ewes on it."

"It's a big area, I can't believe its all mine."

"Aye it is Miss, y've got a lot on y' plate, but I'm sure y'll cope alright."

Elfie gave Edgar a brief smile. She knew it was an enormous task and she would need all her resources to make it all work. And yet, it was everything that she dreamed of for her and Mick, perhaps much bigger, but nonetheless, an exciting challenge.

"Most of it takes care of itself round here. Main part o' works around farmhouse." Edgar went on. " as you'll know, lambing and clipping are busy times and then they get on with themselves. But with cows it's constant all year round, see."

"That's with the dairywork and milking and that?"

"That's right, it doesn't ease off. Milkings a busy time, got to get it all done and then lass an' mrs get on with butter an' that. We could do with another in dairy, Nell's finding it hard. She's not as young as she was, y' know, all of us are really."

"So you're saying we need to get some more help then?"

"We do miss, we've been struggling to keep going since Mr John passed on."

"Then we'll have to sort things out as soon as I've got a good idea of what goes on. But I'll give a hand in the dairy to make things easier and I'll learn about it as well."

"Be a big help if y' did, miss."

They continued on eventually making their way back to the farmhouse.

"The fields below the house are mostly for hay," said Edgar, sweeping an arm in the general direction. "Then beyond them is the woods and that's extent of land there."

"Really," replied Elfie, "so there's a number of fields here as well."

"Aye, nine in all, four of 'em are big uns an' all."

It was approaching noon by the time the two had completed the walk around the farm.

"Thank you Edgar, it's going to take a while for me to get to know everything but you've been very helpful. It's so different from shepherding, what with cows and the dairy and things going to market. You and Mrs Hawkins have worked hard to keep things going and I shall see that you have things easier as soon as I can.

"Well, thank you miss, owt to make it a bit easier for these old bones would be welcome."

Edgar trundled off in the direction of his cottage whilst Elfie made her way to the dairy.

"Oh, y' back from y' trip round then, miss?" said Nell on seeing Elfie approach.

"Yes, we are, I'm amazed how big this farm is. How are you getting on in here?"

"Oh it's alright today, sometimes it goes well, sometimes it don't, depends on t' weather y' know."

Elfie went round to where Hannah was scraping out the cream from the separating bowl. These rested on a long stone shelf, which had a hole in it so that the skimmed milk could run off into a pail below.

Elfie stood watching the dairymaid for a few minutes. Conscious that she was being observed, the girl's face reddened up.

"How long have you worked here, Hannah?"

"Bout two years now, miss."

"Do you like what you do?"

"Yes miss, I like the milking best of all, it's easier than in the dairy."

"That's because y' sat down," joked Nell.

"No it aint," replied the girl, somewhat indignantly.

"Tell me, what do you do with the cream?"

"It goes into that churn, an then it's turned and turned until it forms butter, sometimes it takes all day if it goes t' sleep."

"What do you mean, if it goes to sleep Hannah?"

"That's when it won't come into butter, then we have to put warm milk with it and that's when it gets boring, just stood here turning."

"Right, then what do you do with it?"

"We clash it with us hands in a butter bowl to remove the buttermilk. Then we shape the butter into pounds, then its ready for market."

"Well, now I see, I've never done dairy work before. Mrs Hawkins tells me you did a few jobs in the farmhouse when my uncle was alive."

"Yes miss, I did a bit of cleaning and that, I like doing things like that."

"Well then, when you've finished here you can come over and help me.

There's quite a few things want doing and I need to move things round a bit, would you do that?"

"Oh, yes miss, I'd be glad to help."

"Good, that's settled then, you come over when you've done and then you can tell me all about dairy work. Then tomorrow, I'm going to work with you."

Hannah seemed to warm to Elfie and gave a wide smile in reply to her last remark.

Elfie left the two women and walked back to the farmhouse. It was quieter here. She gazed out of the window at the distant hills. Her head was buzzing with the morning's events and the scale of things. I've got to get some extra help, then we can do things better. If only Mick was here, he'd know what to do. Her thoughts drifted off to the ewes. "At least we know what we're doing with them, don't we girl?" her hand reached down and fondled the soft ears of Tess. "Yes, I think we'll be alright with them, the rest we'll just have to learn, won't we?"

Chapter twenty-eight

The month of March had been of a very wet and windy nature. There had been prolonged periods of heavy rain followed by squally showers as the month progressed. The ground was now thoroughly soaked, unable to absorb any further rain and easily churned up in to mud. The ewes has been gathered from the surrounding moorland and brought down into the fields adjacent to the farmyard in preparation for lambing. Life on the farm had settled into an orderly routine as Elfie's influence on everything steadily came into being.

A young girl has been hired to ease the workload in the dairy and enable Mrs Hawkins to have an easier existence. Hannah took great pride in teaching the new girl, Molly, the rudiments of dairy work.

Elfie had called a meeting of all the workers on the farm to outline her proposals. She was of the firm opinion that it was to be a partnership and that everyone should feel valued. To that end, she had given everyone a modest rise in wages with promises of further money as the farm became more efficient and successful.

Although she was no accountant, she has the ability to manage her finances and was confident that she had sufficient money to pay everyone appropriately. There was a steady income from the dairy and soon there would be further income from the sheep side through the sale of lambs, wool and the like. There was also her own money left by her father and a more substantial amount from her uncle's will.

With the money that she had accrued she could have enjoyed a relatively easy life without the need to work for a living. But this was not Elfrida Mason; she was driven by success, firstly by her moderate success in Fusedale and now on a grander scale as farmer and landowner.

Her coming to Catrigg Farm had lightened the workload of Edgar and he was truly grateful for that. The two lads, Danny and Ed worked well with Elfie and she thoroughly enjoyed the rapport and fun that had developed between them. They were reliable and worked hard for her and were more than willing to do anything to please her, particularly Ed, the older of the two.

The girl was well aware that he was attracted to her and whilst willing to tease him a little, she also ensured that he did not overstep the mark.

Since her arrival at the farm she had worked hard through all the daylight hours and often late into the evening keeping records of the farm and planning changes and improvements. She had not been away from the farm at all but planned to accompany Edgar to the market in Settle once lambing was over.

She had written to the Jarrow's telling them about how things were going and she had received a reply written by Liza. The letter was full of stories about what was going on at the foot of Fusedale. Reading it brought back a longing to be there and also a further sadness that there had been no information about the whereabouts of Mick. Liza said that she would be finishing school in the summer and enquired if she might come and stay for a while. Elfie had subsequently replied to say that she would be delighted to have her and would contact her nearer the time to make arrangements for her to travel down to Catrigg Farm.

Lambing was now in full swing and Elfie worked tirelessly with Edgar, Danny and Ed. It was easier work than in Fusedale in that the ewes were contained within the fields and accessible terrain. Although there were more ewes she was not working single handed as before. A sizeable proportion of the ewes produce twins, something uncommon with the mountain sheep of Lakeland. There were the usual difficulties with malpresentations and stillbirths but Elfie was able to demonstrate her prowess to the men when these problems arose. Edgar was heard to remark on a number of occasions that 'mistress knows what she's about with them ewes'. Her enthusiasm and skills rubbed off onto the two farm-workers who both eagerly assisted and developed their own shepherding skills.

Come the end of April all the ewes had produced and there were some fine lambs, growing stronger and steadier everyday. There had been some losses, a handful of lambs and a couple of ewes, but overall, Elfie was more than pleased with the outcome of the season. Now she had a good crop of lambs to further increase the size of the flock and she would be able to sell on the draught ewes at market to lowland farmers.

In May the cows were put out to grass in the fields and the ewes and their young returned to the moorland surrounding the farm.

"Mr John were allus pleased when cows went out t' grass," remarked Edgar.

Elfie looked enquiringly at Edgar. "Why was that, Edgar?"

"Well, y' see, when they're in field they gives off better milk which makes better cheese. We call it grass cheese, hay cheese is inclined t' be a bit tough."

"I didn't realise that there was a difference!"

"Oh, aye, an' after they've eaten the aftermath of the hay we call it fog cheese an' that tastes as different again."

"Really, I've just got so much to learn."

"Well, y've done well so far, miss, y've shown lads a thing or two about sheep y' knows. Cows will be calving soon an then y'll 'av summat else to learn then."

Edgar was right, the cows started producing that week albeit more intermittently than the ewes. Elfie was checking on some lambs when Dan came looking for her. "Edgar wants you, miss, says beds out but calf's not coming through."

Elfie followed the agitated lad back to the farm and into the barn where the cows due to calf were being kept.

"What is it Edgar, what's the trouble?"

"This un 'ere, miss, we're going to have t' 'elp it along. Thought you ought t' see it so's y'd know f' future like."

"Good idea Edgar, I've helped the ewes along but never a cow. What do we have to do?"

"We use this calving rope." He pointed to a length of rope which had two loops attached to a wooden pole.

"See, legs are through, but she's not pushing enough. We 'av t' get these loops around t' forelegs, as high as possible, otherwise we might pull its feet off."

Edgar took the rope and placed the loops around the exposed legs, making sure it was as high up as possible. "Now, Ed, you pull on that pole."

The lad strained at the pole whilst Edgar pushed around the rear of the cow.

"Bit 'arder, lad, give 'im a hand, Dan."

With the extra effort the head appeared, the cow bellowed and groaned loudly under the effort.

"Pull away steady, lads."

Within a couple of minutes of further effort, the body came through and the new calf slithered down onto the bed in the straw. Edgar immediately cleaned away around the newborn's mouth and nose to enable it to breath. The slimy creature took its first breath of air.

"She'll soon clean it up, y've got a fine bullock there I reckon," said Edgar.

"He's lovely," remarked Elfie in awe. "It's a lot harder than when a ewe is struggling."

"Right, you stay with 'er till cleansing comes away, don't want 'er eating it, some of 'em do," added Edgar, knowingly.

Elfie knelt down beside the calf which was already trying to stand up. "Nature is unbelievably wonderful, isn't it?"

"Aye. Miss, it is," replied Edgar, "and thanks lads, y've done well."

With lambing and calving over, Elfie, having some spare time so she accompanied Edgar on his trip to the market in Settle. The old cart rocked and bumped over the rough track, which led up to the narrow road to Langcliffe. The horse juddered and scraped as it descended the steep hill down into the village.

"I'm allus frightened it'll run away down here, but it never has."

"I hope it doesn't, we'd be killed if it crashed off the road."

"She's a good un, our Sal," said Edgar, nodding his head in the direction of the horse between the shafts. "She's a sturdy animal."

"I've never driven a horse and cart Edgar."

"Well, miss, y' can take reins on way back, it's easier up hill. There now we're nearly down,"

The horse and cart passed the church and went on through the village. Soon they were in the market place in Settle, and met up with the factor who bought most of their butter and cheese. Leaving Edgar to go for a well-earned drink before the return journey, Elfie wandered around the market square and eventually ended up in Elijah Hall's shop.

"Eh, lass, I'd been hoping you'd come in afore long. I've had a young man in here enquiring of your whereabouts," said Elijah, on seeing the girl in his shop. Elfie's heart raced at the announcement. "Who was it, what was he called?" she asked in an eager voice.

"Hang on a bit," he fumbled through some bits of paper stuffed in a cranny at the side of the cash-till.

"Was he called Mick?"

"Mick, don't think it was, wait a minute, ah here it is – yes – Irving, Mr James Irving."

"James Irving," repeated Elfie, rapidly trying to bring the name to mind. She had been so busy that she had practically forgotten about him.

"Oh, yes," she conceded in a disappointed voice. "He's a teacher at Giggleswick School, I remember him now. What did he want?"

"I don't rightly know, he was just enquiring after you. I told him you were up at Catrigg Farm. Was that alright, miss?"

"Oh, yes, he's alright, I met him on the train when I first came down here."

"Seems a right gentleman," commented Elijah.

"Yes, yes he's nice I suppose," she replied in a somewhat distant voice. If only the enquirer had been called Mick Jarrow, she thought inwardly.

"So, how are you getting along at your new farm, miss?"

"It's hard work, but we've just finished lambing and the cows have produced some fine calves, yes it's fine really."

"That Edgar's a good man, I've known him a long number of years, you can depend on him."

"Mn, yes," she replied, somewhat absent-mindedly, as she purchased a number of items.

"What shall I tell him if he comes in again?" Elijah asked, as she was about to leave.

Elfie thought for a moment, he was harmless enough she was sure. "You can tell him he's welcome to call at the farm if he's a mind to one day."

"Very well miss, good day to you and I hope to see you again soon."

"Yes – er thank you, now that lambings over and I've settled in I shall be back in Settle soon, good day to you, Mr Hall."

Elfie made her way back to where the horse and cart had been left. Edgar was waiting for her..

"You'd no need to rush back Edgar, you deserve a break after all that work."

"Nay, miss, I'm not a great drinker, don't mind an odd un, but not too much. Anyway, I'd be in trouble with Nell if I came 'ome worse for drink.

Elfie giggled impishly.

"Right then miss, you can take the cart back, I'll show you how to get on."

They climbed aboard and set off back on their journey to Catrigg Farm

It was a few days later and around midday, Elfie had just returned to the farm from checking on the ewes and their new lambs on the upper fields.

An excited Hannah greeted her. "There's been a right gentleman asking after you, miss," she exclaimed.

Elfie immediately put any thoughts of Mick to the back of her mind as 'gentleman' was not descriptive of him. "Did he leave his name, Hannah?"

"Yes miss, he were called James Irving, do you know 'im then?"

"Yes, I do, Hannah, he's a teacher at Giggleswick school."

Hannah giggled mischievously. "He's just someone I met on the train when I was coming down here. Did he say what he wanted?" Elfie enquired the obvious.

"No, miss, said 'e were going to look at force and called in on his way there."

"How long ago was this?"

"Only about half hour ago, miss."

"I'll have a walk over there and see if he's about," replied Elfie in a somewhat uninterested tone of voice. She set off in the direction of Catrigg Force.

So James had taken it upon himself to look her up, she couldn't help feeling a little pleased inside to the fact that he had taken an interest in her.

Heading down towards the beck she soon spotted a figure near the great cleft of rock that the water plunged in to. She covered the ground quickly and was behind him in a matter of minutes. He was obviously unaware of her presence, any sound being masked by the roar of the water cascading down the force.

"You be careful young man, folks have fallen down there afore today and never got out," she said in a deep, gruff voice. He startled and turned to face the speaker. He was even more shocked when he realised that it was not some irate farmer in fact but part of the object of his visit to the area.

"Good heavens, you made me jump." The startled expression changed to a warming smile.

"Serves you right, wandering about my land without asking."

"Do you own this waterfall?" he asked, rather incredulously.

She nodded, her face taking on a warm smile.

"It's an good geological example of a limestone gorge and how the water has cut away at the rock, you know."

"Really."

"Oh, yes, it's very deep and the stream disappears underground and emerges further down the valley, I called at your farm but the girl said you were out somewhere. So I thought I would have a walk down here and then call on my way back to see you. You don't mind, do you?"

"No, not at all, Elijah at the store in Settle said you had been in enquiring about me."

"That's right, that's how I found out where you were, you didn't write to me?"

"No, I didn't, I've just been so busy with lambing and everything else, I just never got around to it."

"Or didn't want to?" he questioned with an enquiring expression on his face.

"No, no it's nice to see you again, how are things going at your school?"

"Oh, it's fine now, I've got settled in to the routine, yes I'm enjoying it very much, and you with your farm, how is it?"

"Well, it's taking a lot of getting used to, there's such a lot to do and learn, but I'm getting in to it. There's so much going on, we've some three hundred or so new lambs and several calves to look after and then there's the dairy work as well," she replied somewhat excitedly. "If you've done here you can come back and have a look round."

The two headed back up towards the farm, chatting away about their experiences since their last time together on the return train journey north.

"Well I must say you've done very well for yourself," said James as he relaxed by the fire in the kitchen. "I can see now when you say that it's been a busy time."

"Mm, do you want another pot of tea?" replied Elfie.

"No, but thank you very much, you make delicious scones you know."

"I didn't make them, they're Nell's, she bakes all sorts of things, she's like a mother to me, don't know what I'd do without her really."

"You are very lucky to have her around."

"Yes I am, but I can cook," retorted Elfie as if to dismiss any views that it was something she was not capable of. "But not as good as Nell," she added.

"Maybe you'll have to show me sometime," said James with a twinkle in his eye.

"Are you inviting yourself to tea – cheeky beggar?"

"Only if you want to," came the reply, but I would like to see you again."

Elfie giggled, "You're so polite, James, but yes you can, though you will have to earn it."

"I don't get it, what do you mean?" he enquired.

"Well, you could come and milk the cows, or help make cheese."

James looked a bit taken aback. "I've never milked a cow," he replied, a hint of nervousness in his voice.

Elfie burst into laughter, "Oh James, I'm only joking."

An expression of relief came over the young man's face. James got to his feet, "I must be getting back now."

Elfie walked to the gate of the farmyard with him.

"Shall we say a week on Sunday then?"

"Yes, that's fine."

"And get here early, we milk at seven o clock in the morning."

"You are a bit of a tease young lady, aren't you?" he grinned at her.

Elfie opened the gate for him, "you'll see, won't you when you come next time."

"I shall look forward to it."

"And I too," she replied.

She watched him as he set off up the lane from the farmhouse. He turned and gave her a wave, which she reciprocated, then she went back the farmhouse.

Later that evening she sat by the cosy warmth of the kitchen range and thought back over her time with James. He was so different to Mick, so polite and well mannered so positive and assured. If she was truthful to herself she had to admit that she was attracted to him. But still in her mind was Mick. And yet, it was some considerable time since she had seen him and she wondered if she would ever see him again. She still loved him of that she was certain, but for how long should she wait for him on a faint chance that he might show up again. For all she knew he might have found someone else by now, why should he think about her. In his eyes she had deserted him for Jacob Farrington, so logically, he was unlikely to be concerned about her anymore let alone seek her out. Her only hope was that he might return home and if he did they would tell him what really happened, then he might realise that he had got the wrong idea. She knew that she was clutching at straws and wondered whether she ought to let go of her hopes and perhaps take advantage of James's interest in her. She would have to see how things worked out. The thoughts continued to drift in and out of her mind as her head hit the pillow of her comfortable bed until finally she succumbed to sleep.

As the year progressed and with lambing and calving over the farm work settled into a routine. Hannah and her new assistant Molly worked well in the dairy and practically ran things themselves with occasional help from Nell who still liked to keep her hand in. This gave Elfie and Edgar time to maintain and improve things around the farm.

James had visited the farm on a number of occasions and wasn't averse to getting his sleeves rolled up and giving a hand. Indeed, he seemed to have a good grasp of how things worked and how improvements could be made. Elfie teased him saying that 'he would make a better farmer than a teacher.'

He countered this with the comment that it was his parents wish that he followed an academic occupation and that he had chosen geography because of his love of the countryside. James was happy to enjoy her company and friendship. He knew from conversations with her that she had not given up hope of finding Mick and that she still loved and wanted him. If that was how it was he was content to go along with it but he knew that he wanted more than just a friendship with her. Maybe, in time she would relinquish her love for Mick and perhaps turn to him, he could but play the waiting game. For her, she was glad of his company and enjoyed the attention he paid to her, which was never overbearing or in any way demanding. In some ways they became more like brother and sister, each knowing and accepting that there was a barrier to any further development at least for the time being.

It was one day near the end of May when Elfie accompanied Edgar into Settle to deliver some produce and collect some supplies. She called in at Elijah Hall's shop to purchase groceries and other items, which were running low.

"Ah, Miss Mason, good morning to you, I was hoping I'd see you afore so long." He paused.

"Oh, were you Mr Hall, why was that?"

"Well I've a bit of news for you, I were going to send up word to your farm if I didn't see you soon."

Elfie gave Elijah an enquiring look. "What is it, Mr Hall?"

"Right, well I were talking to a fellow from up Austwick way that I know and he were telling me he'd been helping with lambing at old man Mitchell's farm at Feizor. In the conversation he mentioned a lad called Mick who were working for old Mitchell and I wondered if it were same fellow as you knows, you see."

Elfie's heart pounded rapidly, "is he still there, where's Feizor, how long ago was this?" the questions came out in rapid fire.

"Now hang on a minute Miss, I'm not saying it's the same fellow, but it might be."

"Yes – yes, but where's Feizor? I must go and see."

"Aye, well it'll be about seven mile or so from here."

"Is it a big village?"

"Oh, no Miss, just a hamlet of two or three farms, that's all, Mitchell's is first one you come to."

"Well, thank you very much Mr Hall, I will go there right away and see if it's the same person," she replied excitedly.

Elfie made her purchases and hurried outside to find Edgar who was loading up the cart. As they returned to the farm she told him about the news from Mr Hall. "So you see, Edgar, I must go and find out if it's him. Do you know where it is?"

"I do Miss, it's a fair way round by road, but there's a bit of a track goes over from Stainforth by way of Smearsett Scar. Reckon it'll be two or three miles from here."

"Right, then I'll go over there first thing in the morning, I suppose it's a bit late to set off there today."

"Aye, it will be now, best thing to go in morning."

Elfie barely slept that night thinking about Mick and Mitchell's farm at Feizor. Would he still be working there? How would he react when he saw her? She tossed and turned in her bed anxious for morning to come. When it did she awoke bleary eyed but excited. She was quickly out of bed and dressed hurriedly, a quick breakfast and she was off before the sun had time to rise over the flanks of the distant Fountains Fell. Having got directions from Edgar, she set off to descend the path down through the woods to Stainforth. She slipped and slithered down the mossy path, twice falling and banging her arms and elbows. Tess barked excitedly. "Its alright for you with your four legs," she teased to the eager dog.

Soon she reached Stainforth which was only just awakening from its slumbers, no-one was about to witness the passing of the girl and her dog. On reaching the packhorse bridge over the River Ribble she paused and looked at the spot where the river plunged into Stainforth Force as it was known. I wonder if James has been and looked at that waterfall she thought to herself. James drifted through her thoughts, she had seen him on a number of occasions now and was developing a steady friendship with him. But now, Mick had emerged to the fore and she set off again on the track that led past Knight Stainforth Hall and over the high ground beneath the craggy limestone form of Smearsett Scar. Soon she could see a small hamlet in the valley below. That must be Feizor she thought.

She almost ran the last half mile down to the houses. Now which was Mitchell's farm? An elderly man stood leaning on a gate drawing on a pipe, which smoked heavily sending out a strong smell of tobacco into the morning air.

"Excuse me, sir, but could you tell me which is Mitchell's farm?" she enquired.

The man looked her up and down. " You seeking work, like?"

"No, I just need to see Mr Mitchell," she replied a little impatiently.

The man took a long draw on the pipe and blew out a haze of smoke, and then he pointed with the stem. "Second house on there." The pipe returned to his mouth.

"Thank you very much," she hurried off anxiously in the direction that he had pointed. The door to the farmhouse was open. Elfie knocked and called out "hello." Presently, a rather large woman wearing a bonnet and apron appeared at the door. She smiled at Elfie and said "what can I do f' you lass?"

"I – I was wanting to see a Mr Mitchell, does he live here?"

"Aye, he does lass, but 'e's in bed poorly like, were it urgent?"

"Well, yes it is really."

"Best come in an' sit down," she led the way to the kitchen. "Sit th' self down then.

Elfie pulled back a chair and took a seat. "Are you Mrs Mitchell then?"

"Aye, f' me sins I am, now perhaps I can 'elp you, Albert's too poorly to see anyone today."

"It's not serious, I hope, is it?" enquired Elfie in a sympathetic voice.

"No, 'e gets these headaches and dizzy do's, takes to 'is bed for a couple o' days and then 'e's right again. 'E's getting too old for this job really, but 'e won't give up." Elfie nodded as if in agreement. "Now, what is it lass?"

"Well, I'm enquiring about a man called Mick who I was told was working for you at lambing time."

The woman smiled. "Ah, yes, Mick, 'e were a right grand lad, 'e didn't half work hard, Albert were right pleased with 'im."

"Is he still here?" asked Elfie, in an anxious tone.

"No – no 'e isn't, left a few weeks ago when lambing were over."

"Oh, where did he go to, do you know?" the girl couldn't conceal her disappointment.

"Ee, I don't rightly know, were 'e a friend of yours, then?"

"Yes he was, that's if it's the same person, did you know his last name?"

"Nay, I can't just remember, wait a minute, no- it were an odd sounding name, er-"

"Jarrow, was it Jarrow?"

"Aye, now I think, it might 'av been, wait on, I'll go an' ask Albert, he'll know."

Elfie waited anxiously as the woman went off to ask her husband. Presently, she returned. "Aye, lass, Mick Jarrow, Albert knew it, says 'e were going up north, but not sure where, said 'e came from Cumberland like."

Elfie proceeded to tell the woman a bit about her circumstances and why she was seeking Mick.

"Well, lass, I 'ope y' find 'im an' if we 'ere anything we'll get word to you," said Mrs, Mitchell.

Elfie stepped out into the farmyard. "Thank you very much, for all your help and I hope Mr Mitchell is soon well, goodbye."

Elfie's heart was torn between elation and despondency as she headed back home. Mick was alright and had only been a few miles away from her, so near she could hardly believe it and yet he was gone to who knows where. Perhaps, if he was going north maybe he was going back home. The first thing was to write to the Jarrow's and tell them all about it and hope against hope that he would turn up.

Two weeks later Elfie received a letter from Liza. Her heart sank when she read that there had been no news of Mick. The letter went on to tell her about happenings in Fusedale. The Jarrow's continued to tend the flock of sheep that Elfie had previously been responsible for. No new shepherd had been set on and the croft at the top of the dale had fallen into disrepair. Liza finished her letter with a reminder of her proposed visit to see Elfie in the summer.

Somewhat despondent, she read the letter through again and then put it to one side. She went over to the window and looked out. The countryside was so beautiful here, the farm was running well under her management and she now had a thorough grasp of most aspects of the work. She was happy and content with her situation and yet her heart ached for the one person who could make everything complete. He had been hers and then she lost him through no fault of her own and now he had been but a few miles away from her, if only she had found out earlier. Nagging thoughts plagued her, even if she found him, would he believe her story, would he still want her after all this time.

Chapter twenty-nine

Early summer brought another letter from Liza asking if she could come and stay as school had finished for the summer. There was no mention of Mick so Elfie assumed that he had not returned to Dale End. Elfie subsequently obtained all the necessary information on train times and wrote back to Liza to set a date and to tell her which train to catch so that she could meet her at Settle station. As the date approached, Elfie became quite excited at the prospect of Liza's visit and had spent some time preparing one of the bedrooms for her stay.

James continued to visit the farm almost in the role of a patient suitor.

He sympathised with Elfie when she had told him how she had been so close to finding Mick but had also put forward the argument that she might never find him and that perhaps she would have to look towards a life without him. He never pushed himself, being content to enjoy her company and play the waiting came. Perhaps, one day she might relinquish the idea of finding Mick and then he might get his chance. He had become very fond of her over the last few months and she certainly did not make any attempt to dissuade him from visiting her.

For Elfie, James was a good friend, becoming almost like a brother, she enjoyed discussing ideas relating to the running and improvement of Catrigg Farm. She was somewhat impetuous at times and often over eager to do things. James could act as a brake, being a logical and careful thinker, he would often analyse her ideas and then make suggestions to enable her to put things into practice. She respected his views and in many instances she would wait until she saw him and then would excitedly put forward her thoughts and ideas and try to anticipate his views. He was a calming influence on her and she valued his support. At times she toyed with the idea that he might wish to join her in the running of the farm, as his interest developed. With her ideas and his logic they could look to expanding further but these where her inner thoughts and a present she did not share them with him.

It was a fine July afternoon when the Dales was at its prettiest that Elfie waited on the platform at Settle station for the arrival of the train bringing Liza down from Cumberland. The sound of the engine's whistle was heard in the distance signalling the imminent approach of the train. Elfie's heart beat excitedly as the train swept into the station. It would be lovely to see Liza again she thought, as life in Fusedale has paled into the distance after the hard work and excitement of Catrigg farm. She looked anxiously for the girl as the train came to a halt. Then she saw her at the far end of the train alighting from a carriage. She looked bewildered for a moment and then she saw Elfie frantically waiving and running towards her. They met in a big hug, Elfie almost lifting her from the ground in her excitement at seeing her again. "Oh Liza, I'm so pleased to see you again."

"Elfie – Elfie I've seen him, I've seen him," cried the girl excitedly.

"Seen him, who have you seen Liza?"

"I've seen Mick."

"Mick, where?"

"On the train."

"The train, this train?" asked Elfie, her eyes rapidly scanning the windows of the carriages.

"No – no, I mean from the train, on the way here."

"Calm down, Liza." She took the young girl over to a seat on the platform and sat her down.

"Now, slowly, tell me what you've seen."

"Oh Elfie, he was there, as close to me as that train there is an' I think he saw me. He sort o' half waived at me. I couldn't believe it Elfie, but it were definitely Mick I'm sure."

Tears started to stream down Elfie' cheeks, Liza looked directly into her eyes and she too started to cry. The two hugged each other for several minutes until Liza composed herself.

"Now, where did you see him?"

"Well, we'd just set off from this station and just as it were getting going we passed a gate an' there 'e were, leaning on it like. I saw him an' waived, but I couldn't get window open to call to 'im but I'm sure 'e saw me, he – 'e sort of waived back. There were a lot of ewes round 'im an' a dog as if 'e were waiting for train to pass, so 'e could cross line like."

"Can you remember the name of the station Liza?"

"Let me think, yes it were a funny name, er bent I think, yes bent."

Elfie thought for a moment, "was it Dent?"

"Yes, that's it, not bent, Dent, I were near though weren't I?"

"You were Liza, that's very good, can you remember anything else?"
Liza thought for a moment and then looked up and giggled at Elfie.
"Now I think on, yes. The train went over a long bridge an' then we were in a right long tunnel, it were dark for ages. Then when we came out other side it went over a long bridge an' then stopped at another station, it were last 'un afore here, yes that's it

"That's wonderful news Liza, it sounds as if he's working up there."
"I know, it does, don't it, we ought to go back straight away an' see if he's still there?"
"We must, but I don't think he'll still be there, but if we go and make enquiries at the farms thereabouts we should be able to find him, oh I can't believe it Liza. What we'll have to do is find out when there's a train to Dent, I think it will be next day now."
They made enquiries at the ticket office and found out that the next train would be in the morning at ten thirty.
"That's settled it, we'll go back tomorrow and then you can show me where you saw him, then we'll see if we can find him. Now we must get you to the farm, Edgar's waiting outside with the cart, come on now."
She took hold of Liza's bag in one hand and the girl's hand in the other and they hurried out of the station to where Edgar sat waiting.
Liza chatted incessantly all the way back to the farm telling Elfie all that had been going on back at Fusedale. After Elfie had shown Liza around and introduced her to Nell they went back to the farmhouse for supper.
"You aren't 'alf lucky to be given a place like this Elfie, I wish I lived here, can't I come an' work here for you?"
"Hang on a bit, Liza, you've only just got here."
"I know but it's grand."
"Yes, you're right, I am lucky, but it has been hard work and still is, keeping everything going and that."
"D'you think we'll find Mick if we go back tomorrow, I'm sure I'll know the place where I saw 'im?"
"Well, if he was with some ewes there's a good chance he'll still be there, I do hope so, I've missed him once already," she added in a sad tone of voice.
"I know, I can't wait till morning to see if 'e's still there."
"Mm, But he won't be where you saw him, we'll have to go to the nearest village and make some enquiries. It might take us some time."

The following morning the two of them boarded the northbound train. Elfie had explained the purpose of their journey to Edgar and told him to expect them back in a few days. Both he and Nell wished them good luck.

Liza looked anxiously out off the window not wanting to miss any clues as to the location of Mick. The train crossed the big viaduct over Battye Moss and then plunged into the darkness of Blea Moor tunnel. Little sparks from the engine whisked past the carriage windows as the train proceeded through its confines underground. Then as sudden as the carriage had been plunged into darkness the train emerged and the carriage was flooded with sunlight.

"It's not very far now, I think we go over another bridge and then we're there." Liza craned her head forward to see ahead.

The train started to slow down as it approached Dent station.

"There, there, that gate, that's were 'e were, did y' see it Elfie?"

"Yes, I did," replied Elfie excitedly, "you're sure though?"

"Yes – yes, I'm certain that were it."

The train pulled into Dent station and the two of them left the train and made their way to the ticket office.

"How far is it to the village?" enquired Elfie.

The man behind the counter scratched his head. "Be all of four miles miss."

"Four miles, is that to Dent?"

"Aye, it is miss."

"It's a long way from the station, isn't it?"

"Reckon it is, but that's how it is, couldn't get lines up to village, so this is as far as y' get."

"I see, so which way is it?"

"Turn left out of the station and follow the road down to the bottom of the hill, then you'll join road along the valley. Go right there and just follow it on."

Elfie thought for a minute. What is there if we turn left along the valley?"

The man scratched his head again. "Bottom of the hill is Cowgill, just a few houses there then not much else for miles really."

"Are there any farms that way, you see, were looking for some-one who works on a farm near here, he's called Mick, Mick Jarrow, I don't suppose you've heard of him, have you?"

"No miss, can't say that I have, but there's one or two farms along the valley before you get to the moor, then there's nowt for miles after that."

"Well, thank you for your help," replied Elfie.

The two of them set off down the road towards the valley, their eyes scouring the fields as they went in the vain hope of seeing Mick, but without success. Soon they reached the tiny hamlet of Cowgill.

"We might as well start here and work our way along the valley, Liza, you try these houses here and I'll try at the houses over there. Their enquires proved fruitless except for the information that there was an inn half a mile along the road.

Maybe they'll know something there, or at least we can get something to eat and maybe a bed for the night if we need one," said Elfie.

They carried on along the road enquiring at any house that they passed, again with no luck.

"These aren't farms Elfie," remarked Liza after returning from the door of one of the cottages along the way.

"I know, but we've just got to try everywhere."

Eventually the two of them reached the inn. It was a quaint little building, which looked like it had formerly been a couple of cottages. A stream bubbled down the hillside and under a small bridge before joining the main river, which ran, down the valley. It was very dark inside and it took some time for the girls to accustom their eyesight. There were only three elderly men sat at a table, Elfie went over to them.

"Excuse me, but have you heard of a Mick Jarrow working hereabouts, he's a shepherd?"

The three men looked at the two girls, obviously surprised to see females in there, then one spoke. "Can't say I 'ave, lass, 'ave you 'eard on 'im?" He directed his eyes at the two other men. They both shook their heads.

"Well, thank you gentlemen, " said Elfie "is the innkeeper about?"

"'E'll be int back, Alf, Alf, there's some young ladies t' see y.

After a moment or two a large, jolly looking man appeared. "What's that you say Dick?"

"These two lasses are looking for a fella, what did you call 'im?"

"Mick, - Mick Jarrow," replied Elfie.

The innkeeper thought for a moment, "No, names not familiar, who is he?"

"My brother -" replied Liza a little impertinently.

Elfie interrupted, "Yes he's working as a shepherd around here, Liza saw him from the train as it left Dent station.

"Mm, now Wilf Baxter's land goes up Brant Side an' onto Great Knoutberry, line cuts across there. Now 'es got biggest flock o' sheep hereabouts, I'd try 'im if I were you."

"Well thank you very much, where is Mr Baxter's farm?"

"Oh, aye, its at bottom o' Artengill, nobbut ten minutes along road."

"Right, we'll try there Liza, oh, by the way, can you find us a room for the night, there isn't a train back till tomorrow for us?"

"Aye I'll tell missus, she'll sort it out, so where y' from then?"

"I've got a farm near Settle."

"I see, I thought you were a bit landed."

"Landed?"

"Aye, a bit posh like, I can tell by way y' talk, see."

Elfie smiled at him, "It's a long story, but we'd best be off, we'll be back later and thank you for your help."

"Aye well, good luck t' y'."

The two of them left the inn and went outside.

"Never been inside an inn before, Elfie, are they all like that?"

"I don't really know," came the reply.

They set off along the road again and soon reached a huddle of buildings at the foot of a great cleft in the hillside. A big stream tumbled down the rocky ravine.

"This must be it," said Elfie, "lets see if we can find anything out here."

They made their way to the farmhouse up a short track, which lead into a sprawling farmyard. There were buildings of all shapes and sizes, farm implements and straw seemed to abound. Hens and ducks ran back and forth as the two girls approached and knocked on the door of the farmhouse. The door was partly open but soon creaked back on its hinges to reveal a large, red-faced woman wearing an apron. She had flour on her hands and arms and was obviously in the middle of baking.

Elfie smiled and said, "good afternoon, is this Mr Baxter's farm?"

"Ee, tis that lass, are y' wantin' 'im, cos 'ees no 'ere at moment, 'ees up at Gillhead, farm over yonder," said the woman inclining her head in the direction of a farmhouse further up the road.

"Oh, will he be long?" enquired Elfie.

"Nay, once 'e gets talking there's no telling, y' know, what did y' want 'im for anyway?"

"Well, you might be able to help us, were trying to find someone called Mick Jarrow and the innkeeper said he might be working here."

"Mick, 'e's a right grand lad' 'es-"

"You mean you know him, is he here?" interrupted Liza.

"Aye, 'e is." The woman peered at Liza. "Eh, tell me, are you related, y've got 'is eyes?"

"Yes, yes he's my brother, where is he."

"It's not many minutes since 'e were 'aving a pot 'o tea with me in kitchen," said the woman, in no hurry to divulge where Mick was.

"Is he still here?" asked Elfie in an anxious voice.

"Oh aye, reckon 'e'll be int barn, one o' dogs 'ad pups a few days since, spends a lot 'o time looking after 'em. One of 'em int doing right good like, an 'es been keepin' an eye on it."

"Which barn is he in?" asked Liza, excitedly.

"That un, cross yard, doors round side, go on then, see if 'es there," said the woman almost teasing them.

The two of them hurried across the yard, as they reached the door Elfie suddenly grabbed Liza's arm and pulled her to a halt.

"Come on Elfie, what's up?"

"I – I don't know," she stared the ground. "I don't know whether I can face him,"

Liza took hold of her hands, "He'll be so pleased to see you."

"No, I'm not sure he will after all that's happened." Tears started to well up in her eyes. "You go on Liza, see how he is first and then I'll see him if he wants to."

Liza hugged her, "It'll be alright, I'm sure it will, you wait here then."

The girl went in through a low door at the side of the barn. It was quite dark inside. The sweet smell of hay permeated the air. As her eyes grew accustomed to the dim light she could just make out a figure sat on a bale of straw.

"Mick, is that you?"

The figure rose to its feet and turned towards her.

"Liza! How have you got here, how did you know I was here?"

He took hold of her and cuddled her almost squeezing the life out of her.

"It's so good to see you, but how did you find me?"

"I saw you when I were on the train, I waved to you."

"So it was you, I saw you but I weren't sure if it was you. Oh it's so good to see you again, are mother and everyone back home alright?"

"Yes —yes they are but why didn't you come back Mick, we've all missed you so much, why Mick?

He hung his head almost as if in shame. "I couldn't lass, couldn't face it anymore up there, so I thought I'd start afresh. I were going to come back eventually when I'd sorted m'sen out, I were really."

"Well it don't matter now, main thing is that you're alright, we didn't know what 'ad happened to you.

"Im not so bad now."

He reached down into the straw and picked something up, placing it in Liza's lap. "I've got these to look after now."

Liza took hold of a small bundle of fur and cradled it in her arms.

"She were struggling at first, but she's doing right good now."

A collie rose from the straw and came over to Liza and started to lick at the puppy in her arms.

"It's alright old girl," he stroked the dog's head and it went back and lay down contentedly with its other pups.

"They're so sweet, how old are they Mick?"

"They'll be three weeks or so now."

Mick looked up to see a figure silhouetted in the doorway. "Is somebody with you Liza?"

"Yes," she replied, almost in a whisper, "its Elfie."

"Elfie, but, what's she doing here?" He rose to his feet.

Liza tugged on his arm and he turned towards her, "It's not how you thought it was Mick, she's come with me, to find you."

Mick pushed her arm away and walked over to the doorway where Elfie was standing and stood before her in a confrontational manner.

"What do you want, Farrington got fed up of you, has he, thrown you out eh?" he glared at her almost threateningly.

Elfie just stood there, rooted to the spot, tears starting to stream down her cheeks.

"Go on I don't want you around here," he almost pushed her out of the door.

She turned and went outside sobbing loudly.

Liza was quickly over and pushed Mick to one side. She put her arms around her and held her close.

"Come, come on, Liza, I want to go," she sobbed loudly.

Mick stood there glaring at the two girls. "What did you bring her for?"

"You don't understand Mick, you –"cried Liza.

"I don't want to."

Liza let go of Elfie and stood directly in front of her brother.

"Listen you stupid idiot, Elfie didn't run off with Farrington, he took her away and held her prisoner for weeks until she escaped, and you, you just took off without knowing the truth."

"Yes, but I went to the manor and they said she was living there."

"Yes she was, but she were locked in a room. Anyway Farrington's dead now." She spit the last few words with contempt.

"Dead, you say, Farrington's dead?"

"Yes, he's dead alright, fell off his horse chasing Elfie across Askham Moor."

Mick slumped against the wall and put his head in his hands. There was a long silence broken only by the choked sobs of Elfie.

"It's no good, I'm going back Liza," she turned and started to walk slowly away.

"Mick," Liza almost screamed the word out.

He looked up, first at Liza and then at the figure of Elfie walking away.

"Elfie – Elfie," he shouted out to her. She carried on walking. "Elfie, wait," he ran over to her, grabbing hold of her arm. "Is it true, tell me, is it true?"

She turned and looked him directly in the eyes. Her face broke out into a helpless smile as if her fate were sealed.

"Yes, - yes it's true," she spoke in almost a whisper.

"But, what happened, why did you ride off with him, I saw you, I saw you?"

"I was ill, Mick, I nearly died, I was on the fell getting the ewes in when the snow came and I slipped and knocked myself out. When I came round I was in a snow-hole with Tess and the ewes. I managed to get back to the croft and then just crawled into bed. I was so poorly. Jacob Farrington found me and took me back to the manor and got a doctor. I suppose he saved my life really, but he kept me locked in a bedroom for weeks and weeks. Then I got away and he came after me, his horse stalled at a gate and he was thrown off. It was so awful, he died right there. I got to your farm, but you'd gone. I've been trying to find you ever since."

Mick just stood staring at Elfie with an incredulous expression on his face.

"I went to Feizor the other week, remember, you worked there at lambing."

He nodded his head.

"Then Liza saw you from the train and that's how we came here."

"But what was Liza doing on a train?"

"Oh Mick, she was coming to stay with me, you don't know do you, I live in Yorkshire now."

"Yorkshire?"

"Yes, near Settle."

He was still gripping her arm, he released it gently.

"I must be dreaming," he said shaking his head.

"No Mick, it's no dream, it's true," she replied with a tenderness in her voice.

Now it was Mick's turn to cry, the anger left his body to be followed by one of amazement and wonder.

"I just thought I'd lost you," he choked the word out.

"No Mick, you never lost me, it all went horridly wrong, just horridly wrong, but I never stopped loving you and wanting you."

"I – I don't know what to say, what to do Elfie, I didn't know, honestly, I didn't know."

Then he pulled her towards him and held her tightly. The warmth of his body coursed through hers. He nestled his face in her neck.

She pulled away from him slightly and looked up at him.

"Do you still want me Mick?"

He looked into her eyes, "I've been such a fool Elfie, can you forgive me, and I was so awful just now."

"It doesn't matter, but you haven't answered my question," an air of her former self-returning. She cocked her head on one side. "Well?"

"He smiled broadly, "you haven't lost your bossiness have you?"

He pulled her towards him and kissed her gently. "You're all I ever wanted Elfie, all I ever wanted and still do, I just can't take it all in. You know, I'd given up hope of ever seeing you again, I just thought I'd lost you to him."

"Well, now you know, you haven't."

They kissed again, this time lingeringly.

The two were interrupted by a coughing sound; it was Liza, a big grin on her face. Elfie grabbed hold of her, "Oh, Liza, I'm so happy, if you hadn't been coming to stay this would never have happened."

The three of them just hugged together for what seemed an age.

As they parted, Elfie caught sight of the little fluffy bundle nestled in Liza's arm. "Oh, the little thing, here, let me hold it." She took the puppy from Liza and cradled it against her. "He's so beautiful, aren't you?"

Mick looked on approvingly, "It's a bitch, she were runt, but she's pulled through, tough like you I reckon."

Elfie smiled up at Mick, "Do you know, this must be the best day of my life, I was fast giving up hope of ever finding you again."

"Lets go and look at the other pups," said Liza, who was now getting a bit embarrassed by the endearing looks that the two were giving each other.

They went back into the barn and knelt in the straw and played with the little creatures. Mick just knelt there gazing at Elfie until finally he said, "best let 'em rest a bit now, eh?"

"Yes, oh they're so sweet, reminds me of when we first saw Tess."

"How is Tess?" enquired Mick as they walked out of the barn.

"She's fine, she's back at the farm at the moment."

"The farm," asked Mick in a puzzled voice.

"Yes, my farm, it's called Catrigg Farm, it's up on the moors above Settle.

"How do you mean, my farm? Do you mean your working on a farm now?"

"You probably won't believe this but I own the farm. It was left to me by my father's brother who died last year –"

"You should see it Mick," chirped in Liza, "it's enormous."

"Well, I wouldn't say that," retorted Elfie, "but it is quite big, I've over three hundred ewes, dozens and dozens of lambs. Then there's the cows and the dairy and, oh you must see it Mick, you'll just love it, won't he Liza?"

Mick stood, staring, his jaw dropped in amazement. "This can't be real, I'm dreaming aren't I?"

"No Mick, you're not dreaming, though I can't believe it really. I've such a lot to tell you, so much has happened."

They walked out of the barn and into the farmyard. Mick took hold of Elfie again and looked into her eyes. "You've made me happy again Elfie, never thought I would ever be happy again. I used to think back on our times in Fusedale, things were so good then. I never reckoned they could ever return."

"I know, Mick, It was the same for me, I'm never going to lose you again.

But now things will be even better, we have our own farm, just like we said we would –"

"I know, but hang on a minute, Elfie, are you sure you still want me, now that you're a lady of means and that?"

"Course I do, as long as you promise to work hard on the farm," she replied with a mischievous twinkle in her eye.

Mick grinned at her, "You're the same old Elfie I knew, hey, but you used to say it were going to be a partnership, remember?"

"That was before I became a lady of means."

"Yes but even then you reckoned we'd have our own farm didn't you?"

"I did, but what I never told you was that I had some money, remember the old chest of my father's?" Mick nodded. "Well, there was some money in it enough to get us started, I was about to tell you, then it all went wrong. Anyway, that's all in the past, my uncle left me some money as well, so I'm quite well of now."

The conversation was interrupted by the appearance of a stocky, middle-aged man. "What's going on then, 'oo are these lasses?"

"Hello Mr Baxter," replied Mick. "This is my sister Liza, and this is Elfie" he said, putting his arm around her. "The girl I told you about back home."

Baxter peered at the three of them for a moment or two and then a broad smile spread across his face. "S'pose I'll be losing you eh, y'll be off back up north then?"

"Well sort of," replied Mick, with a very apologetic expression on his face.

"Aye, well I reckon I can't blame y', y've got a right bonny un there. Reckon I'll miss y', been a good worker, like, but I'll non stand in y' way lad."

"Thank you very much Mr Baxter, you're very kind," replied Elfie.

"Ee, y're a posh un an' all, eh?

"She only talks like that, she's not really posh," Liza interjected.

"I'll get me things," said Mick, excitedly and headed off in the direction of a low building adjacent to the barn. In a few minutes he was back clutching a bag.

"Is that all you've got?" enquired Elfie.

"Aye, that's about it," grinned Mick. "We'll get off then, if that's all right," he looked expectantly at Elfie.

"We're staying at the inn tonight, then we'll get the train tomorrow."

"Thanks very much, Mr Baxter, you'll look after them pups won't you?"

"Aye, I will lad, an, good luck to y"

The three of them gave him a cheery wave as they headed off down the lane from the farm.

That evening the three of them were seated around the fire at the inn having enjoyed a hearty meal. Elfie had related at length all the details of her escapade, her time at Thornthwaite Hall and how she had escaped. She described in detail how Farrington had met his death and the vision still brought tears to her eyes. Then she told of the circumstances surrounding the inheritance of Catrigg Farm and how she had spent the last few months there. When she had finished she sat back in the chair looking contented.

"So now you know what happened, now you can tell me what you were doing."

Mick was enthralled by her tale and was silent for some time as if digesting it, then he spoke, "it's unbelievable really, I mean, I know it's true but it's – it's, well I don't know what to say."

"Well, come on Mick, you know all about me, I want to know about you."

Mick thought hard for a moment and then he launched himself into his tale. He told how, after seeing her with Farrington he had gone home devastated, but his father would not let him pursue her for fear of trouble. It was when Farrington came over and instructed his father to take on the Mason's flock that he decided to go to the manor only to be told that Elfie was now living there and he could not see her. He went on to tell of how he did not return to the farm but set of southwards, sleeping rough for nights on end and scrounging food where he could. Eventually he got a lift with a carrier and ended up near Settle. He described how he got work as a farm hand doing odd jobs through the winter and sleeping in the barn. Eventually, he arrived at Feizor where he helped with the lambing before, moving on again to Dentdale.

"You see, I just didn't know what to do, I suppose I'd 'ave eventually got back to Fusedale but, only when I felt I could face everyone again."

Elfie took hold of his hand and squeezed it.

"I were beginning to like it here, they're nice people, the Baxter's an' then you turned up. Eh, I right sorry for being rotten to you when you came."

"Well, there's no need, I understand, really I do."

"What you going t' do now, Mick, are y' coming back to Dale end?" asked Liza, who had been unusually quiet throughout.

"No he's not, he's coming to Catrigg Farm aren't you Mick?"

Mick smiled lovingly at her, "If you'll have me."

"Try stopping me, I'm not letting you out of my sight ever again."

"Does that mean you're going to get married?" asked Liza.

Mick and Elfie's eyes met and the warmth and understanding passed between them as if forming a bond. "Yes, we are," replied Elfie.

"And as soon as we can," added Mick.

They continued talking for some time in the now empty inn until Mick said, "isn't it time you were off to bed Liza?"

The girl flashed him an impertinent look, "Nothings changed has it Mick, still trying to get rid of me? But I'll leave you two alone."

Liza got up from her chair, "come here Liza," said Mick. He then gave her a cuddle and a kiss.

"Ger off, y' daft thing," protested the girl.

"I'm just so happy to see you again." A tear ran down Mick's cheek.

Liza ruffled his hair, "see you in the morning."

Elfie and Mick sat together by the fireside for some time. Neither of them spoke, there was no need to. They just soaked up each other's presence.

Eventually, Elfie got up and sat on Mick's knee.

"I can just see us back at Catrigg, sat by the fire in the evenings when the works all done," she said dreamily.

Mick kissed her gently, "and I'll be the happiest man alive, just like I was before you went away. You've no idea how I've missed you, longed for you, even though I'd given up the idea of ever seeing you again I never stopped loving you and I never will."

"Me too. Mick, I used to lay awake at night just thinking of you and just hoping that we'd meet up somewhere. You've no idea how much I love you."

"I have El, otherwise you'd not have come looking for me, you could have had any man you fancied, I'm just so glad it's me."

They kissed lingeringly for some time and then she pushed him back slightly, "You'll have to wait until we're married before you can kiss me again," she said almost triumphantly.

"Nay El, I can't wait so long."

"Then you'd better hurry up and marry me then."

She leaned forward and kissed him again.

"Mm, I've decided what we'll do, first thing when we get back to Catrigg I shall send a letter to your Mother telling her you're at the farm. Then when Liza goes back home we'll go with her and then we'll get married at St Martin's church." She thought a moment, "yes that's what we'll do. I'd like that."

She rose to her feet and pulled Mick to his. They kissed briefly.

"That alright with you, Mick?"

"Whatever you say El, you're the boss, always were, I suppose.

Chapter thirty

On a beautiful autumn morning the train pulled steadily away from the station in Settle. It carried Elfie, Mick and Liza on their return journey to Fusedale. In the preceding two weeks since returning to Catrigg Farm the couple had put in hand arrangements for their marriage. They would obtain a license and then stay at Dale End Farm for two weeks to comply with the requirements, and then they would marry at St Martin's church. Arrangements were in hand for Nell and Edgar to travel to the wedding, indeed Nell had hardly stopped talking about it since she was informed.

Elfie had written to James at Giggleswick School to tell him that she had found Mick and to inform him of their forthcoming marriage. She received a letter back almost immediately. In it James expressed his best wishes for their happiness and promised to visit them on their return from Cumberland, adding if that was agreeable to her new husband. Elfie again replied that it most certainly was and that she valued his friendship and help. She had previously told Mick about her meeting and friendship with James emphasising that it was just a friendship. Mick happily accepted this. As he remarked, "You wouldn't have carried on searching for me El, would you if you'd wanted someone else?"

Her smile confirmed all he wanted to know.

"I still can't believe this is all happening El," said Mick as the train plunged into the depths of Blea Moor tunnel.

"Well you'd better, because next time we're on this train we'll be coming back to Catrigg as Mr and Mrs Jarrow," replied Elfie

"I know, but it's still like a dream," said Mick, pulling Elfie to him and giving her a kiss in the privacy of the darkness of the tunnel.

Soon the train was flooded with daylight as it emerged from its confines.

"There, there," said Liza excitedly, "That's were I saw you on the way down."

"That's the best thing you've ever done Liza, if it hadn't been for you we might never have met up again." He reached across and grasped the young girl's hand.

"Ger off" said Liza giving him an impish grin." You can repay me by letting me come to stay again, only for longer this time."

"You can come whenever you want," said Elfie, "as Mick said, all this is down to you."

At length, the train arrived at Appleby and the three of them were soon on the coach to Penrith. It was there that they obtained the marriage license that would enable Rev Winterburn to perform the marriage ceremony at St Martin's. Finally, they then hired a carrier to take them the last few miles to Dale End.

Young Andy was sat on the wall outside the farm as the carrier approached. Seeing the occupants he leapt down and ran into the farmhouse shouting.

"They're 'ere, they're 'ere."

"Davy," hollered Mary as she hurried out into the farmyard to see Elfie, Mick and Liza getting down from the carrier's wagon.

She stood there speechless at first, wringing her hands together, tears just rolling down her cheeks.

Oh my lord, it's so good t' see y'." she grabbed Mick in her arms and just held on to him for what seemed like an age. Then letting go she turned to Elfie and held out her arms to her and then almost squeezed the life out of her. Holding her at arms length she gazed at her. "My – my y' look such a lady now, y' so lucky t' get 'er back y' know lad. And Liza, love, 'av y' 'ad a nice time?"

Liza gave her mother a kiss and the cuddling commenced all over again before they went into the farmhouse.

"Where's y' father?" demanded Mary, "go an' find 'im Andy."

Presently, Davy appeared. He stood for a moment witnessing the scene of reunion in the kitchen before entering.

"Y' were a daft beggar f' going of like that, caused me no end of problems, but bye 'eck I'm glad t' see y' again, an' you lass, its all come right in t' end. More embraces followed until they were all seated at the table with mugs of tea in front of them and a plate of Mary's scones were rapidly disappearing from the plate.

"Ow long y' stopping for?" asked Davy.

"Couple of weeks till we're married and then we'll be going back to Catrigg," replied Mick.

"Sounds like y've landed on y' feet, y'll 'ave t' make sure he works 'ard Elfie."

"Don't worry Mr Jarrow, I'll see to it that he does," replied Elfie with a twinkle in her eyes.

"Well, see 'e does, 'e were a bit of a slacker at times –"

"Hey, I never was, I-"

Mary interrupted, now don't start you two, everything's in past, Mick worked 'ard 'an you know it. If owt it were you, mooching about sometimes."

Davy was about to protest.

"That's end on it," said Mary giving him her best scowl.

"Now you two tell us all that's been going on."

The tales extended through supper and late on into the night before Davy eventually rose to his feet. "Some on us 'av to be up in morning, work t' do."

He said this with a grin on his face.

"Aye, y' right, we'll leave y' to it, come on Liza, Andy, time you were away an' all.

They all trooped of upstairs leaving Elfie and Mick alone in the kitchen.

Elfie got up and went to sit on Mick's knee; she draped her arms lovingly around his neck and planted a big kiss on his forehead. His arms went around her waist and he pulled her close.

"I must be the luckiest man alive."

"And I the luckiest girl."

There lips met and lingering warmth passed between them before they finally made their way to their beds.

A couple of days later Mick and Elfie were seated in a hired carriage speeding through the countryside.

"I'm not sure we should be doing this Elfie."

"Well I am, Mick, I promised Suzie I would repay her and I intend to do just that. She looked after me when I was ill and let me escape from Farrington. I've nothing to fear from that family now."

"All same, I don't know that it's right going there."

"Come on, Mick, I'll do all the talking, anyway, look, we're almost there."

The words had barely left her mouth as the carriage swept down the drive to Thornthwaite Manor. The driver pulled on the reins and the horses came to halt in the courtyard. The couple alighted and looked about them.

"That's it, that's the door to the servants quarters," said Elfie setting off in its direction. Mick followed on hesitantly.

Reaching the door, Elfie knocked on it loudly. There was no reply, she knocked again. Presently the door opened and the figure of Mrs Riley was framed in the opening.

"Good morning Mrs Riley, I'd like to speak to Suzie if I may."

The housekeeper stared at Elfie for a minute, "I know you from somewhere don't I?"

"Yes you do, It's Elfie, remember now, I was kept here against my will, remember?" she said in an almost vindictive tone of voice.

The colour drained from Mrs Riley's face.

"It's alright, said Elfie in a softening tone, at the same time placing her hand on Mrs Riley's arm.

The woman pulled away, "what do you want her for?"

"It's a private matter, now, can I see her please?"

"I'd better see what Barker says," replied the housekeeper, a hint of defiance in her manner now.

"I don't think that we need to involve him, would you go and get her, please,"

Mrs Riley lowered her eyes, "you'd better come in then."

She showed the couple into a room adjacent to the kitchen.

"Wait here, I'll go and fetch her."

Mick shuffled about uneasily. "I don't know how you dare do this Elfie, you-"

He was interrupted by the return of Mrs Riley.

"She'll be with you presently," said the housekeeper who then left.

"At least she hasn't fetched Barker, I don't like him."

A few minutes elapsed and then Suzie peered cautiously round the door.

"Suzie," exclaimed Elfie, stepping forward and giving the girl a great hug.

"What, what are you doing 'ere, Miss?"

"I've come back to see you," then lowering her voice to a whisper, "I said I'd repay you for helping me."

"Well I never expected to see you again an' after all that with his lordship an' that." Suzie beamed excitedly.

"This is Mick, Suzie, remember me telling you about him, we're getting married next week?"

The girl wrung her hands, "I'm so happy for you miss."

"Well, what I've come for is to offer you a job as housekeeper for me, I've inherited a big farm in Yorkshire and I'd like you to work for me now, I'd pay you well, what do you say?"

The girl looked stunned, "do you mean that, miss?"

Elfie smiled at her, yes I do, and what's more I want you to be a bridesmaid at my wedding." She took hold of the girl's hands. "Well?"

"What will Mrs Riley say?"

"It's not up to Mrs Riley, Suzie, it's up to you."

The girl filled up and tears started to run down her cheeks, "I'd love to work for you miss, I don't really like it here anyway."

"That's settled then, go and fetch Mrs Riley and I'll explain to her, then you go and pack your things, you might as well come back with us right away."

Suzie hurried off, after a short time she reappeared wearing a rather tatty dress and carrying a bag. "I don't have much miss."

"No, I can see that, but we'll soon get you fixed up with some decent clothes, now, where's Mrs Riley?"

What seemed like an age elapsed before the return of Mrs Riley, she looked first at Suzie and then at Elfie.

"What's going on her, what's she doing in that dress."

"Suzie's coming to work for me, Mrs Riley, I'm taking her back with us."

"You can't do that," stormed the housekeeper, "I'm going to get Barker, see what he says about it all."

"It doesn't really matter to me what Barker thinks or says or his lordship for that matter, after what went on here, locking me in that room all that time. Come on Suzie, we're going we've got a carriage waiting outside."

The three of them walked past Mrs Riley who just stood there, her mouth open and an incredulous look on her face.

As the carriage pulled away from the manor, Suzie giggled mischievously.

"Did you see her face, Miss, I've seen her look sour but not like that. D'ye think it'll be alright?"

"Of course it will, Suzie, you're working for me now," said Elfie grinning equally as mischievously.

"I don't know how you dare Elfie, to stand up to that woman like that."

"Well that's the difference between you and me, you're just soft and I'm strong and determined." She winked at Suzie before giving Mick a nudge in the ribs with her elbow. "He's quite good with sheep though, aren't you?"

"Now, what about your parents, we need to go and see them, where do they live?"

"I haven't got any, I lived with my aunt in Askham, my mother died a long time ago and I never knew my father."

"I'm sorry about that, but we'll call and see your aunt on our way back," replied Elfie.

"That's alright miss, what about you, have you got any family?"

"No, Suzie, I'm a bit like you, I never knew my mother and my father died the year before last. Mick's lucky though, he's got his parents and a brother and sister, haven't you Mick?"

Mick nodded. "And that's where we're going now," said Elfie contentedly, settling into her seat in the corner of the coach.

Chapter thirty-one

The bright rays of the early autumn sun filtered through the window dappling the faces of the two sleeping girls. Its increasing brightness was sufficient to cause one of the two slumbering in the cosy bed to awake with a start. Elfrida Mason raised her head from the pillow and looked around the room. In her dreams she had been pursuing an endless trail through remote country in search of Mick only to find that as she drew near to him he repeatedly moved on. Now awake, she realised her dream was not reality. She looked down at the sleeping figure of Liza and shook her quite rigorously.

"Um, ey, what's up?" muttered the young girl, "it's too early to get up."

"No its not," retorted Elfie, "its today, my wedding day, at last, at last."

She sighed the last words as if she had been waiting an eternity.

"Come on Liza, there's a lot to do," she said excitedly, half pushing the girl out of bed with her feet. Soon the two of them were downstairs and into the kitchen where Mary was preparing breakfast.

"Where's Mick?" enquired Elfie, "I thought he'd be up by now."

"Aye, he's up alright, an long away now," came the reply.

"Away, where to?"

"Out o' way on you," replied Mary with a twinkle in her eye.

Elfie looked puzzled and alarmed.

"Oh, nay lass, 'es not gone for good, but I've sent 'im off, its bad luck t' see bride on t' wedding morning, so next time y' see 'im it'll be in t' church. Hey come 'ere luvvy," she reached out and put her arms round Elfie and held her close. "Y' know, this is one of the 'appiest days o' m' life.

Elfie remained still in Mary's embrace for some time as if drawing the love and warmth from her.

"And it's mine, too," she half sobbed.

"Come on then, lets get some breakfast down y', y'll need all y' strength, it's a busy day t'day."

Elfie smiled at Mary, "but where have you sent him to?" she asked, still with a hint of anxiety in her voice.

"E's gone t' village to meet up with y' friends staying at t' inn, what they call 'em, er Edgar an' er-"

"Nell," Elfie added.

"Aye, Nell, that's right, memory's not m' strong point y' know. Then 'e's seeing 'em t' church. Now you get this down y," she said pushing a steaming bowl of porridge towards her, "then we'll 'av t' be getting ready, carriage 'll be 'ere afore we know it.

Within an hour two carriages drawn by grey dappled mares drew up in the farmyard.

"Their here, there here," cried Liza who for once was ready on time and had been stood anxiously at the door of the farmhouse.

Elfie was stood in the parlour, dressed in a flowing muslin dress with long sleeves and a high neck. She wore a white bonnet decorated with delicate hand stitched flowers, similar ones were worn by her two bridesmaids, Liza and Suzie. In her hand she clutched a bouquet of large, white daisies interspersed with roses. Suzie fussed around her dress, "there, y' look perfect miss, y' really do."

At that point Mary's head came round the door, "You ready luv?"

Elfie nodded and gave her a nervous smile, then walked out into the hallway.

Davy was stood waiting there; he came forward and took hold of her hand. A tear welled in the corner of his eye. "I've never seen anyone look as lovely as you do lass." He leaned forward and kissed her on the cheek. "I wish y' all the luck an' happiness in the world, y' deserve it y' knows."

Elfie smiled at him too emotionally overcome to utter any words.

"Come on then, lets get y' t' church, else our Mick 'all be getting worried.

Soon the little procession was underway, travelling along the track and into the village of Howtown. Word had spread quickly of the forthcoming marriage and many of the villagers were out to see the shepherdess from the wild dale get married to local lad Mick Jarrow. There were smiles and nods and calls of good luck as the party progressed through on its journey to Martindale, several of the locals followed on behind the carriages anxious to see the wedding ceremony.

Mick was anxiously waiting outside the church gate as the wedding party came into view.

"Come on now lad, get yourself into church, you shouldn't see your bride till she walks down that aisle," said Nell, taking hold of his arm and half pushing him in the direction of the church door.

Reverend Winterburn was at the church door to greet Elfie as she arrived. He took hold of both of her hands and squeezed them gently.

"It' good to see you at this church again, this time in happy circumstances."

Elfie gave him a brief smile.

"And who is going to give you away my dear?"

Elfie looked a little puzzled at the question.

Edgar stepped forward, "Im going to do that honour, my wife Nell here and I looked after Elfie when her father worked on his brother's farm, so I think it's fitting that I do."

"That's fine," replied Winterton, "may God bless you all." He waved his hand in the direction of the altar where Mick stood waiting. "Shall we-"

Some twenty minutes later the newly wed couple stood in the doorway of the church, smiling and waving at the people gathered outside.

"I can't believe it's all over so quickly," said Mick smiling down at his radiant bride.

"Nor I," replied Elfie, squeezing his hand.

"S'pose we go back to Dale End now, eh, for something to eat?"

"That's typical of you, you've just got married and you're already thinking about your dinner."

Mick grinned happily and gave her a kiss.

"There's just one thing I need to do before we go, Mick."

"What's that, El?"

Without answering him Elfie left his side and walked round the rear of the church and over to the large yew tree in the corner of the churchyard. There she stooped and placed her bouquet of flowers on the raised mound that was the grave of Robert Mason. She took a couple of steps back and stared hard at the ground.

"Well, father, I'm the happiest person on earth, and I want you to be happy for me, wherever you are. Mick's a good lad, I know he'll look after me, he's all I'll ever want."

She turned to see Mick standing just a few feet away, hurrying over to him she threw her arms around his neck and kissed him lovingly.

Mick looked into her eyes, "Mrs Jarrow, I love you so much."

Arm in arm the two of them walked back round to the front of the church and out to the waiting carriage.

Chapter thirty-two

It was late spring, the lambing season was all but over and again it had been very successful. Now, in the kitchen of Catrigg Farm, Mick paced up and down, clearly in an anxious state. There had been much activity, back and forth and particularly upstairs, but he was excluded, banished to the kitchen until further notice. Then from somewhere above he heard the sounds of a different birth. Familiar he was with the ways of nature and its amazing way of recreating life but this was something he was unsure about, how to react to it. Then Suzie appeared at the kitchen door, a smile stretching from one ear to the other.

"Nell says you can come up know."

Mick stood as if his feet were stuck to the floor.

"Come on then, come and see your daughter."

"Daughter?"

"Yes, it's a little girl."

Suddenly the reality set in and Mick half knocked Suzie to one side as he raced along the hall and upstairs to the bedroom.

There he beheld what was for him a most amazing scene. Elfie was propped up in the bed on a large quantity of pillows, cradling a small bundle in her arms. She looked up at him and smiled, a tired smile.

"Mick, just look at her, isn't she the most beautiful thing you've ever seen?"

Mick walked over and sat on the bed besides her and gazed at the tiny baby.

"She – she's just like you, same eyes, same hair, she's just lovely Elfie, just lovely.

"Now we're a complete family, we've got everything we want."

Her head fell back on the pillow and her eyes closed. Nell came over and gently took the baby from Elfie's arms.

"She's had a hard time, she needs to rest now, leave her be."

Nell placed the sleeping child in a cot at the foot of the bed.

"Now you just rock it gently Suzie, whilst the baby sleeps so Miss Elfie can get some rest. We'll go and have a pot of tea, its been a long morning," said Nell, ushering Mick out of the room before her.

For the first time in weeks it was a clear, sunny, warm day. The month of May had been unseasonably wet, making the routine on the farm more arduous. Now, some weeks after the birth of her daughter, Elfie was feeling well and anxious to spend some time involved in the day to day running of the farm rather than receive reports from Mick. The lad had been patient with her constant questions and queries about what was going on and he had promised that as soon as the weather improved he would go round the stock with her to show her how things had faired.

Seeing Edgar go past the window, Elfie went to the door and called out to him. "Have you seen Mick about anywhere, Edgar?"

"Aye, miss, he's gone up to top fields to let some of the ewes back onto moor with t' lambs, reckons their ready now."

"Oh, I see, thank you Edgar."

"Miss."

Elfie went back into the kitchen where Suzie was sat in the rocking chair cradling the baby.

"I wish 'e were mine miss."

"Well one day you'll meet someone Suzie and have a family of your own."

"Oh, I don't know miss, don't reckon anyone 'll want the likes o' me, miss."

"Of course they will, you're a pretty girl and sensible at that, you've been a big help this last few weeks. Now, listen, whilst she's asleep I'm going out for a bit to see Mick and have a look round, I won't be away too long."

"That's alright miss, she'll be safe with me."

Elfie gave her a smile as she pulled on her coat and boots and then set off outside. She headed off through the fields taking note of the ewes and their lambs, which appeared, healthy and contented. Reaching the last field she cast an eye around for any signs of Mick but could not see him anywhere about. Perhaps he's headed over towards the upper reaches of the beck, which was more fertile than the open moorland and a better grazing area for the ewes feeding their new lambs.

The faint track led over rough pasture and tussocky moorland which was boggy in places. Eventually she reached the head of the shallow valley, which the beck meandered through before joining forces with another watercourse to form the main flow into Catrigg Force. Although there was no sign of Mick there was evidence that he had been here by the number of ewes and lambs grazing thereabouts.

"Well, it seems that he's been here Tess, probably gone back to the farm the bottom way. Never mind eh, it's good to be out and about again."

Tess gave a couple of happy barks as if acknowledging her mistresses comments. Heading downhill, she soon reached the beck, which was still running high after all the rain of the previous weeks.

Reaching a large rock she sat down and looked across towards Penyghent.

She mused on the fact that as yet she had not climbed that particular hill as she had thought she might when arriving at Catrigg Farm. Since taking over the farm she had had very little spare time. Now that she was a mother the demands on her time were even greater. Elfie reflected on the events of the last twelve months or so and concluded that they had been the happiest times of her life. She had inherited the farm, found Mick and got married and now had a beautiful little daughter. I'm so lucky she thought, beyond my wildest dreams.

"Come on then Tess, we'd best be getting back."

Tess gave an excited bark. The girl and dog continued down the path beside the beck. As they approached the part where the beck narrowed before rushing into the force her attention was drawn to a scraping sound and something moving below a clump of tree roots, which overhung the beck. On closer inspection she could see that it was an ewe which had somehow slipped down the bank and got one of its horns tangled in the roots rendering it unable to move but a few inches back and forth.

"Silly creature, what do you want to go and do that for?"

She climbed down the banking towards the ewe intent on rescuing the animal. As she got nearer she could see the anguished look in its eyes.

"Poor thing, how long have you been stuck here?"

Tess scrabbled down the banking towards her.

"Back off Tess, we don't want to agitate her any more, back."

Tess duly moved back a little further upstream.

"Alright, old thing, let's see if we can get you loose."

Hanging on to the tree roots with one hand she tried to pull the animal's horn free with the other. Each time the ewe struggled.

"Ooh nearly, it's no good, I'm on the wrong side of you."
With some tentative manoeuvring she managed to half climb over the animal so that she was directly next to the entangled horn rather than trying to reach over its head.

"There, that's better."
Now she hung on with her right hand with her feet perched precariously on a large length of tree root. Taking hold of the horn she pushed down and twisted at the same time releasing the animal's head. Grateful for its release it bucked violently and headed up the bank. This sudden action pushed Elfie backwards and out over the beck causing her feet to slip off the tree root. She screamed out loudly as she hung by her arms. Her legs scrambled at the banking, but the rock was greasy and she could find no purchase. She was now hung at arms length over the abyss that was Catrigg Force. Try as she could she was unable to pull herself up and her arms tired at every attempt.

"Tess, Tess," she screamed the words out at the dog that was now directly above her looking down anxiously at her mistress's plight but unable to do anything to help.

"Tess, go and get Mick, go and get Mick," she sobbed the words. The dog looked puzzled not wanting to leave her in this predicament.

"Go, go and get Mick," she implored. With a couple of hesitant looks Tess turned and ran of up the hillside in the direction of the farm.

"Just got to hang on, hang on," sobbed the girl, wincing at the ever-increasing pain in her arms.

Mick was sat in the kitchen enjoying a pot of tea and gazing at the baby, which slept contentedly in Suzie's arms.

"How long she been gone?"
"She set off about half an hour before you came back," replied Suzie.
"Well I never saw her, mind you I could easily have missed her."
He took a sip of his tea, then he heard a frantic barking outside.
"Blooming 'eck what's that dog barking for, is there someone out there?"
He got up and went to the door to find Tess barking frantically and running back and forth.
"What's up with you then, there's no-one here."

The dog continued to bark frantically.

"What is it Tess, where's Elfie?"

Tess made off towards the gate barking continuously and then ran back to Mick and jumped up, tugging at his clothing; she then released her hold and ran towards the gate again.

"Summats up, summats up," he cried and set off in hot pursuit of the dog, which had now jumped over the gate and was heading off across the fields.

The dog increased its speed now and Mick gasped as he tried to catch up. On they went through the fields and across the open moor until they reached the track that led down towards the beck, Tess turned and gave a bark as if to confirm that Mick was still following her. Soon they reached the valley leading down to the beck and Tess raced on with Mick in breathless pursuit.

The dog soon reached the place where she had left her mistress and stopped and barked loudly. Mick caught her up and then came to a halt, gasping for breath. Tess continued to bark, looking in the direction of the force.

"What is it Tess, I can't see anything, what is it?" anxiety now very evident in his voice. Tess went nearer the edge, her bark now receding into a whimper. She pawed frantically at the tree roots. Mick looked at the place that the dog was indicating and then saw the disturbance to the ground where the ewe had made its escape. He stared hard at the waters of the beck as it crashed down into the greasy abyss of Catrigg Force.

Tess lay down on the banking and wined steadily. Mick looked at her puzzled.

"No –no," he screamed the words out at the top of his voice, "no, it can't be –no."

The awful reality now coursed through his brain. He scrambled down the banking to where Elfie had effected the rescue of the ewe but could see nothing.

"Elfie, Elfie," he called loudly, but there was no reply. He leaned out over the force and tried to look down but from his vantage point he could not see the bottom of the waterfall. His body shook and he felt sick with terror. He scrambled back up the bank and onto the path. He stood for a few minutes in a helpless state, then, pulling himself together he set off along the path, which first climbed up around the edge of the force before descending to the calmer waters of the beck where it escaped the confines of the gorge. He was consumed with panic as he stumbled on down the path with Tess now in pursuit. He slipped a couple of times on the muddy track but quickly picked himself up and continued on down until he reached the point where the beck emerged from the gorge.

In his mind now was an ever-increasing fear that something terrible had befallen Elfie. He looked about him but could see nothing. Then Tess took the lead and started to head into the gorge itself. Mick followed, slipping and sliding about half in the water half on the rocks until they reached a point where the beck widened to form a pool. It was but a short distance from the fury of the water where it plunged over the waterfall. Tess barked loudly as Mick approached, still he could not see anything.

"What is it lass, what is there?"

Then he saw what looked like a bundle of rags partly submerged in the water between the rocks. He splashed his way through the waist deep water until he reached the object. Then his worst fears were founded, what he saw was a body face down its lower half in the water.

"No – no," he screamed, "God no."

Tess pawed at the lifeless form as Mick approached. He bent over the body and lifted its head to see the face although he already knew who it was.

He reached down into the water and lifted the pathetic form up into his arms. Tess whined gently, she knew she had done all she could but it was too late. Carefully, Mick made his way through the jumble of rocks with Elfie in his arms. He moved slowly and carefully until he reached the end of the confines of the gorge. He climbed out and lay Elfie's lifeless form down on the grassy bank.

Then he lay down beside her and cradled the wet body in his arms, he wept out loud. The heat from his living form passed to the still, forlorn figure in his arms and all the joy and happiness within his heart slowly ebbed into the ground on which they lay.

Tess shuffled up close on the other side of Elfie, resting her head on Elfie's lap she wined gently.

The Pantheists Gods had come down to the earth and taken the shepherdess back to their heavenly abode.

Chapter thirty-three

It was a beautiful spring morning, the sun shone down on the valley bringing with it the much-needed warmth for this time of the year. The fell tops were still cloaked in snow and the sun shimmered and reflected from their whiteness. Ullswater was as still as a millpond. The summits reflected in its clear, blue water. Daffodils and snowdrops grew in profusion around the shores of the lake, bringing that splash of colour needed before the buds, now well advanced opened to reveal this years growth of leaves.

A man and a girl walked up the track to the upper reaches of Fusedale. He was of middle age, with a weathered face from years of exposure to the outdoors. He was also slightly stooped as if world-weary.

The girl would be about sixteen years of age; she had long blonde hair, which fell, about her shoulders in a carefree manner. Her cheeks had a rosy complexion and her eyes were a vivid blue. They had a slightly rebellious look about them, which was easily softened by her smile.

Climbing up the steep section of the track, they soon reached the point where the upper valley widened and the track passed through a cutting in the rocks. The man stopped and climbed up onto a small outcrop and looked up to the head of the valley. He reached down and offered his hand to the girl and pulled her up along side him.

"There Helena, I promised that one day I would bring you here. It's taken me a long time I know."

The girl squeezed his hand.

"That little building you can see over to the right, that's where she lived."

"It's so wild and remote, how did she manage?"

"Oh, she managed alright, she was a tough un."

The two of them climbed down from their viewpoint and carried on along the track. The girl's eye was taken by a profusion of daffodils growing around an earthen mound.

"Look at all those flowers, nowhere else are there any except here," she remarked.

"Aye, that's where Moss were buried, one of your mother's dogs. I can

298

still see him now; him and Tess worked well as a pair on these hills. Aye I can still see them."

A tear ran down his cheek.

"And your mother, she's still up here, I can see her plain as day wandering about these fells, with a flock of ewes, Moss and Tess working back and forth. There isn't a day goes by that I don't think of her you know," he said, in a saddened tone.

Helena put her arm around her father and they walked on slowly to the now derelict croft.

The End

Printed in the United Kingdom
by Lightning Source UK Ltd.
130769UK00001B/292-318/P